SO-BZI-564

EX
LIBRIS

_____

_____

_____

Romance
Treasury

THE ROMANCE TREASURY
ASSOCIATION

NEW YORK · TORONTO · LONDON

These stories were originally published as follows:

THE HOUSE CALLED SAKURA
Copyright © 1974 by Katrina Britt
First published by Mills & Boon Limited in 1974

CHATEAU IN PROVENCE
Copyright © 1973 by Scribe Associates Ltd.
First published by Mills & Boon Limited in 1973

THE DREAM ON THE HILL
Copyright © 1974 by Lilian Peake
First published by Mills & Boon Limited in 1974

ROMANCE TREASURY is published by
The Romance Treasury Association, Stratford, Ontario, Canada.

Editorial Board: A. W. Boon, Judith Burgess, Ruth Palmour,
Alice E. Johnson and Ilene Burgess.

Dust Jacket Art by Len Goldberg
Story Illustrations by Len Goldberg
Book Design by Charles Kadin
Printed and bound by R. R. Donnelley & Sons Co.

ISBN 0-373-04058-X

Printed in U.S.A.   AO 58

CONTENTS

THE HOUSE CALLED SAKURA

The House Called Sakura

Katrina Britt

Never before had Laurel met a man like Kirk Graham, but after his brief English holiday Kirk had returned to his job in Japan. Then months later he had written to Laurel and proposed, and Laurel, still deeply in love with this man of her dreams, had gone to Japan and married him.

But time had changed Kirk. Instead of the close bond that had previously existed, it was as though a wall had been erected between them—a wall that puzzled Laurel.

That is, until she met the beautiful Countess Nina Wanaka, a women whose relationship with Kirk gave every indication of being much more than merely platonic!

CHAPTER ONE

SLOWLY THE MIST LIFTED and the sea that hitherto had been a choppy gray changed miraculously to an enchanting blue, giving Laurel an exciting glimpse of Fujiyama as the ship approached the superb harbor. Oriental sampans came into view, their decks alive with dark-haired, small Japanese men.

Then came the big ships from foreign ports, mingling with those flying the flag of the Rising Sun. From the deck of the ship Laurel's first impression of Japan was that of a lovely siren gaily executing the dance of the seven veils.

Provocatively, tantalizingly, she discarded them one by one to reveal scenes of incredible beauty, each one more lovely than the last. Lightly the veils of gauze mist were tossed away on the breeze to frolic and curve around the branches of pine trees gracing the delicate lines of the hills now touched to gold by the sun.

Through her linen suit, Laurel could feel its warmth as it blazed down onto the innumerable islands caressed lovingly by the inland sea. On one oasis of greenery a beautiful old temple pricked the blue sky in isolated splendor while the liberating breeze whisked away the last of the misty veils to frolic around the fishing fleet setting out in full sail.

Their junk sails, held together by intricate interlacing of ropes, strained against the breeze as the picturesque craft glided over the surface of the water like silver-veined butterflies on blue glass.

The scene photographed itself on Laurel's mind with an endearing clarity. Everything was so fresh, so young, so gay, so utterly different from anything she had ever seen that she found herself smiling at the faces beneath mushroom hats bobbing up and down industriously between bales of rice straw on the quay.

With quickening heartbeats she scanned the crowd awaiting the ship's arrival and the heat rose in her cheeks. There he was! A wild thrill shot through her. He had not changed. He was still larger than life with a careless grace about him, a quality that, while it arrested and charmed, also gave confidence. He looked tanned and very fit, unlike Laurel, who was pale, tired and a little overwhelmed upon reaching a country that alternately charmed and frightened her by its strangeness.

The sun glinted upon the crisp tobacco-brown hair combed back from an intelligent forehead as the keen gray eyes, inscrutable beneath straight dark brows, pinpointed her slender figure. The lean, sardonic face relaxed suddenly into a white smile that gave the well-cut mouth and slightly hooked masculine nose a boyish look. But there was nothing boyish about Kirk Graham. He was a man in complete control of his own destiny. It showed in his arrogant stance, the proud bearing and the nonchalant wave of a firm brown hand, Laurel thought as she fluttered her small one in greeting.

Even from a distance, with the blue water still dividing them, she felt his magnetism. Suddenly she trembled with the realization that she was shy of this man who was soon to become her husband. Was it only a year since their first meeting, a year in which her life had so irrevocably changed? The crowd of unfamiliar faces swam before her eyes. It all came back as clearly as though it had happened yesterday.

It had been one of those days for Laurel, that fateful day when she had decided to spring-clean the living room of the cottage. Everything had gone wrong from the moment she had stripped the room to wipe down the ceiling and walls. It had developed into one of her mother's off days, and to make matters worse, the doctor was late in coming. Laurel had finished the room and was about to hang the freshly laundered summer curtains when he arrived.

After he had gone, she had rushed out with the prescription, hoping to reach the drugstore in the village before closing time. It was essential for her mother to have the newly prescribed drug, for the previous one had made her feel ill.

Evidently the doctor had not had a good day, either, for he was well over an hour late finishing his rounds and the cottage had been his last place of call before driving home for his evening appointments. Pity he had been going in the opposite direction, or Laurel could have asked him for a lift to the village. A glance at her watch told her she had just a quarter of an hour to reach the drugstore before closing time at five-thirty. Failing that meant going to the next drugstore on the roster for late-night closing at Sabridge five miles away. Of course the car had refused to start, and in exasperation at all that had gone before, Laurel set off to walk the considerable distance to the village.

She had hurried out just as she was in jeans and workaday top, her dark hair covered by a gay scarf. Half walking, half running, she had not seen one chink of light in the black clouds hanging over her since the train accident that had cost her father his life and caused her mother severe head injuries.

She was so engrossed in her troubles that the long, sleek car approaching had pulled up smoothly beside her before she was aware of it.

"Excuse me. I'm looking for Dr. Machelle. I believe he lives somewhere in the vicinity."

The charming, cultured voice had come from a dark, well-shaped head emerging from the open car window. Laurel, gasping for breath, had stopped precipitately, torn between hurrying on and helping this stranger. Her small, firm bust rose and fell agitatedly as she pictured the pharmacist putting up his shutters because of the delay.

"Oh, dear!" Her words came out in a rush. "I'm in a

dreadful hurry and it's rather complicated to explain. You keep straight on—"

She had broken off abruptly. The man's eyes, gray as steel in a suntanned face, held an amused twinkle.

"Is someone chasing you or are you going someplace?" he drawled, taking in her slim figure and the scarf tied nurse-style on her head.

"I'm going to the drugstore in the village and it'll close at any moment. Where was I?"

Slowly he had released the catch on the car door and opened it. "You were telling me how to find my Uncle George. Hop in and you can tell me on the way to the store."

There was a kindling appraisal in his look and his manner was kindly in a way that instilled confidence. Laurel, piteously in need of a helping hand, had stammered, "But . . . but it will be taking you out of your way. You must have just come from there."

"I have. Shall we go back?"

She wondered afterward why her embarrassment had fallen away as she complied. She had taken an awful risk accepting a lift from a comparative stranger whose gorgeous tan could not possibly have been acquired through the rigors of an English winter. Had it not been for the almost imperceptible air of aloofness behind the gray eyes, she would never have accepted. As it was, she had sunk into the luxurious upholstery to give him a steady look.

His profile had presented the outline of a Roman gladiator who had attained near perfection in everything he had undertaken. His air of alertness, his immaculate city-going suit, his firm hands on the wheel of the car coaxing it to speed had mesmerized her.

"Well, is the summing-up satisfactory?"

He had continued to keep his eyes front as if to spare her any further embarrassment.

Touched, Laurel had given a little chuckle, completely reassured. "I might not be a very good judge of character, but I'm not worried."

"Thanks. I can usually be relied upon, although, as they say, self-praise is no recommendation."

He had smiled at her then, a smile that was somehow breathtaking. It had reminded Laurel that not only was her face minus makeup but she was also disheveled and very tired. She had told him everything about her parents' accident with the feeling that he had a right to know. He had listened gravely without comment until she had finished.

"So you're left to pick up the pieces, as it were," was his brief observation. "Hard luck on your own. Poor child!"

The drugstore had been on the verge of closing when they had arrived and in a short time Laurel was back in the car with the precious prescription.

"Lovely day," her companion had remarked when they had left the village behind.

Laurel had agreed, feeling the heat of the sun through the car windows. Wretchedly sticky, she longed for a leisurely bath, realizing her foolishness in trying to cram all the work into one day. No wonder her head throbbed from sheer exhaustion. But she managed to give him the directions to the doctor's residence.

"Thank you. You've been very kind," she had told him as he drew up the car at the gate of the cottage.

"So have you," he replied with his smile slowly changing to a frown of concern on seeing her pale, strained little face. "Are you all right?"

"Yes, thanks. It's been a warm day for working. Goodbye and thanks again."

Somewhat unsteadily, Laurel was leaving the car when the ground suddenly rushed up and hit her. She opened her eyes later to find herself lying in a chair in front of the uncurtained window in the living room where she had toiled so laboriously all that day in between looking after her mother.

He was standing slightly to one side of her chair, chafing her hands while allowing the fresh air from the open window to reach her. With a swift cry of distress Laurel

had looked up into the gray eyes watching her so intently.

"Oh, dear!" she had cried. "Did I pass out? I've never
done that before in my life."

"It's all right. Lie still." His tone and touch were absolutely gentle but firm when she tried weakly to sit up.
"I'm going to make you a cup of tea."

And because she felt so utterly exhausted and ill,
Laurel had leaned her aching head back against the cushions he had thrust behind her, and closed her eyes.   She
opened them again when he had entered the room with
the tea tray.

The sunlight from the uncurtained window gave a cop-
pery sheen to his crisp dark hair. It was the kind that
curls when wet, and his eyes were the sort that danced
when he smiled. He was, as far as she could judge, on the
outer rim of his twenties, which accounted for his mature
looks. Looking at him made her heart feel as light as her
head.

"I managed to find everything in the kitchen," he said,
placing the tray on a low table and carrying it near to her
chair. Adding milk to a dainty eggshell china cup in gold
and yellow, he proceeded to pour out the tea. "My guess
is you've been working without a break. Now be sensible
and drink this."

It was much stronger than she liked it and he had
dropped three cubes of sugar into the cup before handing
it to her. Laurel closed her eyes and drank it gratefully,
ignoring her revulsion of sugar in her tea. Then he was
handing her the homemade shortbread she kept in a biscuit tin colorfully painted with Japanese geisha girls.

She took one to please him after insisting that he pour
out a cup of tea for himself.

"Ever been to Japan?" he had queried with the quirk
of a dark brow at the tin as he took a shortbread. She
shook her head and he went on, "It's a delightful country."

He had a deep vibrating voice and he spoke in clear,

precise English. Listening to him, Laurel forgot the living-room window minus curtains and the cup of tea she had intended taking up to her mother before bringing her downstairs for tea. She learned that his name was Kirk Graham. He was thirty-one and was a secretary at the British Embassy in Tokyo. He had been on vacation with another six weeks to go and had decided to look up his Uncle George, known to Laurel as Dr. Machelle. They were deep in conversation when Laurel's mother walked in with a hostile expression in her blue eyes.

Kirk had risen immediately as she entered the room, and Laurel, who had now fully recovered, went to meet her.

"Darling," she said, taking her mother's arm, "I'm awfully sorry to have forgotten your cup of tea, but I've managed to get your new prescription, thanks to Mr. Kirk Graham here who so kindly gave me a lift to the village before the drugstore closed."

Laurel had introduced them and Leila Stewart had acknowledged Kirk's greeting in a clear, soft voice. The blue eyes, once so warm and eloquent, were blank. She returned his smile without really smiling. Laurel had gently taken her mother to a chair, choking back the tears and wishing that the charming stranger had known her real mother and not this broken, joyless woman whose mind was practically empty of memories. She had been such a dear.

To her surprise, Kirk seemed to understand. Charmingly, he plied her mother with tea and shortbread. There was no mention of Laurel's collapse. Leila had lost the capacity to hold any information long enough in her mind for her poor bruised brain to assimilate. Her eyes regarded him blankly, taking in the immaculate suit, the handmade soft leather shoes and his well-groomed appearance accentuated by his charm.

For his part, Kirk had seen a woman as slim and dainty as a girl of twenty-five with blue eyes and brown hair untouched with gray. But her cream and rose complexion

was marred by the scar that meandered from her hai
across her forehead and down her cheek. The tailore
simplicity of her soft beige dress had given her an air c
delicacy and charm. He had been enchanted to find him
self in the company of two of the most charming wome
it had been his pleasure to meet since arriving in Eng
land. They had talked, what about Laurel could neve
have remembered. But she did remember Kirk's kee
eyes taking in the curtains she had been in the act of pu
ting up when the doctor had paid his visit. Taking ther
from the back of the chair where she had left them, h
had put them up, making short work of it with his lon
arms.

After that he had dropped by every day at the cottag
to take them out for a run in his car—sometimes to th
coast where Laurel bathed with him in the sea while he
mother sat on the beach. He had borrowed his uncle'
boat and taken them both for a sail, or he dined with then
at the cottage.

Laurel prepared chicken delicately golden, tender
sliced young beans, small new potatoes and fresh youn;
green peas from the kitchen garden. She felt ridiculousl
pleased when he had asked for a second helping of he
apple strudel. Sometimes in his company her mother re
sponded to his wit and charm before the shutter cam
down again over her face and it took on again
heartbreaking blankness.

The shock of her father's death and the constant atten
tion on her mother had sapped Laurel's energy unti
there were no reserves; but she was recharged by Kirk':
vitality. She discovered that he was an excellent golfer
getting up at six in the morning to play on the links wit!
his Uncle George before breakfast. He was also a stron;
swimmer and took a delight in fast driving.

When he had gone back to London after a month's sta\
at his uncle's, Laurel had ached for a sight of him. The
the letter had arrived in his strong masculine scrawl invit
ing them both up to London for the last week of his leave
Her joy had known no bounds. He had booked them in a

a hotel, and that week was one Laurel would never forget. They had gone to shows, visited parks and art galleries, dined in all the smart places. She had danced with him in the intimate glow of dimly lit luxurious places until she had not been herself anymore.

She became hopelessly lost in his charms, his low chuckle, his casual, easy acceptance of the best wherever they went, his sense of humor, congenital courtesy and slow, tantalizing smile. All these and his unfailing kindness and attention to her mother bound her heart in silken cords, imprisoning it against all comers.

That last night in London when he had delivered them to their hotel rooms he had taken her aside after her mother had gone to her room. Keen-eyed, he had looked down into her flushed face.

"I leave early tomorrow for Japan. I'll find a mountain of work awaiting me, so I'll be busy for the next few weeks. I'll give you my address and I want your promise to write to me." From the pocket of his dinner jacket Kirk had given her an envelope with his address and had pressed it into her hand. "Will you write?"

Laurel had been near to tears. She knew that when he had gone she would die a little. He was her knight errant, riding in a sleek black car instead of on a white charger. Now he was going away forever out of her life. She had looked up at him, valiantly hiding her feelings. *I love everything about him*, she had thought despairingly, *his leashed energy, his outrageous charm and devastating smile and the way he has walked into my life to give it a new meaning*. He had seemed reluctant to leave her, putting a firm finger beneath her chin and masterfully lifting her face to his. The long, hard kiss had continued despite the elderly couple who had come up in the elevator to pass them in the corridor. Laurel had wanted to go on clinging to him, but her sense of delicacy prevented her. He had been very kind to her mother and to herself. It would not be fair to mistake his courtesy and kindness for something more personal.

A man in Kirk's position and with his ability did not need a wife—at least not Laurel Stewart. He was quite capable of making a successful career without the help of a feminine hand. So Laurel had waited for him to write to her first before committing herself. His letters had been short because of the pressure of work. Then gradually they had lengthened, demanding all her news in return.

But Laurel had not told him that her mother had grown worse and had become violent at intervals. The injury to her head had resulted in a piece of bone penetrating her brain. An operation had been out of the question and Laurel had flatly refused to send her mother to the hospital. When his proposal of marriage came several months after he had gone back, Laurel read it through a mist of tears. It took a few days of sleepless torment and many sheets of writing paper before she finally wrote her refusal.

The following months taxed her strength and courage to the utmost. Dr. Machelle was away on a course and without Kirk's letters to sustain her, Laurel became a shadow of her former self. Scenes with her mother, in which for no apparent reason she would throw the first thing on hand at Laurel, became a nightmare. The climax had come on the day Dr. Machelle returned. He had called at the cottage with his locum to see how his patient was, and had found Laurel unconscious and bleeding profusely from a wound in her temple. She was lying on the floor of her mother's room not far away from the silver candelabrum that her mother had thrown at her.

Leila Stewart died that night, and Laurel lay for weeks in a twilight world. Dr. Machelle had taken her to his home in the care of his housekeeper, and gradually she began to gain strength. When she was strong enough the doctor sent her to a cottage in Cornwall where she was looked after by an old aunt of his. She was there when Kirk sent a second proposal of marriage.

Laurel had carried the letter back home with her to the cottage unanswered. While she longed with all her heart

to go out to him, something seemed to be holding her
back from answering the letter. In the end, his Uncle
George approached her in his forthright way, telling her
he knew of the proposal and that he was taking care of all
the arrangements for her departure.

With her feelings in cold storage, she had bought her
trousseau after sending Kirk her acceptance of his proposal, and now here she was on the deck of the ship bringing her nearer to the man who had taken her heart for all
time. Nervously Laurel tugged at her white gloves, adjusting her shoulder bag and glanced down at her neat
navy suit and white pumps. All unnecessary actions, she
knew—like patting the Grecian-styled coils of hair when
not a hair was out of place.

By the time the ship docked, her heart was hammering
against her ribs and her mouth was dry. Then she was
holding out her hands to him and looking up into his face
with the tears running down her cheeks.

He gripped her hands before drawing her against him
with a look of concern. "Eh, now! I hope those are tears
of happiness."

He dealt swiftly with the tears and the handkerchief
was back in his pocket as he took her arms in his strong
hands and looked down into her pale face. To her tired
spirit he was the embodiment of youth, strength and vitality, bringing with him a fresh tang of mountain air mingling pleasingly with the masculine fragrance of good
grooming. He was even more devastating at close quarters than she remembered and it made her feel weak just
to look at him.

"Are you better, my sweet? You look tired. I hope the
journey hasn't proved too much for you."

He bent his head to kiss her cheek like a brother might
have done. It occurred to her then that his Uncle George
had been keeping him well informed.

She gave a pale smile. "I'm much better. I'm going to
love Japan. It gives an impression of being all fun and
gaiety. I feel I want to laugh and cry at the same time."

He watched the frank enchantment of her face. "And are you pleased to see me?" he whispered.

Laurel trembled as she stared up at his dark feature and firm leanness, trying to believe he still loved her, a woman who had been remote and almost a stranger for so long, a woman who must be persuaded to give herself unreservedly into his keeping, who would be expected to love him as he loved her. It was all there mixed up in her mind. Giving him her love and trust would help her to restore her lost faith in life, in herself. Her need for him was like a searing pain.

Her smile was misty but ineffably sweet. "I've dreamed of nothing else."

Again she felt the spell of his magnetism, finding him as wonderful as at their first meeting. The look in her eyes must have convinced him, for his eyes softened as he looked down on her forlorn slim figure. From then on he took charge and to Laurel it was heaven.

If Yokohama had fascinated her, Tokyo filled her with delight. In Kirk's long, sleek car they cruised along narrow winding streets past clusters of unpainted crazy warehouses and brown toy dwellings that actually housed families. Kirk told her that the Japanese did not favor painting their wooden houses. They believed that exposing the wood to the weather preserved it better.

The scene through her window was like a film—mushroom hats, gay kimonos, parasols and cotton trousers hurried along on bare feet in wooden clogs. They clip-clopped along the pavement to pause at open-air stalls overflowing with market produce, fish and household goods. Strapped on their mothers' backs, fat little babies nodded in sleep, and bicycles did miraculous curves around the traffic as the narrow, shop-lined streets gave way to wide boulevards.

Here Europeans in Western clothes mingled with the Oriental kimonos and clogs. Presently Kirk drew up at the New Otani Hotel where Laurel was to stay until her marriage. The foyer was filled with a happy, laughing, chattering throng of Orientals in all their finery.

"A wedding party," Kirk whispered on their way to the reception desk. He took charge of her hotel key, ordered tea to be brought up and accompanied her to her rooms.

"Poor sweet, you looked tired out," was his comment. "We'll talk tomorrow when you've had a good night's sleep."

Laurel could have gone to sleep there and then, for Kirk had surrounded her with cushions on a bamboo chair in the Western-style room with its expanse of gleaming wood floor and the minimum of light, unpolished furniture.

His lean, capable fingers dispensed the Japanese green tea into small delicate cups from an enchanting teapot with a dragon's open mouth for the spout. She found the tea wonderfully refreshing and to please Kirk she ate two of the small cakes made from rice flour, a wafer-thin one flavored with caraway seeds and a vanilla-flavored one smothered in nuts.

The sense of strangeness slowly diminished. Kirk was as cool and managing as ever with that experienced look that defied things to go wrong. His smile was tolerant and teasing and at times grave and interested. Before he left her he stood looking down at her for a fleeting second and said with a crooked smile, "I'm still trying to convince myself that you're here." He bent his head to kiss her lips lightly. "I want you to go to bed now and rest. I'll be around in the morning. Sleep well, and dream of me."

Her heart soothed, Laurel found herself loving him as a reality far more than she had loved him as a fiancé faraway. Being with him would take away all her sadness and sense of loss. He was hers now—or would be quite soon. How soon?

CHAPTER TWO

THAT NIGHT Laurel slept the sleep of exhaustion and awoke with a sense of strangeness to find her hotel room flooded with sunshine. The first thing in her thoughts was the wedding dress in her wardrobe. Kirk had not said how soon they were to be married. Was it possible that he had changed his mind since seeing her again? Laurel stared up at the ceiling with a scared feeling rippling along her nerves. Had Kirk changed in his feelings toward her since he had made his second proposal? After all, he met many beautiful women in his own circle of friends who would flock around him, drawn irresistibly by his charm and good looks, while she was just a shadow of her former self.

The thought of those women made her feel a bit sick at what was before her. Could she face up to meeting all his friends? Moreover, could she marry Kirk and be all that he expected in a wife? Cold sweat broke out like dew on her forehead, and in putting up a pale little hand to her temple, her fingers came in contact with the scar left by the blow from the candelabrum. A fraction of an inch to the left and the blow would have been fatal. But she had been spared to be Kirk's wife. Her pulse hammered at the thought of being in his arms. She loved him—there was no doubt about that. Why, then, should she have the feeling of being hurried into something for which she was not quite ready? The loss of her parents had left her unsure and the world had become alien and frightening without their reassuring presence. Was that the reason?

Laurel had not found the answer when she left her bed to wash and dress. It occurred to her as she dressed her thick silken hair at the back of her head in the Grecian style that suited her so well that, had her eyes been almond-shaped, she could have passed for Japanese. Of medium height, she had the velvety skin of a camellia plus a delicacy of wrists and ankles that was pleasing. Moreover, the black silk, flower-printed pantsuit in a size ten fitted her perfectly, outlining her softly rounded bust and tiny waist enchantingly. The low open neck revealed the slender column of her young throat and the enchanting curve of her chin. But her eyes were shadowed and her small face looked drawn.

Breakfast was brought to her room by a blandly smiling Japanese waiter—rolls, butter, honey, crisp toast and a boiled egg. The typically English breakfast ordered by Kirk the previous evening was set down on the lacquer table.

His knock on her door came around ten o'clock. Laurel rose with unspeakable relief from her enforced inactivity to open the door. He strode in with a bouquet of flowers, rosebuds with the dew still on them. His eyes, gray as steel in his tanned face, twinkled with amusement and more than a little appraisal at the pretty pantsuit before they narrowed on her flushed face and sweetly curving mouth.

"Good morning, my sweet. I bring you flowers when you're like a flower yourself. What are you, an English rose or a Japanese orchid?"

Laurel accepted the flowers with a feeling of agitation that she knew had to be checked before it came too apparent. She had been lucky that the breakdown she had suffered after her mother's death had only left her with frayed nerves that would heal with time.

"Both, I hope," she said, burying her face in the sweetness of the roses. "They're lovely. Thank you, Kirk."

She turned to place them on the lacquer table and he looked down tenderly at her bent head.

"No kiss?"

Gently he turned her around to face him, his voice, his face, his lips a command as he bent his head.

Laurel trembled in his arms. The kisses of a year ago were never quite like this one. His lips were transmitting an electric current through her whole being, touching every nerve in her body. She became glowingly alive and her whole being responded to his nearness. She clung, and it was Kirk who drew away. His gray eyes met hers fully for a breathtaking moment in a look that made her quickly lower her own.

He spoke, she thought, a trifle unsteadily for him. "I mustn't forget that you're still not a hundred percent fit."

Subduing the wild beating of her heart, she said breathlessly, "I'm all right. What did . . . Dr. Machelle tell you?"

"Enough," he answered laconically. He looked suddenly grim. "Why didn't you tell me about your mother instead of turning down my first proposal as if you didn't care?"

Laurel moistened dry lips. "But I did and do care enormously. Too much to tie you down to a wife who could never have been one while mother was alive."

"So you shut me out."

"Could I have done anything else? Wouldn't you have done the same?"

He shrugged. "With me behind you, you would have been better equipped to fight the undercurrents, whereas we've wasted so much time. And now it's—" He broke off suddenly and her heart went cold.

Her overwhelming love for him urged her to throw herself into his arms and tell him how shattered she had been. But a sense of delicacy held her back. Laurel braced herself for what was coming.

Piteously, she held out her hands. "I . . . I did what I had to do. Kirk, I'm sorry."

He took the small, hot, quivering hands in his strong grasp, drew her in his arms and, kissing her hair, let her go.

"You've had a bad time of it, my sweet. I hope I'm not rushing you." A finger beneath her rounded chin was compelling her to look at him. "Still want to marry me?"

Laurel's blue eyes searched his; she wished heartbreakingly that she knew the real reason behind the question. But his eyes remained enigmatic.

"I came all this way to marry you, Kirk," she answered soberly.

"So you did." He released her chin with a playful tweak. "And now suppose I show you around the hotel?"

"This hotel?" she queried in bewilderment.

"Of course." He was smiling now, that smile of extraordinary charm which did things to her heart. "We're getting married and the Japanese specialize in weddings. The New Otani is a rather special hotel where weddings are concerned."

Kirk escorted her down to the ground floor where Laurel saw not only banqueting halls, but everything required for a wedding. The banqueting halls ranged from modest ones catering for a small party to enormous places spacious enough to cater for a thousand or so guests buffet-fashion.

Everything the Western world could produce was there, from television to all kinds of electronic equipment. There were photographic studios for wedding pictures, makeup rooms, dressing rooms and shops selling everything from wedding presents to wedding attire. A shop that interested Laurel rented out wedding clothes. Thus one could enter the hotel in a business suit, change to rented wedding attire for the ceremony and reception, then change back again before leaving the hotel.

Laurel learned that the Japanese wore a morning suit complete with carnation in the buttonhole for their wedding. She also fell in love with the bride's traditional white kimono with its elaborate trimmings and the beautifully coiffured wig lacquered to firmness and decorated with flowers.

"Do they marry in church?" she asked Kirk as they

gazed at a splendid six-tier wedding cake in an illuminated alcove.

"They marry in the Shinto Wedding Ceremony Hall.
Come on, I'll show you."

He led her into a beautifully decorated wood-paneled
hall containing all the accoutrements for a Shinto wedding. A white-robed priest was already there and it was
obvious that a wedding would soon be taking place.

From there they were taken to the kitchens by a super-
visor who, on recognizing Kirk, came forward to take
them through. Bowing low from the waist, he explained
in English that the hotel kitchens were apart from those
catering for weddings, for which they employed a special
staff. They were the last thing in efficiency and up-to-
date equipment.

The reception after a Japanese wedding was much the
same as in the Western world with the exception that an
orchestra was hired even for the smallest gathering, although often on a smaller scale with fewer instruments.

"Well, what did you think of it?"

Kirk asked the question lazily, but his eyes were keen
to see her reaction.

Laurel shone up at him. "I think it's fabulous. Shall . . .
shall we be married here?

"You don't mind?"

"I'd love it."

They had lunch in the Rose Room of the hotel where
Kirk chose a Western-style meal.

"Enjoying it?" he asked when, having finished the
meal, they were waiting for their coffee. He had lighted a
cigarette and was leaning back in his chair surveying her
face mockingly.

"Very much," Laurel smiled. "It tastes different, but
deliciously so."

He leaned forward to tap the ash from his cigarette into
an ashtray provided. "Amazing, isn't it? But I can see
you're going to like Japan. You'll like the Japanese
dishes. They have a certain gastronomic delicacy offer-

ing a new world of cuisine. I found it both adventurous and pleasing. I still do.''

"Even raw fish?"

He grinned. "Yes, raw prawns, octopus and eel liver are extremely palatable."

The waiter brought their coffee. When he had gone, Laurel asked casually, "Shall we have a place of our own or . . . or shall I move in with you?"

"We have a place of our own, which I'm keeping as a surprise—a new house that we'll move into when we return from our honeymoon." His eyes met hers suddenly and pierced her with their steeliness. "Are you looking forward to it, or are you worried?"

"I much prefer a place of our own, of course." She wanted to add that anywhere would be home with him, but found herself tongue-tied: Besides, he was looking at her with a strange glitter in his eyes that affected her oddly.

"Afraid?" he mocked.

"Should I be? Perhaps I am a little."

He laughed softly as though at some secret joke. "I think we're going to be very happy. By the way, I'm not taking you to meet any of my friends yet. Time enough when we return from our honeymoon." He stubbed out his cigarette. "What would you like to do this afternoon?"

"I'd like to go around the shops," Laurel said, adding hurriedly at his raised eyebrows, "Not to buy, only to look."

"Why not to buy? I was hoping you would say that, because we have an important bit of shopping to do."

That afternoon strolling through narrow streets of shops with Kirk's hand clasping hers was something Laurel never forgot—the clip-clop of wooden clogs mingled with the high-pitched tinkling voices of vendors selling their wares in narrow streets closed to traffic where brightly colored Japanese lanterns swung in the

warm air alongside picturesque street lamps and English
names over shops.

Shop fronts were open to the weather, displaying their
wares with lantern-lit dim interiors like Aladdin's caves.
Laurel would have liked a camera to take the scenes as
they passed by them—the old fortune-teller in the dim
recess of a shop leaning over a pretty kimonoed girl's
hand beneath an orange lantern, the wizened old man
roasting chestnuts over a brazier and the boy in a beautiful kimono of hand-painted birds and sunsets carrying a
fairy temple of white wood rather like a Christmas tree
with little drawers that opened out and contained can-
dies.

Now and then Kirk looked down on her enchanted,
glowing face with mocking amusement as she gazed on
these delights, imprisoning them for all time in her heart.
Occasionally he drew her closer to his side when children
and dogs dashed madly along the pavements as they will
do in any country. Leisurely they strolled by displays of
household goods, market produce, flowers, fish, confec-
tionery, rich silks, kimonos, jewelry, real pearls, Shinto
shrines and little Buddhas carved in silver, jade and
wood.

At a small jewelers, Kirk bought her a necklace,
bracelet and earrings in jade and was highly amused
when the little old shopkeeper with a face like a walnut
presented her with a jade comb to wear in her hair.

Laurel was so touched by the gift that she felt tears
welling in her eyes.

"Honorable lady not like?"

The little walnut face with two very concerned shoe-
button eyes regarded her pathetically.

"Oh, yes! It's beautiful, and so kind of you." Laurel
blinked back the tears as she groped for the appropriate
Japanese words. "*Arigato gozaimasu.*"

She then bent forward to kiss the parchmentlike cheek
and looked up to see Kirk smiling at her mockingly.

"That old rascal was evidently smitten with you," he

said when they were making their way back to the car. "I can see you being very popular with the males. You will find them very eager to please—only don't go around kissing them for doing you a favor!"

Kirk jealous? A delicious thought. Laurel hugged it to her, hoping it was true.

"He was a sweet old man, and quite harmless."

"I'm not so sure. The average Japanese male is very much a man, and don't forget it," he said dryly.

They had reached his car and he opened the door for her to slip inside.

"I'll take your word for it," she said.

His lips twitched. "I wasn't aware that you could speak Japanese."

"Only the essentials for good manners," was the demure answer as she entered the car.

Their next place of call was a high-class establishment in the Imperial Arcade. A young man in a black morning suit came forward to greet them, bowed his beautiful sleek black head and escorted them to a small private room, where they were seated in ornate gilt chairs. He then proceeded to place trays of wedding rings on the glass counter before them. Laurel's finger was measured, the correct size offered for Kirk to choose one, and he promptly slipped it on her finger.

"Comfortable?" he asked, highly amused at her flushed cheeks. She nodded. The wedding rings were withdrawn and trays of engagement rings winked at them.

"You choose, my sweet," Kirk said. "I'm sorry I couldn't send you one. I had no idea of your size."

Laurel leaned forward, wondering about their cost. That they were real diamonds she had no doubt. She settled at last on a diamond solitaire. Kirk pushed it on her finger. His firm mouth tilted.

"I was about to choose that one myself. Do you like it?"

"It's beautiful," she assured him, smiling up into his

gray gaze. Then while the young man whipped away the
rings she drew his head down and kissed him on the lips.
"Thank you."

"Tired?" Kirk was setting the car off at speed and they
were leaving the shops behind.

"Of course not."

Laurel looked down at the engagement ring sparkling
on her finger. Already she felt part of Kirk. How could
she possibly be tired on such a singularly beautiful day,
savoring the delights of being alone with him in exploring
a beautifully strange new world? She already felt
stronger and for the first time since her parents' tragic
accident was carefree and happy. There was a breathless
expectancy in the air too new to dwell upon, but it
thrilled her all the same.

She found herself shining up at Kirk with joyful anticipation when he suggested taking her to a Buddhist temple for the tea ceremony.

"I think you'll enjoy it," he said.

He drove through open thoroughfares between
streams of traffic until they reached a high stone wall enclosing many carved picturesque pagoda roofs, Leaving
the car outside the gates, Kirk and Laurel entered the
grounds. To Laurel it appeared to be a garden of temples
and as they strolled past the first one, she had a glimpse
of brass and gold shining in the dim interior.

The second beautifully carved, unpainted wooden
building had many pagoda roofs curling against the blue
of the sky. The main entrance door was guarded by two
stone dragons. At the top of the steps they slipped out of
their shoes to put on the canvas slippers provided, then
Kirk opened the door of an officelike room and guided
Laurel inside.

Instantly a beautifully painted paper door in the far
wall was drawn along and a thin, ascetic-looking Japanese
strode in wearing a long black lace robe over a white silk
undergarment.

"The high priest," Kirk whispered to Laurel as he
walked toward them. A thin strip of obi cloth in scarlet

and gold was draped around his neck to hang down the front of his robes. His hair was cut in the manner of a monk and his clean-shaven face was wreathed in smiles.

"Kirk-san! How good to see you," he said in excellent English, bowing low.

Kirk introduced Laurel and after several more courteous bows the priest led them across the room to the painted paper sliding door. Along corridors and through a hall they went to yet another painted paper door.

At first the room they entered appeared to be empty except for the gold-edged tatami mats on the wooden floor. Then across an area of gloom Laurel saw an enormous golden Buddha with the usual large head, heavy hooded eyes and enigmatic expression. On each side of this awe-inspiring figure with its halo of golden flowers were beaten gold lotus flowers holding lighted candles.

The smell of incense burning stung Laurel's nostrils as her eyes followed elaborate golden frescoes that leaped and twirled over the altar in the shape of flowers, lambs and saints. There were cabinets of treasures around the room, but the smell of incense was overpowering and Laurel was thankful to feel the comforting grip of Kirk's hand on her elbow as they left the room.

They walked with the priest through another long hall and through yet another paper sliding door. This opened onto a garden of miniature trees and lawns. Kneeling on cushions on the lawn were three young Japanese girls in kimonos facing an older woman in a black one.

"Enjoy your tea ceremony," siad the priest smilingly as he motioned Kirk and Laurel to cushions by the girls on the grass then he left them.

Kirk folded his long legs with the ease of long practice. Laurel met his ironic gaze as she sat down gracefully beside him.

"The lady in black is teaching the girls the tea ceremony," he whispered. "It's one of the essentials in learning to be a good wife."

As he spoke one of the girls gave her attention to a ket-

tle about to boil over a charcoal burner in front of her
Almost reverently, she poured a little of the water into
small porcelain bowl to heat it as one would heat
teapot. Then, beneath the eagle eye of the teacher, sh
measured out green powdered tea into the bowl. Th
boiling water was then poured over it and whiske
around with a small bamboo-whiskered brush. Gravel
the girl took the bowl in her left hand, turning it aroun
slowly twice, and gave it to Kirk.

He again turned it around twice before drinking it. Th
same procedure, making the tea in the small bowl an
whisking it into a green froth, was gone through again
this time for Laurel. Carefully, she turned the bow
around twice and raised it to her lips. The slightl
pungent flavor was delicious. So were the tiny jelly cake
served on toy plates.

The teacher watched the girl making every move witl
her dainty hands, nodding and smiling graciously at Kirl
and Laurel as they received the tea. She spoke Englisl
fluently and conversed with them, keeping one eye on he
pupil as she did so. Laurel enjoyed it all immensely.

That evening they dined out at the Fontaineblea
Restaurant on the top floor of the Imperial Hotel. It wa:
expensive and elegant. Later they walked in the gardens
It was a lovely evening with the silver sickle moon low ir
the wide expanse of sky. Earlier they had looked dowr
on the glitter of Tokyo by night, a mixture of the old anc
the new with modern neon lights nudging the Japanes
lanterns of centuries-old design.

As she strolled beside Kirk along the gravel path
Laurel's heart began to beat painfully, not because the
were hurrying but because he appeared to be strolling ir
the gardens with her for a purpose. Leisurely they hac
passed over small bamboo bridges spanning rock pool:
until they reached a dainty pagoda-roofed pavilion
where they paused at the top of the steps to admire the
view.

They stood without contact but close enough fo

Laurel to wonder if he could hear the beating of her heart. Tremors ran along her nerves and she shivered.

He stood motionless for a second. Then he gripped her shoulders and turned her around to face him. "Are you cold?"

"No. Not in the least," she hastened to reassure him. "It's not a cold night, is it? Perhaps it's all the excitement of a strange country."

Her face, very earnest and appealing, was lifted to his, and she saw him smile oddly.

"Are you sure that's all?" he asked softly. "You're not afraid of me, are you, Laurel?"

"Of course not." She grew suddenly rigid under his hands. "Only I'm not the girl I was twelve months ago. I'm almost a stranger to you."

He said roughly, "We would have been married by now if you'd accepted my first proposal."

"I know. But I've been ill since then . . . and . . . Kirk, you're not marrying me because you feel sorry for me?" Her voice held the sound of tears.

"No, I'm not. I asked you to marry me for the usual reasons. Incidentally, I've never asked a woman to marry me before."

For a moment Laurel could have sworn the look in his eyes was one of regret. But it went as quickly as it had appeared. Nevertheless she seemed to sense his sudden withdrawal. It was all wrong. She should be laughing up at him, telling him that she was a scared idiot. With every fiber of her being she wanted this cool, lean, arrogant man with his strength of character, his steady gaze of gray eyes beneath dark brows, his nonchalant grace of movement and his charm.

"You . . . you don't regret it, then? After all, twelve months apart is a long time."

"You're not trying to wriggle out of it, are you, my sweet? You know, you *are* afraid of me." The hands that held her arms closed with a steady pressure. "I know we've been apart for a while, but I promise you won't regret marrying me." His eyes twinkled down at her. "I promise not to beat you more than twice a week."

He had evaded her question. His reply had been too absolute for her to admit any doubt on her part. If only he would follow up his teasing with taking her in his arms. Then she could have told him her fears. But he did not.

Laurel made a valiant attempt at humor. "That's what I call a very generous offer, Kirk-san."

"And you accept, my little lotus flower?"

He was smiling down at her with the smile that rocked her heart. He was so tall, so dear with his dark head silhouetted against the night sky. She wanted to put her arms around his neck and know the comforting warmth of his embrace.

Instead, she gave a heroic little smile. "Unreservedly," she answered.

Was the sudden intake of breath one of relief on his part or dismay? Laurel wished she could stop torturing herself as he took her hand.

"Come on, sit down. I want to talk to you."

He led her inside the pavilion and she sank down on the wooden seat. He did not sit down beside her but stood leaning against the door frame showing her his rather stern profile as he gazed out into the night.

"I had intended us getting married immediately upon your arrival. However, on second thoughts I've decided that it wouldn't be fair to you after an exhausting journey, especially as you're recuperating from a run-down condition."

"I'm much better. Dr. Machelle said I would soon pick up again."

"Undoubtedly. You're young and resilient. But you've had a rough time. We must get you well, and that means no extra exertion until you can take it in your stride."

"I've never been ill in my life before. . . ."

"I know," he cut in somewhat impatiently. "You're the kind of little idiot that would keep on until you dropped."

"But I'm well now, honestly, Kirk."

"Are you?" Without having moved he was bending over her in one swoop, looking down at her in the gloom with an expression that stirred her pulses alarmingly. "Are you?" he repeated. "Well enough to marry me this coming Saturday?"

Laurel's heart lurched near her throat. "This . . . this coming Saturday?" she echoed weakly.

"That's what I said." He frowned. "Is it too soon? Do you feel I'm rushing you?"

"No."

He straightened but he did not smile. "We won't discuss it now. You've done enough for one day. I'll make all the arrangements. And you're not to worry. I'm taking time off for the rest of the week to show you around—unless you'd rather rest until Saturday?"

"No." Laurel rose to her feet to put a hand on his sleeve. "I'm not an invalid, Kirk. I never have been."

His frown disappeared and he gave a semblance of a smile. "Even so, there'll be no late nights for you, my sweet, for a long time to come."

CHAPTER THREE

KIRK WAS CAREFUL not to subject Laurel to any degree
of strain during the next few days and she was so happy
to be with him that the time simply flew. He took her out
to dine most evenings, sometimes in an expensive plush
restaurant like Maxim's in the Ginta, a replica of
Maxim's in Paris with French cuisine and the old-world
atmosphere. Other times they went to an inn to dine
Japanese-style or to one of the many night spots where
they could dance in between courses in the warm intimacy of shaded lights.

Their days were spent leisurely in the parks or in the
country where they picnicked with a basket made up at
the hotel. And each day Laurel became more and more
enchanted with the fragile and delicate charm of a
strange and beautiful country. She loved the dainty
snow-covered peaks piercing the blue skies, the beautiful willow-pattern gardens, the Japanese farmers in their
mushroom hats patiently wading in the mud of their rice
paddies to plant the delicate green shoots, and hardworking mothers carrying their fat little babies strapped to
their backs and the round, bland, smiling faces of the
shopkeepers frankly admitting their pleasure to be of
service.

Looking back afterward on those few days with Kirk
Laurel realized that she was beginning to recover her
former health and strength, to pick up the threads of life
that the tragedy of her parents had unraveled.

Saturday morning dawned with Laurel waking up to
her wedding day. She was up early for breakfast in order

to go downstairs to the hairdressing salon. Keeping her mind a careful blank, she put on the black silk pantsuit, found it impossible to eat a thing and drank several cups of coffee.

Her appointment had been booked and she was greeted by the proprietor, a small gold-toothed young man who bowed her ceremoniously to a chair in one of the cubicles in the salon. In excellent English he complimented her on her beautiful hair as he dressed it up expertly. The salon was filled with clients and Laurel wondered how many brides there were among them. Her pulse was rapid despite her outer calm and she was thankful her hairdresser was not a chatty female who would want to discuss her wedding.

Last-minute jitters—that was what she had. Did Kirk have them, too? She doubted it, although, like herself, he would be glad when it was over. The thoughts ended as the proprietor excused himself to answer a personal call on the phone and Laurel's wits were sharpened when she heard Kirk's name mentioned by a voice coming clearly through the paper-thin wall of the next cubicle.

The first voice was saying, "I'm surprised he hasn't introduced his future wife to his friends."

"Who, Kirk? She's probably in this very hotel. It seems he's kept her out of the way. No one knows where she's staying."

"I asked Bill to find out something about her when he went to the stag party Kirk gave last night at the club," said the first voice.

"And did he?"

"No. I believe Kirk was as close as an oyster and refused to be drawn. By the way, Kirk wouldn't get to bed before four this morning. It was close to four when Bill came home, and Kirk was still there."

"Well, there won't be anything bleary-eyed about Kirk at his wedding. He's so full of health and vitality that one late night won't make much difference to him." The second voice was cynical for a woman. "Dennis came home smashed and he'll have bags under his eyes all day to prove it. I wish he had a bit of Kirk's strength of character.''

The first voice heaved a sigh. "Bill wasn't too bad. Do you know, I'm sorry Kirk is getting married. He's such a good sport. And all the women had their eye on him, even the married ones. I bet his wife will be one of those jealous possessive creatures who'll watch him like a hawk.''

"If she is, it won't take her long to keep a certain female at bay.''

"You mean Countess Nina?''

"Who else? She's regarded Kirk as her property for long enough. I shall enjoy seeing someone put her in her place. You don't think Kirk is marrying for a blind, do you? I mean, Nina has been very obvious in her preference for his company of late. Kirk might be starting as he means to go on and keep his wife in the background, so to speak. Maybe she isn't the possessive kind. She's probably docile and will turn a blind eye to Kirk's friendship with Nina.''

"Do you think so? You could be right. I could imagine a girl being glad of having Kirk on any terms. He's so exciting, so everything. Not feeling jealous, are you, Jean?''

Jean's laugh grated. "Maybe I am at that. I'm ready to bet that she's starry-eyed and so blindly in love that she can't see where she's going. I know because I was the same. Look where it got me.''

"Well, you would go in for looks. You should have gone in for a bean pole with a face like a bad ham and been gloriously happy like me with my Bill.''

"Well, the girl has certainly done well for herself. Everyone knows that Kirk is on the way up—the emperor will see to that. He's very fond of him.''

"I wonder if he's told His Nibs he's getting married. Funny he should decide to get married when he's away.''

"Yes, it's all so hush-hush, isn't it? Kirk's taken no

leave, either, for twelve months apart from that little business trip to Honolulu when he came back with that millionaire and his two pretty daughters. I'm surprised Kirk didn't marry one of them. They were crazy about him.''

"He could be saving his leave for a long honeymoon. This girl he's marrying is English, isn't she?''

"As far as we know. Well, it won't be long before we see what she's like. I'm terribly disappointed we couldn't get the boss to do our hair. Apparently he's with some important client.''

Laurel took this to mean herself. She longed to be able to see the speakers who had inadvertently pricked her bubble of happiness. She was remembering Kirk's bitterness about her refusing his first proposal of marriage. Had he wanted to tell her then that he had found someone else who was more his kind—Countess Nina, beautiful, rich and influential? Laurel felt the perspiration of doubt on her temples. The perfumed salon suddenly became overpowering, unbearable.

Then the proprietor was back, apologizing profusely for the delay. He picked up the comb and his deft fingers plaited the dark locks of hair into a thing of beauty. Laurel recovered her composure enough to smile when he held the jade mirror at the back of her head to show her the result of his labors. She showed the correct degree of enthusiasm and marveled that she could be so calm outwardly when she was trembling within.

Taking off the protective cape from her slim shoulders, he brushed off all imaginary hairs from her suit and retreated in horror when she offered to pay for the service.

"No. Kirk-san very good friend," he insisted in his Pidgin English. "Honored to do honorable lady's hair."

Laurel pleaded, "Please take something."

But he was adamant. "Happy to be of service. Wish honorable lady much happiness and many children."

The gold teeth flashed as he bowed her out. On her way back to her room Laurel was a prey to tormented thoughts hammering unceasingly in her head, stealing the color from her cheeks, the light from her eyes and the buoyancy from her step. The menacing cloud that had descended after the tragic accident to her parents had never really lifted. The two voices she had heard were only a part of it. Had Kirk really hoped she would change her mind?

Was it the reason Kirk had not introduced her to his friends? Laurel was too pure-minded to see double-dealing in others and she was sure Kirk would not resort to it. But he was in the diplomatic service and was trained in such matters. During the trying time with her mother, Laurel had not been fully aware of the extent to which he had filled her life. She had cared desperately for him all along. Yet it was not until she had seen him again that her love for him had leaped into flame, a flame that she could not quench.

In vain Laurel told herself to have it out with him and give him back his ring if he did not wish to marry her. She lifted a hand to her throbbing temples. It would be impossible to tear him out of her heart without dying a little. Feverishly, recalling a touch, a certain tone in his voice, she could have sworn he loved her. Then calm reason reminded her that he had hardly behaved like a lover. There had been the cool kiss on the ship and the rather cruel one on her first morning at the hotel when he had brought her the flowers. After that, what? A cool kiss on the hair when he left her at the door of her hotel room.

Laurel's sensitive nature trembled at the thought of giving her love where it was not wanted. Her face burned with shame at the thought. Tears pricked her eyes as she closed the door to her room and leaned back against it. *How weak we are when put to the test*, she thought bitterly. One of the women in the hairdressing salon had said that a girl would be happy to take Kirk on any terms. Was she so devoid of pride as to be that kind of person?

If only she had time to think! But the sudden tap on the door behind her told her she had not even got that. It sounded like the crack of doom.

With a groping movement Laurel found the catch of the door and opened it. A young woman stood there holding the bouquet. She was wearing a very pretty kimono in turquoise. Laurel warmed to the bright smile on her little moon face.

"Your flowers, honorable lady," she said in soft broken English. "I, Mini-san, have come to help you prepare for wedding."

Laurel stepped aside to allow her to enter. First came the exquisite lace and satin bra, panties and matching underskirt. Then the dress, which zipped up her slim back, emphasizing her small, firm bust deliciously. The tiny stand-up collar gave her a demure touch of dignity and the long wide sleeves added an elegant finish to a beautifully modeled dress that fitted her willowy figure to perfection.

"Honorable lady have skin like peaches and cream. Pale now like bride. Japanese bride have whitened face. It is traditional." She peeped over Laurel's shoulder as she sat before the dressing-table mirror. "Not much makeup needed."

Mini-san then proceeded to touch up Laurel's eyelashes. The tiny hands enchanted Laurel as they carried out their task, ending with the tiny coronet of flowers being placed on top of the beautifully coiffured hair to hold the long veil in position.

"Bride beautiful like angel," Mini-san cooed when Laurel was ready.

But no little bluebird of happiness sang in Laurel's cold heart when she surveyed her own enchanting apparition in the mirror. All feeling seemed to have deserted her as she took the bouquet that Mini-san offered.

She wondered if Kirk would be waiting for her downstairs or if he would change his mind and slide out of it at the last moment. But no note came and she went downstairs with Mini-san beside her. At the entrance to the wedding hall stood a very good-looking Japanese in a morning suit with a carnation in his buttonhole, and be-

side him stood two delightful tots dressed as bridesmaids. Around five years old, they were as alike as two
peas in a pod in white organza with two frilly little caps
on their black pageboy-styled hair. They looked so delicious with their pretty almond-shaped eyes and
rosebud mouths that Laurel could have picked them up
and hugged them.

When Mini-san introduced them they bowed almost to
the floor. They were named Ranko (Little Orchid) and
Mariko (Little Ball). The New Otani Hotel certainly had
everything laid on, Laurel thought a little hysterically,
and was torn between laughter and tears.

The good-looking Japanese was introduced as
Kasuti-san, a colleague of Kirk. He was to give her
away. They entered on cue to soft music, Laurel with her
hand on the black sleeve of Kasuti-san. Kirk was waiting
for her with a man in the uniform of a captain in the
British navy. She learned later that his ship was in
Yokohama for repairs and that he was an old school
friend of Kirk's.

As she moved to join Kirk a startled flicker of appraisal
appeared in his clear gray eyes. Then it was gone. He
took her cold hand firmly in his warm one and Laurel
gave herself to him for all time. The English ceremony
was brief, after which Laurel was introduced to a blur of
faces.

Photographs were taken and soon they were sitting in
the center of a long, elaborately set table facing a three-
tier wedding cake in one of the banqueting rooms. A
horde of congratulatory telegrams were ready by the best
man, including one from Kirk's Uncle George; the wedding cake was cut with Kirk's firm steady hand over
Laurel's shaky one; and he made a sparkling speech.

Later, Laurel had gone upstairs to change with the
help of Mini-san, and it was all over.

"NOT TOO BAD, was it?"

Kirk was driving the long, opulent car at high speed on

the first stage of their honeymoon. He looked careless and debonair in a light gray business suit while Laurel sat beside him gazing through the windshield with a pale, set face.

It was a day of soft sunshine and gay, enchanting shade. But Kirk was intent upon speed and the scenery swept by like pictures on a screen. To Laurel the wedding had been one of real beauty—the tiny bridesmaids, the beautifully decorated room filled with enchanting flower arrangements that extended into the banqueting room, the gay kimonos mingling with the European dress of the guests and the soft classical music fron an orchestra, a splendid background for all the courtesy.

She said wistfully, "I thought it was rather lovely. The Japanese are unique in the way they have of putting beauty before everything."

He said carelessly, "I knew you would enjoy it. I know every woman dreams of a wedding with all the trimmings and the photographs to drool over afterward. I didn't want to deprive you of it. For myself I would have preferred something short and sweet."

Laurel eyed him covertly. He looked strong, lean and unshakable, his gray eyes steady and cool beneath straight black brows. If only he would look at her like a lover or stop the car and kiss her! It would be only too easy then to tell him of her fears. But he did neither. He merely presented a dark profile that caught painfully at her heartstrings.

Even if the wedding should turn out to be a mockery, she had to hand it to him for the superb handling of it.

"Thanks for everything you've done, Kirk," she said. "For giving me the wedding every woman dreams of. It's something I shall never forget, especially since, like a man, you wanted no fuss. Are you glad it's over?"

He tossed her a questioning glance. "Are you?"

Again the evasion, she thought. "I suppose so."

During the journey to Japan, Laurel had looked upon her marriage as glorifying everything by its radiance, lift-

ing her to the heights of happiness and ecstasy. Instead
all she felt was a strange unhappy bewilderment, an anguished doubt emphasized by the torture of his nearness.
Here they were sitting side by side yet kept miles apart
by some strange undercurrent that she was powerless to
resist. Perhaps, she thought drearily, she was too feeble
to deal with the unseen barrier that seemed more formidable when they were alone.

The house in which they were to spend their honeymoon was at Kamakura Bay, a little town of historic interest about thirty miles or so from Tokyo. The big car
ate up the miles of potholed roads with an easy assurance, tossing aside little hamlets or brown wooden
houses and Japanese inns enclosed by cherry orchards
heavy with blossom.

Wealthy friends of Kirk had offered the house that
they used mostly as a holiday home. It was situated on
the side of a mountain overlooking the bay. Kirk had
driven with considerable dexterity along bumpy roads
with rolling seas of rice on either side thinning out to hills
that gave glimpses of beaches caressed by shimmers of
blue water. A magnificent stone Buddha looked down
from a hilltop as hills became mountains and tea marched
with rice up the sides.

A road lined with Japanese cedars veered upward and
several curving country roads brought them eventually
to the gates of the house. Evidently they were expected,
for the gates were open to receive them. Laurel saw a
Japanese garden of miniature trees, enchanting small
rustic bamboo bridges over streams with flowers and
stone lanterns placed with Japanese artistry on sloping
lawns.

The house, built of carved wood, rose mellow and
serene in the sun like a showpiece in a garden setting. A
young man in a white jacket over black trousers stood in
the doorway. His jet black hair was brushed back from a
sallow face to which only his eyes gave color. They were
a perfect almond shape and twinkled as he bowed low
from the waist in greeting.

Kirk had helped Laurel from the car. "Darling," he said, "this is Yuseku-san who'll look after us while we are here."

Yuseku-san bowed low again, greeting Laurel in perfect English before fetching the luggage from the car.

"Tired, my sweet?"

Kirk swept her up into his arms to carry her over the threshold, then set her down in the tiny vestibule between the two front doors. Here they faced a row of house slippers, and kneeling down, Kirk took off her shoes to choose her small size from those provided and put them on her feet.

"I'm not in the least tired," she answered as he discarded his own footwear in favor of the slippers. "Please can I see the house? It looks delightful."

Laurel was surprised at the spaciousness of the rooms where sunlight fell slantingly through tall windows onto elegant furniture and highly polished wooden floors. Crystal chandeliers winked, a lacquer cabinet gleamed with objets d'art, a gold Buddha on an ebony pedestal looked mysteriously mellow and flowers were everywhere in jade bowls and beautiful vases.

The house was unusual. Half the rooms were furnished in Western style. The rest, in Japanese, would not concern them since Kirk did not intend to entertain visitors on their honeymoon. It was evident that no expense had been spared on furnishing the house, and Laurel walked through it wide-eyed.

"It's awfully grand, Kirk. Are your friends so wealthy?" she asked as they entered the main bedroom.

"So-so," was the laconic reply. His mouth twitched with amusement as she looked anywhere but at the bed. "This is to be our suite of rooms. I have a dressing room leading off." He inclined his head toward a communicating door. "I'm going to wash and change for dinner. Take your time, there's no hurry."

Laurel walked to the window to see the view across the sea, which delighted her immensely. She imagined them going down to the little secluded beach just visible below a winding path. There was a white curve of foam where the water washed gently on the shore. They would bathe together and get to know each other again. All her fears had been groundless, purely prewedding nerves. It was a big thing to give oneself unreservedly into some-one else's keeping, especially someone like Kirk whom she knew so little about. But it was going to be heaven, Laurel told herself as she swung around to look at the room she was to share with him.

The four-poster bed dominated the room with diaphanous drapes cascading down from the canopy overhead framing the cluster of cushions placed artisti-cally at the head of the bed. Rich dark furniture and a scarlet-fringed bedside lamp looked dramatic against neutral walls. The whole effect was one of warm, en-veloping sumptuousness.

Lightheartedly Laurel unpacked her cases brought in by Yuseku-san, filling available space with her pretty trousseau and placing her frothy nightdress of ribbons and lace on the bed. The last thing in her case was the leather case of masculine brushes, her wedding present to Kirk. She looked down at it thoughtfully for a moment and on a sudden impulse she crossed the room to the communicat-ing door.

Opening it quietly, she crept into the empty room. Yuseku had obviously unpacked Kirk's clothes, as his cases were nowhere to be seen in the masculine room containing a bed, dressing table, wardrobe, writing desk and two comfortable chairs. Kirk was in the bathroom, for she could hear the water running. Somewhat disap-pointed not to find him there, Laurel put the case down on the dressing table. As she did so she saw his pajamas folded neatly on the bed.

Laurel frowned, wondering why they should be there. Then it occurred to her that Yuseku-san had laid them out for Kirk to undress that evening in his dressing room. The incident was forgotten as Laurel returned to her room to wash and dress for dinner. She took care to keep

er hair immaculate in the process and blessed her frock
or zipping all down the back to enable her to step into it.
After she had made up her face lightly the result in the
mirror was pleasing. The long fluid lines of the dress in a
soft shade of rose accentuated her slimness and she was
considering whether to put on the jade necklace to fill the
scooped neckline when Kirk strode in.

The next moment something cold was clasped around
her neck and she saw the fire of diamonds as Kirk lowered his head to look over her shoulder into the mirror.
He smelled of cedarwood soap and his tanned face was
like bronze beside her pale one. His cool lips brushed her
cheek.

"Thanks for the brushes, my sweet. I hope you like
your present."

Laurel fingered the diamonds. "But, Kirk, they look
real. I . . . I'll be scared of losing them."

He turned her around to face him, taking his time in
looking her over, taking in the slender youthful curves of
her figure before concentrating on the braids of rich dark
hair.

"Well, well, Mrs. Graham," he said softly. "You're
full of surprises. This morning you were an angel in bridal
array, now you're a dusky beauty in rose pink who can't
be real. Or are you?" He bent his head as though drawn
against his will to seek her mouth. Suddenly he straightened and laughed. "You're looking far too lovely for my
peace of mind. Come on, we'd better go in to dinner or
Yuseku-san will be wondering what's keeping us."

The dinner was proof of Yuseku-san's skill as a chef.
Kirk provided most of the conversation by talking about
Japan. They went into the living room for coffee and
while Yuseku served it, Kirk put a long-playing record
on the stereo.

They sat together on the settee and Kirk took a
cigarette case from his pocket.

"Cigarette?"

"Not now, thanks," she said. Then, hoping he would

not think her too unsophisticated, she added hurriedly
"I do smoke sometimes, but not very often. In fact,
don't really enjoy it."

He lighted one for himself, blew a line of smoke in the
air and said disarmingly, "Don't be apologetic about i
I'm glad—I hate a woman to reek of tobacco smoke
Come here."

He put out a long arm and scooped her up beside him
drawing her head back on his chest. The soft music
which really was music and not a blaring noise, washe
over them. Laurel closed her eyes. Doubt and misgivin
drifted away. She was here with Kirk and nothing els
mattered.

The next thing she knew was his firm mouth restin
briefly on her own.

She opened her eyes sleepily to find his very close
"Oh, dear, have I been asleep?" she said confusedly.

"For a little matter of two hours," he replied dryly
"What about a little stroll in the garden before bed?" H
put her back against the settee and rose lazily to his fee
"I'll fetch your wrap. Take your time about wakening."

He was back in no time with a jacket, which he slippe
on her shoulders as she stood up. Then he drew her han
through his arm and they strolled out into the garden
Everything was so wonderful in the dusk of a Japanes
night. The sky was a transparent sapphire, against which
the branches of trees drooped like dark shapes cut from
black paper. Overhead the moon looked down o
silhouettes of fishing boats on the calm waters way out t
sea and on the horizon a big Orient liner showed a neck
lace of light along her length.

As they stood at the little wicket gate leading down t
the beach, Laurel's dress billowed lightly out as if sh
was indeed borne on the air. With her hand tucked i
Kirk's arm she was filled with a lightness of spirit, a kin
of dreamlike ecstasy.

"The sea is as smooth as cream," she said.

"What about a sail? There's a boat waiting for us dow
at the jetty."

She shone up at him. "Could we? I'd love it."

"Come on, then."

He took her hand in his and they went down the path to the jetty where the boat was moored. Then they were on the water and Kirk was grinning down at her from the controls. He was all fire and laughter, his teeth gleaming in his dark face, his wide shoulders bracing up to the speed as he sent the boat leaping through the water like a porpoise.

As for Laurel, she shrank back deliciously from the onslaught of spray that took her breath away. Then she was holding up her face, enjoying the tingling sensation on her skin. Returning to the shore was like falling from the heights onto the ordinary plain.

They returned to the living room for a nightcap before going to bed. Kirk had rung Yuseku-san for fresh ice as he poured the drinks. Laurel wandered around the room admiring a lacquer cabinet filled with Japanese dolls in traditional dress before stopping at a portrait on the baby grand piano.

It was the head and shoulders of a beautiful woman in her twenties. Her face, with its high cheekbones, slanting eyes and pretty nose and mouth, was openly provocative. She held a fan just below her chin and there was a flower in the beautifully coiffured hair piled Japanese-fashion on her head. A geisha girl, Laurel thought, or the wife of the owner of the house.

She sauntered to the chair by which Kirk was standing with her drink and sank down in it, accepting the glass. Kirk did not sit down but stood indolently against the wall by the drinks cabinet.

"To us," he said, lifting his glass. "May all our troubles be little ones."

On a wave of shyness, Laurel lifted her glass, lowering her eyes from the gleam in his that filled her with a wonderful trembling joy. When he was like this at his most charming she had neither the will nor the desire to resist him. Her face grew hot, staining her cheeks to a wild rose. Her lips trembled in a smile.

"To us," she murmured, then before she could stop the words, they were spoken. "Who is she?"

"Who?" he asked lazily.

"The lady in the portrait on the piano."

"Oh, that?" was the careless response. "The lady of the house."

"You haven't told me anything about them. I suppose you've been here before?"

"Many times."

"Are they Japanese?"

"Yes—Ishi and Nina Wanaka. To give them their correct title, the Count and Countess Wanaka."

A blast of cold wind swept Laurel from head to toe. The identity of the woman in the photograph smiling on them so mockingly came as a shock. She took a large sip of her drink and marveled at her steady hand as she looked toward the photograph.

"She's very lovely," she said inanely.

"Isn't she?"

Laurel gazed down into her glass—anywhere but at Kirk. "I don't remember seeing them at the wedding." He did not answer for a moment and she raised her head to find him looking down at her enigmatically.

"They're away at the springs of Noboribetsu. It's a famous spa on the island of Hokkaido and a favorite resort with Tokyo residents. I'll take you there sometime. You'll enjoy it."

Bitterly, Laurel told herself she must be unique as a bride who was spending her honeymoon in the house of her husband's girl friend—or was it mistress? Tears choked her throat as she recalled the two voices in the hairdressing salon that morning. There was never any smoke without fire and if the two gossiping women were romancing a little, there must be some truth to what they said. This Nina person was beautiful enough, anyway, to turn any man's head, even Kirk's.

Why, then, had he married Laurel? Because his lady love was unattainable, or to stop the gossiping tongues

until the woman was free? The color ebbed from her
cheeks, leaving her face strangely white; her nerves were
on wires pulling so tightly that they threatened to snap.
She put the glass down on the low lacquer table. The walls
of the room seemed to be closing in on her and she heard
Kirk's voice coming from a great distance.

"Are you all right, Laurel? You look as pale as a
ghost." He was bending over her after putting his glass
down beside hers on the table. His keen gray eyes were
raking hers with concern as he took her trembling hands
in his.

She said, "Yes."

He held her hands gently. "Poor child! It's been a long
and trying day for you. Come, I'm going to carry you to
bed."

Before he could carry out his intention, Laurel was on
her feet.

"Please, Kirk. I'm not an invalid, so don't treat me as
one." How could he know that she did not want him near
her at that moment? She was still trembling a little, but
she had regained her self-control.

His hands gripped her then and he looked at her oddly.
"My dear girl, you're my wife and I intend to look after
you. Come along to bed. You'll feel better in the morning."

Kirk held her arm in a deceptively light hold and she
walked with him to her room, too weary to protest. At
her door she drew away from his hand. He opened it and
followed her into the room.

"I'm all right now, thanks," she told him, her eyes
straying to the four-poster bed. His pajamas were not
there. In that moment all feeling in her died. His hand
came under her chin and she felt the coolness of his firm
lips resting lightly on her own. He felt her tremble and
there was no response.

His hand dropped. "Good night, my sweet. Sleep
well."

Then he was gone into the adjoining room where he

had intended sleeping all along. Laurel stood in th
center of the room trying to gather her confused thought
into some kind of order to review the situation soberly.

Her head was woolly and her heart ached, but sh
willed herself to see things in their true perspective. Sh
was a bride, yet not a bride, a simple naive girl who ha
fallen headlong in love with an experienced man of th
world without knowing the least thing about his life. On
thing was clear—she loved him irrevocably and com
pletely. If he wanted her, she was his for the taking—bu
he did not.

Laurel sank down upon the bed in despair. This Coun
tess Nina had probably held him in her toils long befor
he had met Laurel. Even if the woman had only know
Kirk recently, that provocative smiling mouth and al
that coquetry derived from experience was enough t
persuade any man to forget even honor in his desire fo
her.

Laurel's soft mouth tightened stubbornly. *One thing i.
certain,* she thought, *I'm not afraid of the woman and
don't care if she has had a head start. I've alread*
burned my boats by marrying Kirk, but it won't stop m
from building a new one. I love him far too much to mak
him a laughingstock in front of his friends by leaving hin
now. Besides, isn't that what Countess Nina wanted?

She shuddered to think how much she had changed i
the last twenty-four hours. For instance, taking it fo
granted that the woman was no good. That she of all peo
ple, who had always loved her fellow beings, should har
bor resentment and hatred against a complete stranger! I
filled her with shame.

Granted she was up against a woman who held all th
winning cards. Nevertheless, she was a fast learner her
self. The challenge roused all her old fighting spirit, fee
ble at the moment because her vitality had been draine
by all the events of the past year. It was there, though
responding valiantly to her need.

Calmly Laurel went over her weapons, beginning wit

her clothes. Her trousseau was pretty and feminine enough, though everything she bought from now on would have to be just that little bit more alluring. The flowered black silk pantsuit, for instance, did something to her pale skin and slim figure.

Wearily she lifted a hand to her coiffured hair, surprised to find it had withstood the breeze on the sea. The silken tresses tumbled down, hardened by the lacquer used to keep them in place. That was going to be washed out for a start. Kirk disliked women to smoke and she was sure he preferred her hair to be soft and caressing with its own natural perfume.

Laurel wished she knew more about his likes and dislikes. The effort to please would be worth it for one warm husband's glance from those gray eyes. Deciding upon a line of action lifted her spirits and she felt almost lighthearted when she made her way to the bathroom.

CHAPTER FOUR

LAUREL AWOKE bemused with sleep to look around the
strange room in brief bewilderment. Memory came
flooding back and she looked at the little traveling clock
on her bedside table. Eight o'clock. The house was silent
above the soft swish of the waves washing against the
beach below.

Her head, like the new wedding ring on her finger, felt
as heavy as lead. No sound of movement from the adjoining room reached her ears as she slipped into a frothy
negligee and went to the window. The garden, sloping
down to the sea, brightened here and there by clouds of
cherry blossom and lordly pines with red gold branches,
was backed by the serene lines of hills closing in on the
scene like an old Japanese print. The beauty of the place
struck Laurel as ironic—a veritable Eden that was
owned by the serpent.

Laurel went toward the wardrobe to pick out something to wear. She had no idea of Kirk's plans for the day.
He was probably up by the crack of dawn, out riding or
swimming. At the moment her feelings were too slack for
either. Exhilarating moments beneath the shower
worked wonders and her step was buoyant when she
peered into the adjoining room.

Kirk's bed was immaculate. There was no sign of him
or Yuseku-san. No one in the dining room, either. Laurel
walked down the short passage to the door opening onto
the kitchen garden. She was putting on the wooden garden shoes when Yuseku-san came in with lettuce from
the garden. His round face creased in a delighted smile as
he answered Laurel's "*Oheyo!*" with a spate of tinkling

English that she gathered was all about the weather and his hopes that she had slept well.

She said, "*Hoi. Arigato.*"

The two little words meant "Yes, thank you." The *hoi* was spoken as *hi*, which Laurel thought sounded gay. Her knowledge of the language was practically nil and she was discovering that smiles and gestures did very well for little things. Moreover, these small people with their crinkling, laughing faces were so friendly that one never felt embarrassed when unable to find the right words. They seemed anxious only for her to understand their good will; the rest did not matter.

Laurel was clip-clopping along the garden path when a little brown mouse of a woman arrived obviously to do the chores. She wore a brown kimono and reminded Laurel of a wooden doll with her black pageboy-styled hair and mobile smile lighting up behind spectacles glinting in the sun. On seeing Laurel, she stopped, bowed low from the waist, giggled and hastened indoors.

Amused, Laurel continued along the garden path. Two gardeners were at work, clad in neat blue cotton trousers and jacket with *getas* on their feet. They smiled and bowed low as she passed on her way down toward the beach.

Kirk met her halfway, a tall, wide-shouldered figure in a bathrobe. A towel was flung carelessly over one shoulder and his tousled hair fell on his forehead in boyish tendrils. How extraordinarily attractive and arresting he was, she thought with a painful lurch of her heart. He was so intensely alive with a vitality and fire burning beneath the surface, a quality that excited and challenged.

"Hello there!" He put an arm around her shoulders, smiling down at her as they walked back to the house. "Slept well?" When she nodded, he went on, "I've been for a dip in the sea. I looked in to ask you to come with me, but you were fast asleep. I accepted a loan of this house thinking it would give you the opportunity to relax. A hotel isn't the same; you have to quit your room after breakfast. Here you can rest all day if you feel inclined.''

You can also use two bedrooms without inviting the curiosity of a hotel staff, Laurel thought bitterly. The next moment she was regretting her bitterness, and smiled up at him sweetly in consequence.

"You're very kind," she said wistfully.

"And you're very sweet," he said, hugging her shoulders.

Laurel ought to have felt blissfully happy at that moment, with Kirk's arm around her shoulders, but she wasn't. He hugged her as he would a pal. There was no way of discovering what he thought and what he intended to do about their marriage. It could not go on indefinitely as it was.

Even so, breakfast with Kirk sent her spirits soaring. He gave her his whole attention, ignoring the morning papers that Yuseku had placed beside him on the table. In between seeing that she had a good breakfast, he told her amusing incidents that had happened during his work at the embassy. Gradually all strain and embarrassment left her as she responded to his teasing.

"How much Japanese do you know?"

Breakfast was over and Kirk was leaning back in his chair, having lighted a cigarette. Laurel watched the well-kept hands, the lean brown fingers curling around the cigarette as he sent a spiral of smoke ceilingward.

"Apart from his usual greetings, very little."

His mouth twitched. "Define very little."

"I know that *haro* means hello, *sekken* means soap, *orfuro* means bath and *miza*, water."

He regarded her with tolerant amusement. "My poor sweet," he teased, "you were evidently determined to keep clean! You'll learn as you go along. Japanese is much easier to speak than to write. There's certainly nothing for you to worry about. The average Japanese male, like any other, has an eye for a pretty girl and he'll fall over himself to help you." He leaned forward to tap the ash from his cigarette into an ashtray provided on the low table. "However, you'll be with me most of the time."

He had leaned back again in his chair and Laurel looked up. His expression was quizzical and disturbingly direct. She was growing accustomed to his way of looking people straight in the eye. It was easy for him since he was so good at an enigmatic expression.

Laurel knew she was utterly transparent in her emotions and felt, as now, that Kirk could look through her like a clear pane of glass. Was she a fool to distrust his feeling for her, to be afraid to reach out for her own happiness? She could do it, lure him on and set the match to the flame of his passion. But she did not want him on those terms. He had to come to her with an agonizing love and need. He had to feel for her exactly how she felt for him. That was what marriage was all about.

She found refuge from the ensuing silence in speech. "Talking about Japanese males, I haven't yet seen any of those terrifically huge fat men who wrestle on the television."

"The Japanese call it sumo, one of the oldest of sports. The men who take part are Japanese who go in for this kind of thing if they happen to be tall and husky as youngsters. They deliberately fatten themselves up through the years and do special exercises to develop their muscles. The minimum weight is a good two hundred and fifty pounds. Anything less and he would look thin and puny in the ring. Some of them are a colossal weight, which adds to the entertainment when in the ring. There are tournaments lasting about two weeks in Tokyo, and there's one in May if you care to see it?"

Laurel shivered. "No, thank you!"

He teased. "Wouldn't you like to go just once just to see what it's like?" He was laughing at her revulsion. "Women do go. And they enjoy it."

"I'll take your word for it. Why do they wear their hair in a funny topknot?"

"It isn't a wig, but their own hair allowed to grow long

for the purpose of wearing it in the old feudal style of the daimyos or old feudal warlords.'' He laughed at her mockingly with a devilish gleam in his eye as he added, "Their costume, a kind of loincloth, is supported solely by a belt.'' His chuckle was deliberate. "Now you're blushing.''

"You meant me to.''

"You do it so beautifilly. I shall probably do it often.'' He leaned forward to stub out his cigarette. "You haven't much color since your illness. I suggest we go out in the car this morning and spend the afternoon on the beach. It's sheltered and gets really hot in the sun. We can take the morning papers with us. If there are any magazines or books you'd like I'll order them for you.''

SEATED BESIDE HIM in the big roomy car, Laurel felt happy, and relaxed. The day was delightfully warm and sunny with Kirk suddenly much closer than he had been.

"My friends are a mixture of English and Japanese,'' he told her as they sped through villages of unpainted houses, shops and the usual Buddhist and Shinto shrines. "You'll like them.''

Laurel thought of the two English voices she had heard in the hairdressing salon on her wedding morning. If only she had not heard them! Then their marriage would have had a better start. The strangeness of a foreign country seen through the eyes of a happy bride would have been far different, more bearable. Not that she felt alien. She did not. On the contrary, she felt at home. The small, doll-like, unpainted houses caught at her heartstrings and the way the bright-eyed, hardworking little people smiled on their own modest circumstances made her feel ashamed when she had so much more. They passed farms and orchards where the fruit was protected from the birds by being covered in small bags, each one wrapped religiously, looking strangely like artificial trees. In the paddy fields whole families were working furiously and dedicatedly planting the shoots of their staple diet.

Kirk said, "We had a fortnight of rain before you arrived, a godsend to rice growers. After the negligent growth of a hard winter the spring rain sent up the rice shoots that are now ready for transplanting. These people live frugally, yet they would share their last grains of tea or rice with you if you were to pay them a visit."

He pulled up at a little wooden gate leading up to a small, unpainted wooden house. Against it huddled a greenhouse. Both buildings appeared to be clinging for dear life to the side of the hill. The notice on a post at the side of the gate said Maniki Flower Garden.

"I won't be a minute."

Kirk left the car to stride along the garden path where he was met by a small middle-aged man in muddy boots and faded cotton trousers and jacket. He bowed low and Kirk spoke to him. Almost at once a small doll-like creature appeared beside him. Papa-san and daughter-san, thought Laurel, thinking how lovely and dainty were the Japanese girls almost without exception.

This little creature smiled up at Kirk like a bright little blackbird, comprehending his request intelligently before scuttling away between rows of staked dahlias and gladioli.

Kirk stood hands in pockets, a figure carelessly at ease, talking to the little market gardener. He was no doubt bowled over by Kirk's charm, Laurel mused, watching the sun glint on the thick crop of crisp dark hair and the wide shoulders. Just looking at him brought a surge of longing for his arms around her and his gray eyes alight with something more than his tolerant teasing.

Presently the little girl reappeared with a bouquet beautifully arranged and tied with ribbon. Money changed hands amid much bowing and smiling and Kirk was returning with the bouquet.

Laurel's color deepened as he gave it to her with a mocking smile.

"For me? How nice! Thank you, Kirk. They're lovely."

The dew still clung to the delicate petals of the sweet

peas, larkspur, dahlias and chrysanthemums as she buried her face in them.

"We have a lot of courting to make up," he said, smiling at her pleasure. "Letters are unsatisfactory things."

Better than nothing, though, Laurel thought, and so very, very precious to keep for all time. Her whole being seemed to reach out to him with the premonitory pain that loving, unloved, brings. His thoughtfulness touched her to the verge of tears.

Before lunch Kirk parked the car and they strolled to see the great famous Buddha of Infinite Light over seven feet high and weighing over a hundred tons. It squatted in the open with legs in yoga-style and hands palms upward, thumbs touching in its lap. It had sat there for hundreds of years since the fourteenth century like a great rock untouched by eruptions and the progress of time.

Kirk grinned down at her. "How would you like that in your back garden?"

Laurel quipped in return, "There wouldn't be much light around it if we had it near the house!"

There was much to see in the ancient town of Kamakura, but Kirk, after driving along an avenue for pine, bright azalea shrubs and cherry trees for Laurel to gaze up at a shrine reached by seventy steps, told her that other historic places of interest would be left for another day.

They had lunch at a Japanese inn enchanting in structure and design. Kirk ordered a knife and fork for Laurel, knowing she would find it difficult with the chopsticks. She did try and they laughed at her efforts.

"Not bad for the first time," he said with a chuckle. "I'll teach you."

There was a tender undertone in his teasing that probed her defenses. But although he sounded sincere, his smile did not always reach his eyes. His attitude puzzled her until she wanted to ask him point-blank why he had married her. The violence of her own feelings astonished her.

She said quietly, "I'm always willing to learn," in such

a cool little voice that she wondered if she was really getting as adept as he was at hiding her true feelings.

The afternoon was spent on their own little strip of beach below the garden. They bathed in the warm sunlit water, then stretched out blissfully in the sun. Closing her eyes, Laurel was reminded of the time they had first met when Kirk had taken her with her mother to the coast. They had been much closer then than they were now.

Kirk lay close beside her—too close. If she were to turn her head she would see his dark hair all tousled and drying in the sun, the fringe of his lashes dark against the gleaming bronze of his face and his firm lips closed. The silence around them was profound and restful, yet Laurel felt anything but. Maybe her inner restlessness transmitted itself to him, for she felt him move and bend over her.

"Laurel," he breathed. Not "darling" or any other term of endearment, just "Laurel." Yet the way he said it was like a deep note of music playing on her heartstrings. She held her breath with a sense of painful delight deepening the longing inside her that his nearness was making unbearable.

Then his dark head shut out the light and the feel of his mouth on hers stifled everything but the mad beating of her heart beneath his own. The kiss deepened and became urgent, demanding. He let her go at last, very slowly. Neither of them spoke. Laurel felt in her despair that he could not love her or he would not have been satisfied with one kiss.

I love him so much, she thought. *I always will.* But even as she admitted it there was a conviction that she was reaching out for something that could never be hers. For delicious moments she had imagined her love creating an answering passion in him. Now she knew she had nothing to give that he wanted.

"I'm anxious about you, my sweet," he whispered, hovering over her. "You know that, don't you?"

"I think I understand," she said flatly.

He shook his head. "You don't. Not entirely, because you're not a man. You have to trust me and go along with what I do."

He was right—she did not understand him. All she knew was that she loved him and yearned for him with all her being. He had not kissed her lightly or carelessly, Laurel was sure of that. So what was this conflict in him, this awful barrier keeping them apart? Laurel looked up into his face. Poignantly, for breathless moments, their gaze held, lingering with emptiness. The air grew chilly and she shuddered. Instantly Kirk was looking at the black clouds scuttling along overhead.

"I felt rain," he said shortly. "We'd better go."

Helping her to her feet, he helped her to button up the long skirt and pretty top of her beach suit over her swimsuit. Then, carelessly shrugging into his bathrobe, he scooped up all the paraphernalia and, taking her elbow, piloted her toward the house.

Tears blinded her and she stumbled as they reached the little wicket gate leading into the garden. His grip on her elbow steadied her and he frowned down into her pale face.

"Headache?"

Laurel managed a pale smile. "It will pass."

They went through the little gate. She had not lied, for the tension she had been under had made her temples throb. At the door of the house, Kirk knelt down to change first her shoes, then his own. Leaving the things he was carrying right there, he scooped her up into his arms and carried her into her room. Depositing her on the bed, he unbuttoned the top and long skirt and put her into bed in her brief swimsuit.

"Did Uncle George give you any tablets for these occasions?" he asked as he tucked her into bed.

"They're in a bottle on the bedside table—antibiotics. I don't take them if I can help it."

He strode to the bathroom and was back in seconds with a tumbler of water. Reaching for the capsules, he

ook one and, sitting sideways beside her on the bed, put
n arm around her to lift her up. Obediently Laurel took
he capsule with a drink of water, wishing it had the
ower to put her out forever as he held her to him. It was
. relief when he lowered her down and left her.

Then he was back again, this time to place something
leliciously cold on her burning forehead—a cold com-
ress.

"That better?"

She nodded.

"Go to sleep. You have all of three hours before dinner
his evening. Ring for Yuseku if you want anything. I
hall be in my room in any case, catching up with my cor-
espondence."

He bent to kiss her hair and left the room. The patter-
ng of the rain on the roof must have lulled her to sleep,
ecause the next thing she knew was that Kirk was there
ooking down at her thoughtfully.

"Had a good sleep?" he asked, taking her slender
wrist between thumb and finger.

The sight of his tanned face and keen gray eyes
rought a glow of comfort to her trembling heart. But she
loped he would not attribute her galloping pulse to his
resence. She smiled up at him from clear blue eyes from
which all pain had gone and he straightened to stare
lown at her for a long moment.

"Feel fit enough to get up for dinner?"

"I feel fine."

He hesitated for a moment. "Want any help to dress or
wash?"

"No, thanks. I can mannage."

He was amused at her sudden vehemence. Laurel
made no attempt to get up. For some reason she was shy
of leaving her bed in his presence, which was ridiculous
eeing that she had spent the afternoon in his presence in
her swimsuit.

"Take your time getting up. You have an hour in
which to get ready. It's now seven. Dinner is at eight."

He left her then. He had spoken with an easy tole
ance. The kiss on the beach had meant nothing to hin
she thought. He had been in the kind of mood to seek di
traction and had given way briefly to deeper feelings. H
might even have imagined she was Nina. Laurel drew
deep breath. She had never felt so oppressed, so hope
less. The fact that he did not love her weighed like a stor
in her heart.

CHAPTER FIVE

KIRK WAS WAITING FOR HER in the dining room. He turned from contemplating the view at the window as Laurel was seized by a new and unaccountable feeling of dread. Was it the subtle suggestion of strength and obstinacy in his dark, sardonic face? In repose it looked anything but reassuring to her wavering heart. He had the look of a man who was strong enough to be patient in order to get what he wanted, the kind who never gave up. Was that how he felt about Countess Nina?

Her eyes lingered on his mouth and a faint color stained her cheeks as she remembered his kiss. His eyes looked straight into hers and there was something pitiless, something almost brutal in their regard. Then he moved with that ease and grace that was characteristic of him and came forward smiling.

"All right?" he asked.

She nodded, aware of his look of appraisal as he seated her at the dining table. There were chopsticks with the usual cutlery. The meal began with a delicious ice-cold soup followed by chicken with rice and fresh vegetables. The next course was small slices of raw fish covered by a thick sauce.

"This is where you try the chopsticks," Kirk said with a quick quirk of amusement at Laurel's stare at her plate. "They're easy enough to use when you've once got the idea. But first something to help you to enjoy your Japanese food—sake, the Japanese national drink made from rice." He filled two tiny cups with the transparent liquid and passed her one. "This is the real sake, matured

in a cedarwood cask that gives it its delightful flavor."
He held his cup aloft. "Cheers."

Laurel followed suit. "*Kampai,*" she murmured.

He lifted an attractive brow. "So we speak in
Japanese. Do you know what that means?"

"It means 'your health' as a toast."

"Clever girl!"

Laurel was surprised at the warm glow after she had
drunk the sake. It was quite pleasant.

"Like it?"

She nodded. "Very nice."

He had tossed his down. "Taken in small amounts like
this, it adds to the enjoyment of the food. It hasn't the
kick of spirits, but it is not unlike sherry in its potency."
He refilled her cup and came around to stand behind her
chair. Leaning over her with an arm on each side, he
placed the chopsticks in her hands and, closing his fingers over hers, manipulated them. A portion of the food
was conveyed to her mouth and she discovered that the
fresh fish was extremely palatable with the sauce. Eventually her portion disappeared from her plate, washed
down by the tiny cups of sake. During the performance
her sense of humor had got the better of her and the ripple
of mirth bursting from her lips joined Kirk's deep
chuckle.

Back in his chair, he grinned at her. "How was it?"

"Not bad at all. Thanks for the lesson."

There was a flicker of approval in his gray eyes.
"You're an apt pupil."

"You're a good teacher."

"Thanks. That's comforting."

Laurel caught her breath a little and forced herself to
meet his gaze.

"That sounds as though I had a lot to learn."

"So you have," he replied laconically.

"You mean about Japan?"

"Japan . . . and other things."

He did not enlarge on what the other things might be.
Instead he talked about things in general, disarming her

completely. She recalled his words when they sat in the living room later listening to the stereo. Kirk had put on a long-playing record of Grieg's music and they sat opposite to each other because he had lighted a cigarette.

At least, Laurel thought that was his reason for not sitting beside her on the settee—to keep the smoke away from her. A kind of rumble came first as the floor shook and the chair trembled beneath her. She looked up at the chandelier swinging perilously from side to side; the dolls danced a kind of minuet in the lacquer cabinet and the clock on the mantelpiece did a victory roll.

Laurel gripped the arms of her chair, tremblingly aware that something terrible was happening. She was experiencing the sort of shock of one who, on seeing a mouse, leaps on the nearest chandelier, only this one was swinging madly to and fro like the pendulum on a clock.

The room did a rock and roll quite out of time to the music and Laurel sent an agonizing look at Kirk. He was sitting smoking. His whole attitide was one of complete relaxation, only there was something about him, an indefinable something that calmed her fears and kept her rigid in her chair.

A sudden severe tilt of the room was the last straw. It sent the arm of the record player hurtling across the record, distorting the sound into a wild shriek that somehow mingled with Laurel's. The silence that followed was profound. Kirk had scooped her up into his arms and was now sitting in her chair with her on his knee. She was clinging to him with her face buried in his chest and he was holding her close.

For a long time Laurel knew she was the only one who was trembling. The room had ceased to do so. Everything was static once more.

"Poor sweet," Kirk whispered in her hair. "Your first earthquake."

"Is that what it was?"

Her voice was muffled against him, but she still clung and trembled. His arms tightened around her and they stayed like that for some time, silent and close.

Then he said quietly, "I'm not going to say I'm sorr
for not telling you about them. The best way to find abou
the earthquakes is to experience them firsthand. Had
warned you what to expect you would have imagined a
kinds of horrors, whereas they're just part of everyda
life in Japan. If I'm sorry at all it's for bringing you ou
here before you were fit to deal with this kind of thing.
He gave a short laugh that held no mirth. "You sat ther
looking at me like a terrified child." Laurel felt his kis
on her hair. "Feel better now?"

"Yes, thanks."

Laurel had stopped trembling, although being hel
closely in his arms was hardly conducive to utter calm.

"It was only a baby earthquake." His voice was reas
suring. "If you look around the room you'll see that noth
ing has been broken and that things are only out o
place. Remarkable when you come to think of it."

Laurel lifted her head and looked around the room
Nothing had been broken. No plaster had fallen from th
ceiling, everything was intact. The portrait of Nina ha
slipped perilously to the edge of the baby grand piano
Her presence in the room seemed almost tangible.

She looked away, made an effort to be normal. "You
did right not to tell me about the earthquakes. I would
certainly have been on edge waiting for my first one. I'n
glad you were with me, though."

He drew her against him. "There'll be many more, bu
you'll get used to them. There's less risk of collapsing fo
wooden houses built on piles than for those built of bric
and cement with cellar foundations. The biggest hazar
is fires. Again these people have a wonderful system o
battling with them." His lips moved down to her cheek
"Not sorry you came, are you?"

His mouth was seeking hers. He kissed the corner of it
The next moment he would have kissed her. But Laure
could not bear a kiss given to comfort her distress. She
turned her face away. He had probably felt her stiffen
although his hold on her remained perfectly still. Confu-

sion swept over her in waves of despair. Her mouth was dry as she sought an excuse for her action.

"I can hear the record player still running. Hadn't you better see to it?"

Kirk looked down at her, his face strangely set. "Oh, yes," he said with an ominous quietness. "We mustn't forget the record player. It's most important."

Wincing at the sarcasm in his voice, Laurel felt herself released. She stood up and he strode across the room, looking up darkly from his task when Yuseku tapped on the door.

Curtly, Kirk bade him enter. With his round face beaming, Yuseku-san gave the kind of glance around the room that sums everything up in a couple of seconds, and began to restore order. In his swift noiseless way he went around the room putting it to rights in a manner born of experience.

"Coffee?" he asked brightly when he had finished.

"Please. Make it good and strong," Kirk commanded.

Yuseku went on a bow and Laurel said swiftly, "Not for me, thanks. I think I'll go to bed."

Kirk closed the lid of the stereo and straightened. "Sure you won't have a drink of coffee laced with brandy? It would do you good, settle your nerves and make you sleep."

Laurel shook her head. "No, thanks. Good night."

He strode across to the door and opened it for her. "Good night. Sleep well. There won't be any more eruptions tonight."

CHAPTER SIX

AFTER THE EARTHQUAKE Laurel was prepared for anything. According to Kirk, spring in Japan usually brought
a spell of fine weather. It did that week of their honeymoon, making it possible for them to go out on all kinds
of jaunts. They dined out most nights at Western and
Japanese eating places.

Laurel learned to use her chopsticks and she really enjoyed most of the Japanese dishes. She enjoyed the
sukiyaki dinner taken in the company of other diners sitting on tatami matting minus shoes around a low table.
Watching the meal being prepared was an entertainment
in itself, with the lady presiding over it looking very
charming in her colorful kimono and bright silk obi
around her tiny waist.

First, in a heated iron pan over a charcoal brazier, a
soy sauce was made, into which was cooked a potpourri
of meats, vegetables and herbs. Eaten with chopsticks
and washed down with sake, it was very palatable.
Laurel, flushed with sake and using her chopsticks to
good account, would meet Kirk's mocking gray gaze and
feel that life was good.

The parks, to Laurel, were enchanting places at their
best in the spring with the cherry blossom in full bloom.
More enchanting still were the endless crowds of school
children who were always around with their teachers,
sightseeing and learning all about their country. They
would crowd around anyone like Laurel and Kirk to
practice their English, the girls in their little pleated
skirts and sailor collars, the boys in black suits and small
caps on black hair.

They laughed easily with their small almond-shaped eyes twinkling in their round little faces. They cluttered up the park among the many stalls and sideshows, buying candy floss, local sweets and marine delicacies from nearby seaside resorts, and added to the atmosphere of lightheartedness and gaiety.

Laurel blossomed in the sun like a spring flower; her clear eyes glowed and her skin had the pearly transparency of health. Most of the time was spent outdoors swimming, sailing and sightseeing away from the city beneath vast blue skies. She was caught in an enchanting wave of happiness that without wish or volition of her own swept her into a sea of bliss.

Kirk was the ideal companion, lazily tolerant, unperturbed yet giving the impression of smoldering fires underneath. He looked at her often, broodingly, intently, as though he was studying a mathematical problem. Yet his manner was infectiously gay, a surface gaiety not without an endearing devilment.

The nights ended on the same routine of him striding to the adjoining room with a finality that struck a chill to her heart. So the honeymoon ended. Kirk stowed their luggage in the trunk of the car and Laurel, from the open car window, breathed in for the last time the air from the garden tinged with the tang of the sea, wet moss and pine—a mingled scent, bittersweet.

Their new house was in the suburbs of the city and they reached it in record time after an uneventful drive. The suburbs were lovely with avenues of stately cedars, cherry trees and acacias. Suddenly it seemed to Laurel's enchanted eyes that the avenues became a garden brilliant with flowering shrubs, superb trees and blossom-laden branches thick as snow.

Looking eagerly through the car window, she saw the roof of the house curling up gaily at the edges as though smiling a welcome. Long carpets of grass set along an elegant avenue of trees led them between the double gates along a driveway. Kirk drew up smoothly at the front door. The house, set against a background of wooded hills, overlooked a delightful valley. Down below, the lake lay like a discarded mirror reflecting the blue sky and trees etched black on the surface.

If Laurel thought the house they had just left exquisite, she was spellbound by her new home and its setting. It was a semicircular building facing the sun and cuddling the willow-pattern garden that appeared to stray over the patios into the house. And what a garden, treated as a gift from the gods and planned with Japanese artistry. Water tinkled merrily over lovingly laid stones; little bamboo bridges and fringed trees studied their reflection in the water surrounded by flowers, rocks and green velvet lawns, a quintessence of subtle perfume and poignant beauty.

Laurel held her breath with delight and shone up at Kirk, who stood beside her watching her enchanting small face.

"I'm speechless. Oh, Kirk, it's heavenly!"

"I thought you'd like it." He laughed easily and lightly. His gray eyes teased. "You can make what alterations you wish, of course. Japanese tradition demands that a house is built with sloping ground in front and the hills behind. The front must face a southwesterly direction, as this is looked upon as the gateway between heaven and earth. In Japanese it's called *jinmom*, meaning,'man's gateway to heaven.' "

He followed Laurel's gaze to the letters carved over the door: *Sakura*.

Laurel's soft mouth quivered. It was absurd that his voice, even when he said words he might or might not mean, should do things to her heart to cause her such intense pain. It was not how he looked that counted. It was what he was. He had a rare quality of abundant energy, a magnetism that changed the atmosphere. His charm was immense, heightening all impressions, vitalizing feelings. No matter what he said or did, she loved him, would always love him.

She stared up at his dark, intent face. Then he framed

her face in his hands and his lips came down on hers in a hard kiss. Her mouth responded sweetly to his demanding lips. He felt her tremble as the magic got through to her. When he released her, Laurel was aware without seeing it of his battered, quizzical smile.

"I've waited a long time for this moment, Mrs. Kirk Graham. Welcome home!"

Again she had nothing to say. Her lips felt bruised, as bruised as her heart. Yet when he picked her up in his arms to carry her over the threshold with the mocking comment that the occasion still called for it since this was their real home, Laurel had to fight the urge to put her arms around his neck and kiss that mocking mouth.

If beauty was outside the house it was surely within, a cool elegant beauty of highly polished wooden floors covered by Oriental rugs in delicate pastel colors. Flowers were everywhere, in floor vases, in exquisite bowls, tall graceful gladioli, feathery fern, magnolias, enchanting twigs arranged with a master hand. Their subtle perfume and delicate artistry appealed to Laurel's sensitive perception, becoming part of her innermost being. Suddenly a door to their left in the hall slid along and a houseboy entered. A classical study in black and white, he came forward noiselessly in heelless slippers. His intelligent face creased into a smile that revealed several gold teeth among a perfect set. He bowed low from the waist, presenting a shiny cap of black hair trimmed neatly above the white immaculate jacket.

Kirk said, "Laurel, this is Reko who was with me in my bachelor quarters. Reko, my wife, Laurel."

Laurel smiled warmly and inclined her head to acknowledge his bow. The Japanese, it seemed, did not shake hands. She had seen the look amounting to hero worship Reko had given Kirk, who towered above them both, lean hipped, broad of shoulder with eyes as gray as an English winter.

While Reko went to carry in their luggage, Kirk escorted Laurel on a tour of the house. The kitchen, behind

the door through which Reko had entered, was light, airy
and scrupulously clean.

Kirk said, "Like most Japanese homes, we have elec-
tricity for lighting. Cooking is done with charcoal and we
have a refrigerator." Leading off from the kitchen was
the pantry and food stores. The dining room came next,
overlooking the garden, then the living room and, next to
that, Kirk's study.

Here there were the usual book-lined walls, desk and
comfortable chairs. On the desk was a pile of correspondence and Kirk strode to this to sort it out quickly and
efficiently. As he did so a small envelope fluttered to the
ground at Laurel's feet. She bent to pick up the perfumed
letter with a sense of foreboding. A woman's handwriting without a doubt, and a Japanese postmark. Countess
Nina's! Laurel could only hazard a guess as she passed it
to him with trembling fingers.

"Thanks, my sweet," he said, pushing it absentmind-
edly into his inside pocket with the air of a man whose
thoughts were elsewhere. To Laurel, the careless acceptance of the letter and the way he had segregated it from
the rest was condemnation enough.

Her face had paled. She drew back. The action, rather
than the letter, was hurting her more than she would have
dreamed possible. He put down his mail.

"You all right, my sweet? You've gone very pale."

He gripped her small, cold hands, and although Laurel
recoiled inwardly from his touch, something radiantly
proud came into her small face. In a small voice, cool and
smooth as silk, she said, "I'm all right."

If Laurel had envisaged his past at all, it was to imagine
him striding through a sequence of trivial love affairs, a
few pretty girls, the usual college dances and the fun of
blind dates. He was a man now with a man's feeling and
passion. So far, Laurel had not seen the passion. But it
was there, nevertheless, somehow linked with the perfumed letter lying near his heart.

"You're tired. Come along, let's have tea. Reko will

have made it by now. We can see the rest of the house later. There's no hurry."

He put an arm around her shoulders and they went to the living room. Reko was there within minutes with the lacquer tray. Kirk placed a low table in front of the settee as easily as he had placed Laurel on it. Reko put down the tray and Kirk took over.

Unhappily, Laurel tried not to think of the letter in his pocket and accepted her tea. The living-room window, like all the others, looked out over the garden. It opened on a patio and everything looked beautifully peaceful, but Laurel was discovering that the heart could know torture even in beautiful surroundings.

The tea was refreshing. They had lunched on the way back to Tokyo, so neither of them was inclined to eat the little delicacies Reko had brought in along with the tea. Kirk had a cigarette.

He was studying the glowing tip when he said casually, "I don't expect you to settle in here right away. You're sure to feel a bit restless. I know how you're feeling." His tender smile down at her was loaded with charm. "It must have been an appalling ordeal losing your parents in such tragic circumstances. The aftermath was pretty rough, too. The kind of illness you've had always leaves a certain amount of depression. Fortunately, we have a good doctor on hand, a personal friend of mine. He and his wife were away in Germany when we got married, so they were unable to attend. Otherwise you would have met him."

Laurel put down her empty cup. "I don't need a doctor, Kirk. I'm well. It's . . . as you say, a matter of adjusting myself to a new life." She shook her head as he picked up the teapot to replenish her cup. "No more, thanks."

He stubbed out his cigarette into an ashtray on the lacquer table, said carefully as if he had already said too much, "We have a Japanese room—I know you'll want to see that right away. Shall we go?"

Laurel was on her feet, eager to be moving. Somehow being alone with Kirk only increased her restlessness. He had risen, too, to look down at her with an expression that she could not read, searching, quizzical. There seemed to be a trace of bitter humor and she wondered why.

Like the other rooms, the Japanese room overlooked the garden through a wall consisting of sliding floor-to-ceiling glass doors. It was a cool, bare room with pale walls, in which nothing was contrived but everything was plain to see. The yellowish green, thick tatami mats, with their surface of very finely woven rushes stretched over a base of crude rice straw, harmonized with the mellowed tones of the room. On the inner wall facing the garden was an alcove with a step containing an arrangement of twigs rather like pussy willow in an elegant vase. Above it all on the wall was a painting of Fujiyama.

"Every Japanese has a similar alcove," explained Kirk. "It's called a *tokonoma*. Years ago it was used for sleeping in, being warmer than sleeping on the floor of the room. The floors were then concrete. Now they're wooden and much warmer. The built-in cupboards around the walls contain cushions for sitting on, also the brazier, kettle and things for the tea ceremony."

Laurel shone up at him, thoroughly interested. "I'm aching to see you in a kimono. I suppose that's why the men wear them, because they're easier to sit down in."

"They are warmer, too, in the winter—worn in layers. I have a kimono. I wore it for judo and karate, for which I hold the black belt. Personally I prefer my own clothes, but you'll look delicious in a kimono with your dainty figure and tiny waist. Most Western women buy one; they can't resist the beauty of them."

He left her at the door of the first bedroom. "There are four bedrooms. This one is yours and mine. I'll leave you now to unpack. Dinner is at eight, but I'll see you before then."

Laurel entered the prettiest room she had ever seen,

magnolia walls with touches of palest pink in the dainty lace bed cover, in the pillows and sheets, in the beautiful wall clock and in the pretty arrangement of tea roses in a vase on her bedside table. There was a card propped up against the gold and cream bedside lamp.

"To my darling wife. All my love, Kirk."

How could he? Laurel crushed the card in her hand. With misty eyes she looked around the room to stare at the pink and white silk-corded bell rope beside the bed. Everything laid on, she thought bitterly, even to a tasseled bell rope to summon morning tea. Then she stared down at the card in her hand. She was too weak willed to destroy it, of course. Despising herself, she straightened it out and put it into the dressing-table drawer.

It was a few minutes before she began to unpack. It occurred to her long before she had finished that Kirk's suitcases were not there. *Here we go again*, she thought, *in the other room*. Leaving the empty cases to be taken away by Reko, Laurel left the room to peep into the next bedroom. This one was more austere, a bedroom suite in dark wood contrasting dramatically with the pale walls. The cream wool bedspread was unadorned and the masculine set of hairbrushes, her wedding present to Kirk, mocked her from the dressing table.

Laurel had not the heart to look in at the other two bedrooms. Returning to her room, she washed off the dust of travel in a bath of warm water perfumed from the cut-glass bottles and jars arrayed beautifully along glass shelves. Here again she felt the subtle touch of a woman. Who, Laurel pondered, dressing mechanically. Countess Nina?

Kirk had not said whether there would be guests for dinner, so to be on the safe side she chose an elegant, slim-fitting black velvet dress with an extravagantly simple, high-fitting bodice painstakingly made from tiers of white lace. She dressed her shining coils of hair Grecian-style on her head, adding light makeup, a whisper of blue to her eyes, lipstick and a dusting of powder. The ruffle of blue lace around her slim throat did away with the need for a necklace, but the small cameo—her mother's—looked demure at her throat.

Kirk would no doubt be wearing a business suit if they were dining alone. But the dress gave Laurel confidence; besides, it would be good practice for when they did entertain or go out to dine with his friends. No doubt he had been regarded as one of the most eligible Englishmen in Tokyo, and she had carried him off right under the pretty noses of all the women who would have been angling for him. Her cheeks warmed at the thought of meeting their critical gaze.

The effect upon Kirk as she entered the dining room was balm to her sore heart. A swift gleam in the gray eyes, enough to electrify the atmosphere, was gone before she could swear it had been there at all.

"You look lovely, my sweet."

He caught her hands as he strode forward. She felt his arms around her and they kissed. He released her quickly.

She hesitated, then began, "I didn't know if we were to have guests or not." Her blue eyes, bewildered and unhappy, took in his gray business suit. "You didn't—"

"I'm sorry, I ought to have told you. Don't look so upset." His sardonic grin relegated her concern to the depths. "Is it so surprising to want you to myself on our first evening home?"

He took her hand to lead her to a low table containing two parcels.

"We've received a great many wedding presents, which we shall have to go through sometime in the future. These two are from the emperor. I thought we'd better see what they are before putting them away. All the presents have been acknowledged. These arrived while we were away."

Both parcels were wrapped in the manner of Japanese wedding gifts, tied with the traditional knot in white and gold cord and a paper *noshi*, the Japanese sign of a gift.

'here was also the royal insignia. Kirk parted the wrap-
ings on the first to reveal two beautiful cloisonné vases.

"Very nice," was his bland comment.

"They're lovely," murmured Laurel wistfully.

The enclosed card was a rather splendid affair in gold
eaded with the Imperial crown. "From Their Imperial
Majesties, the Emperor and Empress."

The smaller parcel contained a bottle of sake and three
liminutive cups. Kirk replaced the lid of this rather
quickly and minus a smile, but not before he had read the
extra words written by hand on the card enclosed.

"What did the card say?" Laurel asked curiously,
hinking it odd he had not let her see it.

He shrugged. "A little joke between the emperor and
myself. I'll tell you about it sometime."

Laurel flinched inwardly. She felt as though a door had
been slammed in her face. She took it on the chin. "How
nice of Their Majesties. We shall have to thank them."

"They've already been thanked. The emperor is
away." He pinched her cheek. "He'll receive his wedding cake when he returns."

She gave a small laugh. It was either that or flippantly
ry, "Just like that!" So far she had only taken part in the
wedding ceremony. Had it not occurred to him that it
was her wedding, as well as his, and that she would have
found pleasure in acknowledging the gifts herself? Apparently it had not. The eyes she raised to his were bright
with unshed tears. "Remind me to have you at my next
wedding."

She turned away then to blink back the tears and was
otally unprepared for the savage grip on her shoulders as
he swung her around to face him.

He spoke with impersonal and hard deliberateness.
"Don't ever say that again, even in jest. What I have I
hold."

He kissed her then. It was the kind of kiss Laurel could
not define, like no other she had ever received. There
was no love or desire in it, only plain cold anger. It told

her she was his as long as it suited his purpose. It seeme
to go on and on, bruising her lips as well as her heart.
discreet tap on the door parted them, and Reko entere
to say that dinner was ready.

The dinner was perfect. Reko, with a snow-white na
kin on one arm, trod silently around the table offering th
superbly cooked food, the ice-chilled beer for Kirk, th
sherry for Laurel. Later they went into the living roo
for coffee and Kirk unexpectedly placed a large book i
her lap as she sat down on the settee.

"Our photograph album of the wedding," he sai
dryly. "It arrived today."

Laurel took it from him with a gasp of pleasure as sh
admired the gold tassel down the spine and the gilt-edge
pages. "Ours?"

Her look was so unbelieving, he laughed. "Wh
else's?"

He lowered his long length beside her and Laurel b
her lip. The New Otani Hotel took care of everythin
where weddings were concerned, she knew. But the
would not prepare a wedding album of the photograph
unless specially requested to do so. Kirk had obviousl
requested it and his thoughtfulness touched her an
made her feel too full for words. Her hands trembled a
she opened it. They looked at it together, Kirk with a
arm along the back of the settee behind her, his face clos
to her hair as he looked down.

All the photographs were excellent and the two tin
bridesmaids looked adorable. The one showing th
bridal couple cutting the cake caught at her heart. Wit
that smile of extraordinary charm, Kirk was the devote
bridegroom, gazing down at her absorption in the task a
hand with a look of tenderness that Laurel felt was in
tended solely to impress.

"There are several pictures of the wedding in the
Japanese magazines. One in particular has exclusive pic
tures of the house and garden and an article on the fur
nishings. I've ordered them for you."

Kirk told her this later as they strolled in the garden before going to bed. The moonlight splashed inky shadows beneath the trees and the perfume of the garden was the essence of things Oriental, stinging the nostrils and stirring the emotions to a vague yet drowsy excitement. The sky was sapphire, casting a blue haze over the lake, and the hills gave a sense of unreality in the hazy background. To Laurel it was a dreamworld, an ideal place for two lovers who had been parted to meet and find their dreams come true.

Nature could not have presented a richer, more wonderful bit of heaven than this garden of Eden in which they walked. But behind all the combined perfection of the time, the place and the loved one was the shadow of a wall as impenetrable as a light through thick fog. It drew closer and closer around her, affecting her both mentally and physically, attaining substance.

Kirk had spoken seldom and was completely unobtrusive as if he was aware of her secret longing for him and was avoiding any action that might fan it into flame. He was smoking a cigarette and was gazing out across the valley. A breath of tobacco wafted toward her and she watched his arrogant profile, held by a creeping fascination. The situation was incredible. It could not go on, she told herself wildly.

Presently he crushed out the cigarette with his heel and smiled down at her. "One of the most wonderful things about you is that you don't talk a man to death. It's so restful to be with you." His gray eyes raked her face. "You're beginning to look much better since you arrived."

"Am I?" she responded tonelessly, and clenched her hands.

"Don't you feel better?"

The shadow was still there between his own gravely searching eyes and her wretched ones. Suddenly she could not bear it.

"I . . . I . . . ." Laurel stopped, unable to go on, and to

her horror she began to weep hopelessly and quietly as she had done in the weeks following her mother's death, her face in her hands.

"Stop it," Dr. Machelle had commanded her sternly when he had found her in tears. "This kind of thing is no good for your recovery."

Now Kirk was saying it. "Stop it, Laurel!" He said it firmly and harshly, yet with a gentleness beneath the harshness. He drew her against him. "This isn't like you. You've always been such a brave little thing, sticking to your determination to nurse your mother against all odds. You'll get over it." He kissed her hair. "Don't want to go back to England, do you? You're not homesick?"

She shook her head against him. Gradually she grew quiet.

"Laurel." He spoke her name gently like a caress. "This is something we have to face together. You can face it if I can. You can trust me to do the right thing. We do belong to each other, you know."

Laurel used her handkerchief. "I'm sorry," she said in a husky voice. "I think I'll go to bed."

"Yes. I'll come along with you." He put an arm around her shoulders and they walked back to the house.

Reko met them in the garden—Kirk was wanted on the phone. Instantly he was on the alert.

"Thanks, Reko. I was expecting it. I'll take it in my study." His smile down at Laurel was apologetic. "Shan't be long, my sweet."

The next moment he had gone, with his graceful long stride.

Laurel stayed where he had left her; the emotion with which she was filled was unbearable. All kinds of thoughts were seething through her brain, thoughts of Kirk and Nina. Unfair thoughts? She had to find out. If it was not Nina, he would have taken the call in the hall. But no, it had to be in his study where no one could hear.

Mechanically her footsteps were guided in that direction, working along to where the study window overlooked the garden. He was there inside at the phone. Laurel drew back against the side of the window in the shadows.

He was saying, "What you suggest, Nina, is impossible. I know you're eager to get it over, but you must leave it to me. I have to see it through myself. We must think of Ishi and there must be no scandal." A pause. "I agree. It does put me in an intolerable position, but there's nothing I can do about it. You must see that." Another pause. "No," very firmly. "That's the last thing you must do. You'll have to be patient. I'll be back at the office on Monday. We can discuss it then. . . ."

Laurel did not wait to hear any more. She had heard enough. She paused at the door before entering the house to pull herself together. Her attitude was one of utter dejection. It was clear enough even to her way of thinking that Kirk had married her for a purpose. But what purpose?

Things were, perhaps, more painful because she was so physically near him, sleeping in the next room; it intensified the face that he made no effort to break down the wall of reserve between them. In fact, where personal contact was concerned, he might be a hundred miles away.

Thinking about this, Laurel, who had been standing with closed eyes in melancholy contemplation of her intolerable position, opened them to see Kirk standing on the threshold of the door.

"Sorry about that," he said. "Come to the living room for a nightcap to make you sleep."

Pale, unsmiling, like a stone statue, Laurel felt him take her cold hand and lead her through into the hall.

"I'd rather go to bed. I'm tired," she said, and even her voice sounded like a stranger's.

Kirk had spoken in level, teasing tones. Now he was frowning down at her, puzzled at the coldness of her look. "Are you?" He smiled. "Well, don't be too serious

about it. You know I won't disturb you. I know you have
to get well before we begin our married life together in
earnest.''

Laurel looked up at his dark face. The conversation
she had just heard had plowed a painful furrow through
her brain until it hurt unbearably. Exasperation mingled
with her pain and torment of loving him blocked her
throat.

''Get well?'' she echoed blankly, two perpendicular
lines appearing between her delicate brows.

He gestured with a hand as though she was behaving
stupidly. ''Didn't Uncle George say anything to you
about taking things easy for a while?''

''He gave me tranquilizers, if that's what you mean.''

Kirk gazed down for a long moment into her unhappy
eyes and a wave of compassion made him speak very
gently as though to a child. ''Forget it. Go to bed. Good
night—sleep well.''

Laurel never remembered how she got to her room.
Awareness came back when she lay in bed, smothering
her tearless sobs of anguish into the pillow.

CHAPTER SEVEN

IT WAS EIGHT O'CLOCK when Laurel opened her eyes.
She lay hovering between sleep and wakefulness, listening to the chatter of the birds outside her window and the
soft brushing of dew-wet leaves against the pane.

Myopically she gazed around the beautiful dreamy
room which looked tender and undisturbed with the
pretty window curtains framing the beginning of a new
day. Sunshine sent beams of dancing gold dust across her
bed and voices from the garden cleared her brain of the
last remnants of sleep. Reaching for her negligee, a
frothy lace and ribbon affair to match her nightgown,
Laurel slipped it on and went to the window.

Reko was there talking to a man in faded cotton trousers and jacket. He was digging, bending over his spade to
show the black hair curled up into a duck's tail at his
neck. He was tubby and elderly and was obviously the
new gardener. Reko went indoors and the man bent
down to take up a piece of the newly dug soil and break it
gently, almost reverently in his fingers.

Laurel watched him with a tender smile. Very large
farms did not exist in Japan. Most of them, she knew,
were no more than an acre and small enough to work by
hand. The poor gardener probably did not possess even
an acre. He could belong to one of the families to be seen
tending the narrow tracts of land, no more than six feet
wide, that rose in shallow tiers on the slopes.

She walked to the bathroom thoughtfully, taking in the
luxury of shell-pink and black ornate fittings, fluffy rich
towels and the gleam of tiled walls. What a hard life the
Japanese peasants enjoyed compared to this! Yet they

smiled so readily even when up to their knees in ice-cold muddy water in their rice paddies. Could it be that in the very simplicity and humbleness of their existence they had found the key to real happiness?

Even with her own problems still unsolved, Laurel was beginning to feel the utter tranquility, the sense of infinite quiet and unity creeping into her being like a healing balm. She cleaned her teeth, ignoring the fact that the bathroom looked too feminine in the morning light without Kirk's shaving gear and toothbrush.

She had not heard him leave in the car to go to his first day back at his office. No doubt he had, after peeping into her room to find her still sleeping. Laurel thought while dressing of the duties she would have to undertake as his wife—entertaining his friends and colleagues and visiting them in their homes. She was not looking forward to it, although she had reconciled herself to living one day at a time until her problems resolved themselves.

She was ready when a tap came on her door and Kirk entered in a smartly cut, dark city-going suit and pale blue shirt that did something to his gray eyes and bronze skin.

"Good morning, my sweet. Ready for breakfast?" He bent his dark head and kissed her lips lightly. "Hmm, you smell delicious."

He exuded a freshly groomed masculine fragrance. Was it cedar soap? And was he as pleased to see her as he looked?

"So do you," she said, adding hurriedly at the pained expression her remark put on his face, "In a masculine way, of course."

"Thanks." His gray eyes laughed down at her. "Did you sleep well?"

"So-so. Aren't you going to your office this morning?"

"Yes, after I've had breakfast with my wife."

"But won't it make you late?"

"Undoubtedly. However, since it will be the first time, I shall manage to arrive before they recover from the shock. We're having breakfast on the patio. It's warm enough and you'll enjoy it."

The early-morning meal with Kirk in a teasing mood and a panoramic view of Tokyo at her feet was heaven to Laurel. The city was surrounded by thick walls and numerous shallow moats stapled with bridges. To Laurel it was one of the most beautiful places she had ever seen, with its wooded hills and valleys, quaint buildings and small doll-like dwellings set amid pines, weeping willows and cherry blossom. She gazed at it entranced until, aware of Kirk's eyes on her, she turned to meet his intent look.

His charm was irresistible when he chose. "Come on, you can do better than that. You're eating nothing. The view is hardly as sustaining as breakfast, so eat, there's a good girl."

He pushed a dish of fruit toward her and refilled her cup. He ate what he wanted and lighted a cigarette. Laurel looked at the strong brown throat as he set a line of smoke heavenward.

"You're used to the views by now. To me they're new and enchanting. I don't imagine myself ever looking at them and remaining unmoved by their beauty," she said.

She peeled a banana and he smiled at her lazily. "I agree, I love this country and all the fundamental values simmering beneath the surface that only people who live here can really appreciate. I've never felt an alien, and while I keep very much to myself, I feel part of the community. By the way, the building reaching for the sky on yonder hill behind the trees is the Imperial Palace of the emperor."

He indicated the roofs of a magnificent building perched regally in isolated splendor on the top of green slopes surrounded by shallow moats. It was half-hidden by a boscage of trees and high walls. Grassy banks sloped from the walls down to the moat. They were planted with willow and cherry blossom, some of which gave the impression of having slipped down to the edge of the water to bend Narcissus-fashion to admire their own reflections. Swans cruised elegantly along on the water beneath them and the high walls surrounding the palace had wide gateways at intervals with carved wooden gates and brass fittings.

Laurel said, "Isn't the emperor supposed to be a divine being to his subjects?"

"Not so much since the last war," he answered lazily. "Before then he was looked upon as something out of this world and practically indestructible. The war changed all that by proving he was as prone to destruction as his subjects. You'll enjoy making his acquaintance."

"You mean we shall go to the Imperial Palace?"

"The emperor is away, but the empress is at home. You'll probably be requested to go to tea."

In her mind's eye Laurel saw Countess Nina looking at her patronizingly with the mocking regard of a woman who had nothing to fear from Kirk's wife. The woman's affair with Kirk would be court gossip, and Laurel shrank from the thought of meeting all the critical eyes.

"Do I have to go?" she almost pleaded.

"Naturally. What are you afraid of? Your taste in dress is impeccable, you have that quiet and enviable quality of speech and manner of which the Japanese so highly approve. You're also slim, dainty and pretty." He tapped ash from his cigarette into an ashtray on the low table and leaned back again in his chair to survey her with approval. "Pretty enough to hold your own against the best of them. You'll have a store of beautiful memories in years to come because I can assure you that you'll enjoy yourself here.

"Things are changing here fast, but we in the diplomatic service have the privilege of moving in the old Japan that the Imperial Palace still holds almost intact." He smiled with a gleam in his eyes that made Laurel's heart turn in her breast. "By the way, Japanese women are by age-long tradition obedient and subservient to their husbands."

"But how dull for the husband to have a wife who's afraid to say boo to a goose!"

"Do you think so?"

"Of course I do. How can one respect a doormat? Half the fun of marriage is the battle of wills between husband and wife."

"Really?" he responded, lifting a quizzical brow. "Sounds interesting. Tell me more."

Laurel saw his lips twitch and was sunk. *He has got me absolutely*, ran the devious tenor of her thoughts. *It's something bigger than myself . . . like the air I breathe . . . my life's blood, my whole being.*

"Why should I make it harder for myself by letting you know my opinions on the subject?"

"Touché," he said lightly. "Do I detect a challenge? Can it be possible that my sweet fragile-looking wife is both passionate and chaste?" He threw back his head and laughed at the sudden rush of color staining her cheeks to a wild rose. "It's not fair to tease you. The important thing at the moment is to see you don't get bored being on your own while I'm at the office. I'm buying you a horse. I remember your saying you used to help a neighbor sometimes with her riding stable. My horse is stabled with friends at the moment until we have a stable built here."

Laurel felt the prick of tears behind her eyes. How much more did he remember? Did he ever think of those all too brief ecstatic hours they had spent together a year ago, how happy they had been? Now his feelings were more or less under lock and key. She had once possessed that key and could not, even now, believe she had lost it.

"I'd like that," she said evenly. "I did a bit of riding when I went down to Cornwall after my illness."

"Good. Riding will be more relaxing for you than driving a car at the moment. Fortunately, we have the sum-

mer to look forward to and you can go swimming in the
lake and take a book to laze in the sun. I shall feel easier
knowing you're near home for the first week or so. Reko
will be here and a woman is coming in every day to do a
few chores, so you won't be alone." He smiled, a tender
smile transforming his dark, sardonic face in which the
gray eyes allured and startled and made her heart beat in
thick, deep strokes. "As for the earth tremors, they will
persist, I'm afraid, owing to the alluvial soil. Think you
can stand them?"

She nodded. "I think so. I've never been afraid of
thunder and lightning, so I suppose I'll get used to them.
Anyway, I love the country."

"That will help, because you can regard the rumblings
as being some kind of message from the earth saying it
reciprocates your love."

Achingly, Laurel wanted him to add, "As I do." *Why
don't you tell me that you love me?* her heart cried piteously. *Then I can face earthquakes and anything else,
however terrifying.* In the ensuing agonizing moments
she ceased to draw breath, so great was her longing. But
she could not reach him. A sob rose from deep down inside her as he looked at his wristwatch, then stubbed out
his cigarette.

"Duty calls. Feeling all right now?"

He was on his feet, pushing back his chair and towering above her. In spite of his height and breadth of shoulder, his hard leanness and experienced charm, he looked
so boyishly endearing, so unconsciously aware of her
love for him that Laurel loved him more in that moment
than she had ever done.

"Yes, thanks."

His mouth gave a cynical twist and he shoved his
hands into his pockets. "The Japanese have a saying that
means 'bend with the wind.' I think it helps."

Laurel felt a lump in her throat as bit as a goose egg.
"Thanks, I'll remember that." Her smile was wavering.

He grimaced wryly and continued to contemplate her,

his eyes narrowing. "I'd like to see you smile more," he said gravely. "Don't come to see me off. I'll have to rush. Relax and look at the papers. See you at lunch."

He planted a kiss on the top of her head and was gone.

AMONG THE MORNING PAPERS Laurel found a glossy magazine. To her surprise, the picture on the cover was that of their new home. Inside were further pictures and an article about their marriage. She was deeply interested in it when Reko came in to announce their first visitor.

The Countess Wanaka. Hastily Laurel smoothed her hair and made her way to the living room. A young woman in a beautiful kimono in pale gray embroidered in white flowers with a pale pink obi around her slim waist bowed as she entered. For several seconds the two women eyed each other with no change of expression.

Laurel found herself looking at the original of the photograph that had watched her groping through her honeymoon, constituting an ever present threat to her own happiness. Laurel's first astounding thought was that Countess Nina was not really beautiful. She was the kind who was photogenic. She gave an instant impression of beauty because she knew how to use every trick to its best advantage. Her skin had the Oriental texture of a ripe peach. Her eyes, amber and dark lashed, her rather retroussé nose and full lips added up to a strange face, a sensuous face that rivited and demanded attention.

"Countess Wanaka?" Laurel smiled pleasantly as the women bowed. "I feel I already know you from the photograph on the piano at your home. It was kind of you to lend us the house. Please sit down."

"Not at all. Kirk is a very close friend of ours." Nina sat down gracefully in a chair while Laurel took one opposite. "Ishi adores him."

A strange feeling of crisis made Laurel choose her words carefully.

"I believe you've been to the hot springs at

Noboribetsu? I hope your husband feels a benefit from
his visit there?''

Between the thick black lashes came a calculated
gleam of amber. Small white teeth showed in a smile that
was no smile. Perceptively, Nina's voice hardened. The
American accent became more marked.

"Ishi is quite well. The Japanese males look after
themselves well—or rather, they see that their wives
do.''

"You're American?''

"I was. Since knowing your husband I realize what
I've missed in marrying a Japanese.'' Nina gave her a
long speculative look from under curling lashes. "You
don't know how lucky you are, Mrs. Graham.''

"Thank you.'' Laurel maintained a steady look.

Beneath it Nina said amiably, "Actually, I came to
see Kirk.''

"Surely you knew he would be at his office this morning?''

"Of course. That's why I'm here.''

Laurel smiled. "I don't understand.''

"Its quite simple,'' Nina vouchsafed as if Laurel was a
complete idiot. "My husband is a Minister for the Interior and we have a town house not far from the government building in Tokyo. It was important for me to
see Kirk this morning and I phoned his office to find he
had not arrived. I called the house to find the line engaged, so I decided then to come to see him.''

"But why all the haste?''

"Kirk has never been late for work before. It was most
unusual.''

Nina had taken off her gloves to show magnificent
rings on her fingers, which flashed in the sun filling the
room.

Laurel watched their glitter. "I'm sorry you missed
Kirk. I'm also surprised that you didn't wait for him at
his office. Reko would be using the phone when you
called here—to order provisions, most likely.''

"I'm afraid I'm a little impulsive and I didn't pause to think," Nina said smoothly. "You see, Kirk has always been such a close friend of mine and I was hoping his marriage would not interfere with our friendship."

Laurel kept her eyes now on the other woman's calm mask of a face. She disliked her and her kind, her beautiful insolence, her brazenness in trailing after another woman's husband when she was married herself.

Her smile was sweet, almost gracious. "You must see that having a single man for a friend is not the same as having a married one. Naturally, his wife will come first. I see no reason, though, why you shouldn't remain friends providing your friendship is kept within bounds. Actually, it was my fault that Kirk was late at his office this morning."

Nina's smirk was one of satisfaction. "I knew it was no fault of Kirk's. He's much too exacting in his work to show any signs of weakness."

"Being late for work is hardly a sign of weakness in a married man. Often unforeseen circumstances arise—the wife could be indisposed or there could be a baby on the way."

The amber eyes narrowed, the peach-bloom face darkened in color. "I would hardly think the latter was so in your case, Mrs. Graham, though I've heard that you are very much the invalid. I trust it won't injure Kirk's career. He's very highly thought of in diplomatic circles and he has a great future."

Laurel's heart plunged painfully. "Indeed?" She felt bewildered, but her quick wit was busily assessing the strength of the grapevine encircling the English community. Like every other country, it thrived on gossip.

Nina made a gesture with a perfectly manicured hand, flashing her rings to give weight to her words. "Surely that was why Kirk guarded you like a hothouse plant before you were married? He was so careful to keep you away from prying eyes or anything in the least upsetting."

Laurel met her amber eyes calmly. "There could have
been other reasons. He could have wanted me to himself.
After all, we were apart for a long time."

"Exactly."

Cold air rippled over her skin. "What do you mean?"

"For a man who wanted to keep you to himself, he behaved very oddly."

Pale with anger and disgust, Laurel said quietly, "In
what way?"

"Kirk had two months' leave coming to him, yet he
only took one week of it for his honeymoon. Doesn't that
strike you as odd?"

"There could be a reason."

The woman's words had filled the air of the quiet room
with a venom from which Laurel recoiled. For a moment
she was angry, then common sense prevailed. A sense of
humor was called for in a situation like this. Her visitor
had been trying to make her angry, to loosen her tongue
and thus reveal the true relationship between her and
Kirk. So far Nina could only guess at it.

Nina smiled, well pleased with the way the conversation was going. "I hope we can be friends. I have an influential position at court—in fact our house comes
under the protection of the Imperial Palace. I can do
much for you."

"So it seems," Laurel said dryly. "Thanks for the
offer, but I'm sure I shall get along admirably as Kirk's
wife. As you mentioned earlier, a man who is destined
for a great career can surely take care of his own wife. I
must apologize for not offering you refreshment, but it's
a little early and you're in a hurry to see Kirk, so I won't
detain you. Good day, Countess Wanaka. Reko will see
you out."

Laurel walked to the door, opened it and gave a short
gracious bow. She was trembling when the woman rose
to her feet with a look of hauteur and swept to the door,
passing her with an icy-cold travesty of a smile.

Laurel had gone to her room when Reko knocked with

a glass of milk and rice biscuits. Kirk had apparently left
his orders. She sat down by her window to drink, but left
the biscuits. Nina would now be going posthaste to
Kirk's office. Maybe she ought to have treated the
woman with an amused tolerance, but it was not in
Laurel's makeup to pretend friendship where none existed. Her own courage, her respect for others demanded
the same respect for herself. This woman had none.

If Nina was having an affair with Kirk, and it certainly
looked that way, then Laurel would fight it at any cost.
She refused to be browbeaten by such a woman, whether
her love for Kirk would be the same afterward was
something to be proved. Laurel wondered despairingly
how some men could be so blind to a woman's true colors. They probably found it out too late.

Kirk did not come home to lunch. He called to say he
could not make it. After lunch, Laurel wrote several letters home, including one to Kirk's Uncle George, Dr.
Machelle. In it she told him how wonderful the country
was, thanked him for the check he had sent for their
wedding present and altogether wrote like a happy bride.

Three o'clock brought two more visitors, the two
voices she had overheard in the hairdressing salon on the
morning of her wedding. And although these women
were responsible for much of her heartache and the dis-
ruption of her marriage, Laurel liked them on sight. To
begin with they looked so comical together when she entered the living room that she was inclined to giggle.

One was tall and rangy with brown hair and horn-
rimmed spectacles covering gray eyes set in a long sallow
face. Her companion was small, plump and blond, rather
like a robin in her suit of cherry red. For a fleeting moment Laurel imagined them in kimonos. The result was
so hilarious that she found herself suppressing a chuckle.

"Good afternoon," said the tall one. "We hope you
don't mind our coming by. Kirk phoned me and asked us
to call on you. He thought you might feel lonely on your
first day at home. We met at the wedding, but you'd be

too bemused to remember us." She smiled, her brown eyes warm with friendliness. "I'm Jean Summers and this is Susan Smithers."

Laurel shook hands with them. "How nice of you to come over. Please sit down and I'll ring for tea."

But Reko was there as if on cue, setting down the tray between Laurel and her guests on a low table. Laurel dispensed tea and cakes. Jean had a cigarette and Susan, like Laurel, was content to nibble at the small delicious cakes.

Jean's husband, Dennis, managed one of the big international banks in Tokyo. Susan's husband, a writer, was working on the memoirs of a well-known Japanese man of letters.

"Think you'll like it here?" Jean asked amiably, leaning back in her chair and exhaling smoke carefully away from her companions.

"It's a beautiful, strange country, but one in which I'm beginning to feel at home," Laurel vouchsafed.

"My husband, Bill, and I love it here," Susan said, finishing her fourth little cake with an air of satisfaction. "There's heaps to do—golfing, tennis, sailing, climbing, riding, badminton, even hops in a helicopter."

Jean agreed. "There are lots of laughs on the way, too, if you look for them. The laughter wrinkles I've encouraged since coming here don't bear thinking about—as if my marriage lines aren't enough!" Her smile emphasized the wrinkles on her good-natured face. "I'm thirty-five, Susan is twenty-four, more about your age Laurel. May I call you Laurel?"

"By all means."

If Countess Nina had sent her spirits down to zero Jean and Susan had sent them up again with mercurial swiftness. On first-name terms, they got on like a house on fire.

Jean started her third cigarette. "We're all going on a climb of Fujiyama this weekend. Has Kirk told you about it?"

Laurel shook her head. "No. It sounds fun. I suppose Kirk is an expert at it."

"Kirk is an expert at anything," Jean vouchsafed without rancor. "He's good fun to be with, too—never gets in a panic in an emergency and is completely unperturbed by caustic remarks, adverse weather conditions or any other obstacle that would make another man hesitate. You're going to be regarded with envy by all the females around, including several in kimonos."

Laurel smiled. "Do you think I'll survive?"

"Kirk married you, didn't he?" Susan took a breath between chewing her fifth cake. "I'm glad he married you. We're going to be great friends."

Jean was amused at Laurel's sudden flush. "Susan's right. You have nothing to worry about regarding Kirk's being a good husband. He's the kind we all dreamed of marrying—good-looking, tolerant, humorous and a perfect gent. He'll treat you like a precious piece of porcelain. I'm not surprised he's chosen someone like you, sweet and unspoiled. He's seen so many of the other kind—in his own circle, I mean. Frankly, you were lucky to come out here and find him still single. These little Japanese women, for instance, can charm the ducks off the water. They wait upon their husbands hand and foot, are hardworking, artistic and have never heard of women's liberation."

"They will," chipped in Susan darkly.

Before her guests left, Laurel escorted them around the house. A surprise came for her when, on taking them to see the bedrooms, she discovered that the third was a nursery.

"Very nice," Jean said, her amused glance flickering over the pretty bamboo cot with its frilly drapes tied with blue ribbon. "Blue for a boy, too! Trust Kirk to presume the firstborn will be. He'll get his wish, too, I'll be bound."

Laurel had another peep into the nursery when they had gone, gazing around it wistfully. All part of the setup, of course. And yet this room did not seem to have Countess Nina's touch. Maybe she had not been consulted about the furnishings after all.

Steady now, Laurel admonished herself, *your visitors have sent you up in the clouds. Nothing has changed between you and Kirk. But he did ask them to come and see me,* she argued. *And they saw nothing odd in having a week's honeymoon.* After the unpleasant incident with Nina that morning, her feelings had verged on despair. Now, in a new light mood, Laurel felt years older in experience and not so shattered.

THE LIGHT MOOD PERSISTED when she dressed for dinner that evening in the black silk flowered pantsuit. She was ready when the slam of Kirk's car door heralded his arrival. Quivering a little despite her determination to remain calm, Laurel waited for his footsteps. Would they pass her door or would he peep in to see her?

She heard him greeting Reko, the short conversation, then his footsteps passing her door. Some of the spirit went out of her then. Leaving her room, she went to the living room to fetch the glossy magazine containing photographs and an account of their new home. *In later years it would be something to keep, of a marriage that never was,* Laurel told herself bitterly.

Back in her room, she waited for Kirk to leave his and opened her door.

"Hello, there," he said breezily. "Sorry I couldn't make it for lunch. Had a nice day?"

His arm was around her slim shoulders and they strolled to the dining room. To Laurel's sensitive perception there was a strange undercurrent, as though Kirk was being charmingly polite against his will.

"Yes, thanks," she replied coolly. "It was kind of you to ask Jean and Susan to call."

"I thought you would enjoy their company." He led her into the dining room and seated her at the table.

"I did, very much."

Laurel spoke with lowered lids, shaking out her table

napkin, aware of his well-tended, flexible fingers doing likewise in the seat opposite.

"They're both intelligent and sensible young women. You'll find them good friends. Their husbands are equally likable." Kirk raised his eyes across the table to meet her blue ones. "They have bikes, as well as cars, so I suppose you'll be wanting the same."

Laurel met his mocking gaze and wished he did not look so critical. Was that the word? Funny she should feel something about her displeased him. He had not mentioned his reason for not coming home to lunch, but she knew instinctively that he had dined with Nina.

"A bicycle sounds fun, and they're popular here," she said evenly.

Reko came in with the first course and went out again. Kirk picked up his soup spoon. "There's plenty of time. Some of the roads are deplorable, especially in rainy weather. You can take things easy for a while. I expect you'll be making changes around the house. I want you to go ahead in that respect and do whatever you want. The shopping facilities in Tokyo are wide and varied. What you can't get we can always send away for."

Laurel's lips, stiff and cold, curved to receive her soup. In some strange way the house and its contents did not seem to have anything to do with her. Everything went on oiled wheels without her help. Reko was up at five every morning, going through the household chores like a clean breeze before preparing breakfast. The soiled laundry was taken away and returned beautifully done in a matter of hours. Her own underwear, put out that morning, now lay in softly perfumed folds in her bedroom drawers.

How was she ever going to get close to Kirk without sharing any intimate little pleasures like trying out a new recipe and waiting to see his reaction? She looked down at the golden brown portion of chicken Reko was placing on her plate. It was perfectly cooked. So were the vegetables she added to her plate.

"I shall have to look around before I dare to make any

alterations. In fact, there's so much beauty both indoors and out that I feel I can never improve upon it," she said, passing him the vegetable dish.

Kirk leaned over to add more vegetables to her portion. "That's better. See you eat it." Taking his own share, he put down the dish and continued with the conversation. "Even so, a house no matter how excellently furnished invariably needs the woman's touch."

They ate in silence. Laurel was thinking of Nina and wondering why he had not mentioned her visit that morning. He must know she had been to the house. Yet for the life of her she could not mention it, nor her surprise on seeing the nursery. They were in the living room having coffee when Kirk mentioned the countess.

His first words, clipped and to the point, jolted her severely. "Why were you so rude to Countess Wanaka this morning?"

Laurel's nerves stretched to shrieking point. Although she had expected him to mention the visit, the accusation came like a bolt from the blue.

"I beg your pardon?" she said with youthful dignity.

"I asked you why you were so rude to a friend of mine this morning," he repeated with the air of a man being reasonable against his will.

She put down her coffee cup with trembling hands. "Since you're convinced that I'm the guilty party, why not ask her?"

"I don't remember saying you were to blame," he said with a dangerous quietness.

"No, but your manner implies it. Your precious Nina—"

He cut in sharply, "She's not my precious Nina!"

"No?" Laurel was deathly pale and shaking. The only color in her face was her eyes dark with indignation and anguish. "Strange I should have that impression, just as you have that I'm to blame."

Kirk was studying the glowing tip of his cigarette. He was a little pinched around the nostrils, a sure sign that he was angry. But he controlled himself, leaning forward to flick ash from his cigarette into the ashtray on the low table.

"Maybe I deserve that," he admitted evenly, leaning back in his chair to look at her angry eyes. "While the last thing I want is to upset you, I must know what went on. I didn't mention it before because I wanted you to enjoy your dinner. You can't afford to miss a meal because you don't eat enough as it is. Nina was most upset when she came to my office this morning. Apparently you were hostile from the moment she arrived."

"Then that made two of us. To begin with, she didn't come to see me, she came to see you."

"Laurel! How can you say that about a woman who couldn't wait to welcome you and make friends?" He spoke sternly.

She rose to her feet, hands clenched by her sides. She looked young and vulnerable, but there was a quiet dignity about her forlorn slim figure that was infinitely touching.

"The woman came here to see you and to make mischief—I can see that now. And you had lunch with her after she'd maligned me, instead of coming home."

His face darkened at the contempt in her clear voice. "I can't see what that has to do with it."

Laurel laughed—it was either that or cry. "You only see what you want to see." She drew herself up to her full height and took a deep breath. "Well, let me tell you this, Kirk Graham: had it been the other way around and a man friend of mine had made accusations against you, the last thing I would have done would have been to dine with him afterward. So drink that down with your coffee."

Her voice wavered on the last word and she ran from the room. She heard him call her name as she ran, and once in the haven of her room she locked her door, leaning back against it and trembling uncontrollably. Sweat oozed on her temples like dew and the palms of her hands were damp with moisture.

How could he take that woman's part against her? The

silence mocked her as she threw herself on the bed to stare up at the ceiling. Kirk had not followed her. If only he had, to show that he cared about her! Taken her into his arms and given her the love she so badly needed from him.

Laurel closed her eyes, too cut to the heart to cry.

"Laurel, I want to talk to you."

Kirk's voice, accompanied by a rap on the door, came through the mists of sleep. She opened her eyes to a darkened room and memory stabbed like knives.

Another peremptory tap at the door and Kirk's voice demanding entry made her push herself up into a sitting position on the bed. Wearily, Laurel put a hand up to her head.

"Go away! You've already made up your mind who you want to believe. Now leave me alone," she said.

Another turn of the doorknob, then silence. Laurel lay down again and wept.

CHAPTER EIGHT

NOTHING EVER SEEMS SO BAD in the morning light, thought Laurel, awakening to find that it was eight o'clock. She had overslept, which meant that Kirk would have left the house for his office. Hastily she left her bed to unlock the door, hoping Reko had not already come with her early-morning tea, only to find it locked. Whatever happened, no breath of scandal must be circulated about her marriage. Not that Reko was likely to talk; he was much too devoted to Kirk to hurt him in any way.

He came with her breakfast as though he had been listening for the sound of the unlocking of her door. There was a note on the tray from Kirk. It read, "Have a good rest in bed this morning and take things easy. I shall be home to lunch. Kirk."

But Laurel was not the staying-in-bed type. In any case, she felt much too restless to stay immobile. The first round of a battle with Nina had not been very successful. Nothing had been solved.

Going for a walk to think things over, Laurel strolled along leafy lanes looking out on panoramic views. Little smoke signals spiraled up into the blue sky from bonfires of dead winter grass, along the banks of a stream. Here and there fishermen, balanced precariously on rocks, tried their luck in the shallow waters. On the slopes the narrow paddies were beautifully sown and tended, and down in the valley small figures moved across a golf course, their bright red and yellow golf bags giving a gay touch of color to the scene.

Laurel saw it all vaguely as in a dream. Her thoughts were confused. It was so difficult to know what to do for the best. If she had been rude to Nina, it had been the woman's own fault as much as her own. *I could have been more diplomatic about it*, she mused. Yet her more chastened mood did nothing to bolster her morale at the thought of meeting Kirk at lunchtime.

The walk up the mountain pass in the laughing sunshine took on new dimensions. Gradually Laurel relaxed to gaze on the most surprising views as peak after peak of the hills rose before her. Then they were forgotten in the breathtaking view of distant Fujiyama, white, dazzling, an unforgettable cone-shaped image piercing the blue sky. Thick mists swirled around the base, rising again to circle it. Entranced, Laurel wondered if she had really seen it and she continued with wings on her feet along the narrow mountain road.

The little brown house appeared as if by magic around a bend in the road. The room was open to the garden and inside a girl in a pretty kimono was toasting bread on chopsticks over a charcoal fire. Laurel watched, fascinated by the delicate movements of her hands. Now the girl was making the tea, and she suddenly looked up and across the small garden to where Laurel stood.

Ashamed of herself for being so rude as to stare, she turned away after offering a little apologetic smile and hurriedly retraced her steps homeward. The touch of a hand on her arm halted her and the girl with black, shiny, built-up hair and a merry face was gesturing for her to walk back again into the house.

Laurel was by now feeling a little exhausted and the offer of tea proved too much. Willingly, she allowed the girl to take her back. She shed her shoes at the door and walked on the soft tatami mats to sit on a bright silk cushion. The tray, in the form of a lotus leaf, held the teapot and matching cups painted gaily with birds flying over mountain peaks.

It was not until they had sat down that Laurel discovered the girl could speak English. Shyness had kept her silent until then. While she plied Laurel with tea and the delicious crisp brown toast, she talked about herself. Her name was O-mea, she was sixteen and looked after an old lady who was bedridden in the house. She seldom saw anyone except the tradesmen, and it was heaven for her to see Laurel.

O-mea did sketches in her spare time and she fetched her sketchbook for Laurel to see. The sketches were good and the girl obviously had talent. Time went on wings, till Laurel realized with dismay that she would have to hurry to get back home in time for lunch.

"*Sayonara*," cried O-mea, waving her on her way and standing in the road until Laurel turned a corner out of sight. Fortunately, the road back was downhill. She ran until she saw the roofs of the house and something more. Kirk was walking nonchalantly up the mountain pass to meet her. The incline, however, was too steep for her to slow down and she found herself hurtling down into his arms.

For blissful moments her slim suppleness was pressed against him as she took in deep breaths to replenish her lungs. He felt the fragrance of her hair beneath his lips before she lifted her head.

"Oh!" she exclaimed on a breathy laugh. "I'm so sorry I ran into you like that. Am I late for lunch?"

He looked down at the warm, smooth rose of her cheeks, her bright eyes, her soft throat and the pink mouth slightly open to help her breathing. Then he was bending his head and quietly, gently was kissing her. For a moment she stood tense and trembled.

He let her go, his face revealing nothing of his feelings. But his slow, lazy smile rocked her heart.

"No, you're not late," he said, placing an arm around her shoulder as they walked on. "I came to look for you, only too pleased that you're out enjoying the fresh air. You look blooming."

The rose flush deepened. "Do I?"

To cover her embarrassment, Laurel told him about seeing Fujiyama and taking tea with O-mea, then, not wishing to bore him, she spoke about the golf links they were now looking down on in the valley below. As a bachelor he would go freely to play as the mood took him. Was he already chafing against the bonds of matrimony, which were anything but satisfactory in their present state?

"That looks a very good golf course down there. Are you a keen golfer?" she asked tentatively.

He tossed a negligent glance in that direction. "Not particularly. It's only one of my many pursuits. As you enjoy most of my activities we shall in future share them."

"Are we going climbing this weekend?"

His glance was quizzical. "You know about it?"

"Yes. Jean and Susan mentioned it when they were here."

"Done any climbing?"

"No, but it sounds fun."

"You will enjoy it. Although it can prove exhausting on a hot day. Fortunately, we have the cool spring weather as yet. I've been up myself on more than one occasion when I felt the need for solitude."

The incidence of the previous day was forgotten as he talked about climbing. To Laurel's relief he did not allude to it during lunch, a lunch that he took control of, slicing cold meat and putting a generous portion on her plate. There was a poignant sweetness at being taken care of by Kirk.

"I've a surprise for you," he told her. "You're summoned to the Imperial Palace tomorrow afternoon to meet the empress."

Laurel watched him dumbly as she reached across to pile salad on her plate. The tea and toast at midmorning had already taken the edge off her appetite. Now this.

"Oh dear!" she cried.

He put down the salad bowl after taking some himself and Laurel knew her eyes betrayed her utter dismay.

"It's quite an informal gathering," he vouchsafed, adding a delicious sauce to his plate. "You really ought to try this sauce."

She shook her head. "I shall go with you, of course."

"I'm afraid not." He smiled at her reassuringly. "It's an afternoon tea party for a few pretty ladies, yourself included." A pause. "Countess Nina is to present you to Her Highness."

"I see." The temperature in the room took a decided plunge. "What shall I wear? It's rather short notice, isn't it?"

He grinned. "Not in Japan. They can produce a tailored suit in under twenty-four hours. Which reminds me—" Kirk slipped a hand inside his jacket pocket and drew out a checkbook made out in her name "—there you are. You can buy anything you wish." He pushed it across the table.

She stared at it woodenly. "Thanks."

"Don't look so worried," he teased. "I'm going to take you to a sweet little lady who'll make you a suitable dress. She's a court dressmaker and knows exactly what it requires. I'll drive you there after lunch on my way back to the office. We can call at the Imperial Palace on the way to give you a closer look at it!"

ON THE GREEN WATERS of the moat surrounding the Imperial Palace, the swans looked beautifully white as Kirk drove to the Ohte gate. Laurel was aware of pine-clad slopes, massive gray masonry and white watchtowers. The usual daily sightseers were there taking pictures of the grounds through the bars of the closed gates.

Kirk was instantly recognized by the black-uniformed guards who saluted and allowed him to drive through the huge gateway to follow a fifteen-foot thick high stone wall topped by a watchtower. This curved around to a large lawn on which cars were already parked. Kirk parked the car and they strolled beneath trees laden by cherry blossom looking like blobs of snow through which the sun frolicked.

The grounds were really lovely. Kirk had said they would have time for a quick look around, so they did not linger until Laurel heard the sound of men's voices and a spate of stentorian laughter. It was coming from a field behind tall pines and there were sudden glimpses of gay colors worn by men on horseback. There were eight of them, four clad in red coats and white shirts and four in blue jackets and pink shirts.

"Polo players," Laurel said. "They have long bamboo poles with nets on the end."

Kirk was grinning down at her. "I know."

"You play polo?"

He nodded. "Another of my vices," he mocked.

She said, "I know so little about you."

"You know enough," was the cool reply. "Come along, we have to go."

"Does the emperor play polo?"

They were back in the car approaching the gates when Laurel asked the question. Kirk did not answer. He was leaning out of the car window having a word with the uniformed guards at the gates. He spoke swiftly in Japanese and they replied, showing gold teeth among white ones as they saluted.

Evidently they had shared a joke, for Kirk grinned as he returned their salute and shot through the massive gateway.

"You were saying?" he said as they left the palace behind and joined the traffic on the main highway.

"It was nothing," she answered, thinking that playing polo could be a cover-up for his affair with Nina. The ladies of the court would be spectators, naturally, and the countess was sure to be one of them.

Kirk swung the car from the main road toward the suburbs. "It's an awful job to trace anyone here. The numbers of houses are like a jigsaw puzzle. Lord knows how the mailmen manage to deliver the letters. The best thing to do if you want to find an address is to go to the police." He slowed down at a crossroads and turned by a tall red post topped by a red light. "This is the road, I think, going by the fire alarm."

Laurel eyed the post apprehensively. "Is that what the red posts are?"

"Yes. We have one in the garden. I'll show you how to use it. They can't afford to play around with fires here. The alarm is rung at the slightest suspicion of an outbreak. Like the earthquakes, fire is another item of everyday life. Either of these hazards can wipe out a city in no time."

The road wound between yew hedges hiding small picturesque dwellings of unpainted wood. Kirk drew up at the first one. A small garden was surrounded by a fence and a little wicket gate. Leaving the car, Kirk opened the gate to the tinkle of a bell, stood aside for Laurel to enter and escorted her along the garden path.

The garden had the sad, dejected look of having battled through a hard winter. Tufts of dead winter grass loomed up between azaleas and the shoots of spring flowers. In a corner by the house a willow tree was sprouting little green shoots along its branches. The bell must have alerted someone in the house, for the sliding door moved and a petite Japanese lady stood there.

Mrs. Pakara was a diminutive four foot ten or so. She had the appearance of a well-preserved geisha girl in her forties. She wore a beautiful kimono with a richly embroidered obi around her tiny waist. Her abundant hair and shoe-button eyes were black in a Malay kind of face and her small hands were covered in rings. She reminded Laurel of a bright little bird, but a knowing one who could sum a person up in seconds and keep what she knew under the elaborate hairdo.

Kirk greeted her charmingly with a slight bow and addressed her in Japanese.

As they talked, Mrs. Pakara's bright black eyes flickered over Laurel's slim form as if she was already taking her measurements. Kirk eventually turned to Laurel.

"Mrs. Pakara is very busy, but she'll be happy to make

your dress for tomorrow. Mrs. Pakara, my wife, Laurel.''

Mrs. Pakara bowed low, Laurel bowed and looked up at Kirk.

He smiled down at her reassuringly. "Mrs. Pakara speaks English, so you'll be able to understand each other. I'll leave you with her and pick you up around five."

As he strode away to his car, Mrs. Pakara smiled at Laurel. "*Dazo*," she said with a bow that Laurel knew meant "please enter." Another sliding door faced her as she stepped into the vestibule. Slipping off her shoes, she stepped into a pair awaiting her on the step and followed her hostess across a beautifully polished hall.

Inside, the house looked more spacious than it had appeared, probably because of the Japanese way of furnishing. Yet another sliding door was pulled along and at a smile from Mrs. Pakara, Laurel removed her shoes and entered to tread on thick tatami mats.

The room was typically Japanese with the elegant spaciousness of walled cupboards and a sea of floor. In the far wall was the usual *tokonama* or raised alcove with its beautiful flower arrangement beneath a pictured scroll of a Japanese landscape. In front of this lay a gurgling baby surrounded by cushions. Mrs. Pakara went across to him, raised him on his fat little legs and spoke a few words in Japanese. The next moment he was bending double with his little black head going down to the dimpled chubby hands on the floor in a bow to Laurel.

He was too fat to get up again and rolled over in the cushions chuckling with mirth.

Laurel was captivated. "Isn't he sweet?" she cried.

Mrs. Pakara smiled. "Son of daughter-san. Name of Fuseko."

Laurel bent down to take hold of one chubby hand and Fuseko pulled himself up into a sitting position. "What does his name mean?" she asked.

"Fuseko means Little Luxury."

Laurel laughed. "A very precious one, too!"

"Sons very precious. Daughters not so precious in Japan."

"Then your daughter has made up for her own sex by having this lovely child. He's delightful." Her smile was tender. "May I pick him up?" She picked him up and cuddled him, loving the feel of his small velvety cheek against her own, then put him down as Mrs. Pakara returned armed with rolls of material and a pattern book.

Sitting among cushions on the tatami mats they chose a pattern and a lovely roll of brocade.

Mrs. Pakara said, "This famous Nishijin brocade is used only in best fashion houses. I will make it nice for you. You have pretty dainty figure."

The material was draped on Laurel and pinned in all the vital places. It was then whisked off, cut and tried on again. The tiny expert hands moved lovingly over the material, reminding Laurel of the gardener who caressed the lumps of soil. Mrs. Pakara was smiling and chuckling as if she was getting the greatest pleasure out of making the dress. The rings on her hands shone no less brighter than her eyes.

Now and then she would leave the room and sew. Then back again she would come for another fitting. In between these outbursts of energy several callers arrived and it seemed to Laurel that the front gate was forever tinkling.

Mrs. Pakara, however, was undismayed by these interruptions, taking them all in her stride. Eventually the basic lines of the dress were complete.

"Dress ready for tomorrow," Mrs. Pakara promised after a last satisfactory fitting. "We have tea now."

Fuesko, or Little Luxury, had fallen asleep. In less time than it takes to look around, everything cluttering up the neatness of the room had been put away; rolls of material, snippings of cloth, pins, scissors, tape measure and pattern book disappeared as if by magic.

Quickly the little brazier, set in the well of the floor

was lighted, the kettle put on and plates of little cakes brought in. Green tea was poured into eggshell china bowls from a matching teapot and they nibbled cakes as they talked.

Mrs. Pakara was a widow who had outgrown her illusions. Her husband had died after three years of marriage, leaving her with a small daughter aged two. Mr. Pakara had owned a bookshop in Tokyo and his wife, having no love or interest in books, had sold it. Now, twenty years later, she was a successful dressmaker.

"Clothes are my life," said Mrs. Pakara, passing more cakes and tea to Laurel. "A plain woman can turn heads if she knows how to wear clothes."

Laurel agreed and the time went on wings. The sound of Kirk arriving brought an end to a visit Laurel had thoroughly enjoyed.

"How did it go?" Kirk asked her when they were on their way home.

"It was delightful." The last few hours spent in Mrs. Pakara's company had made her feel alive and on the edge of laughter. "The baby was delicious."

He gave her a swift glance. "You're fond of children?"

Kirk was concentrating on his driving among a horde of cyclists.

"I adore them. You certainly charmed Mrs. Pakara into making the dress. A constant string of customers arrived during the afternoon."

"Are you glad? You'll have a beautifully modeled dress fit to be presented at court."

"You might not be so pleased when you hear what it costs. Mrs. Pakara assures me that the brocade is very expensive and only used in the best fashion houses," she said dryly.

"So what?" Kirk had rid himself of the cyclists and was putting on speed. "You like it, don't you?"

"Yes, very much."

"Then there's nothing more to be said."

She eyed him covertly, saw that he looked immensely strong and dynamic. Those steel-gray eyes were fixed right ahead. If only he would look at her as she wanted him to look, with a need for her that would turn her bones to jelly! She sighed.

"Tired?"

"Goodness, no!"

"I'm glad."

"Are you? Why?"

"You'll see," he replied laconically.

And she did, staring wide-eyed at the cars parked around their house, in the grounds and on the approach road.

"What . . . what are all the cars doing at the house?" she asked huskily.

"A housewarming party. I thought it was better to give you a surprise instead of having you worry about it beforehand. All right?"

She nodded. "I was wondering when you were getting around to it."

Kirk drove in, passing cars up the driveway to the cleared entrance to the garage, which Reko had kept open. Then, like two conspirators, they left the garage hand in hand to go around to the back of the house and enter by the kitchen-garden door. Inside the door they paused as voices came along the corridor from the bedrooms.

He bent his head and whispered urgently, "Visitors leaving their coats in the spare bedrooms. Quick, in here until they've gone, then we can go and change."

He pulled her into a little cupboard affair at the end of the corridor where Reko kept his overalls. They stood close, so close that Laurel could feel the strength of his hard body against her own. Kirk was all fire and laughter, so endearing. He held her against him carelessly, easily. Yet Laurel could not relax, could not be as carefree. How could she when she did not trust him?

"All clear now, I think."

"Yes." Her voice was quite steady. She even managed a smile.

"Hurry and change. I'll join you when I'm ready."

He came to her room eventually to find her struggling with the zipper of her evening dress.

"Here, let me." He was across the room in long strides and Laurel with her back to him trembled at the cool touch of his fingers as he worked on the zipper. "There you are." The zipper ran smoothly up her back. "No, don't turn around. Look into the mirror."

She obeyed, saw the gray eyes above her own that enchanted while they mocked. He had taken something from his pocket and placed it on her dark hair. It was a small tiara with the glitter of a thousand lights. Then he was clipping the long diamond earrings onto the small lobes of her ears.

"My mother's," he said. "A family heirloom for my bride."

Laurel stared speechless at her own dazzling reflection. Her cheeks were the color of a wild rose, her eyes dark pools of bewilderment.

"But they look valuable. I've never had anything like it in my life!"

His eyes teased her shocked expression of surprise at the beauty of her own image looking wide-eyed back at her from the mirror. "Have they bolstered your morale?" he said softly against one glittering small ear. "I've yet to see a more beautiful hostess about to welcome her guests. Shall we go?"

He held out his arm and she slipped her hand inside it. They walked into a room filled with a bright laughing, chattering crowd that transformed it into something warm and welcoming.

"Here they are," someone said brightly, and the spate of lighthearted chatter was stilled long enough for the guests to swarm around them.

With Laurel beside him, Kirk separated, coupled and introduced guests with his usual imperturbability and charm. Reko was there with several waiters weaving in and out with trays of drinks, and everyone seemed settled to join in and enjoy the housewarming party.

A long table was set at one end of the dining room loaded with food for a buffet meal. There were too many to seat them all. Laurel enjoyed it all immensely. Everyone was so warm and friendly and there were none of the critical looks she had dreaded.

Granted, most of the guests had already attended the wedding reception, such as Jean's husband, Dennis. He was blond and very attractive with blue eyes and even features including a Grecian nose and rather weak mouth. His fair hair clustered in small curls over his head and he had the bold looks of a man aware of his own attractions where women were concerned.

Susan's husband, Bill, towered above his wife like a bean pole; he was pleasantly ugly with a long thin face and looked shy. Champagne bubbled freely, and as the evening advanced, Laurel noticed Dennis taking more than was good for him. Furthermore, he made no secret of his admiration for her; one look from his bold blue eyes made her feel undressed.

Countess Nina had arrived a little late with her husband. She looked ravishing in white and diamonds and her glance at Laurel's exquisite tiara was a cat's gleam of amber between thick lashes.

Her husband, Ishi, was a handsome, distinguished-looking man. They were talking to Kirk when Laurel sauntered into the garden where Reko was attending to the overflow of guests.

She had astonished herself with the ease with which she was able to relax and be her natural self. Her eyes were warmly eloquent, and her voice, accompanied occasionally by husky laughter, was low, sweet and musical as she talked to a young under secretary of the Imperial court, an official of the Ministry of Education and an American from the embassy.

The garden was gay with lanterns and a low sickle

moon was appearing in the darkening sky. Later, Laurel retraced her footsteps back to the house by a side path. She saw Nina with a wrap around her shoulders . . . saw Kirk join her, heard their quiet laughter, their voices and watched them pass in the shadows in the direction of the little wicket gate leading down the slopes to the lake. Her hands clenched at her sides and she drew a deep breath as though mortally wounded. How could Kirk take that woman on a walk on which she herself had gone with him and treasured? She told herself bitterly that he would not be so detached with his present companion, would not even wait until they reached the seclusion of the lakeside before he took her in his arms.

Laurel was shattered by the intense feelings of jealousy and despair running riot inside her. Unhappiness engulfed her like a choking cloud, drying her throat and clouding her vision. She stood for several moments pulling herself together.

"So this is where you're hiding, in the garden."

Drink-sodden breath fanned her cheek. Someone loomed unsteadily behind her. A voice lowered to her ear was slurred. Laurel swung around to look up at Jean's husband, much the worse for drink. He was swaying on his feet. The shock of seeing him so cleared her brain as to give her an ice-cold logic.

She smiled. "I've been talking to my guests, Mr. Summers."

He swayed toward her and she put out a hand to steady him.

"Where do you get this 'Mr. Summers' from? I'm Dennis. I'm one of your guests, too, and I demand your attention."

He looked down on her broodingly. Her hand flat against his chest appeared to be holding him upright.

"Dennis, then," she said lightly. "I didn't mean to offend."

"Don't you like me?"

Laurel recoiled inwardly as he took her hand and raised it to his lips.

"Of course I do. We're friends." She managed a smile, her eyes purely personal, her face serene. "And don't shout," she added gently. "Come on, sit down."

They were near the patio outside the living room. Laurel freed her hand and led him to the bamboo chairs placed by a low table.

He dropped heavily into a chair and made a grab for her. She cleverly evaded him. "I'm not shouting. Come here, you lovely thing."

Laurel adroitly took shelter behind the small table. "Oh, but you are. You're going to have a drink."

To her intense relief Reko was there with a tray, blandly smiling.

"Coffee, madam?" His light metallic-sounding voice was reassuring.

Her smile registered her grateful thanks. "Yes, please, Reko. Will you put it down on the table? I'll see to it. Thank you."

"Who said anything about coffee?" Dennis growled in disgust.

With steady hands, Laurel poured out a cup of strong black coffee.

Dennis accepted it with an ill grace, watching her pour a weaker cup for herself.

"Cheers," she said. "Drink it up like a good boy and tell me about yourself."

To her relief he obeyed and she poured him out a second cup. Gradually she drew him out of his brooding mood to talk about himself until his eyes closed and he fell asleep.

She met a worried Jean on her way indoors. "If you're looking for Dennis, he's asleep on the patio. I'd leave him for a while."

Jean looked immensely relieved. "He hasn't been making a nuisance of himself, has he?"

"Stop worrying. Dennis is enjoying himself. That's what he came for." Laurel linked Jean's arm. "Let's go indoors. I suppose you've seen the housewarming presents?"

"What a nice person you are, Laurel." Jean kissed her cheek. "I know Dennis has had too much to drink. Drink and women are his favorite hobbies."

"We all have our problems," said Laurel.

When the last trickle of guests had gone, she was aware of Nina holding back until the last. Her husband had left earlier in the evening to go to a previous engagement. Laurel had an idea he had gone to keep some date with a geisha girl. Strange she should have that idea of a man she hardly knew. But a great many wealthy Japanese entertained a geisha girl, sometimes taking a favorite one as a concubine.

Reko had brought Nina's wrap and Kirk was helping her on with it. Laurel thanked her for coming, bade her a cool good-night and went along to her room.

With mixed feelings she walked to the window to look out into the darkness unseeingly, every nerve in her body taut. When she heard someone enter the room, she made no move but stood rigid, a catch in her breath. Color had fled from her face, leaving her skin pale with the luminosity of a pearl in the gloom.

"Laurel," Kirk said softly.

Had she but known it Laurel had never looked so lovely, so desirable, with her wide eloquent eyes dark pools in the paleness of her face. Her red lips quivered as she turned to face him and the small tiara was a blaze of light in the gloom.

"Laurel," he said again, his eyes meltingly tender as he looked at her. He placed his hand around the top of her slender arms. "You were wonderful tonight."

Laurel stiffened in his hold. Her voice was husky and well chilled.

"Was I?"

He frowned down at her darkly. "Is anything the matter?"

In that moment she almost hated him. "Has Nina gone?" she asked flatly.

"I'm taking her home."

"Are you asking me or telling me?" was the bitter response.

"Why should I ask you if I can take a friend home?"

"Why should you?" A rush of anger stained her cheeks and she trembled. "Why come in to tell me? You do as you like in any case."

"Of course I do. I allow you to do the same—or haven't you noticed?"

"You'd be surprised what I've noticed." Her sarcasm was as heavy as his own. "Why do you make your friendship with that woman so obvious? I heard her refuse two lifts home from guests. I think—"

He was savagely angry, she knew, gripping her arms so painfully that she winced, as he cut in, "I don't want to hear your opinion on a matter that doesn't concern you. It's not important."

"It's of the utmost importance, since it does concern me."

"In what way?"

"As your wife. We are supposed to be married."

"There's no supposing about it. We *are* married." He released her and pushed his hands into his pockets, surveying her with an insolent mockery that made her long to slap his face. "However, I lead such a monastic existence that I can hardly be blamed if the fact escapes me from time to time. Can I?"

Standing there before him, Laurel felt his deep emotion, knew him to be laboring under gusts of anger that he held in leash. His frowning black brows gave his dark, sardonic face a grimness that was frightening in its intensity. But Laurel was not afraid of him, for a passionate hope was leaping in her breast at his words.

She put out a hand, then drew it back. "You mean Nina is . . .?"

"Nothing to me," he finished for her.

She shook her head. "Nothing?" she repeated woodenly as if trying to convince herself. She stared at him in disbelief and started to tremble.

"Stop it!" Kirk gripped her shoulders. "I married you, didn't I? You have to trust me, or what's our marriage worth? We belong to each other."

Laurel turned away. "Do we? Do you belong to me?"

Suddenly he swung her around, his anger unleashed. "You doubt it? Then let me convince you."

Seizing her in his arms, he took her soft lips, forcing them to obey his own. But she stood passive in his cruel embrace. Suddenly he released her and she was alone.

For a long time after he had gone Laurel stood staring out into the night. Her mouth still burned and she felt bruised and battered when she finally prepared for bed. A slight cut inside her lip was bleeding, so she made do with a mouth wash instead of cleaning her teeth. The double bed seemed king-size in her utter loneliness as she tossed and turned.

She thought again of Kirk's brutal kiss, and because she loved him, Laurel could feel sorry for him. Poor Kirk, loving one woman and married to another. He wanted her to believe there was nothing between them. How could she when his every action pointed to an association with Nina?

It was a well-known fact that the Japanese were not in favor of divorce, which could be the reason Nina had not asked for one. She could be biding her time, knowing it would be easy enough for Kirk to get an annulment.

At least I didn't throw myself into his arms, Laurel thought miserably. *How easily I could have given way to my love for him, begging him to love me, to make my marriage secure so that no annulment would be possible. But I wouldn't want him on those terms. I might even have had his child.* She trembled at the thought. *But I won't take him on those terms, either, much as I would like a child.*

But where to go from here? A burning question, and one that she eventually abandoned in favor of sleep.

CHAPTER NINE

AT SIX O'CLOCK the paperboy whistling on his bicycle awakened Laurel. Drowsily she listened, then slept. It was seven when she awoke again. In the cheering light of a new day the tumult of feeling brought about by the events of the previous day had subsided into something she could face, if not entirely banish.

When she walked into the dining room for breakfast, no one would have guessed the kind of unsettled night she had gone through. At least, not Kirk, who was perusing one of the morning papers. Her heart somersaulted as usual at the sight of him.

His face was a gleaming bronze mask, his hair darkened by his recent swim in the lake. She caught in the morning light his speculative look from clear gray eyes and hung on to her play-it-cool role with considerable effort. The next moment she was lowering her eyes from that smile of extraordinary charm as he pulled out her chair.

"Good morning, my sweet. You have a full day ahead, I believe. First a visit to your dressmaker, an appointment at the hairdressers' and tea in the afternoon at the Imperial Palace. You look bandbox fresh. How are you feeling?"

Laurel sat down and replied that she was feeling all right. He resumed his seat as Reko appeared, relinquished his morning paper and gave his attention to his breakfast and Laurel.

Outwardly they were a normal married couple sharing their first intimate meal of the day together. Kirk was utterly at ease, or so he appeared to be, and gradually his calm got through to her.

He was to drive her to Mrs. Pakara's for her dress and from there she was to get a taxi to the hairdressers' at the New Otani Hotel, then a taxi home. At eight-fifteen Laurel was sitting beside Kirk in the big roomy car watching him drive confidently toward the city.

The Japanese were early risers and already the small brown houses they passed had been swept, cleaned and polished. The little concrete vestibule between the two doors had been scrubbed, the path swept and watered. Papers had been collected from the glass-fronted box attached to the front fence, and so had the bottles of milk in the gaily painted wooden fixture inside the front gate.

Cycles, hundreds of them, weaved their way in and out of the traffic and mothers clip-clopped along on wooden *getas* with their babies strapped on their backs. It seemed to Laurel that every turn of the car wheels revealed a beauty that enchanted. Even in the city one felt the serenity of the old Japan. It lingered like an aura around the Imperial Palace, even among the Western-style office blocks set in the midst of gardens, and even the constant stream of modern traffic failed to dispel it altogether.

Kirk slowed the car as they passed an office block set in immaculate gardens. He gestured toward it with a lean brown hand.

"This is where I work. I'll take you around it sometime."

Laurel looked wistfully at the place where he spent most of his day.

"It looks very nice," she said inanely. "Why did you decide to work in Japan?"

"My father's influence, I'm afraid. He loved it here. He came to study economics at Tokyo university and stayed to lecture and write. He said Japan had taught him how to live and enjoy life. He liked the way the smiling people, instead of growing away from nature, had taken it as part of their lives. They encouraged it to flow like rivers through their homes, purifying the unnatural indoor environment that would eventually poison the human element.

"And your mother? Did she share his enthusiasm?"

"Up to a point. She insisted that I should be educated in England. I won enough degrees to secure a job here, and here I am."

"And your father?"

"He was killed two years ago while playing polo. He fell from his horse and was struck on the temple by the hooves of another horse. My mother, who saw it happen, died of shock. They were very devoted."

"I'm so sorry."

"I've got over it now. Looking back on it, I realize mother wouldn't have wanted to go on without my father."

They had reached Mrs. Pakara's house and he dropped her off. Mrs. Pakara was at the door as the gate bell tinkled. She looked stricken. She greeted Laurel politely, looking very attractive this morning in slate gray with a blue glittering obi around her tiny waist.

"*Dazo,*" she said. "I sad today."

"You mean my dress isn't finished?" Laurel was slipping off her shoes before entering the hall.

"Yes, dress finished last night. Hope you like."

"Like?" Laurel echoed ten minutes later as she surveyed herself in the beautiful brocade dress. She was standing in front of the full-length mirror in Mrs. Pakara's workroom. It was a perfect fit, emphasizing the youthful curves of her slender figure. The silken threads of the material seemed to have woven all the delicate colors of a Japanese landscape into the sheen of it. The obi around her small waist held all the rich colors of a sunset.

"It's beautiful!" Laurel turned to look at a perfect back view. "I've never seen anything so beautiful."

Mrs. Pakara lifted black hopeful eyes, still shadowed. "You really like it?"

"I adore it. What a dear you are to work so hard in order to get it ready for me. I'll take it off while you make out the bill for me."

Mrs. Pakara had the bill ready and she handed it to Laurel as if she expected her to be shocked by it. The bill was so modest that Laurel gasped.

"Mrs. Pakara, are you sure this is all it is?"

"Sure." She declined any extra money. With her spirits partly restored, Mrs. Pakara proceeded to pack the dress almost reverently into a cardboard box, which she tied with gift cord. "Now we have tea," she said.

She led the way into the room in which the baby had lain. It was strangely quiet without him.

"No baby?" asked Laurel with a sense of disappointment.

Mrs. Pakara shook her head violently and knelt to the charcoal fire in the center of the room, heating the kettle. "Not want to talk about it," she said, and scuttled to the sliding cupboards to produce crockery and plates of homemade delicacies.

Laurel watched, perplexed, and worried at the woman's obvious distress.

"I hope nothing has happened to the child," she said.

Mrs. Pakara again shook her head as she measured tea from a canister into the teapot. "Not know."

"You mean he is missing?"

"No, gone away."

Mrs. Pakara made the tea and passed a cup to Laurel. "You mean the baby is not coming back?"

She shook her head and passed the cakes. They munched and drank their tea in silence until Laurel had to say something, for the woebegone face disturbed her greatly.

"Wouldn't you like to tell me about it? Perhaps I can help."

Mrs. Pakara folded her hands meekly in her lap and

stared down at the glitter of her rings. "Daughter-san
very pretty, very talented. Wanted daughter-san to go to
university, perhaps to America to learn more. But
daughter-san headstrong. Wanted to be geisha girl."
Mrs. Pakara lifted shiny black contemptuous eyes.
"Geisha girl is described as being an entertainer. We
know how many geisha have become the playthings of
rich men and are concubines. Tell daughter-san this, will
not listen. She go for glamour." Mrs. Pakara shrugged
narrow shoulders. "Daughter-san go with one rich man
long time, have baby son. Rich man not know of son. But
rich man's wife find out. Wants to adopt baby of husband. Daughter-san say no."

"Poor child," Laurel said sympathetically. "But your
daughter cannot hide forever. She will need money. Can
I help?"

Mrs. Pakara shook her head.

"Has your daughter considered how much better off
her baby will be with the rich man's wife? He will be educated, and what's more important, he will have a name."

"Daughter-san never give baby away."

"Maybe my husband can help. Talk to this rich man's
wife and make her understand."

"Rich man's wife not understand. Not had any
babies." Terror shone in her eyes. "Not tell husband—
promise!"

Laurel leaned forward and patted the quivering hand.
"I promise, and don't upset yourself. Something will
turn up, I'm sure."

"Turn up?"

Laurel smiled tenderly. "I mean something might
happen to help your daughter."

Mrs. Pakara shook her head. "Rich people very powerful."

When it was time for Laurel to leave for her appointment at the hairdressers', the little dressmaker seemed
brighter. She called for a taxi and Laurel left after offer-

ing to help in any way she could. Mrs. Pakara, with tears in her eyes, thanked her.

Her small tragic face was before Laurel's eyes as the taxi racketed along. Most taxi drivers in Tokyo drove like mad, impervious to oncoming traffic. But Laurel was much too preoccupied to notice. During the time she was in the hairdressing salon she thought about the darling little Fuseko, saw him again bowing before her, bottom in the air as his head came down to touch the floor between his chubby hands.

She hoped fervently that something would turn up for Mrs. Pakara's daughter to help her in her dilemma. Her taxi driver had promised to pick her up at the end of her appointment and she waited outside the Imperial for quite a while. When it was evident he was not coming, Laurel was thinking about stopping another when Dennis Summers drew up in his neat gray car.

"Hello," he said, all smiles. "And here was I thinking that this was my unlucky day. Hop in, I'll take you to lunch."

Laurel stood clutching the cardboard box containing her dress. "I'm sorry, Dennis, I must go home to lunch. Kirk will be expecting me."

He frowned in mock dismay. "Are you afraid of him?"

Laurel regarded his wry grimace and realized he was challenging her to go with him. Any other time perhaps she would have done. But after lunch she would have to get ready for her visit to the palace and she wanted everything to run smoothly.

"I'm sorry, Dennis. I simply have to be back because I'm going to the Imperial Palace this afternoon."

He had opened the car door and she made no attempt to get in. He looked gay and uncaring and she tried to remember when she had looked the same—or would ever look the same again.

Dennis leaned forward. "You look very worried. A pretty girl like you should never be worried. Besides, I owe you an apology for behaving so disgustingly at your housewarming. Surely you aren't going to deny me the pleasure of taking you out to lunch to apologize?''

"You don't need to apologize, Dennis. You didn't do anything unmannerly.''

"If you don't come with me for lunch I shall conclude that you haven't forgiven me.''

"Dennis, don't be an idiot. Look, I must get a taxi.''

He shrugged resignedly. "All right, you win. Hop in and I'll drive you home.''

Still Laurel hesitated. "If you're on your lunch hour I shall make you late unless you stay to lunch.''

He reached out for the box she held and tossed it into the backseat. Laurel slipped inside and he set the car off at high speed.

"It's very kind of you," she said. "I'm not exactly wild about using a taxi. They remind you too much of life insurance. I don't know what happened to mine. He did promise to pick me up at the Imperial Hotel.''

He grinned at her. "Probably lost his way. I've never met one yet who knows much more than half a dozen addresses.''

The next moment she was leaning forward and peering through the windshield. "There he is, coming this way.''

She waved and the taxi driver nodded as he flashed by.

Denis said dryly, "Looks as though he picked another passenger up on the way. You can hardly blame him, since they're paid by the number of fares they pick up.''

Laurel sighed. "I don't feel so bad at not waiting any longer. I paid him for the return journey.''

It came to her with a small unpleasant lurch of her stomach that they were not going in the direction she had expected.

She laughed. "Talking about taxi drivers, are you sure this is the right way to Sakura?''

He grinned. "I'm taking you to a Swiss restaurant specializing in Swiss cuisine. You'll enjoy it and it's much quicker than taking you home. We're here now, so don't argue.''

He pulled into a driveway threading among smooth lawns to brake outside a Swiss-designed eating place with the chalet verandas filled with flowers and alpine scenes painted on the walls.

Laurel, hiding her dismay, gave in gracefully. After all, Kirk might not have gone home to lunch, either, but she had to phone to tell Reko in case he was worried.

Kirk had not arrived for lunch when she phoned Reko to say she was having lunch with a friend. The meal was one of gastronomical delight. Along with her companion's flattering remarks and open admiration it gave poor Laurel a sense of pleasure after Kirk's casual treatment. Dennis knew how to entertain a woman and bring out the best in her.

Granted he worked on blatant flattery, but it was balm to her sore heart. He might have been serious in his gratitude to her for what she did for him at the house-warming party, or he saw it as a successful line of approach as he angled to ingratiate himself into her good books.

Whatever it was, Laurel refused to dwell upon it and set out to enjoy herself. She was almost sorry when it was over and Dennis was driving her home. "We must do this again," he said, rather too casually. "Anyway, I'll be seeing you on the weekend when we go to Fujiyama."

They both saw the long opulent car parked in the driveway of the house when Dennis turned in at the gates.

"The lord and master is home," he observed cynically. "I won't stay." He grinned down at her. "Did you know your husband is an expert at judo and karate? He holds a black belt. Farewell, fair maiden. I must dash."

He pulled up to give himself enough room to reverse, and raising an arm to Laurel as she left the car, he was soon away. Laurel entered the house knowing that Kirk would not be pleased at her having dined with Dennis. She grew meditative, realizing she did not exactly like

Kirk's dining with Nina. So it was with complete sangfroid that she entered the dining room to see Kirk still seated at the table.

The casual way in which he put down the newspaper to regard her with those keen eyes sent a wave of color to her face. She was determined to treat the whole thing lightly, yet here she was feeling caught out herself.

"Did you enjoy your lunch?" he asked casually.

His eyes roved over her flushed face, the becoming hairdo and her pretty powder-blue silk suit. A suspicion of a smile hovered around his lips.

"Very much," she answered lamely, taking off her gloves with her shoulder bag in place.

He leaned back in his chair, stretching out his long legs, and continued to gaze fixedly at her face.

"Who was the friend?"

"Dennis. Dennis Summers."

Laurel had advanced into the room to halt a few feet from the table. For some reason she felt glued to the spot. She had the feeling of a child facing an irate parent, for Kirk's eyes had narrowed to pinpoints of steel.

"You're not to dine with Dennis again alone. Is that understood?"

He continued to look into her face and something like a flash of swordplay passed between them.

Laurel was momentarily staggered. "Why not?" she asked, the gloves lying limply in her hand.

"Because I say so," he replied with provoking calmness. "Dennis Summers is a menace no husband wants to deal with as a companion for his wife. His reputation concerning his affairs with women since he came here is not commendable. He spends most of his free time between geisha houses and the wives of English settlers here."

"Then why do you have him for a friend?"

"Because his job as manager of one of the big international banks in Tokyo gives him the privilege of moving freely in society."

Laurel bit her lip. "I see. I had a suspicion of his being that kind of man. But I can take care of myself."

Kirk raised his eyebrows slightly. "You can't mix with shady characters without some of the slime rubbing off on yourself. I want your word that you will not go out with him again nor entertain him here on his own. If Jean is with him it doesn't matter. The man may seem harmless to you; his type usually does. I assure you he is not."

Laurel fidgeted with her gloves, compressed her lips and raised her eyes. He was looking at her with an expression that stirred her pulses profoundly.

"Well?" he asked at last, his charming smile full of that winning quality that made her like putty in his hands.

Even so, it could not abate a feeling she had regarding his own association with Nina. Her deep breath was a call-up for all the fighting spirit she possessed.

"What about your association with Countess Nina? You dine with her."

She was unconsciously standing rigid, meeting his eyes with the gleam of something like war passing between them. He rose to his feet and walked to the window before turning to face her.

"I thought we'd settled that when I assured you that there was nothing between us." After a significant pause, he added with the slightest inflection of a taunt in his deep voice, "You're not jealous, by any chance—are you?"

Laurel dropped her eyes and bit her teeth together hard. She was jealous, terribly so. On the other hand he must never know. She could bear anything but that.

"Why don't you look at me? Are you afraid?"

Laurel took her courage in both hands and lifted her face to look him in the eye. "No, I'm not afraid."

In that moment, like a blinding flash of light, came the realization that she had left her dress in Dennis's car. Seeing Kirk's car in the driveway had driven it completely out of her mind. Her hand flew to her mouth in dismay.

"Oh, my goodness! My dress! I left in on the backseat of Dennis's car. He won't notice it."

The next moment Kirk had strode from the room. Laurel closed her eyes. The sound of his car dying away in the distance was like the tail end of a hurricane that had swept through the house, leaving her limp and exhausted.

She went slowly to her room, dragging the shoulder bag down and swinging it along lethargically, too spent to care what Kirk might say to the hapless Dennis.

LAUREL WAS READY WHEN, at three precisely, the long black limousine with the Imperial coat of arms slid up to the front door. Kirk had successfully retrieved the dress, leaving it with Reko and going off at great speed without a word to herself. To be fair, he could not be blamed for that. The errand had made him late reporting back to work, and he would hate that.

She would have liked him to have seen the dress, though it was just as well he had not. He would hardly have been in the mood to give an unbiased opinion. Nevertheless, as she took a last look at herself in the dressing-table mirror, Laurel saw no flaws in her appearance. The small tiara in her beautifully dressed hair was perfect above the dream of a dress, giving her the feeling of being a fairy-tale princess in full regalia.

A black-liveried driver stood impassively beside the open door of the car, closing the door behind her after she had slipped inside. The car purred along on its luxurious springs and the feeling that it was all a dream continued during the drive. White swans glided silently on the tea-green waters of the moat surrounding the palace as they passed over the bridge through the Ohte gate and on to the grand entrance door.

A master of ceremonies awaited her in the entrance hall. He bowed low over her hand as she presented her card, another liveried footman came forward and she was conducted to a charming powder room. In this charming dressing room of wall-length mirrors pretty girls in fabulous kimonos fluttered around her like dainty butterfiles to take her wrap.

They gazed down in open admiration at her dress and lovingly touched the smoothness of her hair for stray strands, caressing the tiara as they would an open flower. Laurel's smile was as warm as theirs when they bowed her out to where the master of ceremonies was waiting. Another deep bow and she was escorted along corridors of endless length, though strangely cheerful. Spacious, lined with beautiful aromatic wood, they were enclosed with glass walls through which one could see courtyards, gardens, bamboo bridges over streams, flowering shrubs and pagodas. And there were flowers everywhere.

At last they halted outside a door and Laurel was shown into a room of fantastically muted color. Most of it came from a bower of Western and Japanese flowers artistically arranged in the center of the room.

There were fabulous silk furnishings, gilt chairs and divans upholstered in Kyoto silk; lacquer cabinets filled with objets d'art lined the walls. The light and spaciousness of the room was again enhanced by the view through the sliding glass walls opening onto the gardens. Laurel had the sensation of being in an underwater cavern of sheer shimmering beauty.

Cherry trees heavily laden with blossoms were among fountains sending up jeweled sprays in the sun. The ladies of the court, assembled in the room in their beautiful kimonos, were not unlike flowers themselves. There were about a dozen in all, talking and laughing quietly as she entered.

Countess Nina detached herself from a small group and came to greet her coolly. Laurel felt the woman was doing what she had to because she had no choice. Laurel was introduced to countesses, ladies and others with no title. Those who could speak English did so, the others smiled intelligently and drew her warmly into their circle.

Soon they were all trooping out of the room behind a liveried servant to follow him along more corridors to a room in a picturesque courtyard. The laughter and whispering among them ceased when the servant admitted them into a room where deep red roses and white orchids made splashes of color against crimson silk drapes and neutral walls.

Here again was a view of the grounds through the sliding glass walls. As they stood in silence waiting, the empress, a sweet doll-like creature, entered. Everyone bowed as she walked to a beautiful sofa where she sat down. When Laurel was presented to her, her almond-shaped eyes danced as she wished her a happy marriage and many sons.

Laurel sat beside her on the sofa for tea and the empress asked endless questions about London. She had the most enchanting laugh, the quietest of voices, and her dainty mannerisms were all the more fascinating because of her excellent English. Her kimono was white with a blue and silver obi around her small waist. Her beautifully dressed hair was crowned with a tiara of magnificent stones. Laurel was entranced.

She was still bemused by all the splendor when the tea was over and the ladies were trooping once more along the corridors to the reception hall. Suddenly her heart missed a beat. Kirk was there, tall, hatless, dark haired and standing with an easy grace as he talked to the master of ceremonies.

His devastating charm, his sense of humor, his good looks and his congenital gift of adapting himself to anyone bound him to her in unbreakable cords. Nina greeted him first as one who had the right to.

"Kirk, how nice to see you! You have come to collect Laurel?" she murmured with a smile specially reserved for him.

A faint flush stained Laurel's cheeks as Kirk greeted the woman warmly before giving his attention to herself.

"Ready, Mrs. Graham?" he said, raising a brow as he looked her over. "You look lovely."

A few words with Nina, who had scarcely glanced in Laurel's direction after Kirk's praise, and they were off.

"How did it go?"

Kirk had cleared the palace grounds and was now driving carelessly, easily along the main road. Laurel did not answer immediately. She was remembering his gay smile at Nina and the woman's face at the sight of him. A light had been switched on behind the mask and lovely eyes. Her throat worked spasmodically and her words came forth with a gigantic effort.

"I enjoyed it all immensely. The empress is delightful and I wouldn't have missed it for the world."

He said airily, "You'll be seeing more of the palace when the emperor returns. However, I want you to relax most of the time for the present. The entertaining, apart from the essential engagements, can be shelved until later." He tossed her an engaging smile. "You're doing very well. Nina will be a great help to you in introducing you into the shceme of things. She's a good horsewoman and will be a companion for you when your horse arrives."

Laurel felt herself stiffen, though she kept her voice steady. "I'm not sure whether Nina and I have that much in common."

He let a moment or two go by, then demanded, "Why not?"

Laurel moistened dry lips. "Some women prefer men friends, and I think Nina is one of them."

"But you hardly know the woman."

She fixed her eyes on the road ahead and compressed her soft lips. "I'm sorry, Kirk. I have the feeling that Nina is about as eager for my company as I am for hers. Besides . . . ."

"Besides what?"

His voice was clipped with displeasure, sending a tremor through her. She clenched her hands in an effort to subdue it. "I . . . I don't want a woman companion. A married couple should be sufficient company for each other without a third party."

"I agree." Kirk sounded like a man being reasonable against his will. "Circumstances, however, alter cases. You've left behind all your friends and acquaintances. Here you're a stranger with no real friends as yet. I'm not attmepting to find you friends, I'm merely suggesting you cultivate the right kind of people. By that I mean those in my own particular sphere."

"I won't let you down by becoming entangled with the wrong people," she said bitterly.

She felt rather than saw the tightening of his jawline. "You're being deliberately awkward. I don't know what's gotten into you. I don't suppose it's occurred to you that I shall be away at my job all day and there'll be nights, too, when I have to be on duty. I don't want you to be too much on your own."

"I'm intelligent enough to fill in my time without becoming bored. There's so much to do here, and to see. I can join the library and go to flower-arrangement classes."

He said no more, but the shutter was down firmly between them. They were turning into the driveway when he said in an offhand way, "I shall be busy for the next couple of days, so this will be our last evening together for a while. Shall we dine out, or are you tired?"

Kirk had drawn up at the door, shut off the engine and turned to look down at her. While he looked immensely fit and virile, to Laurel's loving eyes he also looked fatigued and much too lean. He looked as though he was under a great strain. Instantly she put it down to his seeing Nina again.

He was resenting her being where Nina ought to be— by his side. *I'm a coward*, she thought fleetingly. *I ought to have it out with him here and now, end his torture and mine. But I can't. Not yet. I love him too much to lose him, even without his love.*

"No, I'm not tired. I'd like to go out to dine if you don't mind."

Did he seem relieved? Laurel stumbled from the car.

Wildly, she wanted to fling herself into his arms and beg him to stay at home. But the intimacy of an evening together would be too big a strain for them both.

"Have a good rest," he said. "It will freshen you up for the evening."

She nodded and walked blindly indoors to her room.

CHAPTER TEN

TOKYO HAD EVERYTHING to offer in the way of excellent cafés, restaurants and eating places, often in beautiful and luxurious settings. Kirk drove out that evening to a place set in many acres of exotic gardens. Tables were set outdoors beneath gay lanterns, tinkling fountains, shallow streams stapled by bridges, pagodas and rock gardens.

After parking the car, they were conducted to a table near a picturesque pagoda by a kimonoed lady who gave them hot towels to wipe their hands and face and large white aprons to put on before they sat down. In the center of the long table, which seated six people, a brazier was heating iron bars, which the pretty cook was brushing with oil.

The beef steaks she laid on them were done to a turn and handed around to the diners. The meal was unhurried with endless courses. After the succulent beef, there was veal, sweet corn, lotus root and so many more delectable dishes that Laurel lost count. Eating with chopsticks made dining a leisurely and more enjoyable thing, for in slowing up the process, the food was given time to digest because it was not crowded into the stomach.

Thanks to Kirk, Laurel had mastered the art of handling the chopsticks with a light firmness instead of the rigid gripping that sent the food shooting off from between them at a tangent.

The table had filled as the meal commenced, and a Japanese couple sitting down next to Kirk greeted him cordially. He introduced them to Laurel as Mr. and Mrs. Matsu. Mr. Matsu was an expert in marine biology and

went around the schools giving lectures, which he illustrated with slides. He was an alert thirty-five or so with
sleek black hair, a high-cheekboned face and a cheerful
grin.

His wife, petite with a round baby face and a very
pretty smile, looked charming in her kimono and always
seemed on the verge of laughter. It appeared they were
going on to a dance at the Imperial Hotel afterward and
they begged Laurel and Kirk to accompany them.

Laurel's cares were forgotten that evening, for the
Matsus were an exhilarating couple to be with. Mrs.
Matsu was delighted to dance with Kirk. He towered
above her four-foot-ten-inch frame like a giant, and she
giggled uncontrollably as they circled the ballroom together.

Mr. Matsu, at five feet six, was an excellent dancer
and Laurel discovered he had a great sense of humor. It
was quite late when Kirk gave the Matsus a lift home. Of
course, they had to go in for a drink. The neat brown
house was spotless and the little squeal of laughter coming from Mrs. Matsu as Kirk caught his head against the
bronze overhanging lamp in the hall gave a happy note to
their visit.

He had to bump his head yet again on the lamp in the
living room before lowering himself down onto the
tatami mats on the floor. His deep chuckle as he ruefully
rubbed his head mingled with Mrs. Matsu's. If the Matsus were entertaining in themselves, their spontaneous
laughter was encouraged by Kirk's easygoing charm.
Wherever he went he brought an indescribably lightness
of spirit, a natural charm, the hallmark of a good mixer.

Laurel found herself loving him more than ever in a
kind of despairing sort of way. The Matsus obviously
adored him. Mrs. Matsu brought out her best robin's-egg
blue china and the pick of her own delectable cooking—
sugared fruits and tiny rice cakes, deliciously
flavored—with chopsticks wrapped in colorful table
napkins.

While Kirk and Mr. Matsu touched lightly on politics

and culture, Mrs. Matsu gave verbal recipes for the delicacies at Laurel's request. Before they left, Mrs. Matsu gave her a Kokeshi doll, a quaint little wooden doll wearing the national costume of Tohoku.

At last the Matsus had waved them off with a reluctant "*Sayonara*," and Laurel took with her the picture of two warm faces wreathed in smiles, feeling a little sad at parting.

Kirk glanced down at her with a slightly amused expression when they went indoors after putting the car away. A gleam of cynicism came into his eyes as he took in the small doll in her hand. Her sudden need for him made her breathless and weak. She wanted so much to tell him how much she loved him, and only the fear of being repulsed held her back. Scorn for her own weakness and lack of pride steadied her.

THE NEXT FEW DAYS were empty ones for Laurel. She lunched and dined alone, sleeping next door to Kirk's silent, empty room. He phoned often to speak to her and let her know he would not be coming home. She hung around waiting for his call, the sound of his deep voice. It usually came when, tired of waiting, she had gone out for a walk or to the lake for a swim. Reko would give her the message and she would long for the sound of the voice she had missed. Her walks gave her a sense of lightness and freedom, with her whole being absorbing the surrounding peace and harmony of the countryside.

Laurel loved the mornings when she went down to the lake for an early swim. The air was aromatic with fresh green crops, humidity rose from freshly tilled fields and hedges and color mounted from deep within the valley where the brilliantly gay *futons* and bed covers were spread out to air on roofs and balconies of little brown houses. The lake dazzled the eyes with sunbeamed sparks flying up from the flashing water.

In the mornings she awoke in her pretty bedroom feeling refreshed, tranquil and at peace. On the second morning several reporters arrived from the daily paper. Her visit to the Imperial Palace had been noted. They were very polite and gracious, wanting to know her impressions of their country, whether she liked it and her views of the different way of life.

Reko made them tea and pictures were taken of Laurel in the garden. Then, after much bowing and many thanks, the men departed. She spent the afternoon walking in the little woods decorating the mountains with their carpets of bluebells, violets and anemones. She found a Shinto shrine gay with purple banners bearing the white chrysanthemums of the emperor, and breathed in deeply of the hedges of wild flowers lining the lanes.

That evening Jean phoned to ask her to tea the following day. Then Kirk phoned, asking how she was but not asking if she missed him. His call was a brief one in which he told her to expect him when she saw him. He could have been using one of the office phones, hence his brief message. But it was poor consolation to Laurel's shaky heart.

Jean's house was a sprawling building set in a garden. It was tastefully furnished with good paintings on delicately tinted walls and light Oriental rugs. Susan was there and the conversation was mostly about the climbing expedition to Mount Fuji. Their bright company lifted Laurel's spirits, but by Friday morning she was beginning to wonder if Kirk really was being delayed in Tokyo because of his work.

The morning had begun with bright sunshine, which Reko observed with frowning skepticism.

"Sun too bright. Rain soon. Madam not go far today."

He was clearing away the breakfast things and Laurel said brightly, "I won't go farther than down to the lake!"

The sun was really hot, the sky a shimmering blue haze, and Laurel bathed for the second time that morning, lying to dry out on a towel at the lakeside. She must have fallen asleep, for a barely perceptible movement beside her awakened her with a start. The next moment a shadow moved over her noiselessly like the sun.

Laurel sat up swiftly, instantly alert to see a petite
Japanese girl, chic and elegantly lovely in a blue kimono,
with beautiful dark hair piled high with knitting needles
and ribbon threaded in it artistically. Her oval face was
covered in dead-white makeup that gave it the appearance of sweet serenity.

But her eyes looked tragic and haunted. The next instant she had gone, passing swiftly along the edge of the
lake and around a bend out of sight. She had looked back
at Laurel only once, when a few feet away from her.

For her part Laurel felt she had been part of a dream
that had not vanished entirely with her wakening. The
sky darkened very swiftly in the next few minutes, taking
on an ominous blackness, and the first drops of rain
began to fall heavily as Laurel rose to her feet to gather
up her things. And not a moment too soon, for the rain
was coming down in earnest when she reached the
house, wetting the cloud of her loosened hair cascading
over her shoulders.

The house was quiet and dreamy when she went indoors, wondering what Kirk was doing at that moment.
Sometimes, as now, she had the feeling that he was with
Nina. The thought weighed heavily in her breast as she
slipped off her shoes at the back door and entered, to
make her way to her room.

"Good morning," said Kirk.

Laurel's heart lurched painfully. Something like pride
struggling with radiance came into her face as she tossed
back her hair to look up at him. But it was in a voice cool
and as soft and smooth as cream that she said, "Good
morning. So you do come home sometimes."

He had recently shaved and changed and he was lounging against the lintel of her door with an easy elegance.
Apart from the tiredness of his eyes, he looked as virile
and attractive as ever. Fearful of her own delight at his
unexpected appearance, she scanned the dark, sardonic
face as if she expected it to have altered in some way.

Dimly, she was aware of his tired, battered smile.

"Miss me?" he asked softly, lifting up the curtain of her hair and letting it slip through his fingers. "Your hair is like silk."

His deep voice acted like fingers plucking the strings of her heart, coaxing them into melody. Her heart was responding madly in tune with the patter of the rain now falling in a deluge on the house. Kirk was here, it sang. Was it a trick of the morning light or did his face look thinner, more bitter?

If this was love, this hurt for him when he looked tired, the tormenting ache to see him when he was absent and the anguished longing when he was present, then she did indeed feel sorry for him, too. No wonder he looked aged with longing, like herself, for something he could not have.

She said lightly, "You're here, and that's everything."

He looked down at her long slender legs beneath the terry jacket.

"I would have come down to join you in the lake, but I had a soak in town." He grinned endearingly. "I boiled with the rest of my colleagues like a lobster in the communal baths."

"You mean the mixed bathing?"

He laughed at her scarlet face. "You must try it sometime. No one takes the slightest notice of you. You just arm yourself with a bowl, soap and towel, scrub off all the dirt and jump into the caldron of hot water." His fist made a playful feint under her chin. "It's very exhilarating. Don't look so disapproving. You're in Japan, remember."

She nodded. "All the same, I think I'll swim in the lake."

"What have you been doing with your time? You're looking a lot better. Do you feel better?"

Laurel lowered her eyes from his intent look. "Yes, I'm fine. I'll go and dress for lunch."

Laurel joined him in the living room ten minutes later.

He greeted her with a charming smile, saw that she made a good lunch and, having eaten his share, lighted a cigarette.

"No plans for today?" he asked, leaning back in his chair and blowing out a line of smoke away from the table.

"No."

"Tell me what you've been doing with your time."

She told him, and ended with tea at Jean's house. "Are we still going on the climb?"

"Yes, of course." He leaned forward to knock the ash from his cigarette. "Did you bring your riding clothes with you?"

"Yes, why?"

"Because that will be one of the items we shan't have to buy if you're already set up. We'll go three parts of the way up the mountain on horseback. It will be too tiring for you to walk up all the way."

"Can we do that?"

"Oh, yes. Horses will be provided. They're big, strong creatures and docile enough. Feel like shopping this afternoon? It's pouring with rain, but we shan't see much of it in the car."

"I never let the weather keep me in," Laurel said stoutly "I've enjoyed walks in the rain, especially the summer rain. It's good for the complexion."

He took his time taking in the freshness of her skin, the clear eyes and pink lips. "It certainly did you no harm. You grow more beautiful every day."

A cool and deliberate compliment, agonized Laurel, like throwing scraps to a starving animal. He could not be so detached if he were in love with her.

With a flippancy brought on by despair, she said, "Since we're going shopping I should be making the compliments, not you."

She enjoyed the shopping spree. Kirk was humorously patient, rejecting anything he felt did not suit her and directing her choice to the more expensive range of clothes, which, he said, were more profitable to buy in the long run. The rain pelted down all the afternoon and it was fun holding hands and dashing through the deluge to the shops.

In the course of the afternoon they strolled into a fashion house to find a show of fashions in progress. Kirk bought several of the really beautiful model dresses, suits and beachwear for Laurel.

"Wear that peacock-blue thing for dinner this evening," he commanded.

It was an expensive dress, dramatic in its simplicity and hauntingly beautiful in the soft rich colors. With her slender figure she carried it off as effectively as had the pretty girl who had modeled it that afternoon.

Kirk, appearing in evening dress at her door, leaned against the lintel, eyebrows raised in approval.

"Not bad," he murmured, strolling across the room to tweak the small stand-up collar embossed in pearls. His firm fingers brushed her flushed cheek as he looked down at her clear eyes, the soft youthful contours of her face and the delightful curve of her chin.

Laurel stiffened her knees at his touch. She thought, *When he comes into the room he brings something dynamic with him . . . something challenging, daring and . . . and exciting.* His hand had dropped to her shoulder and he bent to kiss her temple lightly on the tiny scar where the candelabrum her mother had thrown had left its mark.

She raised her eyes to his dark face, the hand resting on her shoulder tightened and a spark ignited between them. The next moment it had gone, his hand dropped.

"We're having guests for dinner this evening. Guess who?"

His mouth quirked humorously, but his eyes, those tired gray eyes which, like now, could look almost black, did not smile.

Laurel smiled. She had to. "The Matsus?"

"Clever girl! I had no idea there were back in Tokyo. They've been to Honolulu for more marine biology. That was why you didn't see them at the wedding and the housewarming. We shall entertain them in Japanese fashion. Reko has everything prepared in the Japanese room.'' He dropped his hand and pushed it into his pocket. ''There's something else. I found a letter from Uncle George among the correspondence in my study. He's taking a holiday soon and is thinking of looking us up.''

''How nice,'' she said, and meant it. Dr. Machelle belonged to the saner part of her life when she was a whole unto herself and not an unwanted appendage of Kirk's. ''I'll look forward to seeing him. Did he say when he would be coming?''

''Actually, he's waiting for a locum to take over his practice while he's away before he can fix a date.'' He strolled over to the window to present his wide shoulders in evening dress. They were square and militant as though he was bracing himself to say something he found difficult to put across. ''He's probably coming to see how I've been treating you.''

Laurel stared at the back of his well-shaped head. ''Why should he do that?''

A shrug. ''He's very fond of you. Did you know?''

Two little vertical lines appeared between her neat brows at his tone.

''I like him, too, as he likes me, as a very good friend. I wish he'd marry. He's a lonely man even though he's blessed with an efficient, attractive housekeeper.'' Suddenly she brightened. ''You know, it's only just occurred to me. They would make an ideal couple. She's younger than him, about thirty-five.''

His tone was unbearably mocking. ''Touché, a marriage of convenience from you! Don't tell me you're in favor of them. I thought it was only the cynics who believed in them.''

''Not only cynics,'' she replied with spirit. ''Circumstances alter cases, and your Uncle George is getting on.'' Dead silence. Laurel wished she could see his face, but he kept his back to her and she hastened to add, ''What I mean is, he's mature and past the passionate age.''

Kirk turned around slowly to face her. His lips had thinned. "Do you know how old Uncle George is?" he asked evenly. "Thirty-eight. Seven years older than I am."

Her eyes widened up at him in disbelief. She was remembering the fair hair receding from the high intelligent forehead, the almost perceptible droop of his shoulders. "I thought he was nearer fifty. Why, he's almost bald!"

"His family are all the same in the male line. He married my mother's youngest sister. She died from an embolism after an appendix operation while they were on their honeymoon."

He waited for her to digest his words, his expression enigmatic.

"How dreadful," she whispered. "Poor Uncle George! I didn't know he'd been married."

She looked beyond him through the window to the garden. The rain had stopped and the sun glittered on wet leaves catching sparks from the drops of water, dazzling the eyes. A large black-winged butterfly hovered, then settled on a wad of blossom.

"Tell me," Kirk was saying, "do you regard me as past the passionate age, too? After all, I'm only seven years younger than Uncle George."

Laurel went scarlet. "I . . . of course not," she gasped, looking anywhere now but at him.

"Thanks. I'm glad of that." A pause. "You see, you would be in for a shock if you did," he vouchsafed dryly.

Before Laurel could define what he meant, Reko came to say that their guests had arrived. If she had been perturbed by Kirk's last remark, she very quickly forgot it in the gay company of the Matsus. Their faces beamed no less brightly than Reko's, who cooked and served a superb Japanese meal. In his immaculate white jacket over dark slacks, Redo was charged with energy. All his movements were quick and light, giving the impression that he, like the Matsus, had lived for this moment.

Mr. Matsu talked animatedly to Kirk on his latest discoveries in marine biology and Mrs. Matsu chatted animatedly to Laurel about the beauty of Honolulu. When their guests took their leave, Reko stood with them to wave them off.

"A delightful couple," Laurel said, when they returned indoors.

"Made for each other," Kirk observed absently as though his mind was on something else. "I'm going to the living room to sit down and stretch my legs after being cramped up on those tatami mats." They halted at the living-room door. "What about you, my sweet? Care to join me? It's much too damp to take a walk in the garden after all that rain."

Her heart moved queerly at the challenging gleam in his eyes. They had drunk sake with their meal and the diminutive quantities they had consumed could not have made Kirk in the least inebriated. Thank goodness he took everything in moderation. Why then the gleam?

She said hurriedly, "No, thanks. I think I'll go to bed. Do we have to be up early in the morning?"

"No earlier than usual. Reko will bring you tea at seven. So you won't join me in a nightcap?" His eyes meltingly sought an answer.

Her heart said yes; her common sense, no. She shook her head.

"I really am tired after all that shopping. Thanks for everything." She had to say something.

Kirk, with dark face inscrutable, was ice cool. He gave her a long searching look. "So be it. Sleep well."

CHAPTER ELEVEN

LAUREL OPENED HER EYES to a morning sun caressing her eyelids like a warm kiss. She yawned, stretched her slim arms above her head and sat up abruptly. Sleep had fled and she glanced at her watch on the bedside table, thinking she had overslept. Six-forty-five.

Time to wash and dress before Reko came with her tea. He had brushed and pressed her riding clothes, polishing her boots to the sheen of glass. They were there waiting for her, along with the thick, beautifully soft, knitted cream sweater to combat the chills of the mountain air.

In the bathroom after cleaning her teeth, Laurel thrust out her right arm and was delighted to see that her hand did not quiver. She could hold it perfectly still. Her nerves had improved enormously since her breakdown in health. And she felt marvelously fit, thank goodness.

Kirk was in the dining room when she entered. He, too, wore a cream sweater and his riding breeches revealed the long supple lines of his body, giving him an indolent grace. A fugitive thought ran through her mind that she could have got up earlier and gone swimming with him in the lake.

Most husbands in the same circumstances would have asked their wives to accompany them. Evidently Kirk had no desire for her company or he would have done so. Her level brows contracted.

"Good morning, my sweet. The gods are favoring us with the weather. The dip in the lake this morning was worth getting up for," he observed mildly.

"Oh!" Laurel went scarlet. How remarkable. He might have known what she was thinking.

"Alas, you were fast asleep when I looked in," he went on placidly as though she had not spoken. "The early bird catches the worm."

There was a veiled flicker of amusement in his quiet regard as he pulled out her chair at the table.

"I'm sorry. You should have wakened me."

"And scared you half to death to find a man bending over your bed?"

He sat down in his chair opposite, the amusement quickening in his eyes. There was a kind of challenge in them—a derisive gleam of laughter rousing her to instant fury. How dared he? He had been the one to remain aloof, not her. It was his place to take the initiative as a man.

"Why should I be scared of my own husband?"

"You tell me." Those gray eyes of his brought the color to her cheeks.

She gasped, then pulled herself together. "I could never be afraid of you, Kirk," she said quietly.

"That's something anyway."

As he spoke Reko entered, bringing the savory odor of breakfast with the tray he carried. The delicious smell assailed her small nostrils. Laurel was all at once aware that she was hungry.

They were lingering over their last cup of coffee when Jean and Susan arrived with their husbands in a station wagon. Reko made fresh coffee and they all sat down to relax over a drink and a smoke before starting on their journey.

Kirk was checking the supplies he had put into the trunk of his car and Bill, Susan's husband, was talking to him when Laurel came out of the house. She had left Jean and Susan in her room repairing their makeup.

"Hello there!"

Dennis stood blocking her way, looking lively and uncaring in his riding clothes, for which he was obviously getting rather fat. He was still attractive with his peaked cap set rakishly on his fair curls, but his good looks were, in the clear morning light, obviously taking a bashing from his way of life.

Laurel smiled. "Hello, Dennis, ready for our jaunt?"

He stood very near to her and spoke in a low confidential tone. "Sorry about your dress the other day. Kirk swooped upon me like the avenging angel—or should I say devil? I'm sure his brows were winged."

"You should take up judo and karate, Dennis. You wouldn't be so scared of him then. Besides, it's good for your figure."

"Perhaps I prefer other company."

Impudent little devils danced in his eyes. But Laurel refused to take any notice of them. She had to laugh, though, at his colossal conceit in his own charms.

"You mean you prefer to span a feminine waist rather than a masculine one?"

"Yes, a size twenty-two inch, I should say." His bold blue eyes took in her small waist emphasized by her riding breeches.

Laurel laughed again. He was so ridiculous and obviously clowning. His correct summing-up of her waistline, however, was proof of his experienced eye and the way it roved over the feminine figure. She would have to tread warily to keep their friendship purely platonic.

"Thanks for the compliment. I can hear Jean and Susan coming. Shall we go?"

Before Jean and Susan emerged from the house, Dennis bent his head and whispered in an urgent undertone, "Let me know when you're in town again and we can have a meal together or go to a show."

They set off, with Kirk taking the lead. Seated beside him, Laurel eyed his dark profile, her love suddenly protective.

"Climbing, my sweet, is the most relaxing of pastimes to a lover of the great outdoors. We shall spend the night at one of the stone huts on the ascent and sleep the sleep of the just. Consequently, we shall all return feeling refreshed with all the cobwebs of a week in the city blown away.''

"But you've climbed the mountain before. It won't be any novelty to you.''

"So I have, but only once have I seen the wonderful panoramic views of the Japanese Alps and the Pacific from the summit. It's an unforgettable sight and one few climbers are privileged to see, since Fuji is so high above the clouds that she's only on nodding acquaintance with aircraft.''

"It must be a terrific height,'' she said.

"Twelve thousand three hundred and ninety-seven feet, to be precise. It's a little early for climbing since the top is still covered with snow, but the weather this last fortnight has been much warmer than usual for this time of the year and parties of pilgrims have been going up this month to visit the shrine at the top.''

They left Tokyo behind and with it the modern world, for outside the city lay the real Japan of thatch-roofed farmhouses and peasants in conical coolie hats, swathed black leggings and split-toed canvas shoes eking a meager living from the soil. Fujiyama at close quarters was a most impressive sight, a near-perfect cone rising sheer out of the plains, uncluttered and free from neighboring peaks from base to summit.

According to Kirk the climb to the summit took between seven to nine hours on foot, the descent between two and five. But they were going most of the way on horseback. Kirk had stopped in the village of Subashiri to telephone through to Ichi-Gome, the station where the climb began, to reserve horses and a guide.

When they reached Ichi-Gome the air grew much cooler, with the scent of mountain pine. The horses were waiting for them, looking strong and well fed, and after sitting down for refreshment they prepared for the climb.

At the stores an alpenstock called a Fuji-stick was purchased for each of them. It was an octagonal white-pine staff to use when they reached the steep lava paths nearer the summit. The guide was quite young, around twenty, not so tall, but as strong as an ox. He cheerfully took a lot of their kit and the rest was put on a horse.

Laurel was helped onto her mount by Kirk, who rode beside her as their guide went on ahead. The trail began to steepen once they left the base, meandering through pine woods that were now filled with veils of mist frolicking through the trees. It grew more dense as they climbed and Laurel felt difficulty in breathing. Presently only the trail underfoot was visible in the thick mist.

The distance between the stations seemed endless to Laurel, but she enjoyed the stop at each for tea and refreshment. Kirk had laced the tea in the flask with whiskey, and snug and warm in her woolly lined sheepskin coat, Laurel felt less of the cold.

After they left the fifth station an icy wind sprang up. The trail grew steeper into switchbacks and hairpin bends and at the sixth station the horses went back. Laurel, stiff with riding in the icy cold air, was lifted from her mount and her limbs massaged by Kirk, who rubbed a cold nose against her icy one and grinned down at her.

"Well? Want to go back with them?" he quipped.

Laurel looked around to where Jean and Susan were stamping their cold feet and swinging their arms to encourage circulation. Their husbands were busy shedding their load.

Laurel's lips were parted, her throat parched with the effort of replenishing her depleted lungs with air. All the poignancy and hopes of the day had dissolved into night, icy wind biting her cheeks, Kirk's arms around her, everything strange, hurtful but sweet.

"You think I can't take it?" she said.

"No. Giving you the choice to go on or go back."

"We'll go on." His gray eyes raked her face, his arms slackened to release her. "I am enjoying it, you know."

"That's all I wanted to know. We go on to the seventh station from here. Then we bed down there for the night."

Laurel nodded, content to be taken care of by Kirk.

Taking in the sweet cold air was less painful now. Behind Kirk's dark head the vast stretch of sky had changed to a deep, darkening blue and a lone star looked very near.

A star of hope? Laurel wanted it to be. In that moment it seemed worth all the heartache to be there on top of the world with Kirk. That star would shine through the years, clear and bright with a poignant pain in its wake that would never be forgotten.

Their stay at the sixth station was a short one. The air was piercingly cold and Kirk wanted to reach the seventh station early to make sure of a place in the hut in which they were going to spend the night. Station Seven was near enough to the summit for them to rise early and reach the top in time to see the sunrise.

It was a long, low building hewn out of the mountain with a roof weighted down by rocks against the force of the winds. Anywhere would have been a haven to Laurel, who was feeling the cold in her fingers and toes. All around them was the blackness of night with the lights of villages way down below twinkling up at the stars in the gloom.

She blinked at the carbide lighting in the hut as they entered to see the usual tatami mats strewn around the well in the center of the floor, giving out warmth. Only two people were there and they had already rolled themselves up in their *futons*, the edges of which were visible beneath the curtains partitioning several alcoves from the room.

Laurel did not remember much after that. She was too tired, and was out like a light as soon as she was in her sleeping bag. Jean awakened her to the light of the carbide lamp and, Laurel came back reluctantly into the life of the hut from a dreamland of warmth. Her watch said two o'clock, so it was not yet dawn, and that was what they were rising at this unearthly hour for.

The men were getting the breakfast. In the fierce carbide light Kirk looked fresh and virile, as if he had thrived on the arduous climb of the previous evening. The breakfast and hot coffee laced with rum tasted surprisingly good. Laurel wriggled her toes in her riding boots, every movement painful. Before they began the walk to the summit, Kirk knelt beside her, a slightly cynical smile around his lips.

In his hand he held sandals of woven rice straw. "Fastened on top of your boots, these will give you a better grip on the lava paths and they're quite durable." He grinned up at her. "You're taking it on the chin. That's what I like to see." An eyebrow lifted as he secured the covering over her boots, his keen gray eyes speculative. "Still want to go to the top?"

She looked into his dark face. The maddening stiffness in her aching limbs was forgotten. "What do you think?" she answered gallantly.

Their guide, Totaki-san, gathered up and lashed together larger pieces of their equipment and, attaching smaller ones to his belt, swung the large pack on his back.

Outside the air was sweet and pure with the stars still winking at them from the dark sky. Below them, way down below, lights came into view weaving upward between the volcanic ash to the tinkling of a bell. Their figures showed up a ghostly white in the gloom.

Kirk said, "A party of Fuji-san worshippers making their yearly pilgrimage to the summit. They're clad in white, hence the illusion of ghosts."

He had put an arm around Laurel's shoulders and they walked to the winding path taking them upward. Now the way was much steeper, a tortuous zigzagging climb so steep in places that wire cables had been stretched beside the path to hold on to.

Kirk lifted Laurel up the steeper stretches with no sign of exhaustion. But Dennis and Susan had difficulty in getting their breath because both were overweight. After frequent rests Station Eight was reached, and they rested there for another warm drink.

Said Dennis in Laurel's ear, "Fuji is a wonderful sight from afar. But one is disillusioned on climbing it."

He had sat down beside her. The pilgrims had caught

up with them and were sitting with them enjoying a warm drink. Kirk and Jean were talking to them and Bill was massaging Susan's legs.

The warm drink was reviving Laurel, coming in between her and the cold air that made her catch her breath as if she was diving into Arctic water. She was fascinated, even in the harsh conditions, by the vast expanse of sky. It was not black but purple, the rich royal purple of kings, a velvet mantle as befitting what the Japanese regarded as a sacred mountain.

"I find it rather wonderful," she said soberly. "Like nothing I've ever experienced before. I feel richer because of it."

Dennis jeered, "You say that now. Wait until you have to go up the rest of the way. There's a sharp incline of about thirty-two degrees that will make you long to stop for an honorable cup of tea."

Laurel had to laugh, a delightful quiet twinkle that brought several pairs of Oriental eyes appraisingly in her direction.

"I'll survive," she said.

The last lap was certainly treacherous, with a steepness demanding herculean efforts from heart and lungs. The wind had dropped and Kirk had hauled her against him, pushing her upward with a deceptively careless strength. When their path had suddenly taken a U-turn over an awe-inspiring revine, he had swept her around it before she could see the depths.

Eventually he thrust her through the last *torii* gateway to the summit. Then he went back to help the others. Jean, Dennis and Bill had come close on their heels apparently none the worse. But Susan, cold-driven and panting, almost wept with relief to reach the top.

Kirk teased her about putting on weight and suddenly there they were on top of the world with the thick clouds between them and the earth. It was like looking down into a vast snowdrift into which one could dive.

The dead silence that followed seemed almost uncanny to Laurel, who was aware of climbers joining them in large numbers. Slowly, like a vast bubbling caldron, the clouds began to swirl and disintegrate and the sun rose slowly in a blaze of glory, tinting the heavens in a rosy glow. And then it happened. Below them, as clear as any picture could be, lay the wide expanse of the Pacific Ocean and the glorious range of Japanese Alps, uncluttered by clouds.

Cameras clicked and to Laurel's enchanted gaze Fujiyama seemed to take a bow.

"Well? Was it worth the climb?"

Kirk's voice was near her ear, his arm around her shoulders, his warm breath in her hair.

"It's wonderful," she murmured. "The land of the rising sun."

Laurel felt chastened as they descended after peeping into the vast crater. She had only one regret. It would have been heaven to have gone through it all with Kirk, just the two of them. But one could not have everything. Maybe another time. But Laurel knew it would not be the same.

As KIRK HAD INTIMATED, Laurel's visit to the Imperial Palace sparked off a number of dinner engagements at the houses of government officials. There were the usual state functions where Laurel often found herself seated by someone who could not speak English. But there was always an interpreter close by.

She was never bored on these occasions. Her lively mind and interest were caught up by the beautiful gowns and kimonos worn by the ladies and the resplendent uniforms of the men. Sometimes she would find herself seated beside famous people and would sip her champagne while lending an eager ear to their conversation, much to the amusement of Kirk.

Countess Nina was invariably present at these functions, and one evening they were invited to dine at her home. The house in Tokyo had a spacious garden that gave the impression of being miles out in the country. The food was Japanese and her husband, Ishi, was an urbane host.

As most of the guests were European, they dined in one of the Western-style rooms, high ceilinged with cut-glass chandeliers, period furniture and Japanese objets d'art—carved jade figures, Japanese dolls and priceless vases.

Laurel, seated next to her host, was captivated by his charm. There was a certain nobility of features that added to his good looks and she could not help but be drawn by his courteous manner and his obvious admiration of herself. Even Nina, scintillating with diamonds and a really beautiful kimono that must have cost the earth, did nothing to make Laurel aware of her own inhibitions.

She had none that evening, for she was wearing the dress Mrs. Pakara had made for her visit to the Imperial Palace and she knew she looked her best with the small tiara in her dark hair and Kirk's diamonds at her slender throat. The shadow flitting across her face at the sight of Kirk sitting beside the woman was fleeting as she gave her attention to her host.

Her ego had a further boost when they were driving home.

"Ishi was quite attentive to you this evening," Kirk said dryly. "It's not surprising, since he has an eye for a pretty woman and you were certainly one of the prettiest there."

"Thank you," she said demurely. "Ishi is a good-looking man. I like him."

"He's not a bad sort. But like most Japanese, he's fond of the ladies." Kirk dimmed the brights for an oncoming car, then flicked them up again and said casually, "Haven't seen any more of Dennis, have you, since Fuji?"

The unexpected question was oddly disconcerting. Laurel felt her color rise. "Why do you ask?"

"Because you seem to like him, too. I noticed you were a little flushed when you came out of the house on the morning we left for Fuji. Later, on the mountain, he was whispering in your ear and you were laughing as if you enjoyed it."

"Dennis was fooling. He's much too transparent to be dangerous."

He gave her a swift frowning glance. "That's part of his charm—or hadn't you noticed?"

"No, I'm afraid I haven't, because he isn't that important. In any case, I don't know what this is all about."

Laurel knew a sudden surge of mutiny. How dared he censure her actions? She trembled with anger and her soft lips were pressed together as she stared fixedly through the windshield. He sounded so . . . so self-righteous, when all the time he was carrying on with Nina.

"Don't take it so seriously," he said evenly. "You're sweet and trusting and you happen to have taken Dennis's fancy. I merely wanted to make sure you weren't being taken in by him. Although Japan is fast catching up with the Western world, it's still behind in issues that are taken lightly in other parts of the world. Divorce, for instance. A divorced woman here is regarded in the light of a social outcast, even by her own family, and is unlikely to have the opportunity to marry again."

"But that's awfully unfair if she's the innocent party," Laurel protested bitterly. "What about the wealthy husbands who take geisha girls?"

"The men here go to a geisha house as an Englishman might go to his club. They see nothing wrong in having another woman because they do it openly. It's a way of life. On the other hand, it does keep the wife on her toes knowing she has competition for her husband."

Laurel looked down at her hands in her lap and thought about Mrs. Pakara's daughter, the geisha girl with the delightful little boy whom she was hiding from his father's wife.

"What happens when a geisha girl has a baby by one of the patrons? It does happen, I suppose."

He shrugged as if he found the subject distasteful. "Rarely. These girls are trained and know their jobs. I believe there are some who end up as concubines."

Laurel persisted, "If it did happen, could the father claim the baby as his own? Do they adopt children if they're childless?"

He smiled down at her tolerantly. "What a serious little thing you are, feeling other people's troubles as your own. Yes, a son is very often adopted by a childless couple who want an heir. Boys are thought much of in Japan. There's a boys' festival on the fifth of May. On that day hundreds of paper fishes flutter from poles all over the city. The fish represents a carp, a fish that has to fight the strong currents of the rivers to exist. It's symbolic of a boy's struggles through boyhood to manhood. The shops are filled with male dolls in uniforms, in combat and in the ancient robes of feudal lords. You'll enjoy the festival."

Shall I? she thought. *Or will our marriage be over by then?* Putting her own troubles to one side, Laurel thought of Mrs. Pakara, the dressmaker who was so upset at her daughter's trouble with the baby, and she longed to tell Kirk about it. But she had given her word. Besides, Kirk would probably be philosophical about it.

IT RAINED HEAVILY that night and for most of the following morning. Toward lunchtime the clouds passed and the air was still and warm. Laurel went outside into the garden, enjoying the deep intensity of fragrance after the rain. She wandered down as far as the little wicket gate opening onto the path leading down to the lake, and watched the clear outline of trees overladen with rain-soaked foliage leaning over the water.

Her attention was focused on nothing in particular

Yet she was profoundly conscious of her surroundings, the perfume of flowers, the birds twittering, the pearly light over the distant hills where pines marched along the ridges like Buddhist monks on a pilgrimage. And it was there that Kirk found her on coming home to lunch.

"Penny for them," he said teasingly in her ear, coming upon her so silently that she started, curiously shaken.

There was a confused awareness within her of responding to him, an awareness of feeling everything keenly, his arm around her shoulders, the deep cadence of his voice and his kiss on her hair. It was not easy to answer him with the silly pulsation in her throat until pride eased her out of the disquieting emotional spell onto solid ground again.

"I was thinking how sweet and fresh it always is after rain, like a newly minted world, and a very lovely one," she said in her clear soft voice.

The face she raised to him had the ethereal quality of a pearl. Her eyes were cool.

Kirk's eyes were steady, preoccupied, and Laurel wished he would not look at her so intently.

"It's been a terrible morning, yet standing here in the freshly washed air it isn't important anymore." He looked up into the strangely leaden blue sky. "I can smell thunder, though. Stay put this afternoon. Don't go out. Read a book or something."

After lunch Laurel, as a loose end, wandered into Kirk's study. Sitting down in his chair by the desk, she toyed with his pen and looked around the room at the book-lined walls until her eyes rested upon the smallest of the wedding gifts from the emperor on a shelf. Recalling the card inside the box containing the bottle of sake and tiny cups, she was filled with curiosity.

Why had Kirk not wanted her to read what the emperor had written on it?

On a sudden impulse she rose from the chair and reached the parcel down, untied the gold cord and opened the box. The card was tucked inside between the bottle of sake and the diminutive cups. With shaking fingers she drew it out. The emperor had written in a good hand of English.

> Dear Kirk, as I regard you as both a dear friend and a brother, I send you a bottle of sake without which no Japanese wedding is complete. Please use it, for then I shall regard you as being truly married.
>
>   Your dear friend

Her hand was shaking still more when she returned the card to the box and rewrapped the parcel. The reason Kirk had not wanted her to see it was clear enough. He had no wish to solemnize their wedding in the Japanese way because it was only a temporary one from which he would finally seek an annulment.

Laurel paced the room, her hands clasped together in anguish. What more proof did she need? Where was her pride to stay with such a man who did not want her but who was using her for his own ends? The four walls crowded in on her suffocatingly. She had to get out to think.

The next moment she was on her way to her room to phone for a taxi. An hour or so around the Tokyo shops would clear her brain and give her time to decide what to do. Laurel was not partial to the Tokyo taxis or their drivers. Most of them spoke little English and the streets being without numbers added to the confusion. Furthermore, the drivers seemed intent on committing suicide by the shocking way they drove.

Her practice was to wait until the taxi was approaching the place she had in mind, then tap on the window for him to stop. She had remembered seeing a small antique shop when out with Kirk, a sorrowful kind of a ramshackle building with a more resplendent shop on either side supporting it like two rich uncles. Printed in English over the door were the words Oriental Objets d'Art. Please Enter.

All this ran through Laurel's unhappy mind as she hastily donned a white raincoat and matching small-brimmed hat. Thrusting her legs into high white boots, she grabbed her handbag and went through the hall to wait for the taxi, smiling at Reko's look of dismay as she went.

She reached the city still in one piece, keeping her eyes open for the little antique shop, which was somewhere on her right close to the Ginza. Then she saw it and tapped on the window to the driver, who pulled up with a shriek of brakes several blocks ahead. Laurel paid him and walked back to the shop.

Opening the door to the chime of bells, she stepped into an Aladdin's cave glowing richly with treasures and was greeted by a small genie looking rather like a miniature Merlin. Her black kimono was sprinkled with silver moons and stars, but she was minus a wind.

When Laurel gestured that she was only looking around, the pert little face beneath a bird's nest of black hair nodded to show two gold teeth among the white ones. Laurel forgot everything including the time as she browsed among relics of old Japan, swords, face masks, old jade pieces, antique teapots shaped like dragons, coffeepots, shields, bronze Buddhas and fabulous obis. It was some time before she saw the pictures.

They were tucked away from sight in a gloomy corner as if jealously hidden from a collector's avid gaze. There were delightful sketches on wood blocks and beautiful paintings on silk.

Laurel gazed enchanted and found herself staring at the scene from the little wicket gate in the garden of her new house looking down to the lake and over the valley. The scene was identical. There it was, beautifully and faithfully portrayed even to the winding path down to the lake. The pearly translucent glow was there in soft candy colors and there was a boat on the lake with a couple in it that might have been her and Kirk.

The lump in her throat swelled in size as memory came

rushing back. Tears pricked her eyes. What a souvenir! She would have a bit of Kirk that would always be there when everything else had gone.

"Honorable lady like?" purred the little genie at her side.

Laurel sighed. "It's beautiful. How much, please?"

The little genie stared at her for a moment and said timidly, "Two hundred and fifty yen."

"I'll take it," Laurel said delightedly.

The little genie wrapped it up neatly and gave it to her with a bow, and the door chimes echoed Laurel's pleasure as she left the shop. After making a visit to a nearby American pharmacy for a few toilet requisites, and browsing around a book shop where she bought several magazines, she walked to a prominent corner to hail the first taxi she saw.

It was following a big car and Laurel lifted a hand when it got to within hailing distance. The next moment her hand had dropped like a stone, for she caught sight of the profile of the car driver speeding along. His eyes were fixed on the road ahead. There was no mistaking that dark saturnine profile, those steel-gray eyes. Kirk, with Nina beside him looking ravishing in turquoise. No wonder he had told her to stay indoors!

Her head swam. Her blood burned, rushing up into her cheeks. There was a feeling and a need for something to hold on to. When the car slid beside her to a halt, she stared at it stupidly.

"Hop in before you get drowned," Dennis said cheerfully, and Laurel suddenly realized it was raining.

She slid in beside him. "Thanks, Dennis. If you'll drop me off at the first taxi stand I'll be most grateful."

"At four o'clock in the afternoon? You couldn't be so cruel!" Dennis looked affronted. "At least have coffee with me."

"But have you time? I don't want to be a nuisance."

He grinned and started the car. "I always have time for a pretty woman. What about the roof gardens at the Imperial Hotel?"

"All right," she said.

Even Dennis was a friend in need at that moment, someone who would take her mind off what she had just seen. Recalling his past boldness, Laurel wondered if she was encouraging Dennis into becoming tiresome, but she took the risk anyway. She was too dreadfully unhappy to do anything else.

It was pleasant in the roof gardens. Dennis did most of the talking, referring to people of importance seated near them whom he felt she should know. Friends of Kirk's, too, she thought bitterly, who would note her being with Dennis. But what did she care? She wondered where Kirk was going with Nina. Her heart was numb, but her pink lips were smiling at Dennis.

She refused to allow him to drive her home, but insisted upon taking a taxi. Fortunately, it was the taxi driver who had taken her to Mrs. Pakara, the dressmaker. The amazing thing about the Japanese taxi drivers was that they never forgot a face. She was carried away to arrive home in record time. The house greeted her in silence; evidently Kirk had not yet arrived.

She washed and changed for dinner, hating the thought of seeing Kirk again and having to put on a happy face. However she tried, only one solution seemed feasible. She could pack her cases and leave, end the farce of a marriage herself without waiting for Kirk to do it.

He arrived home ten minutes before dinner. Laurel had stayed in her room until she heard his car, then she opened her door and waited for him.

"Sorry I'm late, my sweet," he said, kissing her on the tip of her nose. "I won't be two shakes." The next moment he had walked off to his room.

Laurel made her way to the living room, ashamed of herself for allowing him to play on her emotions. The glass doors in the gaily furnished room were closed, and she walked over to them to look out into the garden. He was late because he had been out with Nina. Yet what could she do? Tackle him about it?

Ten minutes later, he was seating her at the dining

table. When he exerted his charm she was helpless. He had a way of making her feel she was the only woman in the world, and the most precious. She went through an agony of longing, seeing in his tender smile a hope that if she spoke to him this evening, he would tell her the truth about himself and Nina. But his first remark dispelled the hope for good.

He did not ask how she had spent her afternoon, as he usually did. Instead he waited for Reko to serve the first course of their meal, then said casually, "You remember when you went to Mrs. Pakara the first time? You mentioned a baby?" He smiled at her across the table. "You also asked me whether I liked children. I do. No marriage is complete without them."

Laurel met his look gravely. She even managed a gallant little smile.

"I'm glad." She waited for him to go on.

He did not smile now. "I want to ask you about the baby you saw at Mrs. Pakara's!"

Her heart was thumping, but she had herself well in hand. "Yes. What is it?"

He looked at her squarely. "Was the baby there on your second visit?"

She gazed at him with wide eyes. "Why do you ask?"

"Because it's important."

Laurel remembered Mrs. Pakara's agitation, her fear lest Kirk should know that her daughter had taken the baby away in hiding.

"I don't understand," she said through cold lips.

"I don't suppose you do," he replied coolly. "Well?"

It came to her then like a blinding light. The rich man, the father of little Fuseko, was Ishi. Ishi Wanaka, Nina's husband. Why had she not guessed it before? But why should Nina want the baby?

She looked straight at him. It was no time for shrinking avoidance.

"Why do you want to know?" she said.

He looked at her for a moment or two in silence and

waited for Reko, who had entered, to put down the hot covered dishes. When he had gone, he said, "There's no reason why you should be mixed up in this."

Her face quivered and was controlled swiftly. "Oh, but I am if I give you the information you ask for."

He frowned. "What exactly did Mrs. Pakara say to you? About the baby, I mean?"

Laurel suddenly felt very calm. "Nina is the woman after Fuseko, isn't she? Ishi is his father."

He sat mutely considering her. "So Mrs. Pakara told you?" he said quietly.

They had forgotten the meal and were looking at each other across the table. The silence was profound.

"Mrs. Pakara did not tell me," she said with an odd vehemence. "I'm not as naive as you appear to think. Why . . . do you look at me like that? Am I not to be told anything concerning you?"

Her voice shook. Why was Kirk looking at her with a kind of compassion in his eyes? He looked . . . sorry for her.

He spoke slowly, aware of her sudden trembling. "I'd rather you knew nothing about it."

"It's too late for that. You asked me a question. I refuse to answer it until you tell me what it's all about."

He made a gesture of distaste with a lean brown hand. "I need hardly remind you that I speak in confidence. Nina wants to adopt the baby, give it her husband's name. There'll be a fine future waiting for the boy if she can do so."

"And . . . and where do you come in?"

"Nina only came for my help when all her efforts to persuade the mother to agree to his adoption failed. She's kept up a regular flow of letters to Mrs. Pakara's daughter requesting her to agree, and now she's discovered both mother and child have gone, probably left the country."

"Why doesn't Nina give her husband a son if he needs one that badly?"

"I can't tell you that."

"No? Then I'll tell you. Ishi is as yet unaware that he has a son, so Nina is counting on his delight when he discovers it. She's hoping he'll be so glad that he'll agree to divorce her so that she can marry . . . someone else." Laurel's voice quivered. She put a hand to her throat as if she was choking. Tears blurred her eyes. "I . . . I pray with all my heart that she'll never find the baby."

Then she was running from the room.

"Laurel, come back, you little idiot!" Kirk called. But she ran on to reach her room and flung herself down on the bed in an agony of tears.

"Laurel! Now do you see why I wanted to keep it from you?" Kirk was there bending over her, turning her over into his arms as he sat sideways on the bed. He had her lying across him, his face in her neck. "I knew you would be upset over the baby. Naturally you would want it to remain with the mother."

She tried to push him away. But he had gathered her tightly in his arms. His mouth moved slowly up her neck until he found her mouth. Gradually her sobs were stifled and she grew quiet except for the thick heavy beats of her heart. Kirk's kisses were deepening. His passion was enveloping her like a furnace and her arms reached up to clasp his neck.

He laid her back on the bed to take her lips with a roughness that was dearer to her than tenderness. Then there was an urgent tapping on the door. Kirk said something explosive, released her reluctantly and was on his feet, straightening his tie and smoothing back his hair.

"What is it?" he cried, and strode to the door.

It was Reko. Kirk closed the door behind him and she heard their voices receding. Laurel saw Kirk no more that night. He was out when Reko brought her hot milk at ten o'clock.

CHAPTER TWELVE

LAUREL'S MIND was firmly made up by the time she had washed and dressed the following morning. She was going to leave Kirk. His compassion had urged him to follow her to her room in an attempt to comfort her. His lovemaking had meant nothing to him. He was sorry for her and probably a bit ashamed of using her for his own ends.

Furthermore, he had ordered Reko to doctor the milk she had taken the previous evening to give her a sound sleep. Why else would she have gone out like a light after she had drunk it? Consequently she had overslept, which had its advantages since she was too late to have breakfast with Kirk.

It was half-past nine when she went to the dining room, where she waived breakfast in favor of a little toast—and she had to push that down. There was the usual pile of Japanese and English morning papers on the table and she looked among them uncaringly.

Laurel could not read Japanese, but the word *geisha* caught her eye.

"Reko!" She called him from the kitchen and gave him the paper folded against a column, just a brief announcement. "Please tell me what this says."

Redo read it silently, then lifted a grave face. "Geisha girl jumps into crater of volcano with baby son." He shook his head. "Many suicides in Japan. Many young ones."

"Yes," Laurel said impatiently. "But what is the geisha's name?"

He lowered his eyes and read aloud. "Kiki Pakara, number-one geisha, and Fuseko-san, baby son."

Laurel closed her eyes and the tears trickled through her lashes. Redo was concerned, but she waved him away, shaking her head, and he left her alone with her grief.

So Laurel cried—for Mrs. Pakara who had lost a beloved daughter and grandson, for Kiki whose only sin was being young and headstrong, for Fuseko who had bowed to her so delightfully, then toppled over chuckling. For Kirk whom she had loved and lost.

When she was more composed, Laurel went to her room to bathe her eyes and order a taxi that would take her to Mrs. Pakara to see if there was anything she could do. But the little brown house was all locked up and deserted.

Fortunately Laurel had asked the taxi driver to wait, so she returned to the house. Passing the living room, she smelled tobacco and, peeping in, stared in utter surprise.

"Dr. Machelle!" she cried, going forward to greet him warmly.

Kirk's Uncle George took her hands and kissed her cheek. "How are you, my dear? And how do you like being married?"

Laurel's smile did not reach her eyes and he noticed her swollen eyelids. "Has Kirk been beating you?" he asked wryly. "You've been crying, haven't you?"

She nodded. "A tragedy in the morning paper upset me. I knew the people concerned."

He nodded sympathetically. "Hard luck." Then he shook his head at her ruefully. "You take things too much to heart, my dear. I'm sure Kirk thinks so, too."

Her smile was still sad. "It's the way I'm made. I'm so glad to see you, and I know Kirk will be, too."

"I dropped in on Kirk at his office. He'll be home as soon as he can arrange it." He looked appraisingly around the pretty living room with the charming view of the gardens through the sliding glass doors. "You have a

delightful house and gardens. The Japanese have the
right idea. They derive great joy from nature!"

Laurel listened, her thoughts in a whirl. The doctor's
arrival rather complicated matters, although she was
glad to see him. The thought occurred then that she might
even travel back with him to England.

"Would you like to see over the house?" she asked
cordially.

"I would indeed. Reko has taken my cases to a guest
room. I thought it charming."

Laurel slipped a hand through his arm and escorted
him around the house. He was delighted with the garden
and the view over the valley and the lake.

They walked down to the lake through the little wicket
gate. The doctor asked permission to smoke and took out
his pipe as they strolled down the slopes.

Smoking contentedly, he asked, "How have you been
keeping?"

"Very well on the whole."

"Earthquakes upset you?"

"Nobody enjoys them, but I'll get used to them in
time."

Laurel felt a wariness in his voice and manner and remembered that he had seen Kirk before he came to the
house. She looked across the lake to the distant hills
shimmering in the morning sun, their peaks softened by
blue shadows against a bluer sky. How lovely it was! She
had forgotten for the moment that she would soon be
leaving. Her heart twisted queerly at the thought of it.

Dr. Machelle was saying, "I haven't been here since I
was in my teens. I find it's changed a lot. There's rubbish
strewed around the parks; the disregard of the people for
their environment amazes me. The changes here are a
great pity, although I never was one for sitting *à la
japonaise*. It's much easier for a man who's putting on
weight to use a chair. Kirk takes it all in his stride, but
then he's so amazingly fit and energetic. I'm afraid I was
a little hard on him when you came out here."

Laurel felt suddenly very cold. "What do you mean?"

"Shall we sit down and talk?" he said. They had reached the lakeside and he motioned to a wooden seat set among black trees splashed with persimmons. They sat down. "I told Kirk you were coming out too soon after your illness, that you needed at least a year for convalescence. I sent you out to him on condition that he went easy with you and stressed the fact that you weren't to have any children for at least a year."

Laurel took in what he said slowly, trying to stem the wild hope in her heart. Then she remembered her last conversation with Kirk and his refusal to take her into his confidence and the reason for Nina's wanting to adopt the baby.

"I wonder . . . ." She broke off abruptly.

"Go on. Finish what you were about to say," Dr. Machelle said urgently.

"I'd rather not," she said stubbornly, and twisted her hands in her lap.

"I think you should. This could be very important."

She composed herself. "Kirk and I have separate rooms, have done since our marriage."

"Good heavens! My dear, I'm most dreadfully sorry. You see, I'm to blame. I told Kirk about women patients of mine who, on marrying too soon after a nervous breakdown, had conceived almost right away, with disastrous results."

"But I'm not the neurotic type. I've never been nervous. I've always been healthy. You know that." She looked at him in bewilderment.

He nodded. "I'm sorry. The frustration of being near the man you love and not belonging to him couldn't have helped in your recovery. I see that now." He smote his knee with a clenched hand. "I wish I'd kept my mouth shut." He looked so abject.

Laurel generously patted his hand. "Don't distress yourself. It wouldn't have made any difference to our relationship. You see, Kirk is in love with someone else."

"He's what?" Dr. Machelle exploded. "You're joking!"

She removed her hand from his to push back her hair from her forehead wearily. "No."

"Nonsense! Why, Kirk was determined to have you—I know that. I'll have a talk with him."

Laurel shook her head violently. "Oh, no. Please, Dr. Machelle. This is between Kirk and myself."

He patted her shoulder, saying gently, "I'm your Uncle George, too, my dear. Can't you call me that?"

"Uncle George, then. Please don't interfere. Kirk must do what he feels is right for his happiness. I love him too much to see him unhappy."

"He doesn't know how lucky he is, the young scamp. I suppose you're sure about this other woman in his life?"

Laurel nodded. "Please don't ask me any more about it. I don't want to discuss it."

"Have you thought about yourself? What are you going to do?"

His arm had moved around her and Laurel stiffened. "Shall we stroll back?" she said. "It's getting on for lunchtime."

He put out his pipe and returned it to his pocket as if he had lost the taste for it. "You're not angry with me for doing what I have?" he asked as they strolled back up the incline.

"Of course not. How could I be, since you acted in my interests as a doctor should?"

Laurel smiled at him, but she did not take his arm as she had on the way down to the lake. A feeling she could not describe had come over her from the moment his arm had slid around her waist. Something Kirk had said returned to her, filling her with apprehension.

They had reached the little wicket gate leading into the garden when the doctor put his hand on her arm and looked down fixedly at her.

"You know, don't you?" he said quietly.

She lifted a clear gaze. "Kirk told me you were fond of me."

"Fond!" His laugh held no mirth. "I worship you. I hope you'll forgive me, knowing that."

Laurel was touched. "Oh, Uncle George, I am sorry." She smiled at him tenderly and he turned away.

"You make me feel so ashamed. You're so sweet about it—and I deliberately tried to wreck your marriage."

She laughed lightly. "Forget it. Come on, we shall be late for lunch."

He hung back and gripped the top of the little gate. "You won't be so ready to forgive when you know the whole truth."

"But—" Laurel began.

He cut in sharply, gazing down at his white knuckles. "I set out to deliberately wreck your marriage. I hated Kirk's good looks, his charm and easy way of collecting all the best in life so casually. I told myself that had he not come on the scene when he did, you and I would have eventually come together."

Laurel was staring at him in wide-eyed bewilderment. "I can't believe it!"

"Why did you think I had you at my home to look after you? A doctor doesn't usually take his patients in and take full responsibility for their recovery unless there's a very good reason."

"Don't tell me any more, please."

She turned and walked to the house, leaving him to follow. At the door of the house she paused for him to come beside her.

"Kirk mustn't know a word of what you've just told me. Everything that's passed between us must be forgotten." She had a sweet dignity that emphasized her youthfulness. Her smile was wistful. "Let's forget about it. I want you to enjoy your stay here."

She almost added that she would most likely be going

back with him. But she knew in the face of what he had told her that this would never be. She would travel alone.

Kirk did not come home to lunch. There was no word from him, so they dined together. It was not much of a success—Laurel tried too hard to make it so. The doctor responded as well as he could be expected to.

After lunch there was a phone call for the doctor from Kirk. After he had hung up the phone, Uncle George walked into the living room from the hall to greet Laurel, smiling broadly.

"That's a bit of luck," he said. "Kirk has got in touch with a former chief of mine who's here in Tokyo giving a series of lectures. No doubt you've heard of Paul Glennock, the famous brain surgeon? He wants me to meet him this afternoon at his club, then go along to listen to a lecture. He's sending his car for me."

Laurel was as relieved as he was. "How nice," she said. "I know you'll enjoy it."

When Uncle George had gone the house seemed silent and empty. Laurel dressed for dinner that evening thinking ruefully that even his company was preferable to none. Kirk had not called or put in an appearance and she went into the living room half an hour before dinner to leaf through a magazine.

She had been in the living room ten minutes when the slam of the car door heralded his arrival. Her heart began to beat in thick heavy strokes as she heard his deep voice mingling with Redo's lighter tones.

The next twenty minutes were the longest she had ever lived through. She sat facing the garden trying to pluck up enough courage to face the final scene that would decide everything. Laurel knew with a sinking heart that Kirk had probably got Uncle George out of the way so that he could talk over their future.

Outside, in the perfection of a summer evening, the little birds were singing lustily and the large-winged butterflies fluttered among the flowers, as her heart fluttered when Kirk came striding into the room. He strode in with an easy grace and a gleam in his eyes that made her heart turn over.

Poor Laurel had never seen him so happy . . . so virile and so utterly handsome in his evening dress. He laughed down at her, told her he was hungry, having missed lunch, and teased Reko, who struggled with a bottle of champagne that refused to open until Kirk took it in his strong brown fingers.

Laurel stared at the champagne, tried to laugh lightly back and avoided his eyes. His exuberance unnerved her as he filled first her glass and then his own. There was something lurking behind the gleam in his eyes that she was unable to define . . . something that tingled and sparkled like the champagne.

She had never made him so happy. Lucky, lucky Nina! Then he was looking at her teasingly, saying with a humorous tender laugh, "Come on, eat up. You can do better than that!"

When he rushed her to the living room after dinner, Laurel was aware of an approaching climax. Then Reko followed them in with the emperor's wedding gift in his hand. Kirk thanked him and he withdrew.

Laurel was sitting on the settee as though hypnotized as Kirk unwrapped the gift and brought forth the bottle of sake and tiny cups. Solemnly, he filled the first of the three tiny cups with three distinct pours. Then he raised it to his lips and took it down in three sips. He refilled the cup in like manner again for Laurel, and as he passed it to her he looked deeply into her eyes and she understood. She drank it in three sips as he had done.

The second cup was now filled, Laurel having it first before he had his. The third cup he took first and she took the second. By this time her face was sweetly flushed, her eyes were like stars . . . and Kirk was looking at her as if he was having difficulty with his breathing, too.

All his actions had been deliberate, and the last in

which he inexorably drew her up into his arms was the most deliberate of all.

With his lips a paper's width from hers he murmured, "Now try to get out of that one, Mrs. Kirk Graham. Our marriage has just been solemnized in the Japanese way. So you're well and truly hooked."

Up to now, Laurel had been convinced that she was dreaming. But Kirk's mouth closing possessively on her own and kissing her with all his passion unleashed was no dream. She hung on before the tempest of his kisses, loving his hard leanness against her. A long time passed before he lifted his head to look down into her eyes in the way she had longed for, as though his need for her was as great as her need for him.

"Oh, Kirk!" she said, and put her head against his chest. He felt the fragrance of her hair, the tears against his shirtfront, her slim suppleness pressed against him. And he lifted her face. His lips found hers again and it was like the consummation of their marriage as they clung together, close, fiercely loving.

When sanity returned, Laurel said, "I thought you loved Nina."

"Nina?" He looked startled. "But I told you she was nothing to me."

"I was sure she was, especially when you . . . you left me alone at night."

He said with disgust, "That ass Uncle George was responsible for that. He said if I had any love for you at all I would give you time to recuperate. I knew you weren't fully recovered when I sent for you. But I knew if I didn't work fast he would get you. I realize now what a fool I was to take any notice of him. I had to marry you quickly to make sure of you."

"There was never anyone else but you," she said.

He spoke forcibly, his gray eyes dark with remembered pain. "I've been through purgatory wanting you, and I was puzzled by your attitude. You were so withdrawn, so remote and trembling each time I touched you.''

Her eyes refused to leave his. ''Why didn't you explain about our having separate rooms?''

''Uncle George told me that he would explain to you as your doctor that it was essential for us to wait a while before starting our married life in earnest.'' His smile made him so boyishly endearing, her heart reached out to him. ''I'm afraid, loving you as I do, I couldn't last out. That was why I spent those nights away from you in town when I felt I was cracking under the strain. Thank heaven we're married!''

Laurel's face went rosy red. ''Please tell me about Nina,'' she begged.

''Nina wasn't the reason I didn't come home to lunch. I was settling my affairs at the office in order to take a month's delayed honeymoon. We only had a week before because I knew I couldn't hold out much longer than that. I was giving you a month to get used to me again. But things have happened. Our married life begins as from now.''

Memory stabbed like knives. Her lips trembled and there were tears on her lashes. ''Poor Kiki and little Fuseko. It was in the morning papers.''

He looked grim. ''I know. I was afraid of something like that. That was the reason I asked you if you'd seen the baby on your last visit to Mrs. Pakara. I knew something like that would happen if Nina persisted in her insistence on having the baby. I've been the go-between, holding Nina off and handling the situation with kid gloves.''

Laurel thought of his telephone call that day in his study. It all added up and made sense. Kirk hugged her.

''Come and sit down,'' he said. He led her to the chair in which she had earlier sat facing the window, sat down and drew her upon his knee. ''I think I feel more sorry for Ishi, Nina's husband, than anyone else. He was terribly cut up when he heard about Kiki and the son he never knew about. He deserves someone better than Nina. Although she came from a wealthy Japanese family, she preferred the Western way of life. Her family sent her to America when she was eighteen to study at the university. Ishi was there working at the Japanese Embassy when she met him and they were married on her nineteenth birthday.''

"Did she have children?"

"No, Nina didn't want children. When they came back to Japan, she was restless. Then she met a man she'd known in America, a millionaire industrialist who came over to Japan on business. They met secretly. But she was afraid to ask Ishi for a divorce. Then she discovered he had a child, a son, by Kiki. Knowing his longing for a son, she decided to get Fuseko and present him to his father in the hope that he would be so delighted that he would consent to giving her a divorce.''

"And she asked your help?"

"Yes. Thank heaven she's gone for good. She left Ishi and went to America yesterday to the man she professes to love.'' He stared out into the garden. "I'm afraid the only one Nina is capable of loving is herself. Pity—she was a charming, well-bred woman and quite likable.''

"Which only goes to show that you're like the rest of the men, easily enamored by a pretty face.''

Laurel dimpled up at him and he gave a sardonic grin that consigned Nina to the depths. A sudden gleam came in his eyes as they caressed her face, a face glowing from his kisses.

"You're so right," he whispered. "I was hooked the moment I saw yours for all eternity.''

His mouth was on hers, stifling anything she might have said. Passion flowed over them like an electrical storm. "I love your hair when it's in a cloudy halo around your face. I want to sleep with you and wake up in the morning to bury my face in its fragrance. I love your gentleness, your quiet laughter and your deep capacity for loving. You do love me, don't you?" he whispered urgently.

He looked down into her large eloquent eyes and

found there a love and need equal to his own. His mouth tilted and she touched the corners of it with gentle fingers.

Laurel's smile was wistful. "I can't believe even yet that this isn't some fantastic crazy dream. But I know my love for you is real enough. I do love you Kirk, so much."

"And there's to be no more separate rooms?"

She shook her head.

He whispered, "Nervous?" His eyes held hers with a mastery adding to the terrifying delight of the question.

She shook her head again, her mouth curving deliciously into a smile.

"A little," she said.

He laughed and with little devils dancing in his eyes proceeded to take down her hair.

They were late getting up the next morning with the admirable Reko bringing them tea in bed. They were having breakfast when Reko said, "I will take your cases to the car, Graham-san. I cleaned it ready."

"The devil you did! How did you know . . . ?" Kirk broke off, made a good-humored gesture with a lean brown hand and winked at Laurel. "Yes, Reko, do that, and thanks."

Laurel, with stars still in her eyes, said, startled, "You're not going away again?"

He grinned across the table at her, vital and loving. "We both are, my darling. When breakfast is over, I'm going to help you pack and we're off on our honeymoon to Honolulu. I made all the arrangements yesterday."

"But . . . but what about Uncle George? We can't leave a guest like that."

"It's all fixed, my sweet. Uncle George will only be too delighted to spend his holiday with Paul Glennock, listening to his lectures and going around his old haunts. He's staying at Glennock's club in Tokyo. He's coming to fetch his luggage later. I think Uncle George has delayed our honeymoon long enough!"

Laurel agreed, although she felt sorry for the man because he had loved her. Then she forgot all about him, for Kirk was looking at her and his gaze was like a kiss, promising an increasing joy forever from the endless store of their love.

CHATEAU IN PROVENCE

Château
in Provence

Rozella Lake

After sixteen years' estrangement Miranda Dixon's French grandmother had summoned her to Château Chambray—a summons Miranda acknowledged only to please her father. After all, Miranda was young, beautiful and becoming recognized as a dress designer; being the last of the Chambrays meant little to her.

However, she wasn't prepared for the hypnotic charm of the château, nor for its neighbor, Alain Maury—a man more disturbing than Laurel dared admit.

But Alain, a famous horticulturist, was desperate to buy the château, as only on Chambray soil would his elusive blue rose bear its intoxicating fragrance. And it was obvious Alain would do anything to obtain it. . . .

CHAPTER ONE

ALAIN MAURY was in a foul temper. It was apparent in the set of his wide, slim shoulders, in the tightness of his mouth and the narrowing of his eyes, their warm brown darkened by his thoughts. He had placed his final hopes on the Cromerty Institute in California, and since no one there could help him discover why the blue rose had no scent, he must abandon the project.

Yet how could he bring himself to do so? This rose was his last chance to prove he had not lost his creative talent. Ever since he had propagated it in his laboratory in Grasse, its magic fragrance had haunted him, firing him with the determination to make a new perfume. But incredibly, the blue rose—when grown outdoors under normal conditions—had no scent whatever, and the only other choice—to grow it in special greenhouses—was far too expensive to be practical.

He sighed. It was four years since he had produced Eternelle, and he was haunted by the fear that he might never again be able to create anything that would capture the market in the same way. What a success it had been—still was, for that matter—doing for Adrienne Cosmetics what N° 5 had done for Chanel.

He flung the letter from the institute onto his desk. At thirty he was too young to live on past success; unless he could create more new perfumes, he would return to the pharmaceutical side of the business.

He stared through the windows at the beautifully landscaped grounds that extended for several thousand acres around the house, a tangible sign—as was the enormous white building in Grasse where Adrienne perfumes were made—of his mother's great success. A success he had done nothing to increase since Lucille's death.

Lucille . . . . He clenched his fists. When would her memory cease to torment him?

Hearing light steps across the floor, he swung around, forcing a smile as his mother came in. From a distance she looked as young as her silver-framed photograph on his desk, though as she came closer, he saw the fine lines around her eyes and the speckle of gray in the glossy black hair that curved into a classical coil at the nape of her neck.

Strange, he mused, that a woman who had built her fortune on artifice should use so little herself. Today, he would swear, she wore only a touch of lipstick and her special perfume—the first one he had ever made.

"Why the frown?" she asked, her soft voice troubled.

In curt tones he told her of the letter from the Cromerty Institute.

"Forget the blue rose and concentrate on something else," she said when he had finished.

"I can't forget it." His voice, though light in timbre, had an edge to it, giving an indication of the quicksilver temperament he tried—not always with success—to keep under control. "Do you know how long it's been since I've produced anything worthwhile?"

"You're not idle. You look after the financial side of the business. Why worry about perfume? Anyway, we don't need another one. You want it for *your* satisfaction."

"I'm well aware of that!" he cried. "Lucille's been dead for three years, and since then I've created nothing. Nothing!"

"Give yourself time."

Adrienne Maury sank down on a velvet settee. In everything she did she was elegant, and looking at her serene face, one found it hard to believe that—left a widow with a five-year-old boy—she had had sufficient tenacity to make her own beauty products and sell them door to door until her fame had spread to the point where a local bank had agreed to finance her, setting her on the first step to international success.

She spoke little of the early, back-breaking years, though Alain could remember returning from school and having nowhere to do his homework, so crowded had their tiny apartment been with bowls of lotions in varying stages of completion.

If only he had his mother's perseverance and control, he thought moodily, instead of a fiery Latin streak that exploded when he least wanted it to—the way it had done the last time he had seen Lucille alive. Lucille . . . .

"Come back, Alain," his mother said. "You're miles away."

"I was thinking."

"You think too much. It's time you fell in love again and settled down."

"Is that an order or a request?"

"A hope!"

He smiled, and his face changed as if by magic, showing him to be an unusually good-looking man with the fine-cut features often found in Latins. There was a mixture of delicacy and strength in his physique: broad shouldered, yet slim hipped; only average in height, but so well coordinated he gave the impression of being much taller. His hands were narrow and well shaped, their restless movement belying the sardonic coolness with which he generally surveyed the world.

His mother watched him with compassion. It had been given to few women to appreciate this complex son of hers: so easy to love if you understood him; so impossibly difficult if you didn't. And Lucille never had. Not that she could talk to Alain about it; on the subject of his dead fiancée he brooked no discussion.

"I'm serious about your getting married," she repeated. "Aren't you tired of playing around?"

"No man admits to being tired of that!" He walked to

the door. "I'm going for a stroll. If Colette telephones, say I'll call her back."

"Colette," his mother said with such feeling that he laughed.

"You've just been telling me to settle down!"

"Not with her! She's so domineering."

"Perhaps I need someone like that."

He left the room and, crossing the hall, went to stand on the front steps. The trees were still bare, yet already there was a suggestion of birth in the air, of buds waiting to appear and leaves ready to unfurl.

He descended the steps and strode along the driveway to the greenhouse. Entering it, he made for a distant corner and a flowering rosebush in a terra-cotta pot.

His beloved blue rose.

Exquisitely beautiful, it had unfurled itself in front of him like a graceful woman disclosing her body. The pale blue petals parted to show a tightly closed heart of deeper blue. A heart without scent, like a woman without a soul.

For a long while he stared at it, his expression growing darker until, with an angry exclamation, he picked up the pot and dashed it to the ground.

The violent gesture exhausted his anger, leaving him calmer than he had been since he had opened the letter from the Cromerty Institute. With calmness came regret for his action, and he bent down and picked up the bush. The full-blown roses had broken off and lay on the ground, but several closed buds were still intact, and he touched his hand to them and wished he could appreciate beauty for its own sake, and not be filled with regret because he could not make the blooms produce a scent.

Unaware that he was still holding the bush in his arms, he left the conservatory and walked through the garden. The cultivated lawns were soon left behind, and the landscape grew wilder. Deep in thought, he walked unseeingly, and only the darkening of the day made him realize he had come around the side of the far mountain and was standing on Chambray land.

It was hard to believe that, as the crow flies, he had

barely come a couple of miles, so different was the terrain here from his own property. It was as though it had never known the hand of man. As indeed it had not, Alain mused, surveying the craggy mountainside where stunted trees clung to sharp inclines, and rough boulders marked the precipitous descent to the valley far below.

Even on the brightest day shadows always lay on these slopes, and now, at dusk, the whole area was filled with Stygian gloom, while a coldness seeped up from the icy waters of the mountain stream that rushed headlong through the gorge.

Shivering in his fine cashmere sweater, he turned to retrace his steps. Moving quickly, he stumbled and dropped the rose bush. Once more it lay at his feet, and this time he decided to leave it there. Better to do as his mother had advised and forget it ever existed.

With a sigh he walked on, but after a few steps he halted. He couldn't leave the bush to die. Ashamed of his sentimentality, he went back to it and with quick movements scraped a hole in the flinty ground. By the time he had planted the bush his fingers were grazed and bleeding, and wrapping them in his handkerchief, he stood up and walked on. As far as he was concerned, the blue rose no longer existed.

"ARE YOU SURE you won't change your mind?" Mr. Joseph asked Miranda Dixon. "If it's a question of money—"

"You've already been more than generous," she interrupted. "But I've been here two years, and unless I start on my own—I feel—"

"Time will pass you by, and you'll be a failure at twenty-two!" Mr. Joseph concluded.

Unable to deny the truth of the remark, Miranda smiled, though looking around the large room with its bolts of materials, long trestle tables and rows of mannequins, she knew she was saying goodbye to one of the most satisfying periods of her life.

From the moment she had come to work as a dress designer for Mr. Joseph, she had been a success. Within six months her name was known throughout the trade, and within two years she had become chief designer for the company.

But now she wanted to start on her own, and neither the offer of more money nor partnership could dissuade her.

"You won't produce much of a collection with five hundred pounds," Mr. Joseph said. "If you want to set up alone, at least let me help you."

Miranda shook her head. "I want to be free to design what I like."

"No designer's free," Mr. Joseph responded gloomily. "We might ignore Paris, but we can't ignore the buyers from Selfridges and Harrods!"

"That's *exactly* what I intend doing!"

Looking at the tall, slim girl in front of him, her piquant face arrestingly alive, her wide-apart gray eyes sparkling with determination and her honey-colored hair glinting red in the light, he had no doubt about her future. Success and Miranda were made for each other, and she certainly deserved it more than the young designers he had hired and fired before this hardworking and intelligent girl had come his way.

"I hope you'll come to my first collection," Miranda continued, her beaming smile showing perfect teeth that made her look more American than English.

"Nothing will keep me away," Mr. Joseph assured her. "How else will I be able to steal your designs!"

Standing up all the way home in the crowded subway train, Miranda did not feel as confident as she had pretended and wondered if she had been wise to leave Mr. Joseph. Yet two years was a long time to stay with one firm if you were ambitious to make your own way. Besides, fashions for the young should be designed by the young, and that meant taking a chance before she grew stale and jaded.

The train jerked to a stop, and there was a rush to the

exit. Propelled upward by a mass of pushing shoulders, she was soon breathing in deeply the cool night air, her spirits reviving as she wended her way up Hampstead High Street to the block of old-fashioned apartments where she lived with her father.

"Is that you, Miranda?" Roger Dixon came out of the living room to greet her. A well-built man with thick gray hair and brilliant blue eyes in a tanned face, he looked more like a sailor than the engineer he was. "I thought we'd go out for dinner," he went on. "It'll save you the bother of cooking."

"You mean it will save *you* the bother!" Since she had first started work, they had shared the household chores, and this week it was her father's turn in the kitchen.

"That thought did cross my mind," he admitted, "but there's another reason, too."

"Anything important?"

"I'll tell you later."

When he did, the news was something she had not anticipated, and it was brought to her attention by a sheet of deckle-edged paper that her father held out to her.

Unfolding it, she saw spidery handwriting and did not need to look at the signature to know it would show the word Chambray. Emilie, Comtesse Chambray.

Miranda dropped the letter to the table. "What does grandmother want?"

"Read it."

She did so. The letter was short and to the point. Written in precise English, it expressed sorrow at not having seen Miranda for many years and hoped that this would be remedied by her coming to spend a holiday in Provence.

"What's the point?" Miranda asked. "I haven't seen her since I was six, and *that* was only for an hour!"

"You reminded her of your mother," Roger Dixon said softly, "and it brought back memories she wanted to forget. That's one reason she didn't see you again."

"I still look like my mother," Miranda replied. "So why should she change her mind?"

"Old people frequently change their mind. Be kind, my dear. You're young and you can afford it."

"How can *you* be kind?" she burst out. "She practically accused you of killing mother!"

"In her eyes I probably did. She was sure that if Louise hadn't married me and come to live in England, her tuberculosis would have been controlled."

"No one could have guaranteed that."

"This climate certainly didn't help her."

"In those days TB was usually fatal," Miranda persisted.

"We're getting off the subject," her father said. "Your grandmother wants to see you, and I'd like you to go." He took a plane ticket from his pocket. "This came with the letter."

Color flared in Miranda's cheeks. "Does she think we can't afford the fare?"

"I imagine it was sent as a gesture of friendship—not charity. Take it, Miranda. Anyway, France is the home of fashion. You might come back with some ideas!"

"I'm sure to find millions in a village in Provence! Honestly, dad, you'll have to do better than that!"

He shook his head and remained silent, and watching him, she marveled that no other woman had succeeded in capturing him. Was the memory of her mother still too strong after twenty years, or was he afraid of allowing himself to become vulnerable again?

She sighed. "All right, I'll go."

"Good. I'm sure you won't have any regrets."

They were words Miranda was to remember with irony and bitterness many times in the months to follow.

CHAPTER TWO

IT WAS a warm April day when Miranda stepped out of the aircraft at Nice airport, and she found it hard to believe that only two hours before she had been battling with the wind to cross the tarmac at Heathrow. Feeling she had stepped into a fairy-tale world, she had to restrain herself from dancing her way to the white terminal building.

At this time of the season the airport was quiet, though as she passed through Immigration, the arrival of a domestic flight from Paris was announced.

Soon the air was alive with voluble Gallic voices, and she was pleasantly surprised to find her French was good enough for her to understand what was being said. Perhaps having a French mother had given her an ear for the language.

Clutching her passport, she went in search of her two red cases—a generous going-away present from Mr. Joseph—and then followed the porter to the taxi stand.

A solitary yellow cab was parked beneath the sign, and she pointed to it urgently. The porter nodded but did not increase his pace, and from the corner of her eye she saw a dark-haired man striding in the same direction. She quickened her pace, and as though guessing her intention, the man did the same. With a defiant lift of her head she broke into a run, nylon-clad legs barely touching the pavement, honey gold hair flying. Simultaneously, they reached the cab and simultaneously, put their hands on the door: scarlet-tipped fingers almost touching strong, tanned ones.

"So sorry," Miranda smiled sweetly. "Perhaps you'll wait for the next one."

"Perhaps you would wait instead," the man barked.

"I was here first."

"A debatable point, *mademoiselle*. You know I wanted the taxi, and you deliberately ran ahead of me."

"*You* ran ahead of *me*." Keeping her hand firmly on the door, she signaled to the porter to put her cases in the trunk.

"Do not let us argue about it." The man was equally firm. "The taxi is mine." He swung around and gave a sharp command to the porter who, about the put the red cases in the trunk, stopped in midair.

"You can't deny you saw me running ahead of you," Miranda said in her calmest tone.

"No one could have missed you in that ridiculous getup!" Brown eyes raked over her emerald suit and jaunty hat with its single scarlet feather.

"Just because I run faster than you," she said furiously, "there's no need to be rude!" She swung around and gave the taxi driver her most ravishing smile. "Please tell this *gentleman* that I was here first."

"But of course, *mademoiselle*." The driver scrambled out of the car, took the cases from the porter and dumped them on the seat beside him.

Only then did Miranda turn to her vanquished neighbor. "I'm sure you won't have long to wait for another taxi."

"You British!" he exclaimed, and turning his back on her, walked away.

Fuming, Miranda settled herself in the seat. So much for French gallantry. And so much for a Frenchman's appreciation of fashion! Ridiculous getup indeed! This green suit had been the most successful design in her last collection.

"Where are you going?" the driver asked.

"Bayronne," Miranda replied. "Near Grasse."

"That's a long way."

"I know," she replied, to reassure him she understood the journey would be expensive, and then lapsed into silence as she watched the passing scene.

Towering apartment buildings and sprawling two-story motels marked by gaudy neon signs bordered the seafront. It was a far cry from the luxury atmosphere she had anticipated, and she realized that this stretch of coastline was the Mecca of the package tour.

The car swung sharply left, sped for several miles along a wide highway and then branched off onto a winding country road, lined on either side with row upon row of greenhouses.

"Flowers," the driver explained. "We send them all over Europe."

"Don't they grow flowers in Bayronne, too?" she asked.

"Around Grasse the flowers are used for making perfume." The man swung around for an instant to grin at her. "*Mademoiselle* is like a flower herself."

Miranda's ruffled feelings were mollified by the compliment, and only then did she realize how irritated she had been by the argument at the airport. Used to being admired by men, she had found the Frenchman's fury surprising. As if it had mattered all that much for him to wait an extra few minutes for another taxi! Not that she couldn't have waitied, too, she thought, and probably would have if he had not been so unnecessarily rude. Pushing him from her mind, she concentrated on the countryside.

They were climbing continuously, the narrow road winding its way farther and farther from the coast. The garish brightness of the sparkling sea, dark green palms and hard yellow sand was replaced by the muted greens of hedgerows and fields, the faded rust of ancient tiled roofs and the dusty gray of crumbling stones. Here was the countryside of Cézanne, though the occasional clumps of purple bougainvillea and showering cascades of pink and red roses brought Bonnard to mind.

Village after village swept by, some a mere cluster of
houses and some a cobbled square set with a fountain, a
church and the inevitable *bar tabac*. And over it all was
the mellow wash of spring sunshine and air fragrant with
orange blossom.

Just after one o'clock they reached Bayronne, a single
street of houses and shops with several cobbled alleys
branching from it. The Chambray château stood at the
end of a winding lane outside the village, and they swung
through a pair of tall, decaying pillars and along a
dilapidated driveway that only became more carefully
tended as they neared the house.

Having only her father's vague description of it,
Miranda was unprepared for the fairy-tale splendor of
the château. In such a place must Sleeping Beauty have
lain for a hundred years—might still be lying, she thought
fancifully as she took in the crumbling stone facade and
the four turrets whose pointed domes were capped by
gray tiles. At the ground- and second-floor levels the
windows were masked by faded wooden shutters, but
those in the turrets were narrow slits, more fitting for
peepholes.

Before she could appreciate any more, the heavy,
nail-studded door opened, and an elderly woman came
hurrying down the steps to take the cases from the
driver.

After paying the man, Miranda went to help her, but
the woman shook her head and beckoned her to come inside.

Miranda did so and waited by the door, expecting to
see her grandmother, but the hall remained empty, and
she stared at the enormous tapestry that hung on one wall
and stretched from the high, vaulted ceiling almost to the
ground. Ahead of her wide stone stairs swept up to a gal-
leried second floor, while at ground level some half
dozen closed doors gave an indication of the size of the
interior. What a large home for one old woman to occupy!

"The *comtesse* would like to see you as soon as you are ready," the servant said. "If you wish to wash first, I will show you to your room. . . ."

Anxious to get the meeting over with, Miranda shook her head, and the woman led her across the polished tiled floor into the salon.

Expecting the same decay evident in the rest of the château, Miranda was surprised by the room. Straight-backed gilt furniture mingled happily with bow-fronted satinwood chests and brocade-covered settees. A profusion of tables was scattered on the Aubusson carpet, several of them holding bowls of flowers whose colors matched the flowers beneath her feet. Narrow windows, their edges softened by faded damask curtains, afforded a view of a terrace, beyond which could be glimpsed sloping lawns and tall grass rippling in the breeze.

But it was the woman lying on a pink settee in front of an enormous marble fireplace who commanded her attention. Emilie, Comtesse Chambray. Her grandmother in name only, who had commanded her presence here.

"Come closer, child," a reedy voice requested. "My eyesight is not as good as it used to be."

Slowly Miranda moved forward, realizing how false her memory had played her as she looked into the lined face. Here was not the majestic, silver-haired matriarch of her imagination, but a diminutive woman with wispy gray hair, a face as lined as old parchment and liquid brown eyes—her most beautiful feature—set above a high-bridged, aristocratic nose. She was as fine boned as a sparrow, and not even the cashmere shawl around her shoulders could disguise the thinness of her body.

"Come closer still," the *comtesse* commanded and held out her hands.

Miranda was obliged to take them and found their grip surprisingly strong. Dutifully, she placed her lips to the lined cheek. "How are you, grandmother?"

"All the better for seeing you." She motioned to a chair. "Sit down, child."

Miranda did so and found herself being carefully scrutinized.

"I like your suit," her grandmother said unexpectedly. "Your father wrote and told me you design clothes. You must tell me how you became interested in fashion. I have so much to learn about you."

"Why do you want to bother after so many years?" Miranda asked bluntly.

"Is it ever too late to admit one is wrong?"

"Certain things can never be put right."

"You sound bitter."

"I don't mean to be." Miranda stared at the floor and then, as nothing was said, stole a glance at her grandmother. The woman was lying motionless, her face devoid of expression, but her eyes filled with tears that overflowed down the furrowed cheeks. Knowing she was the cause of it, Miranda felt a pang of remorse.

"I don't think we should talk about the past," she said hesitantly. "It won't do any good."

"If talking about it can help you to understand why I behaved the way I did—"

"Not yet," Miranda interrupted. "Let's get to know each other first."

"Very well." The *comtesse* was in control of herself again. "I am sure you would like to go to your room and change. Simone will show you the way."

The *comtesse* rang a hand bell, and the servant who had shown Miranda in appeared at the door and led her up the curving stone staircase.

As she had supposed, several corridors branched off from the gallery, each one giving access to two or three rooms. There were at least a dozen bedrooms here, apart from those to be found in the turrets.

Plenty to explore, she decided, and felt her pulses stir with excitement. There was an atmosphere in an old house like this that could not be found anywhere else. How she would have loved exploring it as a child—would love it now if she gave herself a chance. But she was not going to do so; she was only here for a couple of weeks and had no intention of becoming attached either to the château or her grandmother.

But she was hard pressed to maintain her reserve when, entering a corner bedroom overlooking the back of the château, she glimpsed the view through the window. Rolling slopes stretched for mile upon mile: green fields, gold fields and fields of rich brown earth with trees marking the landscape throughout. Cypresses, tall and dark green, pointed stately fingers to the sky, while silvery olive trees—their small leaves catching even the faintest gust of wind—seemed to be constantly dancing.

A slight cough from Simone drew Miranda back to the middle of the room. "Will you be able to find your way downstairs, *mademoiselle?*"

"I think so."

Abruptly the woman walked out, leaving Miranda to wonder at her unfriendliness. She was obviously an old retainer and might be jealous in case her mistress's affections were usurped by a newcomer.

With a shrug she unlocked her cases and unpacked, hanging her clothes in the hand-painted wooden armoire and putting her underwear in the pine chest that flanked the stone wall beside her bed. And what a bed it was! Large enough to hold four people, with an overhead canopy of flowered tapestry identical to the handwoven rugs on the tiled floor.

Not finding a private bathroom, she ventured along the corridor until she came upon a large, old-fashioned one. The water that gushed from the taps was surprisingly hot, and she washed her face quickly and ran downstairs.

The salon was empty, and she crossed the hall and opened the first door she came to. It was a library, dark and shuttered and smelling of dust and leather. Closing it hurriedly, she tried several more doors before finding herself in the dining room.

It was high ceilinged and rectangular with a long, narrow table at whose head sat the *comtesse*. Tall-backed chairs marked twelve places, and though only two were laid, Miranda had the impression that every chair was occupied by a Chambray ancestor, each one watching her with a disdainful stare.

"How young you look," her grandmother exclaimed, motioning her to sit down. "It's the freedom of dress and hair, I suppose. In my youth we had to be so proper we were old before our time!"

Another elderly retainer—were there no young people in the château, Miranda wondered—served them asparagus, thick and paler than any she had seen before, though tasting delicious, as did the filet of veal with calvados and cream and the wafer-thin pancakes served with slices of lemon, which concluded the meal.

"I am glad to see you enjoy your food," the *comtesse* remarked.

"When other people cook it for me," Miranda admitted.

"Who does the cooking in your home?"

"My father and I share it."

"Most Frenchwomen are taught to cook," the *comtesse* said, "even if circumstances will not require them to do so. A woman who does not understand good cuisine will never have a good table, no matter how excellent her chef."

"English people don't set as much store by food as the French."

"More's the pity."

Miranda bit back a retort, determined to say nothing that might provoke a quarrel.

"We will have coffee in the salon," the *comtesse* was saying. "If you will give me your arm . . . ."

With a strange reluctance Miranda did so, feeling tall and ungainly beside the fragile old lady.

Reentering the salon, she sensed a change in the atmosphere and looked around her as she settled her grandmother on the settee. Nothing appeared to have been touched, yet the room was different.

Of course, it was the smell! She gazed enraptured at

the bowls of roses that had been placed on the lacquered tables.

"You are admiring the flowers?" the *comtesse* inquired.

"I've never seen blue roses before." Miranda tentatively touched a petal. It was the color of a delphinium, though its perfume was even more amazing than its shade. "These must be very special. Do you grow them yourself?"

"We don't grow them at all. They are mine by accident!" Seeing Miranda's bewilderment, the *comtesse* smiled. "I will tell you the story. You may find it interesting. The first rose was planted—though it would be truer to say it was thrown away and *then* planted—by a young chemist who lives with his mother on the other side of the valley. For several years he tried to grow these roses and failed."

"No blooms, you mean?"

"Plenty of blooms, but no scent. Eventually, he abandoned the idea of growing them. He took the last of his plants and threw it away—on my land. A few months later Maurice, my handyman, was out looking for a goat that had strayed and found a bush of blue roses. He picked one and brought it to me."

"You must have been astonished!"

"I was. I decided to take as many cuttings from the bush as we could and plant them in the same area. In a matter of weeks we had a carpet of blue flowers. It was unbelievable."

"Are they a special strain?"

"Yes. Alain's a gifted horticulturist as well as a chemist. It's been of great value to him in his work. He creates perfume," her grandmother explained, "and for that you need flowers. Have you heard of Eternelle?"

"Who hasn't?"

"Alain Maury produced that."

"I see." Miranda pointed to the roses. "But tell me the rest of *this* story."

"Well, for several weeks we had rooms filled with

these roses. They have a scent that invades your senses—almost like a drug.'' The thin voice stopped apologetically. ''I'm afraid you will think me fanciful.''

''I know what you mean,'' Miranda said slowly. ''I can feel it, too. Please go on.''

''There's not much more to tell. I got bronchitis, and Alain came to see me with a gift from his mother. When he saw the blue roses, he couldn't believe his eyes—or should I say his nose! He practically accused me of spraying them artificially!''

''It's incredible.'' Miranda looked at a bowl of roses again. Even from a distance their scent was overpowering. ''His had no smell at all?''

''None. He had tried everything—without success.''

''Until he threw one away on your land.'' Miranda looked at her grandmother mischievously. ''What magic power do you possess? After all, you live in a fairy-tale castle!''

''The magic is in the earth, my child—that much Alain has found out. Millions of years ago this region was volcanic. Many of the boulders you still see around are lumps of lava. The soil in this valley is particularly rich with minerals, and it seems that these are in exactly the right proportion for the blue rose to grow properly.''

''What's this man going to do? Put the same kind of minerals into *his* land?''

''It wouldn't work. According to geologists, it could take years before his land has similar properties to mine; and even then there's no guarantee it will be the same. That's one reason I asked you to come here.''

The change of subject left Miranda confused.

''Alain wants to buy my land,'' the *comtesse* explained. ''I only need to keep a few acres around the château, and he's offered me an excellent price for the rest. But I wanted to talk to you before I made a decision.'' The *comtesse* shifted on her pillow. ''You and my great-nephew, Pierre, are my only remaining relatives.

When I die the château and land will be divided between you both.''

"My home's in England," Miranda said quickly.

"I know. That is another reason I should not have waited so long before having you here." The thin voice stopped, and the silence was heavy with memories. Then the voice resumed, lighter in tone, as if the past had been staved off. "If I accepted Alain's offer, I would have considerably more money to leave."

"Or to spend," Miranda said quickly. "The money is yours."

"I am too old to make use of it. Good food is my only extravagance, and even then I can only eat a little. No, Miranda, the important question is whether we keep the property intact—in case you or Pierre wishes to make it your home—or whether we sell Alain what he wants. He has offered to buy the house, too, if that will help me to make up my mind. He would allow me to live in it until I died, of course."

"How ghoulish!"

"It is practical. You should appreciate the difference."

"You must do as you wish," Miranda murmured, "but I certainly don't want you to leave me anything."

"I am not English enough to leave my money to a cat's home!"

"Leave it to your great-great-whoever-he-is!"

"You will like Pierre. I have written and asked him to come here." The *comtesse* sighed. "I will wait until he does before I decide what to do."

Embarrassed, Miranda sauntered to the window. She had expected her visit to bring some emotional complications, but she had not envisaged the ones now facing her. It was going to be hard to make her grandmother see that one could not turn back the clock, not inculcate a sense of family pride into someone who had grown up without it. "Ask Pierre what you should do," she said. "He's more a Chambray than I am."

"He is not!" There was a flash of fire in the brown eyes. "Pierre's a Chambray by name—you are one by birth!" The thin chest palpitated painfully. "I understand your feelings, but you are not to talk that way."

Miranda ran across the room and knelt by her grandmother's side. "I didn't want to upset you, *grand'mère*. What I meant is that we should discuss it with Pierre when he comes. I'm sure *he'll* know what's the best thing for you to do."

"It's *your* decision, too," the old lady reiterated. "Why must you be so obstinate?"

"I can't help it," Miranda said dryly. "After all, I'm your granddaughter!"

CHAPTER THREE

MORE QUICKLY than she had believed possible, Miranda settled down to a leisurely pace of living. Awakened at eight-thirty by a maid with her breakfast, she wandered downstairs by ten and spent the rest of the morning exploring the countryside, making sure she was back at the château by noon to greet her grandmother, who rarely appeared before then.

Luncheon was served at twelve-thirty and afterward they napped in the shade of the terrace, not waking up until tea with lemon was served at four. By the time dinner was served, the sun had taken its toll of Miranda's energy, and she was more than ready for bed when her grandmother retired at nine.

She was horrified at the ease with which she slipped into the life of a lotus-eater. The exciting days with Mr. Joseph seemed as though they had never existed, and her plans for the future—so strong in her mind when she had arrived here—were already blurring at the edges.

One week more, Miranda decided on her tenth day at the château, and she must return to England.

"I was hoping you would stay for several months," her grandmother said heavily when she was told.

"I can't go on being idle. I have work to do."

"It is interesting that you should have this flair for design. Your mother had an excellent eye for color."

"I wish I could remember her clearly," Miranda said. "She seems so pale and ghostly to me."

"She was already dying when you were old enough to remember her."

The *comtesse*'s voice was ice-cold, and though no mention was made of Roger Dixon, the very omission was significant.

A week before, Miranda would have talked of something else, but to do so today smacked of dishonesty.

"It's wrong to blame my father for my mother's death. It could just as easily have happened if she'd gone on living here."

"You speak from ignorance," came the harsh reply. "In Louise's time the only way to fight her illness was to live in a warm, dry atmosphere. Yet because of your father, she settled in a climate that was bound to kill her!"

"Mother made the choice herself. Why do you persist in seeing her as a silly girl without a mind of her own?"

"Because she was! You shouldn't judge her by the things your father has told you about her."

"I'm judging her by the things *you*'ve said! Since I've been here, you've kept telling me how like her I am. Not only in looks, but in what I say and do. If that's true, I'm not surprised she decided to lead a normal life—even for only a few years—rather than spend a lifetime as an invalid."

"Are you suggesting I *wanted* Louise to be an invalid?"

"Didn't you?"

There was a long silence, punctuated at last by a quivering sigh. "I wanted her to live as long as possible. Was that wrong?"

"Of course not," Miranda said gently, "but she preferred five happy years to thirty lonely ones."

"I realize that now."

Miranda caught the bony hand resting on the cashmere blanket. "It must be awful knowing you were wrong and not being able to do anything about it."

"That is why I found the courage to write to you. Time isn't on my side, and I have to make my peace with those I've wronged."

"Just because you look like a granny," Miranda said with determined humor, "there's no need to talk like one! You're going to live for years yet."

The words were like a wave of cold water on a sea of Viennese *schmaltz*, and for an instant the *comtesse* sat stunned.

"You're not offended, are you?" Miranda asked anxiously.

"No, no. And please don't undo the good work by apologizing!" The old lady struggled to her feet and put her frail hand in Miranda's strong one. "Our talk has tired me more than I realized. I will go to my room."

Hiding her dismay at the fluctuating color in her grandmother's cheeks, Miranda escorted her to the large bedroom overlooking the driveway. Simone—who seemed to have ears like antennae—was already there and immediately took charge, making Miranda feel in the way.

"Come back and see me when I'm settled," the *comtesse* whispered.

"You should sleep and not talk any more," Simone interrupted.

"I'll have plenty of time for sleeping when Miranda returns to England." The voice was gentle, but the brown eyes flashed, and the old servant contented herself by muttering unintelligibly under her breath.

Miranda left the bedroom and waited out in the gallery. Even at night, with only a few lamps to cast a faint light over the gray stone walls, one had no feeling of gloom. It was a house that had been loved, and she was saddened to think that on her grandmother's death it would also cease to function as a home. Unless of course the unknown Pierre decided to live here. She herself could never afford to do so; nor would she have the time.

Her thoughts raced into the future. If she became successful she might be able to make the château her home, her very own castle in Provence, in whose tranquillity she could rest and design her new collections!

Pushing aside the fantasy, she pondered what she had learned this evening. In refusing to see her daughter after her runaway marriage, the *comtesse* had hurt no one except herself, for by the time she had repented her behavior, it had been too late to make amends; her daughter was dead. The hope that her granddaughter would appease her conscience had been doomed at their first meeting years earlier when Miranda—faced with an autocratic, elderly stranger—had burst into a storm of tears and run from the room. Small wonder that her grandmother had returned to France and not contacted her again; and might never have done so had Alain Maury not offered to buy the Chambray land. Only then did pride in her heritage convince the *comtesse* to offer her granddaughter the chance of retaining the family home—something that would be easy to do once they had Maury money.

Miranda walked along the gallery. Even with money to maintain the château she could never live in it. It was a home for a family and deserved more than being used as a weekend retreat from London or Paris. If Pierre Chambray did not want it, either, then her grandmother should accept Alain Maury's offer to buy it with the land; at least then it would remain intact.

Miranda was filled with sadness. If only she could have shared her childhood with the frail, but proud, old lady she was beginning to know and love. How much they would have gained from each other. She glanced down into the hall, savoring the faintly musty odor of brocade and tapestry, the resinous smell of wood lovingly polished over the centuries. What a deep sense of security there was in having a background like this. Yet her mother had left it all for love. Perhaps the very strength of her heritage had given her the strength to leave it.

Would she herself have such strength? It was difficult to know, for she had never been in love. Never had time for it, in fact. Unaccountably, she felt a pang of regret.

Her work might suffice for a time, but it would be wrong to let it become her only way of life.

What was stopping her from remaining at the château and preparing the designs for her new collection? Where else would she find such tranquillity—a library to work in, her every need catered for and a beautiful landscape to give her peace of mind?

"The *comtesse* will see you now." Simone stood in the gallery, her face as long and dark as her dress.

With a murmur Miranda went into the bedroom to tell her grandmother of her decision.

"I can't believe it!" the *comtesse* sighed happily. "It is what I have prayed for. Now we can really get to know each other."

Having made her decision, Miranda was surprised at how contented she felt. It was as if, from the moment of her arrival, the château had laid hands on her heart. Brought up in a London apartment, surrounded by neighbors who came and went, she was astonished that bricks and mortar could mean so much to her.

SHE WROTE IMMEDIATELY to tell her father of her change of plans:

> I'll come home when I've finished my designs. Then I'll rent a workroom and hire a couple of models and someone to help me make up the clothes. But I'll certainly be staying on for the next six weeks. You've no idea how wonderful it is here. Mother must have loved you very much to leave this place.

Within a few days an answering letter came from her father, enclosing an enormous bundle of fabric samples for next spring, which several manufacturers had sent her. Ridiculous to think that this April she was looking at materials for next year.

"How many clothes are you going to make?" her

grandmother questioned, looking with interest at the swatches on Miranda's lap.

"About twenty. That's as much as I can afford. And don't offer to help me, because I'll refuse."

"It's not shameful to accept help. There would be no strings attached to it."

"I know. But unfortunately, I'd supply my own!"

Miranda stood up and dumped the samples onto the chair. Rummaging in the pocket of her yellow dress, she found a matching ribbon and tied her long, honey gold hair away from her face. It made her look like one of Wordsworth's daffodils. "Working here is going to be like an extended holiday."

"May I see your sketches—or do you like to keep them secret?"

"I've no secrets from you," Miranda smiled. "Besides, for a little old lady living in the country you've got a keen eye for fashion!"

"When Louise was young we bought our clothes in Paris—we could afford it then."

Talk of clothes overcame the discretion that had kept Miranda's curiosity quiet since her arrival here. "Were you very rich at one time?"

"Rich enough not to think about money! Henri—your grandfather—never discussed it with me. It wasn't until he died—when Louise was seventeen—that I discovered we'd been living on capital and that there wasn't much of *that* left, either!"

"It must have been a shock."

"I managed."

Indomitable spirit came through in the two words, giving Miranda a clear picture of the penny-pinching that must have taken place in order to conserve money without altering appearances.

"At least you never thought my father was a fortune hunter," she said and instantly wished the words unspoken, for her grandmother's expression grew sad.

"I *never* doubted his love for Louise. I just used to

pray he loved her enough to leave her. It's only in recent months that I realized that even if he *had* gone away, she would have followed him.''

A faint sigh concluded the words, and glancing at her watch, Miranda saw it was three o'clock. ''You're missing your afternoon nap. Have a rest and I'll come back later.''

The *comtesse* was about to reply when the telephone rang. Simone could be heard answering it, and a moment later she padded in carrying the receiver extension.

''Monsieur Chambray is calling from Paris,'' she muttered and plugged the telephone into the wall.

Uncertain whether to go or stay, Miranda hovered by the door until her grandmother fluttered her hand toward a chair. Quietly she sat down, listening to the one-sided conversation.

At first the *comtesse* seemed angry as she answered questions and asked several herself. But as the call continued, her voice softened, and by the time it came to an end she was smiling.

''Pierre called to apologize for not replying to my letter. But he was in the United States and only came back last night. He will be coming down on the weekend to meet you.''

''It's a long way to come just to see *me*,'' Miranda murmured.

''There will be much to talk over,'' the *comtesse* said. ''The future of the Chambray estate rests with you both.''

''Sorry, *grand'mère*,'' Miranda said hastily and stood up. ''Now have your nap. I'll be back for tea.''

''I didn't think you'd be back to see *me!*''

With a soft laugh Miranda touched her fingers to the bony cheek, then walked through the open French doors to the terrace.

It was difficult to believe that in England the skies were gray, and people were still wearing woolens. Here the temperature was in the high sixties, and the azaleas bordering the lawn were a riot of color. The sun blazed down from an electric blue sky, yet the air was still clear and faintly moist. Did it ever have the aridness depicted in so many of Cézanne's paintings, she wondered, or did the streams that flowed down from the mountain ranges keep this area of Provence moist and lush?

She set off across the grass, her steps making no sound on the springy turf. Maurice, whom she had glimpsed once or twice since her arrival, spent a good part of each day tending the grounds in sight of the château windows, but even this barely kept the weeds at bay. He made no attempt to do anything with the land that could not be seen by the *comtesse's* vigilant eye, and the farther Miranda walked, the more she felt she was entering a landscape untouched by human hand.

No sound broke the stillness of the day; neither a droning insect nor a bird, and it was not till she had been walking for about a half hour that the chatter of water came to her ears. The ground had begun to slope sharply and she was not sure if she was still on Chambray property. Several large boulders and many small rocks lay scattered around, and she picked her way carefully past them. The descent was steeper than she had imagined, and the lower she went the cooler the air became.

Coming around a bend in the path, she found herself on a flat ridge of land that dropped down precipitously to a narrow gorge where water roared along in its headlong flight from the distant mountains. Careful not to lose her footing, she walked to the edge and peered over.

She had to look a long way down.

Several hundred yards below, the water dashed itself against the huge boulders that lay tumbled on the riverbed, foaming in fury to find its path even partially blocked. Moving her eyes from the angry water, she studied the land on the far side. Small areas of the mountainside appeared to be cultivated, and she guessed there must be several paths leading down to the valley. But there was none she easily saw, and unwilling to continue with her exploration, she turned to go back.

A flash of blue caught her eye, and she swung around to look at it. Farther along the edge, almost hidden by a stunted tree that jutted out from the sparse earth, a small rose bush triumphantly flourished.

With cry of pleasure she ran forward to look at it, her amazement growing as she saw several buds and some half-opened flowers. It was incredible that a rose bush should be flourishing at this time of year. She bent to examine it, savoring the heady perfume. No wonder Monsieur Maury had spent years trying to perfect it!

Carefully she pulled off several of the opened flowers—it was a shame to leave them here to die unseen—and cradling them in her arms, she scrambled back up the sharp incline to the more gently sloping land.

Skirting the terrace, she went through the kitchen garden—where herbs stood in neat little rows like sentries—to the large, old-fashioned kitchen that cried out for ten servants and now had to be satisfied with one. Miranda found a plain white china bowl and arranged the flowers in it, so intent on what she was doing that she was unaware of someone watching her until she looked up and saw Simone's dark, baleful eyes.

"I found these on the mountain," Miranda explained. "I thought my grandmother would like them."

"She will like anything you bring her," the old housekeeper said, her voice thin with dislike. "Having you here has given her great happiness. But what will happen when you go?"

"I'm not going yet. I'll be here for at least two months."

"That will only make it worse when you *do* leave! It is wrong of you to stay. Wrong and thoughtless!"

"It is not your business to question what I do."

"It is my business to look after the *comtesse*—the way I've looked after her since your mother ran off and left her! The way *you* will leave her when you've finished using her!"

At last the woman's fears were disclosed, the reason for her dislike openly stated. Knowing it was not jealousy, but the anger of genuine concern, Miranda's own dislike of her faded.

"Even when I go back to England, I intend to come and see my grandmother as often as I can."

"You say that now—while you're here—but once you have gone you will forget her!"

"Wait and see," Miranda replied, and picking up the bowl of roses, walked out.

The front door was open, as it usually was at this time of day, and sunlight streamed into the hall, falling across one wall like a bar of gold and catching Miranda's hair as she skirted the side of the staircase.

The man coming in through the door stopped with a strangled sound. Hearing it, Miranda turned and saw a thin, serious-looking young man in a dark suit. His tanned face was unsmiling, and his amber brown eyes were watching her intently.

"So we meet again," he said.

"I'm afraid I don't—" Miranda said and then stopped with a gasp as she recognized the insufferably rude man she had met at the airport. "What are *you* doing here?"

"I have called to see the *comtesse*."

If he was curious about her own presence, he hid it remarkably well and ignoring her, knocked on the door of the salon and went in.

Miranda heard her grandmother greet him warmly, and wondering unhappily who he could be, she followed him inside.

"I'd like you to meet Alain Maury," her grandmother said. "Alain, this is my granddaughter, Miranda Dixon."

So this was the propagator of the blue rose! Setting down the bowl she was carrying, Miranda made a pretense of rearranging the flowers; anything was better than having to face the man whose eyes she could feel boring into her back.

"My granddaughter was most intrigued by the story of the blue rose," the *comtesse* continued. "She thought it highly romantic."

Miranda swung around before her grandmother could

say any more. "Did you discover the rose by accident, *monsieur?*"

"It took me three years to produce a hardy strain."

"But without a scent?"

"Without a scent," he conceded, "until I discovered it would grow on *this* land."

Miranda crossed to a chair and sat down, wishing she was wearing something more sophisticated than yellow cotton. Having regarded her green suit as a ridiculous getup, he would no doubt find this simple dress more suited to his unsophisticated taste. Not that he himself looked particularly unsophisticated, she thought, studying him from beneath her lashes; for at close quarters his manner was aloof, and his features as well cut as his navy jacket. Not an easy man to know, she surmised, seeing temper in the nervous flaring of his nostrils and impatience in the twitch of his thin, but well-shaped, mouth. Too well shaped, she thought; there was something almost effeminate in its curve. Not effeminate, she amended quickly as, aware of her regard, he stared back at her. There was too much steel in his character for that.

"I have told Miranda you wish to buy my land," the *comtesse* was saying, "but I cannot give you an answer until she and Pierre have talked it over."

"Indeed?" The tenseness of the man's body belied the unconcern of his voice. "I was under the impression that Pierre made his home in Paris."

"He has. But if Miranda wished to live here . . . ."

Miranda stirred restlessly, wondering if her grandmother was deliberately trying to forget that she had already turned down this suggestion. But before she could speak, the man had swung around to face her, his amber-colored eyes gleaming like topaz in his dark face.

"I had heard that you were here only for a holiday, Miss Dixon. The land can mean nothing to you."

"It's Chambray land," she said coldly, determined that though she would eventually concede he was right, she would at least make him sweat a little.

"But you can have no use for it," he insisted, "and I

have told the *comtesse* I am willing to increase my offer.''

"I will discuss it with Pierre. He will be here this weekend.''

Alain Maury looked at the *comtesse*. "I will come and see you next week, if I may.''

"Miranda will call you," the *comtesse* said, extending her hand.

Alain Maury raised the bony fingers to his lips. The old-fashioned gesture became him surprisingly well, turning his superciliousness into courtliness.

"*Mademoiselle.*" Amber eyes, no longer solicitous, but hard as agate, looked at Miranda. "I hope your stay here is a pleasant one.'' With a final bow in the *comtesse*'s direction, he walked out.

Not until his footsteps had died away did Miranda feel free to speak.

"So that's Alain Maury! Do you remember my telling you about that rude man at the airport?''

"Not Alain?" The *comtesse* gave a laugh. "So I wasn't wrong in sensing sparks between you. But I had the feeling it was caused by something more than a disputed taxi.''

"Taxis can be important when you want one,'' Miranda said, "and he was livid with me for getting to the stand first.''

"His humor is not the best," the *comtesse* acknowledged. "He has never recovered from Lucille's death.''

"He was married?" Miranda was surprised that any girl could have been foolish enough to fall in love with him.

"He was engaged," came the correction. "A month before his marriage Lucille fell to her death on the mountain—near the ledge where you found these roses.''

Despite herself Miranda felt shock. "Was Monsieur Maury with her?''

"No. He was in Grasse. She had gone walking on her

own. I am rather hazy about the details, but as you can imagine, the tragedy affected him deeply.''

Miranda was silent. The death of his fiancée might well have affected the Frenchman, yet she doubted if he had been an easy man to get along with even before it had happened. His arrogance was inbred, and though in another person tragedy might have had a softening effect, with him it had had the exact opposite.

But she must not allow her dislike of him to motivate her behavior. If he wished to buy this land, she had no right to prevent him.

"If you are satisfied that he has offered you a good price," she said firmly, "you should sell."

"The château, as well?" the *comtesse* asked faintly.

Miranda hesitated and then decided that bluntness was less cruel than the raising of false hopes. "The house as well—unless Pierre wants to live here. *I* would never be able to."

"When you spoke to Alain, I had the impression you had changed your mind about leaving here."

"I did it to annoy Monsieur Maury."

"I see," the *comtesse* said again. "I hadn't appreciated that you disliked him so much."

"Neither had I until I saw him again," Miranda said slowly. "I don't think I've met anyone I've disliked more!"

CHAPTER FOUR

IN A bright red sports car as exuberant and dashing as its owner, Pierre Chambray arrived at the château late on Friday afternoon.

In her bedroom, where she had gone to read a book on fashion she had discovered in the library, Miranda heard him mount the stairs, his voice amused as he teased Simone.

Excited at the prospect of meeting another member of the family, she decided to wear one of her more sophisticated dresses that night. First impressions were important, and she was determined to show this man that she was too sophisticated to succumb to her grandmother's matchmaking; that this was in the *comtesse*'s mind had become increasingly obvious in the last few days. Pierre had undoubtedly been given all *her* vital statistics and a character outline, too—and she was going to make it clear that she had every intention of remaining her own mistress. Certainly never mistress or wife to a Frenchman!

Alain Maury's face flashed into her mind, and she tugged a comb furiously through her hair. What on earth had made her suddenly think of him?

Opening the wardrobe, she debated between black crepe and geranium jersey. The jersey won, and she zipped herself inside its clinging folds and clasped a wide, tightly fitting band of glittering jet around her waist. To suit the almost medieval simplicity of the dress, she brushed her hair into a pageboy, the ends curving toward her chin and emphasizing her high cheekbones and the delicate planes of her face.

It was the first time since her arrival that she had worn a long dress, and the skirt floated behind her as she went down the stairs, making her feel like a chatelaine in her very own castle. As indeed it could be if she said the word. Quickly, she pushed the tempting thought aside and went into the salon.

The *comtesse* had also dressed for the occasion, her usual pastel wool replaced by black taffeta, with a sparkle of diamonds at her ears and throat. But it was the man standing beside her who commanded Miranda's attention, for he looked more like an explorer than the advertising executive she knew him to be. He was tall, broad shouldered and blond, with freckles spattering a wide forehead and reddish blond brows marking the palest of blue eyes. His nose and mouth were large, as were his hands, which reached out and caught hers in a warm clasp.

"So you're Miranda." His voice suited his appearance, being deep and reverberating. "Admirably named, I may say. I can see why *Tante* Emilie was so insistent about my coming here."

"I'm glad we can meet," Miranda replied. "After all, we're the only Chambrays left."

"A saddening thought. At the turn of the century there were at least fifty."

She was surprised. "What happened to them?"

"More daughters than sons—and two wars, of course. I'm the last male in the line." He grinned. "I try not to think of it, but every time I come here *Tante* Emilie reminds me of it."

"It hasn't done much good," the *comtesse* commented.

The man's reply was forestalled by Simone who came in to announce dinner, and Pierre escorted his aunt to the dining room.

He displayed the same deferential attitude toward her as Alain Maury, though he was more humorous with it. This might have been because he was a member of the family. The French were sticklers for etiquette, Miranda knew, and no stranger would have dared tease the *comtesse* the way Pierre was doing.

As always, dinner was excellent, and Pierre made appreciative noises at every course, particularly at the superb claret. "Is the Latour in honor of Miranda's presence or mine?"

"It honors you both," the *comtesse* said. "You are of equal importance to me."

He relaxed visibly at the words, and Miranda wondered if he had been afraid that her presence here would affect an inheritance he had always regarded as his own. Not that there was all that much to inherit. A decaying château too big to be used as anything other than an institution or school, and acres of barren land that had only acquired value because of their use to Alain Maury.

Alain Maury. What a difference he could make to their lives!

Coffee was served in the salon, and Pierre entertained them with a racy account of his stay in the United States.

"Do you have many clients there?" Miranda asked.

"The one I just got is the first. Two other agencies were competing for the business, but we got it because we were French."

"Then the client's either in perfume or fashion!"

"Fashion," he grinned. "He has 300 stores and is planning to open up in Europe."

"Do you know much about fashion?" she asked.

"For a million-dollars account, I'll learn!"

"That sounds rather—most expedient," the *comtesse* chided.

"Business *is* expedient." Pierre Chambray was lighting a cigarette, and he paused with a match in his hand. "Believe me, *Tante* Emilie, it doesn't matter whether you're making tractors, selling groceries or working on the stock exchange; once you're dealing with people for profit, you have to watch out for the main chance!"

"You sound as if you've no ideals at all," Miranda could not help saying.

"Ideals and making a lot of money are not good bedfellows!" His smile was sly. "Excuse the metaphor, but I'm French!"

She smiled back. "I still think it's possible to be a success and keep your principles."

"In a profession maybe. Not in business."

"Alain is a man of principle." The *comtesse* entered the conversation, though her remark seemed momentarily to end it, for there was a long silence.

"Alain's in a different category," Pierre said at last. "He may not be unscrupulous in monetary terms, but he is as far as his emotions are concerned. He puts business before everything else. If he didn't, Lucille would still be alive today."

"You're repeating gossip," the *comtesse* reproved. "You should know better than that."

"Forgive me. But you will at least admit that when it comes to business, Alain knows what he's doing."

"He is extremely successful," the *comtesse* agreed, "but he is honest."

Pierre grunted, but the look he cast Miranda spoke volumes.

"We must discuss the land," the *comtesse* said suddenly. "It is one of the reasons for you being here."

"I thought you had agreed to sell," he said sharply.

"Not quite. I wish to make sure that neither you nor Miranda will regret it if I do."

"The land's going to waste," he replied firmly. "Far better to sell it to someone who can use it." Aware that he had spoken before Miranda had been given a chance to reply, he looked at her apologetically. "I take it you agree with me?"

"Yes."

"There you are then!" Pierre said to his great-aunt. "Accept the offer and go on a spending spree!"

The *comtesse* folded her hands in her lap. "It is a considerable amount of money. Alain telephoned me tonight and doubled his offer!"

For the first time that evening Pierre was speechless, and enjoying the sensation she had caused, the *comtesse* went on, "You can thank Miranda for *that*. She gave him the impression she didn't want to sell the land. That's why he increased the price—providing I confirm the arrangement before the weekend is over."

Pierre turned a respectful look toward Miranda. "When it comes to business tactics, you don't do so badly yourself!"

"It was unintentional," Miranda said hastily. "Monsieur Maury got the idea I wanted to live here."

"Don't apologize for what you did," Pierre said exultantly and swung around to his aunt. "This land must be more important to him than I'd realized. Are you sure he only wants it for flower farming? He could buy thousands of acres around here without doubling his offer to *you*."

"He needs the land in the valley," Miranda intervened. "Don't you know?"

"Know what?"

Miranda looked at her grandmother. "I'm sorry, *grand'mère*, I thought Pierre had been told."

"I didn't do so because I was anxious to avoid—" the *comtesse* hesitated "—anxious not to have the sale of my land turned into an auction."

"An auction!" Pierre looked angry. "Good heavens, *Tante* Emilie, what's the matter with you? You've been struggling over money for years, and when you get the chance to make some . . . . If you would kindly tell me the whole story . . . ."

"Those blue roses," the *comtesse* said, pointing to the flowers whose heady perfume filled the room, "cannot be grown with a scent anywhere else except on my land."

"*Enfin!*" Pierre's breath was expelled on a sigh. "At last it makes sense! No wonder he doubled his offer. We must think carefully before we accept it. We might be able to make him go higher yet."

"There's a market price for everything," the *comtesse* reproved. "Alain is no fool. He knows what the land is worth."

"He's already offered you double what it's worth! Everyone up here has land for sale, and it's likely to be that way for the next hundred years. It's only because of these flowers of his that *this* land is important to him. I wish you'd told me about it before. Still, you haven't signed anything, so it's not too late." Pierre was pacing the floor and not bothering to hide his excitement. "It's a good thing Miranda arrived when she did, otherwise you'd have given him the land for a song."

"Alain is our neighbor," the *comtesse* said quietly. "I have no intention of holding him up for ransom."

A wary look came over Pierre's face. "Think what a difference the extra money would make to the château," he said softly. "Neither Miranda nor I could afford to run it the way our finances are now. But with Alain's offer . . . . Don't you see what it means? We could afford to keep the château and make it as magnificent as it used to be!"

"You—you always said you preferred to—to—live in Paris," the *comtesse* faltered.

"Because I can't earn a living anywhere else! But do you think I *want* you to sell the château? I'm a Chambray, *Tante* Emilie—this place is part of my heritage!"

"You never gave me that impression."

"I was trying to pretend I didn't care."

Color came and went in the lined face, and with an effort the *comtesse* composed herself. "You young people are so adept at hiding your feelings. . . . Sometimes it is difficult to believe you have any."

"It often requires money," Pierre replied dryly, "to indulge in your feelings, and that's something we've always been short of."

"And if we had the money—would you be willing to live here?"

"Certainly." The reply was loud and clear. "But

Miranda takes precedence over me, *Tante* Emilie. She is
your granddaughter.''

"My home is in England," Miranda said quickly.

"My estate will be divided between both of you," the
comtesse said imperiously.

"Please don't talk about it!" Miranda cried, putting
her arms around her grandmother's shoulders. "You'll
live for years yet. I want you to spend the money on
yourself."

"I want it for the house."

"Then spend it on the house and enjoy living in it! But
for goodness' sake stop talking about leaving your
money to us." She glanced at Pierre. "Do you agree with
me?"

"Without question. We French are inclined to be too
practical. It leads to morbidity!" Bending over his aunt,
he swung her into his arms. "You must go to bed. In the
morning I will go to Grasse and talk to a few people I
know. I want to find out what makes these roses *so* important to Alain."

"Their scent," Miranda put in. "It's out of this
world!"

"That shows how poor my nose is!" Pierre laughed
and, striding over to the door, pushed it open with his
foot. "Don't disappear, Miranda," he called over his
shoulder. "I'll be back to talk to you."

Left alone, Miranda thought about her newly met
cousin. Even if the sale of the land brought sufficient
money to restore the château to its former glory, she
could not envisage him leaving Paris to live here. Though
she had only just met him, she was positive his only interest was in the money itself.

She ran her hand over the marble mantelpiece. At least
he had the kindness not to let his aunt know he did not
share her love for the château. What would its future be?
A finishing school for rich socialities or an orphanage?
She shook her head. It was too isolated to be practical for
either.

"What deep thoughts are you thinking?" Pierre had returned, as quiet as a panther, giving her no chance to compose her face.

"Just that you're not the type to settle down in the country," she replied bluntly. "You'll be in a fix if *grand'mère* leaves you this place."

"*You* are closer kin than I am!"

"I don't want anything from my grandmother," Miranda said vehemently.

"She has already made her plans. You won't be able to stop her. If Alain buys the land, there'll be a lot of money involved. At least half a million francs. Maybe double before we're finished."

"You're not going to ask for *more?*"

"Who knows? I'll decide when I've been to Grasse."

"And spoken to your spies?"

"My contacts," he smiled. "It always pays to have contacts." He walked over to the sideboard. "Care for a brandy?"

"No, thanks." She watched as he poured one for himself and returned to sit in a chair in front of her.

In repose he was older than she had first imagined, at least thirty-five with an experienced face that added to his attraction, as did the cynicism that touched his mouth. Here was no callow youth, but a man of the world who knew the worth of his charm and would not hesitate to use it.

She considered his remarks about Alain Maury. The pleasure of annoying the young Frenchman was beginning to wear thin, and what had begun as an impulse earlier that afternoon was now developing into a deliberate business ploy that she found distasteful. Worse still, she could almost feel sorry for Alain, whose only desire was to grow his wonderful roses.

"I think there's something nice about using land for flowers," she said. "Flowers and food—that's what land is all about."

"And houses and schools and roads!" He sipped his brandy. "Don't tell me you're a romantic?"

"Half the time!"

"Which half of you designs clothes?"

"Both halves," she smiled.

"I've been told you're very talented."

"Don't believe everything *grand' mère* says."

"She has told me nothing. I heard it from some friends in London."

"Your contacts?" she asked dryly.

"My spies!" he laughed. "They say you'll go to the top."

"Only if I'm lucky."

"Success is all around you," he said confidently. "I sensed it the moment we met." He flexed his hands. "I admire success more than anything in the world."

She remembered the dashing red sports car parked in the driveway. "You haven't done so badly yourself."

"A small salary and a big expense account. In terms of real money I'm a nonstarter." There was unexpected bitterness in his voice. "I was brought up to believe that being a Chambray was the greatest thing that could happen to you, and I was eighteen before I realized that money in the bank—even if it had only been there a few weeks—meant more than a name that had been with you for generations!"

"Most people start their careers without money," Miranda retorted, "and without a family name, either. Take Madame Maury—she began with nothing."

Pierre grinned. "You've put me in my place, *chérie!* From now on I won't complain."

She decided to change the subject. "Have you known Alain Maury long?"

"Since he was thirteen. That's when he moved here. I was already living at the château with my mother, and he used to follow me around like a puppy. Success changed him for the worse. It often does."

"I thought you admired success?"

"Only if it comes from talent. And his comes from a lust for power. That's all he cares about!"

"It's understandable in a way," she murmured. "The girl he loved is dead and—"

"He killed her," Pierre said. "He killed her as surely as if he'd pushed her over the ridge!" Miranda stared at him in astonishment, and seeing it, he shrugged. "I thought you knew?"

"*Grand'mère* said it was an accident—that she fell."

"She jumped. There's no doubt of it. And Alain blames himself. There's no doubt of *that*, either."

"Did he say so?"

"Words weren't necessary. From the day Lucille died he acted as though she'd never existed! She was living at his house at the time, and before the funeral had taken place he had her clothes packed and sent to a welfare mission! He wanted nothing left to remind him of her."

"Grief makes people act strangely."

"It was strange enough to attract comment."

"Villages are notorious for rumors."

"The police made inquiries," Pierre said casually.

"The local constable trying to keep the gossip quiet, I suppose," she said scornfully.

"A member of the Sûreté," Pierre corrected.

Miranda swallowed her discomfiture. "Did you know the girl?" she asked.

"Of course. She was Madame Maury's goddaughter. She had known Alain since they were children and was in love with him for years. But he didn't want to settle down. It was only because of his mother's insistence that he agreed to do so." Pierre frowned. "He changed his mind again a month before the wedding, and she couldn't face being jilted. So she killed herself."

The matter-of-fact way in which Pierre spoke only served to heighten the poignancy of his words.

"What a waste of a life," Miranda whispered.

"I agree. That's why your sympathy for Alain is unwarranted. He has an adding machine where his heart should be.''

''He's made some wonderful perfumes,'' she remarked.

''He's got a nose for business!'' Pierre quipped. ''And we must have the same. I'm sure we can get him to increase his offer for the land.''

Pity for the unknown Lucille destroyed Miranda's earlier sympathy for Alain Maury. ''See what you can find out in Grasse. Then we can decide.''

''Good.'' He stood up. ''Shall I carry *you* to your room?''

She laughed and with a twirl of skirts preceded him to the hall. Together they went up the staircase, pausing at the top to look down at the hall.

''I love this place,'' she murmured. ''I never thought bricks and mortar could mean so much to me in such a short time.''

''You're more of a Chambray than I am,'' Pierre said lightly. ''I wouldn't care if I never saw it again.''

''What will you do if *grand'mère* leaves it to you?''

''Retain it if there's enough money to do so and hope you'll come and share it with me!''

His words made her look at him. In the dim light his eyes were in shadow and his expression difficult to read. The lift at the corners of his mouth could have been tenderness or humor. Deciding to ignore the comment, she walked to her room. Pierre followed her and leaned against the wall as she opened her door.

''I hope I won't wake up tomorrow and find you have disappeared,'' he said.

''You can always find me in the library,'' she laughed. ''I work better there than anywhere else.''

''Work?'' he asked.

''I'm designing a collection. I hope to start up on my own.''

''You should try to persuade Alain to give you the blue rose scent. If you launched your own perfume as well as your own clothes you'd be in the money right away.''

"I'd need a stack of money to do it," she retorted, "but I'll bear it in mind for the future—if I don't end up back in wholesale again!"

"You won't," he prophesied. "I feel it in my bones."

"What else do your bones tell you?"

"Many things." He caught her hand and raised it to his lips, his eyes mocking yet tender. "Many things."

CHAPTER FIVE

Tired though she was, Miranda did not sleep well that night. What she had learned of Alain Maury returned to haunt her dreams, and she awoke at six, heavy eyed and listless.

Padding over to the window, she opened the wooden shutters, already warm from the sun, though the air that flowed over her shoulders held the cool of dawn. This was the loveliest time of day: the grass glittering with dew, the moisture in the air intensifying the colors of the landscape—greening the leaves, browning the earth and making the sky seem a deeper, more vivid blue.

In the pristine light of early morning the dark tragedy of Lucille was already fading. Perhaps it had been the way Pierre had told the story—his every remark about Alain filled with dislike—that had made her feel as if Lucille's unhappiness had been her own personal one. But now she no longer felt it. Alain Maury's past had nothing to do with her, and she must forget it.

It was barely seven when she went downstairs, and quietness lay like a shroud in all the rooms. She went into the kitchen to make breakfast: a jug of creamy milk taken from the large can left at the back door several hours earlier by a farmer, a wedge of yellow butter, crisp, golden *biscottes*—she was too hungry to wait for the warm croissants to arrive from the village—and a jar of homemade apricot jam with the tang of lemon and a subtle taste of fresh almonds.

All this, together with a pot of fragrant coffee, she carried out to the terrace where the early morning sun was just appearing to warm the tiled floor. Basking in the rays, she begn to eat. Around her the landscape was coming to life; a breeze stirred the pointed heads of the cypresses and ruffled the wide skirts of the olive trees, making the lower leaves dance like flounces on a ball gown. An electric saw whirred in the distance, while from near at hand came the bleating of goats as they began their daily wander on the mountainside.

Miranda's tenseness slowly evaporated. There was a magic in this part of Provence that made it impossible for her to be anything other than blissful.

"You look as if you're going to melt into the scenery," a deep voice said, and her cup clattered into her saucer as she looked around and saw Pierre. In tan slacks and a fine spun silk jacket of that particular shade of blue called French navy, he looked more handsome than she had remembered; his eyes a brighter blue, the faint lines fanning out from them indicating humor as well as experience.

Drawing up a chair, he sat beside her. "What brings *you* down so bright and early?"

"Work," she said, unwilling to tell him of her restless night. "You're no lie-abed yourself."

"I'm off to Grasse," he reminded her and fell silent as Simone appeared with a tray.

The woman's taciturn face creased into a smile as she set it down in front of him, and she muttered to him in clipped French, which Miranda could not understand. It was only when he answered, his tone clearer, that she knew they were speaking in the local patois, and it made her realize that for all his world-weary air, he was still a country boy.

"Were you born here?" she asked as Simone went away.

"In Alsace, actually. My father was killed in a mining accident and *Tante* Emilie invited my mother to make her home here."

"Then you must remember *my* mother."

"Very well." He broke a croissant, buttered it liberally and ate half in one gulp, with quick, relishing movements. "Much as I hate to admit it, dear cousin, I'm thirteen years older than you, and I have a great many fond memories of Louise." The smile left his face and his expression grew somber. "And some sad ones, too. It was a bad time at the château when she ran away with your father."

For the first time someone whom she considered outside the family circle was talking about her parents. Though a Chambray, Pierre had been too young to be emotionally involved in what he had seen, and though his opinions might still be clouded by all he had overheard, he had come sufficiently far from the past to have formed a more unbiased opinion of his own.

"Did you know my father, too?" she asked diffidently.

"Louise once got him to take us both out to tea." Pierre ate the other half of the croissant and reached for another. "He struck me as a typical Englishman—solid, dependable and smoking a pipe! I've always remembered that pipe. He lit it when we were having tea, and it made Louise cough. He put it away immediately."

"I don't think he ever lit it again," Miranda told him, "but he still carries one and fills it, as well!" She hesitated and then said, "Do you think he was wrong to marry my mother? Don't spare my feelings, Pierre."

"I'm always truthful to my partners, *chérie*. It's my one virtue! No, I don't think he was wrong. Besides, if he'd run off to Timbuktu, Louise would have followed him. Like most placid types she could be extremely obstinate when she wanted, and there was no doubt she wanted your father."

"Thank you for saying that. You don't know how much you've helped me." Miranda pushed back her chair. "I must get on with some work."

"I'll see you when I get back from Grasse."

She walked to the end of the terrace as far as the open

doors of the library. Only as she reached the threshold did she pause and turn back to look at Pierre. "Why did you say I was your partner?"

"Because we're working together in the business of getting a better price from Alain," he laughed, and laughed again as she gave an exclamation and disappeared.

MIRANDA WAS SEATED at the beautiful marquetry desk, her sketch pad open in front of her, when she heard Pierre drive away. Ruefully, she looked at the blank sheets. Half an hour and not a single line drawn. Resolutely she poised her pencil on the paper, but it remained motionless, and after a moment she flung it away and stood up.

It did not help to have peace and quiet in which to work if one did not also have peace of mind; and if Pierre had done nothing else, he had disturbed her sufficiently to make concentration impossible. The past was too alive to be buried, and memories she had thought forgotten were now surfacing to irritate her.

More than ever she deplored the bitterness that had prevented her grandmother from seeing her years ago. How much they would have benefited from each other! Even after a short acquaintance there was an affinity between them that stretched across the difference in their age and upbringing.

Miranda sighed and ran her eyes over the bookshelves. For a small château, the library was unusually extensive, though many of the books were still so stiff she doubted if they had ever been opened, let alone read.

To her surprise she had found that many of the books were in disorder, as though they had been taken out and then replaced at random. The dramatic works of Victor Hugo stood side by side with the gossip of Saint-Simon, while the brothers Thierry were cheek by jowl with Stendhal and the poems of Baudelaire. It made looking for a book a labor of love, and also an exciting treasure hunt, for she had come across a volume of hand-engraved drawings depicting French dress from the six-teenth to the nineteenth century. The publishing house was a Parisian one, and the author's name appeared on no other book in the library.

When she had shown it to her grandmother the *com-tesse* had professed ignorance about it. "I've never been a great reader, I'm afraid. Perhaps Henri—your grandfather—or Louise bought it." The fine brown eyes were curious. "Is it valuable, then?"

"I don't know. It's mainly that it's very interesting to *me*."

"Then take it back to England with you, my child, and any others you want."

"I wouldn't dream of taking any books. They must remain here—where they belong."

"I wish *you* felt like the books," the *comtesse* had sighed and set about her embroidery again.

Miranda remembered this last remark as she stood fin-gering one of the leather-bound volumes, and she was saddened at being unable to fulfill that wish. Her eyes roamed the shelf nearest to her, and idly, she picked out a Colette novel from where it nestled next to some Théophile Gautier poems. What a mess the books were in! If she had the time she would love to put them in order. Perhaps next year . . . . But next year—if her col-lection was a success—she would be too busy to take a holiday. She yawned. How far away the London fashion scene was from this rural backwater, and how different the musty peace of this room from the brightly lit and over-crowded workroom at Mr. Joseph's.

She walked back to the desk and closed her sketch-book. She was obviously not in the mood to work this morning, and rather than fight a losing battle, she would do better to use the time to complete several errands: mail a letter to her father, see if the local news dealer sold felt-tipped pens and replenish her stock of gouache paints.

Collecting her handbag, she set off for the village. Her

hair swung against her face as she walked, and she drew
out an emerald ribbon from the pocket of her full-skirted
dress and pulled her hair back into a ponytail. It made her
look no more than sixteen, until one saw the provocative
slant of her eyes and the voluptuous curve of her mouth.

The single village street had its usual influx of shop-
pers, elderly women in long black skirts with laced-up
boots and laced-up faces, and younger housewives in
cotton dresses or knitted suits; but all had the common
denominator of bulging shopping bags. Several opulent
cars were parked beside the fountain in the village square
while their owners, casual yet well-dressed women of in-
determinate age, placed their orders with the butcher or
the greengrocer or waited for the arrival of the refriger-
ated fish van, which came from Cannes to sell them shiny
black mussels, gray and coral-spotted shrimp and the
lumpy *loup*—as familiar to the housewife in Provence as
cod is to her counterpart in England.

Aware of several pairs of eyes watching her, Miranda
crossed the cobbled street to buy some stamps at the *bar
tabac* and then entered the news dealer's. But though she
found some pens, she could not find any gouache.

"You'll only get those in Cannes or Nice," the shopkeeper said and turned to serve someone else who had
come in.

Glancing around, Miranda saw a girl of her own age.
That she was French was unmistakable; it was apparent
in the neat figure with its small, high breasts and short
waist. That she was rich was equally unmistakable, for
the short black hair that fell away from the high forehead
and curved forward on the narrow, rouged cheeks had
been cut by a master hand, as had the beautifully tailored
black linen dress and handmade shoes and bag that
shrieked Rome.

Feeling as if she had stepped off a wholesale dress
rack, Miranda returned the other girl's cool stare.

"Would you know if there's an artist's shop in
Grasse?" she asked.

"I should think there must be." The girl's voice, like

her appearance, was careful and controlled, her French perfect and Parisian. "You are English," she added, her face showing its first sign of interest.

But it was a very dispassionate interest, Miranda decided, meeting the steady brown eyes fringed by short, thick lashes that stuck out so straight they gave the eyes a doll-like appearance not echoed either by the aquiline nose or the beautifully shaped, but thin, mouth.

"My accent always gives me away," Miranda smiled.

"It wasn't your accent," came the cool reply, "as much as your tone of voice. All Englishwomen sound like schoolgirls!"

"*Mademoiselle* is the granddaughter of the Comtesse Chambray," the proprietress interrupted.

The French girl looked momentarily discomfited. "I heard you were here, but I'd formed the impression of a—" she hesitated "—of a different type."

"Don't let appearances fool you," Miranda answered. "What you heard might have been right!"

The brown eyes narrowed like those of a lynx. "But you don't know what I heard."

"You obviously hadn't imagined me as a typical English-schoolgirl type!"

"That is certainly true. Quite the contrary, in fact."

The girl picked up a newspaper and went out, giving Miranda a faint nod as she did so.

Miranda followed and saw the black linen figure entering the *bar tabac*. Parked outside it was a silver gray Citroën, the latest and most expensive model, and even as she paused beneath the shadow of a plane tree she saw the girl reemerge from the café and walk toward it. But it was the man beside her who commanded Miranda's attention, for she had not expected to see Alain Maury again so soon.

He was holding a carton of Gauloises under his arm, its blue matching his silk sweater, and as she watched him, he took out a cigarette, lit it and then flung the match away. As he did so, he raised his eyes and stared directly into hers. Even though she was some distance away, she knew he had recognized her, and though she had an illogical desire to turn and run, she realized it would be rude to do so and remained where she was as, with a remark to his companion, he strolled across the road to her side.

"Good morning, *mademoiselle*, so we meet again."

"That's hardly surprising. Bayronne isn't very big."

"Do I detect regret in your voice?"

"Regret?"

"That it is so small that we *should* meet again?"

Staring at him, she saw no humor in his eyes and knew he had asked the question in all seriousness. What a peculiar man he was, she thought, and tilted her head defiantly.

"I can think of more pleasant things than meeting *you, monsieur*. After all, our meetings have hardly been pleasant ones."

"I did not think our second encounter was unpleasant."

"I still remember the first one."

"Surely, *I* am the one who should feel annoyed about it? After all, you *did* take my taxi."

She gasped at his effrontery, and taking advantage of her silence, he went on, "Would it not be more civilized to pretend our first meeting was at the château? One should always be on the best of terms with one's neighbors."

"I'm only a temporary neighbor."

"But you are the *comtesse*'s granddaughter."

Before Miranda could answer, the French girl had come to stand beside them, placing a proprietary hand on the man's arm.

"Do come on, Alain. We'll never get to Grasse by eleven."

"I'd like you to meet Miss Dixon first."

"We met at the news dealer's—though we didn't introduce ourselves." The girl held out her hand. "I'm Colette Dinard."

Miranda forced herself to smile, but as she made a move to turn and walk away, Alain Maury spoke again. "Has your grandmother told you that I spoke to her last night and increased my price?"

"Yes."

"I hope you will persuade her to accept my offer—and quickly. If the roses are not planted soon, they will not be ready for next season."

"The decision is entirely my grandmother's," Miranda said steadily. "I am afraid you misjudge my position."

"I know your position very well," he said emphatically. "I am sure your grandmother will do as you wish."

"I have *no* wishes on the subject."

"Then if you are truly unbiased, perhaps you would be good enough to encourage the sale. At least I could put the land to some use, while substantially increasing the *comtesse*'s bank account!"

Miranda dug her hands into the pockets of her skirt. "Some people don't think money is as important as you do, *monsieur*."

"I *never* think about money," he said gravely. "It is only when you have none that it becomes important enough to think about!"

Her cheeks flamed. "The Chambrays may be poor, Monsieur Maury, but they are rich in tradition!"

For an instant he looked taken aback, then his dark brows drew together in a frown. "I did not mean to be rude, *mademoiselle*. You misunderstood me. I was merely stating a fact. When one has all the money one needs, one no longer considers it. I hope you will forgive me for saying so, but it is well known that the *comtesse* has been worried about her financial position for years. If you could persuade her to accept my offer, she would at least spend the remainder of her life without such problems."

"I have already told you that the decision is my grandmother's," Miranda reiterated, "but if she listens to anyone, it will be Pierre."

"Pierre!" There was no mistaking the anger in the man's voice, nor in the way he turned his back on her and marched to the car.

Scarlet-faced, Miranda continued down the street. Behind her she heard Colette Dinard's laugh, and blindly she opened the door of the first shop she came to and went in. Anything to get away from that infuriating couple!

She found herself in the local *pâtisserie* and debated between buying some hazelnut crescents or a packet of sugared almonds. She decided on the almonds and was paying for them when the silver gray Citroën flashed past the window. Package in hand, she stepped back into the street. Her pleasure in the village had evaporated, dispelled by her meeting with a man whom she had disliked at first sight. What bad luck that he had turned out to be her neighbor! It had been bad luck for him, too, she acknowledged, for had she not disliked him, she might well have persuaded her grandmother to accept his offer for the land.

Even now she knew she would eventually do so, for no amount of prejudice could make her jeopardize the future of those wonderful blue roses. She drew a deep breath, as though the air itself could conjure up the magic of their scent. What a heavenly perfume it would make! No wonder he was so anxious to produce it. She could not blame him for his single-mindedness, for it was a characteristic they had in common, though he probably had more characteristics in common with Colette Dinard.

Was she his fiancée or just a friend? There had been more than an attitude of friendship in the way the thin-fingered white hand had rested on his arm, and there had definitely been possessiveness in the cool voice that reminded him they should be on their way. Yet if she had been his fiancée he would have introduced her as such. That meant they were only friends; though she was convinced this was something the French girl intended to change as soon as she could.

The passing windows gave Miranda back her reflection, and seeing her full skirt and ponytail, she laughed out loud. Now she understood the remark that Colette Dinard had made to her in the news dealer's. Having heard about her from Alain—who had assuredly been anything other than complimentary—she had not expected Miranda to look like a teenager. More probably like a hard-faced gold digger with a decidedly garish way of dressing!

So intent was she on her thoughts that she collided with a woman emerging from a cobbled alleyway.

"I'm so sorry," she apologized. "I didn't see you. My thoughts were miles away."

"So it would seem."

Unthinkingly, Miranda had spoken in English, and she was surprised to hear English in reply.

"I hope they were happy thoughts," the woman continued. "You hit me with such force I had the impression you were wishing you were a steamroller!"

"That would be one way of getting rid of my obstacles," Miranda laughed and looked more closely at her perceptive neighbor.

She was in her early fifties and made no attempt to pretend otherwise. Yet despite her simple wool suit and lack of make up, she was extraordinarily good-looking, with a generous mouth, almond-shaped eyes and flawless skin.

"I'm sorry I turned *you* into one of the obstacles," Miranda apologized again. "I hope I didn't hurt you?"

"Not at all," the woman fell into step beside her. "Are you here on holiday? It's rather early for tourists."

"I'm staying with my grandmother."

"You can't mean . . . you're not the Comtesse Chambray's granddaughter?"

"You have the edge on *me*," Miranda said ruefully, finding it disconcerting to be known without knowing in return.

"I can easily remedy that." The woman held out her hand. "I'm Adrienne Maury. I believe you know my son."

Dismay that this charming woman was the mother of such a disagreeable man kept Miranda quiet.

"You look surprised," Madame Maury said.

"I am. You're not a bit like your son."

"I have the feeling that's meant as a compliment!"

Miranda lowered her eyes. "Was I so obvious?"

"Not more so than Alain," came the amused retort. "You both ruffled each other's feathers!"

Miranda half smiled at the picture it brought to mind: *I'd have yellow or green feathers*, she thought, *but his would be black*.

"Stop looking so fierce," Madame Maury said, "and join me for coffee. At my house," she added as Miranda looked toward the *bar tabac*. "Then I will drive you home."

Miranda hesitated. She longed to know more of this charming woman, yet was reluctant to accept the offer in case it meant meeting her son. Yet he was on his way to Grasse, she suddenly remembered.

"Coffee sounds like a wonderful idea," she agreed. "I'd be delighted to join you."

SITTING BESIDE MADAME MAURY in a small white Mini Cooper, they drove out of the village in the opposite direction from the château, but turning steadily as they did so, which would, Miranda knew, bring them around in a circle to meet the Chambray land at its nearest point to the tall mountain that sheltered the village from Grasse itself.

Massive stone pillars heralded the entrance to the Maury estate; no doubt now of its owners' wealth, for no money had been spared in tending the sweep of lawns that rushed in a tide of green to the smooth walls of an austere, but elegant, house with its long line of deep blue shutters. Bougainvillea cascaded like a purple waterfall around the front door, which was open to the warm day and through which bounded a golden-haired Labrador at the sound of their car.

Madame Maury led the way inside. The house was a

perfect foil for its chatelaine, with cool, tiled floors warmed by richly colored rugs, and elegant furniture in a mixture of antique and Italian modern. There was a wealth of pictures and sculptures from the elongated figures of Giacometti to the smooth curves of Arp and the abstraction of Barbara Hepworth.

"Alain's taste," Madame Maury said, intercepting Miranda's glance. "I prefer more realism."

The abstract would suit Alain Maury, Miranda decided; not for him the sensuousness of an Epstein or the warmth of a Henry Moore.

She found herself in a small sitting room off the main salon. This was obviously Madame Maury's retreat, for fashion magazines littered a low table, together with a pile of lavishly illustrated cookbooks.

"My vice," the woman laughed, pointing to them. "I collect cookbooks the way other women collect diamonds!"

"Less expensive!"

"Alain says it was pure chance that prevented me from mixing cakes instead of cold cream!"

It was Miranda's turn to laugh. "I can't believe it was merely an accident that made you famous."

"My dear, I don't consider myself famous!"

"You're a household name."

"You make me sound like a detergent!"

"Nowhere near as polluting! Your cosmetics are wonderful."

"You use them?" Madame Maury looked pleased, and Miranda was glad she could truthfully answer yes. "You're the type of girl I had in mind when I brought out my last line."

"Modern Miss?" Miranda asked in surpirse.

"Of course. You fit the bill exactly."

"Not in this dress."

"Possibly not—but I've heard about your green suit!"

Miranda sat down quickly. "Your son was very rude about it."

"He was in a temper. When he is, he often says things he doesn't mean."

A maid came in with coffee and biscuits, and not until she had gone did Madame Maury resume speaking. "He was most distressed when he met you at the château last week."

"Why?" Miranda asked, knowing full well what the answer would be.

"Because he was afraid you would try to stop him from buying the land."

"That's ridiculous!"

"I hope so. The blue rose means so much to him. It would be a bitter blow if he couldn't cultivate it."

"Why is it so important?"

"Because it will make a magnificent perfume—you must know that for yourself—and also because it's the first one he's created for several years." A shadow crossed the serene face. "It was a great worry to him that he hadn't done so since . . . . Still, now he *has*." The almond-shaped eyes, their warm sherry brown color so like her son's, saw the look on Miranda's face. "It requires great talent to create a perfume, you know."

"I didn't know," Miranda admitted bluntly. "I imagined you worked out what essences to use and just mixed them up. Perhaps not as simple as that, but—"

"It requires flair and enormous perseverance to develop a new scent," Madame Maury reiterated. "You'd realize it for yourself if you could smell some of the rubbish I've been asked to sell. Alain has the ability to mix one essence with another in a way that will bring out the most unusual bouquet. A great perfume isn't one scent only, you know, it's a subtle blend of many."

"And your son has great subtlety!"

"You two *have* gotten off on the wrong foot! It's such a pity. I'm sure you would have liked each other if you had met under different circumstances."

Miranda stiffened, for the words indicated that Alain Maury liked her as little as she liked him.

"My son is on the defensive with women," Madame Maury continued. "That day at the airport he was anxious to get to Grasse quickly. Some blue rose essence had been distilled in the laboratory, and he wanted to start blending it when it was at a special temperature. He'd timed everything to the split second, and he was worried he'd arrive too late."

"He should have explained," Miranda said lamely.

"It was a lengthy explanation to give while fighting over possession of a taxi!" The generous mouth was definitely smiling now, and Miranda smiled back.

"You make our argument sound very trivial."

"Most arguments are."

The woman poured coffee from a silver pot and handed a cup to Miranda who sniffed the aroma and then sipped.

"This is delicious!"

"Alain blended it."

"Coffee, too?"

"If you've a 'nose,' you can blend anything!"

Conversation became more general after this, though Miranda quickly realized she was being adroitly pumped as to her reasons for coming to the château and her plans for the future. There was no doubt Madame Maury was anxious for her son to grow his blooms, and since this could only be done on Chambray land, what better way of overcoming any possible obstacles than by charming the *comtesse*'s granddaughter. Miranda was faintly disappointed. Her liking for her hostess had been so spontaneous that she had foolishly hoped it had been genuinely reciprocated.

"I'm so glad we have finally met," Madame Maury was saying. "I find you very *sympathique*."

Miranda said nothing and felt sherry brown eyes regarding her quizzically.

"I did not arrange for you to bump into me," the woman chided, the acute perception of her remark belying the languor of her manner. "Nor had I made any plans to meet you. It was pure chance."

"But you used it," Miranda said before she could stop herself. "I don't blame you, of course. I know you're anxious about the perfume and—"

"Not the perfume, my dear—my anxiety is for Alain. If I hadn't found you so understanding, I wouldn't have tried to enlist your help. You see, I admit I am trying to do so—but that is only because I find you understanding. My son has great personal unhappiness, and . . . ."

"My grandmother told me." Miranda set her cup on the table. "Pierre spoke about it last night, too."

"Pierre knew Alain very well—and Lucille, too. But after she died, Alain withdrew from everyone. It was as if he had to remain alone until he had grown another skin."

The words gave Alain Maury another dimension, a deeper more complex character, which, while it did not mitigate the things Miranda disliked about him, at least helped her to see them in a more understanding way. Or was this another deliberate tactic to get her sympathy?

"My grandmother is letting Pierre decide about the land," she said. "I'm sure it's just a matter of money."

"I hope you're right. Alain thinks your grandmother might decide to keep the estate intact for you and Pierre."

"I'm leaving Provence in a few months," Miranda said firmly. "The château can never be my home."

"Nor Pierre's?"

"He *might* keep it if he has sufficient money, but he could just as easily give it up and never come down here again."

"Perhaps Alain should offer to buy the entire estate."

"No," Miranda said vehemently, "I don't want my grandmother to know there's any doubt about Pierre making the château his home."

"I see. In that case we will say nothing. But you might perhaps mention it to Pierre. It may interest him to know that if we had the land we would also be willing to give him a good price for the château—whenever he wishes to sell it."

"That's bribery."

"It's good business!"

"French people talk of nothing else," Miranda sighed and stood up.

"I will drive you back," Madame Maury said, smiling.

"There's no need. It isn't far to walk. I can cut across your land, can't I?"

"Of course. It's a bit complicated until you reach the mountain, but after that you just follow the path around it till you get to the other side."

Madame Maury led Miranda into the garden and gave her further directions that would bring her to the point where the two estates met.

"Don't forget to come and see me again."

"Even though I can't promise to help you?"

"Even though!" Madame Maury smiled.

Miranda set off down the slope. Much as she would have enjoyed seeing her hostess again, she did not feel she would be made welcome if Pierre put a high price on the land.

Yet the Maurys were business people and should expect such things to happen. Once the blue roses were grown, she had no doubt about their commercial success. Neither had the Maurys; hence their determination to produce them. Besides, they were so wealthy it would make little difference if the price were raised, whereas it would make a great deal of difference to her grandmother. And Pierre, too, she admitted. Though she herself had no intention of accepting any financial gain from the sale, she knew he had no such inhibitions. And why should he have? He was not only a Chambray born, but also a Chambray bred, which was more than could be said for *her!*

So immersed was she in thought that she reached the mountain path before she had expected it, and she paused and looked around her.

The grass here was thin and interspersed with rocky outcrops that made a random pattern on the sloping incline. A few stunted trees clung tenaciously to the sparse earth, their branches pointing downward to where the waters of the *vallon* rushed precipitately along the narrow path that cut like a swath of silver between one mountain and another. Yet they were not mountains in the strict sense of the word; for the most part their incline was so gradual that much of the land could be terraced and cultivated, and only here and there were sudden steep sections—almost vertical in appearance—which acted as nature's boundaries to mark one terrace from another.

She was curious to know what had caused these abrupt drops, for it was almost as if giant fingers had haphazardly scooped out sections of earth. It was probably due to erosion and might well mark the path of hidden mountain streams that had washed away the earth until only bedrock was left, leaving insufficient hold for trees. Each succeeding winter's gales eroded the rock even more until, over thousands of years, the land had become barren, developing the dangerous fissures that now existed there.

Was it down one of these that Lucille had fallen to her death? Or been pushed?

Miranda shivered. What had made her think such a thing? Pierre said he blamed Alain Maury for the tragedy, but surely he had meant a moral responsibility and not an actual physical one?

Once again she resumed walking. The path became narrower and more difficult, occasionally crumbling away beneath her feet so that she was forced to hold onto the stunted bushes that had taken the place of the grass. It was much harder going than she had envisaged, and the farther she went the worse it became, the path almost disappearing, so that several times she had to search for footholds on the rocks. The earth was porous and had an unpleasant way of slipping beneath her feet. Several times she felt herself sliding down toward the *vallon*, and only managed to stop herself by digging her hands hard into the ground. Not that any harm could come to her, she kept reassuring herself, as she made laborious progress across the mountain. The incline was steep, but not so precipitous that she would be unable to stop herself if she were unlucky enough to lose her footing. Gritting her teeth, she inched her way forward, wondering why Madame Maury had not warned her what to expect. She would certainly never come this way again.

Out of breath, she paused. Though it was well after midday, the air there was cool. The sun did not penetrate far into this valley, and only the land above her lay basking in its rays. The sound of water was louder here, and though trees and bushes prevented her from seeing it, she could not mistake its rush and gurgle. It was almost as if it had a life of its own and was talking to her. Annoyed at being so fanciful, she continued walking. If anything, it became more difficult, for the ground was so slippery it was like walking on glass, and several times she was forced to sit down and inch forward on her buttocks, which did no good to her dress and even less to her temper.

Rubbing her hands, which were skinned and bleeding, she debated whether to retrace her steps or to continue, but deciding she had come more than halfway, she resolutely pushed on.

A large, smooth boulder loomed ahead, jutting out so far that it blocked her vision. It also blocked off the path she was trying to follow, and she realized she would either have to climb above it or below it. She gritted her teeth and decided to go below; at least if she fell, she would not have so far to go.

Carefully, she began to edge around the rock and, knowing she would not find any fingerhold on its surface, searched out clumps of grass of give her more anchorage.

The stream seemed nearer at this point, and looking down she glimpsed swirling foam some fifty yards below. Would it be better to go right down to the bottom and hope to find a path beside it? She scanned the ground and decided to remain where she was.

Her decision was justified, for laboriously inching

around the boulder, she found herself back on the proper path. But a few more yards of scrabbling and she was once more facing an outcrop of rocks. It did not block her way as much as the first ones had done, and she was able to squeeze past them without difficulty. But nervous tension suddenly took hold of her, and she sank down on one of the boulders and drew deep gulps of air, forcing herself to keep calm. She *must* be nearing the top of the mountain; it was impossible to think otherwise.

But fear rose up in her again, and she felt sweat bead on her forehead. Several strands of hair had escaped from her ponytail and lay in damp, dark gold tendrils on her forehead. With shaking hands she brushed them away from her face, then taking her handkerchief from her pocket, she tried to rub some of the dirt from her palms. But sharp pieces of grit were embedded in the skin and tears of pain made her stop. Putting her handkerchief away, she stood up and resumed walking.

She had gone only a few yards when falling stones made her stop again. Someone was ahead of her, hidden from sight by a turn in the path.

Even as she waited, the steps came nearer. Instinctively, she stiffened and, aware of it, chided herself for being silly. It was probably a shepherd looking for a sheep or goat that had strayed. Yet she had heard no animal bleating, and she took a quick step forward, jerking back as a man came precipitately around the path and bumped into her.

"*Mon Dieu!*" he exclaimed and then stopped. "What on earth are *you* doing here?"

Miranda looked into Alain Maury's astonished gaze. "I'm on my way home."

"Across the *mountain?*"

"Obviously," she said sarcastically. "Or did you think I'd dropped down from heaven?"

"Not in that mood!" he answered, his mouth twitching slightly as he took in the angry sparkle of her eyes. "You look as angry as hell!"

"I might well have ended up there!" she retorted furiously. "Your mother must have been crazy to tell me to come back this way. If I'd lost my footing, I could have broken my neck! As it is, I've ruined my hands." She flung them out. "Look at them!"

He stared at the red, bleeding skin, and instantly the sarcasm left his face. "Wait here," he ordered and disappeared from sight almost as though he had melted into the very side of the mountain.

Only as she looked more closely did she notice a narrow aperture half hidden by an enormous bush, and cautiously she inched forward to peer inside. But the interior was black and gave nothing away, nor could she hear anything.

She stepped back and waited. A moment passed and then two. She drew a deep breath and was debating whether to move on when she heard footsteps again, and almost at once Alain emerged from the cave holding a soaking wet handkerchief.

"There's a little spring back there," he explained. "I want to wash your hands."

"It can wait till I get home."

Ignoring her, he caught her wrists and with quick, but surprisingly gentle, movements dabbed at the skin, removing dried blood and several small flints. He worked intently, seemingly unaware of her eyes fixed on him, and she had a better opportunity to study him than at any time before.

Pierre was thirty-five, so that meant this man was about thirty. He did not look it, for his face was unlined despite its gloomy expression, and there was a faunlike appearance to his physique. He looked up unexpectedly, and she saw that his eyes were an unusual shade of brown. Like sherry that had been poured into a sunlit glass.

Annoyed at her fanciful thoughts, Miranda colored and pulled her hands away from him.

"I don't think you'll find them so painful now," he said matter-of-factly.

Gingerly, she flexed her fingers, wincing slightly. "They're much better. Thank you."

He regarded her, head to one side. "Am I to understand that my mother directed you to return home this way?"

"Yes."

"You must have misheard her—or else you missed the fork."

"What fork?"

"Where the paths meet." Seeing her blank look, the frown cleared from his forehead. "You come to it about a hundred yards after you start walking along the mountainside. A second path cuts across the main one. It descends for a few yards and—"

"I saw that," she interrupted, "but I didn't take it because I thought it led down to the *vallon*."

"It gives that impression, but in actual fact it twists up again and brings you out here." He inclined his head behind him.

"You mean I could have avoided all *that?*" She waved a hand along the path she had just come.

"Completely," he agreed. "The route you took is hardly walkable. Just a track for nimble-footed goats."

"And I'm no goat," she said ruefully. "No wonder I found it hard!"

"I must warn mother to be more careful next time she gives directions. But I don't think she's ever come this way herself, so she doesn't know there are two paths." Once more he looked concerned. "It is most unfortunate you had to be a victim of her lack of knowledge."

"Not a victim," she said, mollified now that her hands were not stinging so badly, "but you should certainly tell her not to send anyone else this way without being more explicit."

"Strangers rarely take this shortcut, and all the locals know it without having to be told."

His words, reminding her that this was not her home, also reminded her that she was not his friend, and with a polite movement she went to walk past him. But he turned and kept in step with her. "I'll see you safely back to the château."

"There's no need."

Ignoring her remark, he continued at her side, and though Miranda quickened her pace, he appeared not to notice, merely lengthening his stride to match hers. Her breath came faster, but she set a quicker pace still, dismayed when she felt a sharp twinge in her side. For several yards she was able to overcome it, but she was finally forced to slow down, irritably aware that her companion showed no sign of discomfort, nor was he breathing any faster than normal.

"Rest a moment." His quiet order indicated his awareness of her pain.

In view of her flushed face and panting it would have been difficult to deny it, and she seated herself on a rock.

He remained standing in the middle of the path, his head thrown back, his shoulders stiff, so that again she was conscious of his tension.

"What were *you* doing on the path?" she asked.

"I often come here. Not many people do, and it gives me a chance to be alone and think." He hesitated. "I hope I will soon be hearing from your grandmother about the land?"

"Pierre will be calling you."

"I had hoped to avoid dealing with *him*."

"His interest is more than mine, Monsieur Maury. You can't expect him not to become involved."

"He hasn't bothered with the estate for years—why should he do so now?"

"Because you have made it valuable."

Alain Maury gave her a strange look. "I wonder if you realize the implication of your remark?"

"Of course I do. But it's no sin to be commercially minded. *You* are."

"I offered your grandmother a fair price for the land."

"Not all that fair if you're willing to double it!"

Color warmed his tan. "I need the land, and I need it at once if I'm not to miss next season. That's why I increased my price."

"I appreciate your urgency, *monsieur*, but you must also appreciate our fears."

"Fears of what?"

"Of regretting the sale once it's been made."

"Or of not holding out for an even higher price!"

"That, too," she agreed.

"Everything has a value," he said tightly. "You would do well to remind Pierre of that."

"If the price Pierre asks is too high, you can refuse to buy."

"Is that what you want? There's no shortage of land in this part of Provence, Miss Dixon. On the coast maybe, but not here." He thrust his hands into the pockets of his slacks. The gesture pulled the blue material across his hips and she could see the taut line of his thighs. "It's only because this particular soil has the right mineral content that I want to buy it. But if *I* don't buy it no one else will!"

"Then my grandmother will be no worse off than she is now," Miranda said crisply.

"Nor will I."

"You want your perfume, don't you? Or do you have another formula up your sleeve?"

"Do you think they grow on trees?" he exploded. "It takes years to get successful ones! Making a new perfume isn't like making a dress. It takes hundreds of hours and dozens of people, and you can still end up with nothing!" His voice shook with fury. "For the first time in four years, I've created a perfume I believe in—one that all women will want. But if I can't get the land to grow the roses, I might just as well throw them away!"

There was so much anguish on his face that Miranda averted her head. She had never realized a perfume could mean so much to anyone that they could look as haunted as this dark-haired Frenchman was looking now. No wonder Madame Maury was so anxious for him.

"I hadn't realized the blue roses meant so much to you," she murmured as lightly as she could.

"You don't realize it even now," he said coldly. "To you and Pierre it's merely a question of money. But to me it's a question of—" He stopped, and when he continued, his voice was without emotion. "If you continue a few yards farther along the path, Miss Dixon, you will come out onto a lower lawn in front of the château."

Without another word he turned and walked away from her. Stones crumbled beneath his feet, and a bush trembled as he passed it, then a bend in the path hid him from sight, and she was left alone.

More moved than she cared to admit, Miranda continued on her way.

CHAPTER SIX

IT WAS ONE-FIFTEEN when Miranda reached the château and, not even pausing to make herself tidy, ran into the dining room where her grandmother and Pierre were already seated.

"I'm sorry I'm late," she apologized, "but I took a shortcut back from the village and got lost."

"We would have waited for you," the *comtesse* said, "except that it was a souflé—and they cannot be held up."

Acknowledging the truth of this, Miranda began to eat, glancing across at Pierre as she did so. She longed to know the outcome of his trip to Grasse, but decided against asking him here. In one thing at least they were in accord: not to do or say anything that might make her grandmother excited or anxious.

Because of her suppressed anxiety lunch seemed to take longer than usual, and she marveled that Pierre could mask his own feelings so successfully. Eventually, the meal was over, and the *comtesse* retired to her room to rest, leaving Pierre and Miranda to take their coffee on the lawn in the shade of an orange tree.

"I had a most interesting morning in Grasse," he said without preamble. "I learned a lot about Alain's activities. Or perhaps I should say his *in*activities! The blue rose essence is the first perfume he's produced since Lucille's death. That's why he's so desperate to grow the flowers."

"I know. Madame Maury told me so this morning." Miranda quickly explained how they had met and what had been said.

"It all bears out what *I* heard," Pierre said triumphantly. "Alain's scared he's lost his creative talent. Perhaps he feels it's retribution for the way he behaved to Lucille."

"Why do you blame him for an accident?" Miranda asked sharply. "It's the second time you've said it."

Thinking of her last encounter with Alain Maury—the way she had suddenly found him barring her path, his face inscrutable, the very air around him filled with tragedy—she could well believe he had something to do with the accident. But she could not believe he had encouraged his fiancée to kill herself.

"I'm sure her death was an accident," she said aloud.

"It was not," Pierre retorted. "Alain quarreled with Lucille and told her he didn't want to marry her. That's why she committed suicide. If you don't believe me, read it for yourself in the back number of the newspaper."

Miranda turned her head and looked at the bright sunshine dappling the lawn. All at once the grass seemed a more arid green and the sky a paler blue. Annoyed at her reactions, she tried to analyze them away. It was ridiculous to be partisan over someone she barely knew and did not like. Yet she objected to having a man maligned in his absence.

"I don't know why you're telling me all this," she said. "Monsieur Maury's personal life has nothing to do with our selling him the land."

"It's got everything to do with it! You have all sorts of scruples about increasing the price, and I'm trying to make you see how foolish it is when you're dealing with someone like him!"

"I've no intention of dealing with him." Impatiently, she jumped up. "*You* make the decision and talk it over with *grand'mère*."

"She won't do anything without your approval. My own inclination is to let him sweat for a bit. Give him a few days, and he'll increase his offer without being asked." There was a twinkle in the blue eyes. "In that way *I'll* be satisfied and so will your conscience—it's obviously bothering you to have to be businesslike toward a handsome Frenchman!''

Color reddened her cheeks. ''You're a handsome Frenchman, too, and I don't find it difficult being businesslike with you!''

''We haven't talked business together,'' he retorted, ''but thank you for the compliment, anyway. I hope you mean it.''

''You don't need *me* to flatter you. I imagine the girls must line up to do so!''

''Only French ones,'' he admitted unblushingly, ''and I've a penchant for the English.'' With one finger he delicately traced the line of her cheek, the tip of his nail coming to rest beside her lower lip. ''What a stubborn mouth you have, my dear and distant cousin.''

His head came lower, but with a deft movement she slipped away from him. ''I must get on with my sketches. I'll see you at dinner.''

''Are you running away?'' he called after her retreating figure.

''Of course. I believe in being safe, not sorry!''

In the library, where she went in order to maintain the myth that she was going to work, Miranda found herself thinking of Madame Maury and her son. There was something mysterious and elusive about them. It came not only from the way they looked but from the very aura they exuded. Curiosity stirred within her, and though she hated herself for the thought, she knew she would go to the newspaper offices and look through the back numbers to check on what Pierre had said.

From the distance the village clock struck four, and determined to put all thoughts of the Maurys from her mind, she picked up a pencil and began to sketch. At first it was difficult to concentrate, but slowly her surroundings and all the people connected with them began to dissolve, leaving only blank sheets of paper to be filled in by swift, sure lines that emanated from her fingertips like ectoplasm from a medium.

NOT UNTIL the darkening of the sky made it necessary for her to get up and switch on the lamps did she realize she had been working for several hours, and she yawned and stretched with a feeling of pleasurable tiredness, then wandered back to the desk to look at what she had drawn.

The designs were good; looking at them with critical eyes, there was no doubt of this. Indeed, they were the best she had yet done, with new ideas bursting from every sketch like buds from a branch.

There must be magic in the air, she thought and flung her arms wide. "You're a magic château," she cried aloud. "My magic castle in Provence!"

"Talking to yourself, or may I join in?"

She spun around to see Pierre, who carried a crystal decanter in one hand, two glasses in the other.

"A whiskey, for *l'heure bleue*," he added, pointing to the window, which dusk was already turning into a sightless eye.

"I rarely get the blues," she said, declining the offer, "and whiskey gives me hiccups!"

Setting down the decanter and glasses, he looked at the sketches on the desk. "May I?"

She nodded, and he bent over the loose leaves of paper. One by one he lifted them up and looked at them, casually at first, but gradually becoming more intent.

"They're sensational," he said finally. "Original without being gimmicky."

"They're not bad," she agreed.

"Are they for your new collection?"

"Hopefully. But I can't afford to make them all up. I'll have to choose a dozen of the best."

"They are all excellent."

"They need a bit more working on," she said, deciding to stem the flow of compliments.

"Agreed." He riffled through the pile and picked out a sketch of a suit and an evening dress. "These don't fit in with your general theme. They're too fussy. Best take out the pleats and cut down on the number of buttons, and they'll do fine."

She was astonished. "Don't tell me *you're* a designer, too?"

"I am interested in it," he said modestly. "Some of my girl friends are models!"

"Girl *friends?*" she quizzed.

"All my ex-mistresses are my friends!"

She laughed and perched on the edge of the chair. "It *will* be hard having to choose twelve from this lot."

"Can't you find a backer?"

"I don't want one. I want to be free to design what *I* like."

"Couldn't you be?"

"He who pays the piper calls the tune," Miranda said dryly.

"*I* know someone who wouldn't. Someone who'd let you play any tune you liked."

"Pull the other one!" she retorted.

"I'm not joking." He poured himself a whiskey and drank it at a gulp. "Have you heard of Christi's?"

"Of course. It was a top fashion house till Jacques Christi died. I've not heard about them since."

"They're still ticking over—just. Two new designers were brought in to take Christi's place, but neither of them was good enough. The last one was fired a month ago, and they're looking for a replacement. I think you would do admirably."

"Now I *know* you're joking!"

"Not at all." Pierre poured another drink. "Christi's is backed by Tissus Maurice—one of the biggest textile companies in France—and Monsieur Maurice is determined to keep Christi's going as an outlet for his fabrics. A successful couturier makes an excellent shop window for the fashion world to look at."

"No fashion house can keep going without a decent collection," Miranda said.

"That's why I want your sketches. Our company handles his advertising, so I know him fairly well."

"You're wasting your time. He'll want an established name for Christi's."

"They brought in two top names and failed with them both! That's why I'm sure it's worth a try. If Maurice likes your work, he won't be put off because you haven't got a big name." Pierre strode over and caught her shoulders. "Where's your faith in yourself? I thought you were convinced you were going to the top?"

"I am," she said staunchly, "but I expect to do it in my own way."

"Wouldn't you accept an offer from Tissus Maurice?"

"Of course I would. It's the sort of thing I dream about."

"Then dream a bit longer. I hope I can make it come true." He bent his head and swiftly kissed her lips.

From the loose way he held her she knew he did not mean to do more, but as he felt the touch of her mouth, his grip tightened and he kissed her again, more slowly and deeply. Miranda tried to resist him, but he was too expert, his touch too skillful, and without being able to stop herself, she was aroused.

"Well, well," her murmured, drawing away from her. "*Tante* Emilie's hopes might not be so farfetched after all!"

"Don't bank on it!"

He gave a soft laugh and, returning to the desk, picked up her sketches and went to the door. "I'll try to see Maurice tomorrow."

"But you've only just arrived here. *Grand'mère* will be disappointed if you leave so soon."

"I won't be leaving. Maurice has a house at Cap d'Antibes. He flies down most weekends. With luck he should be there tomorrow."

She caught her breath. "You make it sound so easy."

"Everything's easy if you know the right people!"

He went out, and after turning off the lamps, Miranda did the same.

As she changed for dinner into a black silk pleated dress that emphasized her creamy skin, she thought of what Pierre was going to do. Tissus Maurice was world renowned, and to be promoted by them could lead to undreamed-of success. Yet despite this, two people had already failed. It was a sobering thought, and she forced herself to consider the dangers that such backing could hold for her.

Her talent might be enough to excite the buyers in London, but was it enough to interest a worldwide market controlled by hard-faced men and women who dictated the tune to which the *couture* carousel turned? It was a frightening thought, and her heart hammered against her ribs. It was not too late to tell Pierre she did not want him to show her sketches to anyone. She could take them back and continue with her own plans in her own time. The thought was tempting—as playing safe always was—but there was not a spark of red in her hair for nothing, and dismissing safety, she decided to leave things as they were and let fate take over.

A MILD INDISPOSITION sent the *comtesse* to bed early that night, and Pierre suggested taking Miranda to Cannes.

"We can be there by nine and try our luck at the tables."

"The best way of trying my luck is to keep *away* from the tables!"

He chuckled. "Then just come and keep me company."

"I'm too tired." She looked at him with some curiosity.

"You can probably find dozens of women to amuse you."

"Dozens," he agreed. "But none as nice as you." He

sauntered across to her, hands in the pockets of his trousers. His stance reminded her of Alain Maury, who was so different in temperament and outlook. But then tragedy had left its mark on him, and she wondered what he had been like before the death of Lucille.

"What are you thinking about?" Pierre asked.

She shrugged, unwilling to let him know her thoughts.

"Are you sure you won't come to Cannes?"

"Positive. But don't let me stop *you* from going."

He looked apologetic. "Even a couple of days in the country gives me the creeps."

"You're obviously no nature-lover!"

"Are you?"

"I love it *here*," she admitted.

"Because you know it's only for a holiday. You'd hate it if it were permanent."

"I'm not sure. I might decide to give up work and settle for marriage and a cottage in the country!"

"Your talent would never let you rest. You've a seeing eye, and you'll only be happy when you're using it."

"You make me sound like a guide dog!"

He grinned. "That's what you are. The seeing eye of fashion—leading those who have no vision themselves!"

It was an ingenious compliment, and impulsively, she reached up to kiss his cheek. But he was too quick for her and turned his head so that their lips met.

Almost at the same moment she glimpsed a movement by the curtain and quickly drew back. But no one came in through the window, and she decided it had only been a breeze stirring the material.

"Go to Cannes for your gambling," she smiled. "I'll come and see you off."

Together they went to the front door where his low-slung sports car gleamed in the moonlight.

"What a vicious-looking thing it is," Miranda remarked.

"Like its owner?"

"You said it, not me!"

She watched as he vaulted into the front seat, switched on the ignition and drove off in a burst of exhaust fumes. Pulling a face at the noise and smell, she turned to go inside, and then changed her mind and went down the steps and across the lawn.

Like a tall, dark shadow she moved over the grass, her long skirt falling gracefully around her, her long, thick hair framing a face that the moonlight blanched of all color. The landscape was colorless, too, with black trees silhouetted against the sky and black shadows lying jagged on the ground. A breeze stirred the foliage near at hand, and a night animal—disturbed in its prowl for food—scampered away at her approach.

Behind her loomed the house, seeming twice as large in the dark as it did in the daylight, while in front of her the undulating hills appeared steeper, reminding her of the mountain and the sharp descent to the *vallon*. She craned her neck, but a bank of trees hid the mountain from sight. Yet its presence pervaded the atmosphere, and though she knew it was only imagination, she was sure she could hear the ice-cold waters rushing on their way to nowhere. A bird called in a tree, a high plaintive sound that startled her, and she picked up her skirt and sped back across the grass.

Straight into the smothering hold of a tall, black figure.

She gave a muffled scream, the sound dying away as the grip relaxed and a quiet voice said, "I didn't mean to startle you."

Astonished, she saw it was Alain Maury. "What are *you* doing here?"

"I came to apologize. I was unnecessarily rude to you this morning."

"So it *was* you on the terrace!" she said involuntarily.

"Yes. You seemed busy and I—I didn't want to intrude."

"You wouldn't have intruded. I was only turning down Pierre's offer to go to Cannes."

"Are your turndowns always so demonstrative?"

"What's a kiss?" she shrugged.

"Something that shouldn't be given lightly."

"You're old-fashioned, *monsieur*." She set off across the lawn toward the terrace.

He kept in step beside her. "I'm sorry if I have annoyed you. I didn't mean to."

"You always annoy me."

"We must have an incompatibility of spirit!" He spoke insouciantly, yet there was nothing uncaring about the look on his face; lit by a sudden shaft of moonlight, it appeared bitter and haunted. "I had hoped we might be kindred spirits, Miss Dixon. That *your* ambition would help you to understand *mine*."

"I understand you very well. But it doesn't mean we're kindred spirits!"

They entered the drawing room, and he carefully latched the window before coming to stand by the mantelpiece. He was elegantly dressed in black: suede shoes, barathea trousers and a cashmere sweater. It made him look very lean and slight, which was surprising, for he was taller than Miranda by several inches.

"I hope the *comtesse* is well?" he asked.

"She has gone to bed. She was feeling tired."

"Not ill, I hope?"

"Certainly not." Miranda spoke sharply, and the man seemed taken aback.

"I do not wish the *comtesse* any harm. It was a genuine inquiry."

Miranda blushed. "I'm sorry. I'm sure it was."

"I have already told you I didn't come to see your grandmother," he continued. "I came to see you to—"

"Apologize for being rude to me," she reminded him.

"And also came to bring you these." He held out his hand, and she saw four tubes of gouache.

"How did you know I wanted them?"

"Colette told me. I happened to have some at the laboratory, and I thought they might tide you over till you get some more."

The thoughtfulness of the gesture left her speechless.

More so because it was unexpected. Contrition warred with the antagonism she felt toward him, and murmuring her thanks, she took the tubes and put them on the table.

"Would you care for a drink, *monsieur?*"

"A brandy would be welcome." He accepted it from her. "Aren't you going to join me?"

"I don't like the taste. The last time I had any it was to stop me from fainting!"

"What a waste of brandy! It can only be appreciated when one has total control of oneself."

"Then you should be able to drink it all the time!"

Deliberately he studied her. "You have a strange conception of my character. Contrary to your assumption, I frequently lose my control. You should talk to my staff!"

He twirled the glass in his fingers. They were long and slender, she noted, yet very strong. He was now looking at the brandy with the same intensity he had deployed on her. It was the sort of look often seen on young children. Not that there was anything childlike in his expression as he lifted his eyes to hers.

"Your hair is the same color as the brandy, Miss Dixon."

"It's lighter."

"Not at night." He held the goblet high so that the light from the chandelier glowed through the liquid. "It's exactly this color," he repeated, "but during the day it is the color of honey."

The compliment embarrassed her, and she tried to make a joke of it. "Brandy and honey. Are your comparisons always centered around food and drink?"

"I'm a Frenchman!"

She smiled and sat down on the settee. For the first time she saw virtue in her grandmother's incessant sewing; at least it kept one's hands occupied. Clasping hers together, she searched vainly for something to say.

However, the silence did not disconcert her visitor, and he sat down opposite her and crossed one leg over the other, his back rigid, his head high.

"Don't you ever relax?" she burst out.

"I'm doing so now."

"You're as stiff as a poker!"

Her words made him consider his position, and he moved his shoulders and uncrossed his legs. "Is that better?"

"Not much."

"I don't find it easy to relax," he confessed so apologetically that she laughed.

"You can say that again. You give the impression of a firecracker ready to go off at any minute."

"That is some kind of firework, is it not?"

She nodded. "It's a special kind that jumps all over the place and keeps exploding."

"I had not realized you thought me so dangerous!"

He chuckled, looking so much younger that she was amazed. Even his features changed when he smiled, his mouth softening into a pleasing curve, his eyes seeming larger when no longer marked by scowling brows.

"You should smile more often, *monseiur*. It makes you look human."

"To be human is to be vulnerable." The smile left his face abruptly. "And to be vulnerable is to leave oneself open to hurt."

"You can't go through life closed up like a clam! You'll miss out on so many other emotions if you do."

"I have no wish for emotion. It robs a man of strength."

"It can *give* you strength. Think of all the wonderful things people have done when they were emotionally inspired; the paintings and music that have been created; the books that have been written and—"

"Not with emotion," Alain Maury said vehemently. "With passion of mind, perhaps, but not with emotion."

"What's the difference between the two?"

"One is mental and of the spirit; the other is earthly and of the flesh."

"You sound like a tub-thumping puritan! What's *wrong* with earthly love? It makes the world go round!"

"You can do better than *that* trite comment."

"Because you had an unhappy love affair doesn't give you the right to mock everyone else." She stopped abruptly, her embarrassment increasing as she saw the lines of bitterness on his face. "I'm sorry, *monsieur*. I had no right to say that."

"You listen to gossip," he shrugged. "I am not surprised. Rural communities thrive on having a villain in their midst."

"Don't you mind?"

He shook his head. "People believe what they want to. I have no intention of trying to alter their opinions. Lucille is dead, and nothing will bring her back. The episode is over."

Miranda was unable to credit his prosaic tones. It was as if he were talking about a stranger and not a girl he had loved. "You make it sound as if she never existed."

"She didn't."

"What do you mean?"

"Forget it. Let us talk about something else."

"You're a hard man, Monsieur Maury."

"I am a realist."

The words reminded her of Pierre, though she could see no similarity between the two men. Pierre was a realist, but he was also warm and spontaneous, whereas this man was cold and calculating.

"I don't think we have anything more to talk about, *monsieur*. It is late and I—"

"We can talk about the blue rose," he said, "and the land I am anxious to buy."

"Is that all you care about? Land for your flowers."

"My blue roses are beautiful. They deserve to bloom."

"No wonder you've not time for emotion," she retorted. "You give it all to your flowers!"

"Do I?" With a swiftness she had not anticipated he was on his feet and gripping her by the shoulders. "Do I?" he said again and pulled her into his arms. There was no tenderness in his touch, no warmth to his kiss, just a deep, raw passion that demanded a response. And how skillfully he drew one from her! Detached and remote he might look, but there was nothing detached about the pressure of his mouth, which, feeling hers move beneath his, became insistent and searching. Held close in his arms, Miranda felt trapped by steely muscles. There was not an ounce of superfluous fat on him. It was as if his driving energy burned him up, giving him a tense vulnerability that added to the complexity of his character.

Not that there was anything complex in his actions, for he was the all-conquering male asserting his strength, arousing her ardor by the depth of his own. What had begun as a kiss of fury was now one of passion, and unable to stop herself, her arms came around his neck to draw him closer.

They drew apart simultaneously and stared at each other, hazel eyes shining, brown ones brooding. Though she was not sure what she had expected from him, she had not anticipated the furious way he put the distance of the room between them. The gesture was more hurtful than any words could have been, and she was dismayed by the hurt she felt. For a brief moment she had believed herself mentally close to this man, and his abrupt withdrawal showed her all too clearly that the affinity had not been mutual.

"I shouldn't have done that," he muttered.

"Forget it." She marveled that her voice could be so unconcerned. "We're in the twentieth century."

"Ah, yes. The permissive society."

"That's an old-fashioned phrase these days, *monsieur*. But then you *are* old-fashioned. It accounts for you trying to use sex to win an argument!"

The remark struck home, and he reddened, looking more saturnine than ever. "You weren't above using it yourself, *mademoiselle*. You deliberately provoked me."

It was impossible for her to disagree, and she was

wondering whether to ignore the remark or make some sarcastic rejoinder when she heard voices in the hall.

She hurried across the room and opened the door. Colette Dinard stood there, elegant in a long black satin skirt and jacket, her pink crepe blouse giving a warm sheen to her skin. Her short hair, sleek as ever, curved into the nape of her neck, showing off the well-shaped head and making her look like an elegantly dressed boy, or one of that strange breed of bizarre young women who had flourished in Germany between the two world wars. She was not at all the sort of person Miranda would have imagined capable of holding Alain Maury's attention, though perhaps this was because in picturing Lucille, the very name itself conjured up someone feminine and childlike, neither of which adjectives applied to the ice-cold Mademoiselle Dinard.

"Forgive me for coming here like this," the French girl said, "but Alain promised to be back in half an hour, and I was worried."

Failing to discern any worry in the hard eyes, Miranda was convinced that curiosity alone had brought Colette here. Was she so worried about holding Alain Maury's attention that she had to follow him to the château?

"Sorry, Colette, but it took me longer to get here than I had anticipated." The man came into the conversation for the first time, sounding faintly amused, as though he saw the truth behind her subterfuge. "You could have saved yourself a journey by telephoning."

"I couldn't get through. You know what village telephones are like."

"Now that you're here, I hope you will stay for a drink?" An imp of mischief prompted Miranda to play the *grande dame*. It would certainly be different from the ingenue she had appeared to be when she had met the French girl in the village that morning!

"There's no need to disturb yourself on our behalf," Alain said quickly.

"I'd love a drink," Colette Dinard overrode him and

stepped into the salon, looking around her with a curiosity she made no attempt to hide.

As she sipped a Grand Marnier she wandered around, picking up and putting down various objets d'art, almost as though she was an auctioneer coming to value the contents of the house. Miranda felt her hackles rise and slipped her thumbs beneath the wide jeweled belt that circled her narrow waist.

"Haven't you seen the château before, Madmoiselle Dinard?" she inquired.

"Only from the outside, and even then not until Alain told me of his intention to buy the land."

"My *hope* to buy it," he amended. "So far the offer has not been accepted."

"Surely it will be?" Colette stared openly at Miranda. "The land's just being wasted!"

"My grandmother cannot make up her mind," Miranda explained, "and she is going to let Pierre decide."

Colette laughed and looked at Alain. "Then you've nothing to worry about. Pierre's a businessman down to his fingertips."

From the remark Miranda guessed the girl knew Pierre, and she wondered why he had not told her so this evening. She would ask him about her tomorrow. She was curious to know Colette's background and her relationship to the man whom she treated so possessively.

"We must be going, Alain." Colette set down her glass and gave Miranda an empty smile. "Thank you so much for the drink, and please give my compliments to the *comtesse*."

"She will be sorry not to have met you." Miranda played the game of formality to its close.

"Another time perhaps." Red-tipped fingers rested on Alain's black-clad arm. "I brought the car with me *chéri*. I didn't think you'd want to walk back as well."

"That was thoughtful of you." He glanced at Miranda. "Thank you for your hospitality, *mademoiselle*. I hope we will meet again soon."

"I see no need for it," Miranda replied coldly. "I expect you'll be hearing from Pierre."

Her answer had the desired effect, for again color ran up into Alain Maury's face. Silently, he went out of the château and took the passenger seat of Colette's low-slung Italian car. It purred away as softly as a departing panther, and not until its taillights disappeared around a curve in the driveway did Miranda enter the hall.

What a strange ending to a strange day! So many incidents flashed through her mind that it was like looking at a kaleidoscope where everything formed a jumble and no cohesive pattern emerged: Pierre's determination to get the highest price for the land; her own ambivalence toward its sale due to her longing to live there, and her equally strong urge to build a career for herself; Madame Maury's devotion to her son, and her son's devotion to the blue rose. And above all, this last meeting with Alain Maury.

How strangely he had spoken of his fiancée. What had he meant when he said the girl had never existed? And how could you love someone who did not exist?

There was no answer to any of these questions, though the questions themselves gave credence to the gossip Pierre had said was rife about Alain's relationship with Lucille. If the girl had never existed for him, it was easy to infer that he had not loved her. Was it this knowledge that had sent her plunging to her death? Somehow Miranda could no longer believe the fall had been an accident.

Disturbed by her thoughts, she tried to rationalize them. No normal girl would end her life because of a broken engagement. Nor would any normal man goad his fiancée into killing herself in order to get rid of her. What had really happened between them? She refused to believe he had become engaged to satisfy his mother's desire to see him married. He had far too much character to be persuaded into doing such a thing. Could it have been a simple change of heart—the realization that he did not want to give up his freedom after all? And could

Lucille—heartbroken—have committed suicide because of it?

Miranda pushed her hair away from her head. Would *she* commit suicide if she were jilted by the man she loved? Would any girl—other than an unstable one—do so in this day and age? Remembering Pierre's injunction that she read the newspaper account of Lucille's death and judge for herself, she decided to do exactly as he had suggested.

"I'm turning into a gossip monger," she thought and said the words aloud, hoping that by doing so she would destroy their credibility. But curiosity remained with her. Nothing gave a man a more glamorous image than to be the center of a mystery, and the only way to stop thinking of him was to find out the whole truth about him.

Destroy the myth, and the man with it.

Tomorrow she would go to Nice and read the newspapers.

CHAPTER SEVEN

SLEEP WAS A LONG TIME coming to Miranda that night, for she kept thinking of the blue rose and what it meant to Alain Maury. When she finally did sleep, he came into her dreams in a far more disturbing way; running with her across a field ablaze with blue flowers and then whirling her around in his arms until they fell to the ground breathless, and she sank into the soft earth beneath the pressure of his body.

She awoke so suddenly that the dream was still with her, and she moved her legs, surprised to find she was lying on a mattress and not on flowers. Quickly she sat up, gaining comfort from the stolid furniture and the daylight seeping in through the half-closed shutters. Clouds unexpectedly marched across the sky, and the air was chilly and damp as though it was going to rain.

Rain it did an hour later when she was having breakfast in the dining room, and she was debating whether to continue with her sketches when Pierre came in, heavy eyed and irritable.

"No luck at the tables," she ventured.

"Positively bad luck," he said glumly.

"You shouldn't gamble if you can't afford it," she said heartlessly.

"There's no excitement gambling with what you *can* afford."

"Can't you find more rewarding excitement?"

"I'm looking," he smiled, some of his good humor returning as he poured his coffee and straddled the chair beside her. "If Maurice likes your designs, I intend to swing myself a job at Christi's."

"I can't see you selling clothes!"

"I was thinking of the business side. Someone has to keep putting the name of the company in front of the public. Publicity doesn't happen by itself. Once you're there I can—"

"Let's wait till it happens."

"That shouldn't be long," he said. "I spoke to Maurice last night, and we're seeing him this evening!"

With shaking hands Miranda set down her cup. "I don't think I'll go with you."

"Nonsense. Maurice isn't just backing a talent. He's backing the person, too. He made that very clear when I spoke to him. He's had enough of airy fairy dress designers and wants to make sure that choice number three has both feet on the ground."

"I wish I had some press clippings with me."

"Forget it. Just see him tonight and sell *yourself.*"

She sighed. "It isn't just a question of a backer investing in a dress designer. It's Christi's cloak being put on the shoulders of an unknown."

"A cloak without someone inside it is just a shroud," Pierre reminded her. "At the moment the House of Christi is a corpse. I'm putting *you* forward as the one person who can breathe life into it."

"I wish you could have chosen a less depressing metaphor!"

"I was fitting it to your mood of self-deprecation!" He stood up. "We'll have dinner in Antibes tonight and get to Maurice around nine. Right now I'm off to Nice. Care to come with me?"

"I'd love to."

Not until she accepted the offer did she realize how anxious she was to learn the full story of Lucille's death and though she despised her curiosity, she was too intelligent to fight it.

The winding road down to the coast was mercifully free of buses, which, Pierre informed her, were the bane of one's life during the summer months. A few miles above Cannes they branched off to take the highway, though it ended when they were still some distance from the city, and they had to continue on a tortuously narrow and congested road into Nice itself.

"If you want to go anywhere special," Pierre said, "I'll drop you off."

Reluctant to tell him what she was going to do, she murmured that she only wanted to do some window shopping, and he left her outside the Galeries Lafayette, arranging to meet her a couple of hours later at the Café Royal on the Promenade des Anglais.

As soon as he had driven off, Miranda made her way to the offices of *Nice Matin*.

Like most newspaper buildings, this one was busy and casual, and her request to look at back issues was met with such disinterest she almost gave up the attempt. But eventually, she found herself in a dingy room facing a mound of yellowing papers.

"Don't get them out of order," an old man adjured her, "and don't tear bits out!"

Promising not to do so, she leafed through the pages. It was disconcerting how guilty she felt, almost as though she were prying into secrets and not something that was common knowledge and available for anyone to see if they wished.

The search was laborious, made more difficult by not knowing exactly what she was looking for, and she had almost given up hope of finding what she wanted when the name Bayronne stared up at her.

Quickly she began to read. It was a short account of the discovery of the body of Lucille Dufy who had fallen to her death while out walking. "Mountain claims second victim in five years," the article ran and went on to state that there had been several accidents at this particular spot, which was made more dangerous in winter and spring by torrential rainfall.

There was also a photograph of Lucille, and for a long moment Miranda stared at it, surprised by the complex-

ity of emotions that went through her as she saw the
plaintive-looking face with its soulful eyes and dark hair.
It was a face made for tragedy, as though the camera lens
had caught the future of this beautiful, yet haunted-
looking, girl.

Somberly Miranda picked up the next edition of the
paper and learned that Alain Maury had been interro-
gated for several hours by an inspector sent from Paris.
For the first time mention was made of a letter found in
Lucille's coat, though the contents were not disclosed,
and she had to thumb through several more weeks' papers before blazing headlines drew her attention to what
the writer of the article called "the tragedy of Lucille
Dufy."

For an instant Miranda closed her eyes, overcome by
revulsion at what she was doing, but she had progressed
too far to stop now, and she opened her eyes and began to
read.

The sordidness of the story emerged from the yellowing pages with an evil life of their own. It was a story that
must have happened many times before, and Miranda
was furious for not having guessed it. Yet its very obvi-
ousness had prevented her from doing so—as if the obvious could never figure in Alain Maury's life.

Lucille had been expecting Alain's child when she
died.

The knowledge filled Miranda with unexpected repug-
nance. She was no prissy Victorian miss who did not
know the facts of life. Why was she surprised that Lucille
and Alain had anticipated their marriage? Was it because
she could not imagine him being overcome by passion?
Remembering the way he had kissed her last night she
knew this was untrue.

Turning back to the paper, she found the copy of
Lucille's letter to Alain. Here at last was what she had
had to see. With fast-beating heart she began to read,
forcing herself to go slowly and not misinterpret. But
there was no chance of doing that. Clearly and concisely,

the letter indicted him, making him as guilty of Lucille's death as if he had actually pushed her over the mountain ledge.

How easy it was to see the turmoil in the girl's mind when, having told him she was expecting his child, he had callously said he did not want to marry her. A person of a hardier temperament might not have been so overcome, but to a girl who, according to the newspaper accounts, had led a sheltered life in a convent until she was eighteen, and then come to live with her godmother, Adrienne Maury, it must have seemed like the end of the world.

Again Miranda read the letter. It was obvious that Alain had never loved his fiancée, as it was obvious that she could not live if he no longer wanted to marry her:

> When you love someone with all your heart, you don't count the cost of what you do or worry about the future. I gave myself completely because it was the only way I could show my love, and even your fury when you learned I was pregnant hasn't made me regret what I did. I always feel in my heart that I wasn't the right person for you.
>
> Knowing the man you are, I know you'll be sorry for all the things you said to me, and I'd like you to know that I'm not angry. I'm not miserable, either. The happiness I've had has been enough for me. My only sorrow is that the child won't—

Here the letter ended, and Miranda wondered what emotions had made it impossible for the girl to go on. How could Alain have behaved so despicably? If he had been so unsure about Lucille that she had guessed it herself, how could he have so callously seduced her? For that was what he had done. Lucille had not been a sophisticated woman, but a trusting innocent who had loved him too much to turn him away.

"Have you found what you wanted, *mademoiselle*?"

The old man had come back into the room, and startled, Miranda turned to look at him.

"Yes, thank you. I was just going."

He looked at her curiously. "You are pale. Can I get you some water?"

"No, thank you, *monsieur*. I'm meeting a friend at the Café Royal, and I'll have a drink there."

Leaving him to his yellowed newspapers, she set off briskly for the Promenade des Anglais.

The day had brightened considerably, but as far as she was concerned the heavens were still weeping, as she was weeping inside for a girl whose tragedy had touched her so deeply. With the stench of guilt in his nostrils, Alain Maury, not surprisingly, had been afraid he had lost the ability to create any more perfume. She quickened her pace, as though by so doing she could leave all thoughts of him behind. But his ghost marched in step with her, and she started to run along the pavement, only stopping as she plowed full tilt into the gray-suited figure of a man rounding a corner. The breath was knocked from her body, and she was only saved from falling by a pair of steadying hands.

"Do you always make it a habit to run like a wild thing?" a quiet voice asked, and Miranda gasped and found herself looking into the brown eyes of the man from whose very thought she had been trying to escape.

"You!" she said. "What are you doing here?"

"We seem to have had this conversation before, too," he said whimsically and took his hands away from her. "I had a meeting with my lawyer, and I'm on my way home. And you, Miss Dixon?"

"I'm going to the Café Royal."

"They do excellent coffee. Will you permit me to share a cup with you?"

Not knowing how to refuse, she nodded and walked in silence beside him.

The café was one of the largest along the promenade, with numerous tables protected from the sunlight by blue and white umbrellas. With the quiet ease that Miranda was beginning to associate with him, Alain found a vacant table, ordered coffee and was almost immediately served.

"Have you been shopping in Nice?" he asked conversationally.

She shrugged. What she had learned about him was still too raw in her mind for her to talk to him with ease, and she made a pretense of being absorbed in choosing a cake she did not want from the trolley that a waiter had wheeled to a stop in front of her.

"I recommend the *framboise*," Alain Maury said, and picking up a plate and fork, took one for himself.

"I'll just stick to coffee," Miranda said, knowing she could not swallow anything.

"Aren't you well?" he asked. "When you ran into me, you looked as though you were being pursued by devils."

Again she did not answer, and after giving her a thoughtful look, he fixed his attention on the passing parade. A motley crowd presented itself before him. Elegantly dressed couples taking the air at their ease; elderly women with frizzy dyed hair and frizzy poodles high stepping past on their way to nowhere; and a spattering of boys and girls, arms entwined and buttocks swinging in tight-fitting jeans.

"I'm sorry Colette arrived when she did last night," he said unexpectedly. "Our conversation was just becoming interesting."

"We had already talked too much!"

"I don't agree with you." Imps of mischief danced in his warm brown eyes. "You have an independent mind, and I would like to explore it."

"Lots of women have independent minds."

"But they are often so aggressive with it." The twinkle grew more pronounced. "*You* have retained your femininity."

"Not enough to arouse your chivalry, *monsieur*. You still tried to race me for a taxi."

"*Tiens!* Must you always go back to that?"

"I don't forget easily."

A shadow crossed his face, and she wondered whether he was aware of her meaning. Yet he could not be, for he had no idea where she had been.

"Did you always want to be a dress designer?" His change of subject disconcerted her, and she nodded. "I'd like to see your work."

"You wouldn't like it." She hesitated. "I designed my emerald suit."

"Ah." He smiled. "Are all your clothes so bright and astringent?"

"I hate labels, *monsieur*."

"But you have labeled *me* in your mind." He rested his elbows on the table, and she noticed how well shaped his hands were. "To you, I am the ungallant Frenchman who insulted your womanhood by wanting your taxi and then made matters worse by insulting your taste in clothes!"

Against her will she smiled, and seeing it he smiled back. As always it transformed his face, his aloofness giving way to unexpected sensuality. No man had the right to look so devastatingly handsome, she thought crossly and pushed her chair farther away from the table. She knew he was flirting with her, and she wondered how she would have reacted under normal circumstances. But the circumstances could never be normal between them. No matter how hard she tried, his past would always form an insurmountable barrier.

"Please don't let me delay you," she said in her coldest voice.

"Why are you so keen to dismiss me? We're neighbors, Miss Dixon. Do you not have a neighborly interest in me?"

Before she could reply a boy stopped at their table. "You are the English lady who was at the *Nice Matin* office?" he inquired.

"Y-yes," she stammered.

"Monsieur Rocchia found this in one of the back copies of the paper."

He held out a blue glove that she recognized as her own, and she hurriedly fumbled in her bag for a couple of francs, all the time aware of Alain Maury sitting beside her as though carved of stone. The boy thanked her and moved away, and only then did the man speak, his voice full of contempt.

"So that's why you came to Nice! You had to satisfy your curiosity." He leaned forward and gripped her arm. "You should have asked *me*, Miss Dixon. I'd have told you what you wanted to know."

"I *couldn't* ask you," she said tightly. "And I—I didn't want to listen to other people's gossip."

"That at least is commendable. The written word, however cruel, is not as cruel as people's tongues." He folded his arms across his chest. The color had not yet returned to his face, and despite its tan it held a tinge of grayness. "I take it you're now satisfied?"

"At least I know what happened."

"Do *you* despise me, too?"

"I try not to judge other people's behavior, *monsieur*."

"An excellent sentiment," he taunted, "but hardly true. I can see from your expression that you too have judged me and found me wanting. You needn't be ashamed of it. You are in excellent company. Like all the other good people of Bayronne, you have the same narrow point of view."

"Is it narrow to have compassion?" she burst out. "Are you so heartless that you don't regret what you did?"

He stood up abruptly, his chair crashing to the ground behind him. Several people stared in their direction, and he bent and picked it up. "You are right, Miss Dixon, we've already talked too much." He placed a ten-franc note under his saucer and turned to go.

As he did so he saw Pierre Chambray approaching, and his face grew even paler.

"Hello, Alain," Pierre said easily. "I'm not interrupting you both, am I?"

"Since when would that have stopped you?" Alain asked harshly.

Color darkened Pierre's cheeks. "Still the same Alain," he smiled.

"Did you expect me to change?"

"I never expect the impossible!" Pierre reached out for a chair from another table. "Don't let me drive you away."

"You haven't," Alain said and, nodding in Miranda's direction, threaded his way through the tables and out of sight.

His going left a vacuum Pierre tried to fill with chatter, but Miranda did not hear a word he said and was glad when she finally found herself in his car driving back to Bayronne.

"What were you and Alain arguing about?" Pierre asked suddenly. "He seemed to be in a flaming temper."

She stared steadfastly through the window, wondering why the sea should look gray when she knew it was turquoise blue. "I went to the office of *Nice Matin* and read about Lucille. He found out."

"So that was it! Still, it's as well he knows you're wise to him. It'll stop him playing on your sympathy to get the land."

"I've already told him *grand'mère*'s leaving the decision to you."

"Alain's a great believer in the power of his persuasion!"

"He must be," Miranda said tremulously and thought of Lucille, who had succumbed to it and been destroyed by it.

"Do you think he *was* to blame for her death?" she asked suddenly.

"Don't you know the answer without my telling you?"

"I suppose so," she sighed, "but I can't believe it. If he didn't love her, why did he pretend?"

"To satisfy his mother."

"It was so cruel."

"He *is* cruel." Pierre caught her hand. "Stop thinking about a past that isn't yours. Think of the future instead. *Our* future."

His exuberance lapped at her depression, and though it did not wash it way completely, it smoothed off the sharp edges so that only sadness remained with her during the long drive back to the château.

MIRANDA'S NERVOUSNESS at meeting Monsieur Maurice forced Alain Maury from her mind. It was all very well for Pierre to talk blithely of her becoming chief designer at Christi's, but was she ready for such a major position? And equally important—would it be offered to her? Would her confidence be destroyed if Maurice turned her down? After all, he had already shown his fallibility by choosing two nonstarters!

Miranda fought against depression by wearing her prettiest outfit: a long skirt and blouse in hand-painted chiffon with ruffles at her throat and wrists. She piled her hair on top of her head, surprised at how defenseless her neck looked when it was bare, as though it could be snapped by a single blow from a lean dark hand. . . .

Quickly, she pushed the thought away and ran downstairs.

"You look like a flower," her grandmother said as she entered the drawing room.

"Like the entire flowerbed!" Pierre corrected and repeated his compliment as they drove down to Antibes. "You look exceptionally lovely tonight. I feel in my bones that things are going to work out well."

"Don't bank on it, Pierre. Feelings can be wrong."

He shook his head, then concentrated on the road. The bends appeared more tortuous at night, but with less traffic they made good time, and soon the lights of Antibes were strung out before them like diamonds around the throat of a dark beauty.

Unlike Cannes, which was busy even late at night, Antibes closed down at eight, and the Place de Gaulle was bare of traffic except for a few cars parked forlornly at the curb, and some solitary figure sitting outside the large corner café.

Pierre drove down a narrow road to a tree-lined square and came to a stop in front of the Relais de la Poste, a subdued-looking restaurant whose interior—with its red-checked table cloths and red-shaded lamps—was far more inviting than its outer facade.

They were served promptly by the *patronne*, who seemed to know Pierre well, and dinner, though not of the three-star variety, was an excellent example of Provençal cuisine, with an abundance of garlic and a profusion of delicious vegetables.

Replete with both food and wine, Miranda was no longer fearful as they drove down the wide, tree-lined Avenue Victor Hugo to the seafront. They went past several large blocks of apartments and up a steep road bordered on one side by the sea and on the other by villas set back on their own grounds and reached only by long flights of steps. They continued to drive for several miles, climbing higher and losing sight of the sea completely until they reached a small square with a fountain set into a wall and a signpost pointing to the Eden Roc Hotel. Here Pierre turned left, driving slowly down a quiet road unlit except for their own headlights.

"This is the most exclusive part of the Cap," he explained. "Every house is owned by a millionaire."

They skirted a high brick wall, and she knew instinctively that this marked the boundary of the Maurice estate. Sure enough, as a pair of gates came into sight, Pierre stopped and flashed his lights three times. At once the gates swung open with an electronic whine for them to drive through.

"A millionaire's answering service," he quipped, and Miranda looked through the rear window to see the gates close behind them.

A moment later they stopped at a wrought-iron door. It opened as if on cue, and a white-coated manservant ushered them into an octagonal marble hall, and then into an immense room overlooking the bay. One wall was of glass, and through it could be glimpsed softly lit lawns with clipped trees and shrubs, and beyond it the glittering jet sea and the silver-starred sky.

The furniture was ultramodern, with giant-sized armchairs in jewel-colored suedes, interspersed with low tables in perspex and steel, and white fur rugs gleaming like snow on the black ebony floor.

A small, dapper man rose from an armchair to greet them. Silver gray hair and a baby-pink complexion gave him a cherubic appearance at variance with the small eyes, that flicked over Miranda like a scorpion's tongue.

"You are younger than I expected," he said.

"Today it's an asset to be young," Pierre put in easily.

Again the gray eyes surveyed Miranda. "I like your designs. They are original, and they have a strong line. You could well be the person we are looking for."

"There's no doubt of it," Pierre intervened. "Miranda has an excellent reputation in England."

"I know. I have already found out." Monsieur Maurice beckoned them to sit down. "I assume you are prepared to work in Paris, Miss Dixon?"

"Of course."

"Good." The man picked up a folder and took out some of Miranda's sketches. "Are these what you envisage for next spring?"

"More or less."

"Don't forget Miranda designed her collection with no specific fabrics in mind," Pierre said quickly. "If she comes to Christi's she'll obviously work with *your* materials."

"Only if I like them," Miranda added, deciding there was no point in not being truthful. "I realize you finance Christi's, Monsieur Maurice, but I couldn't use fabrics unless I liked them."

The man sat as if lost in thought, then he stood up and

pressed a button on the wall behind him. An entire section glided away, and two rails rolled forward, weighed down with samples of fabric.

Never had Miranda seen such a host of colors, nor so many different textures, from cobweb mohair to shaggy tweed, from heavy satin to finest chiffon.

"There you are," he said. "What do you think?"

"They're fabulous!" She fingered a supple jersey that glowed silver one moment and iridescent pearl the next.

"I designed more than half of these myself," Monsieur Maurice said. "I want you to know I am also a creator. My ambition is not only to make money, you understand, but to have beautiful clothes that will show *my* work to its best advantage."

Miranda warmed to the man for the first time since they had met. Here was an ambition she could appreciate.

"I think we would work well together, Monsieur Maurice."

"So do I."

"What are your terms?" Pierre said.

"The same as I gave to José."

"He was a failure."

"When he came to me his reputation was greater than Miss Dixon's."

"Unfortunately *Christi's* reputation is lower now! Two bad seasons have harmed it—one more will kill it completely. You need Miranda far more than you needed José."

"What exactly are you asking for?" asked Monsieur Maurice.

"A bigger profit participation. Miranda would accept fifteen percent in the first year, escalating to thirty in four years."

"That is out of the question—unless Miss Dixon can put up some money."

"Why do you need money?" Pierre asked. "Your company is one of the richest in Europe."

"Would a thousand pounds help?" Miranda inquired.
"That's all I have."

"Wait!" There was excitement in Pierre's voice. "It
might be possible for Miranda to offer something much
more important than money—something that would
bring money into the company."

"Such as?"

"A perfume," Pierre said. "A perfume that would do
for Christi's what N⁰ 5 did for Chanel."

"You have such a perfume?"

"Yes."

Monsieur Maurice sat down and looked at them both.

Not knowing what Pierre was talking about, Miranda
glanced at him covertly. He seemed oblivious to her look
and lounged easily back on the settee as though he did
not have a care in the world.

"May I ask what it's called?" Monsieur Maurice inquired.

"I'd rather not say until we have come to a satisfactory
financial arrangement for Miss Dixon. Then you may
evaluate the value of the scent for yourself."

"That will not be easy to do."

"Throw a cocktail party for a couple of hundred social-
ites and journalists and spray 'em!" Pierre said laconically. "I guarantee they'll go wild over it. Not only will
the perfume give you publicity, it'll bring in a fortune!"

"You are very confident."

"Because I know the scent, and because I'm prepared
to do the publicity for it. Christi's needs *me* as well as
Miranda."

Monsieur Maurice pursed his lips. "So it is the two of
you I must engage?"

"Miranda is the most important one," Pierre said
swiftly, "but I believe I can increase her value to you."

"You may well be right. If I can be convinced that the
perfume is as good as you say, I will give Miss Dixon the
percentage she wants. How soon can you let me have
some of the perfume?"

"Within a few days."

"Good. There is no time to lose. Our winter collection will be shown in August, and that does not give Miss Dixon much time."

"I couldn't prepare a collection for *this* winter," Miranda said flatly. "Next spring is the earliest."

"Unless you can design our *next* collection, I may have to reconsider my decision."

"I'm sorry." She was firm. "I don't intend to let myself be launched unless I'm ready for it."

Monsieur Maurice frowned. "You are obstinate."

"An artist has to be!"

Unexpectedly, he smiled. "I like your honesty, so I will accept what you say. But at least prepare a few new designs for us."

She nodded, but before she could speak Pierre stood up to leave. His impatience surprised her, but she hid it. It was difficult to fathom what was going on in his mind. The perfume was but one example of this.

They walked to the door and were halfway toward it when it opened, and a man and woman came in. Miranda stopped. Alain Maury and Colette Dinard were the last couple she had expected to see here.

"You are back early, Colette," Monsieur Maurice exclaimed.

"Alain promised mother he would be a fourth for bridge." Colette kissed Monsieur Maurice on the cheek. "Why aren't you playing?"

"I've had business to attend to. I'd like you to meet—"

"I already know Pierre and Miss Dixon," the girl said.

Monsieur Maurice looked at Miranda. "I did not realize you knew my stepdaughter."

"We met a few days ago," Miranda said and glanced at Pierre, annoyed that he had not told her of the relationship. Had she known, nothing would have induced her to consider a business partnership with the man. Even now it was not too late to turn it down: it would be embarrassing to do so, but less difficult than having to meet Colette frequently—and possibly Alain Maury, too, if he married the girl! No, the very thought was impossible.

Blindly, she caught at Pierre's arm. "We must go, we're keeping Monsieur Maurice from bridge."

Not until they were bowling along the winding Cap road did she give vent to her anger.

"Why didn't you tell me he was Colette's stepfather?"

"What difference does it make?"

She bit her lip, knowing she was caught out. "I don't like her," she hedged, "and I don't want to be involved with her."

"You won't be. She doesn't take any interest in Monsieur Maurice's business—or Christi's."

"I still don't like it." Miranda tilted her head. "I don't want to be partners with her stepfather. I mean it, Pierre."

He slammed his foot so hard on the brake that Miranda was only saved from the windshield by her safety belt. "You can't mean to let your dislike of Colette stop you from accepting the best offer you've had in your life!" She did not answer, and he swung her around to face him. "We're not talking about your refusing a dinner-party invitation!" he stormed. "We're talking about your future. What does it matter who the hell Colette is?"

Put so bluntly, her reason sounded ludicrous. "I dislike anyone connected with Alain Maury," she said lamely.

"*That* part I can understand!" Pierre replied. "But I can't understand your throwing your future away because of some childish dislike of another woman. You're going to work at Christi's, dear cousin, whether you like it or not!"

He set the car in motion again, and she sat quietly, trying to analyze exactly why the French girl irritated her. It was not simply because she had been unfriendly from their first meeting; rather, it stemmed from the fact that she was a close friend of Alain's. Anxious to concentrate on something else—indeed on anything that would push the man from her mind—she shifted around and looked at Pierre again.

"What perfume were you talking about to Monsieur Maurice?"

"None in particular. It was the first thing that came into my head."

She gasped. "He'll be furious when he finds out you invented the whole thing."

"I didn't exactly invent it. We *will* have a perfume. The blue rose."

"You must be joking!"

"It began that way," he confessed, "but as I kept talking, it started to make sense. If you could launch a perfume like that, you'd be made!"

"I'm sure I would. But how do you suggest we get it? At knife-point?"

"We'll probably have to use a bit of persuasion," he conceded.

"Oh, be serious," she said crossly.

"I am. I've worked out a plan. Alain will do *anything* to grow those roses of his. Not only because it's the first perfume he's created in four years, but because the essence itself will make him a fortune."

"That's why he'll never give it to *us*."

"You don't understand. You can make more than one scent from an essence. The perfume he's got now won't be the *only* one he'll make from the blue rose."

Miranda looked searchingly at the profile beside her, and aware of her gaze, Pierre turned and smiled at her.

"It's true, dear cousin."

She relaxed. "I hadn't realized that. Mind you, I still don't think he'll sell it to us."

"He'll have to—if he wants the land."

"That's blackmail!"

"I prefer to use the word bargain!"

"We can't refuse to sell him the land," she protested.

"Why not? *Tante* Emilie's leaving the decision to me." Pierre frowned. "Stop thinking in terms of one perfume. The blue rose is like sugar. Once you've got it, you can use it to make a hundred different kinds of cakes. All we want is to buy Alain's first recipe. He'll make a handsome profit producing the perfume for us, but we'll get the profit from the sale and—more important still—all the publicity that goes with it. There'll be nothing to stop Alain launching any other perfumes at the same time."

Put like this, the proposition seemed workable, yet she was still doubtful that Alain Maury would agree to it. Even using Pierre's simile, it could be argued that a cook might be more attached to the first recipe he had created than to any subsequent ones—possibly sufficiently attached to refuse to let anyone else have it.

"Creating a perfume isn't easy," she said, remembering Madame Maury's comments on the subject, as well as the bitter anguish Alain himself had disclosed when referring to the barrenness of the years since Lucille's death. "What happens if he lets us launch the blue rose and then can't create anything else?"

"He will," Pierre said confidently. "He's one of the best in his field."

"He hasn't done anything for four years."

"You know the reason for that." Pierre looked at her again. "The fact that he's produced a perfume now shows he's gotten rid of his guilty conscience. It's probably because of Colette. There's nothing like one woman for helping you to forget another!"

The words brought with them a picture of Alain and Colette as she had seen them that evening. There had been an ease between them that spoke of familiarity, and it gave credence to Pierre's statement. Miranda was surprised at the bitterness this evoked in her. No matter how much she disliked Alain for his behavior to Lucille, surely she didn't want him to go on paying for it forever? This was contrary to everything she had been brought up to believe. She sighed deeply, perplexed at the angry emotions that were tossing her around on a sea of confusion, washing away all her normal points of reference.

"Don't look so worried," Pierre said. "Think of the wonderful future ahead of you and leave me to deal with Alain."

"What will you say to him?"

"That he can buy the land on condition . . . . You know the rest. I don't need to say any more."

"No," she whispered and wondered what Alain Maury would say when *he* was told.

CHAPTER EIGHT

NOT EXPECTING TO SLEEP WELL, Miranda was surprised that her night was a dreamless one, and she awoke refreshed and elated. But her first sight of the landscape outside her bedroom window brought Alain to mind, and with it came the thought of his reaction to Pierre's proposal.

The idea was sufficiently daunting to destroy her appetite, and she sat on the terrace sipping coffee and wondering what the future held for her. How would her father react when he heard her news? It was one thing to suggest she come to Provence for a holiday, and quite another to discover that the holiday had led to her becoming a permanent resident of France and the chief designer at Christi's!

Her coffee cup clattered to the saucer. She was mad to have accepted such a position. How could she go from Mr. Joseph's wholesale house to a couturier? Supervising two dozen girls in a workroom could not be compared with controlling a staff of several hundred.

Fear sent her to the telephone to call her father, and hearing his voice on the line, she precipitately blurted out her news.

"It's a big decision for you to make," he said finally. "I'll come out and see you. Then we can talk it over properly."

"I'd love that." She had not realized how much until she heard her father's offer. "When can you come?"

"In a couple of days. I've been wanting an excuse to

see Provence again. It's time I laid *my* ghosts to rest, too.''

His words stopped Miranda from thinking of her own problems. The last time her father had walked these sunny lanes he had met her mother, a meeting that had led to a few years' happiness and far more years of loneliness. If his ghost *could* be laid to rest, perhaps he might find happiness again.

''Come quickly,'' she whispered. ''I'll tell *grandmother* that—''

''I'll book in at the local hotel,'' he interrupted. ''It will be better that way.''

After the call Miranda felt some of her confidence return, and she sat down at the library desk and began to sketch some new designs, raking her memory to utilize a few of the magnificent fabrics she had seen the night before. The silvery jersey had made the strongest impression on her, and this gave creation to a host of evening dresses, all diaphanous and suggesting warm, sensuous nights. So intent was she on her work that Pierre's entrance sent her pencil stabbing across the page, the point breaking in a spatter of lead as she saw Alain Maury behind him. Why hadn't Pierre warned her that he was going to bring the man here?

Color rushed into her cheeks, ebbing quickly as Pierre said, ''Alain's agreed to manufacture the blue rose essence for us.''

She had not anticipated such swift capitulation and, meeting Alain's mocking eyes, knew he was aware of her thoughts.

''Pierre is not the only realist, Miss Dixon,'' he said. ''He knows how important it is for me to buy your grandmother's land.''

''So it's all settled,'' she murmured.

''Yes,'' Pierre intervened. ''Luckily, Alain has several thousand cuttings ready in his greenhouses, and they'll be planted at once. It's a good thing we saw Maurice when we did. If we'd left the negotiations another week, it would have been too late to plant the roses. As it is, the first blooms should be ready by September.''

Surprise drew Miranda's gaze to Alain's. "Are they so late flowering?"

"They flower continually," he said. "That is another of their unusual features."

"It couldn't be more fortuitous." Pierre hugged Miranda tightly. "I told you you wouldn't regret leaving everything to me."

Aware of the slim, dark man behind her, she wriggled free. Not knowing how to change the conversation, yet knowing that she must, she pointed to her sketches. "I've been working, too. I tried to remember some of the materials I saw last night."

Pierre looked at the drawings, and watching his face, she knew he would make an implacable enemy. It was a good thing he was on her side. Yet it meant that Alain Maury was not. She was sure that his agreement to give her the blue rose had been a forced one, and she glanced around and saw him watching her, his mouth so tightly set that the shape—which she had noticed and admired—had disappeared into a thin line.

"Take a look at these," Pierre said, handing him the sketches. "Then you'll realize why it's so important for Miranda to get every opportunity to succeed."

"I'm no judge of women's clothes." Alain Maury held himself stiffly away from the designs, but Pierre thrust the sheets at him, forcing him to take them. Nerves or temper made him careless, and the sheets fell to the floor. Hurriedly, he bent to pick them up, slowing down as he studied them.

Pierre caught Miranda's eye and winked. With the sunlight streaming in through the window to catch the auburn in his hair, he looked the epitome of a red devil, and she knew he had enjoyed forcing Alain to bend to his will. Again she wondered why the two men disliked each other so much. Pierre considered Alain guilty of

Lucille's death, but surely this had not caused the break in their relationship?

With a start she heard Alain talking to her. "I can see why Pierre believes in your future," he said. "You have great flair."

"I'm glad you like them. I'll design a special bottle for the perfume, too."

"Our own company usually does that," he said coldly.

"I'd still like to try. I know what appeals to women, and if the perfume is going to be launched as mine . . . ."

The moment she spoke she regretted the words, for Alain flung her a look of such bitterness that she almost cried out.

"*You* can make the final decision, of course," she said breathlessly. "I'm sure you have more knowledge than I."

"What about a name?" Pierre said. "I've written out a list of suggestions."

"I'd like something simple," Miranda looked at Alain. "What do you have in mind?"

"Does it matter? The perfume's yours. . . ."

She turned away, refusing to be swayed by pity. He had gotten the land he desperately wanted, and to give her just one of the perfumes he would be able to produce from these lovely flowers was a small price to pay for it.

"I rather like the name Tendresse," she said slowly. "It's what most women want from a man."

"Most women don't deserve it," Alain retorted.

"Then at least let them be able to buy it!"

His laugh was sarcastic, and turning on his heel, he walked to the door, stopping as Pierre called after him.

"I'll get our lawyers to draw up a contract, Alain. I'm sure you'd like things settled."

"I don't go back on my word," came the reply, "and I don't expect you to do so, either."

The door closed behind him, and Pierre gave an angry snort. "He went back on his word four years ago, and Lucille died because of it!"

"Oh, stop talking about the past," Miranda burst out. "It's all so morbid!"

"Sorry, my dear. I won't mention it again." Pierre smiled. "The future is much nicer, I agree—especially yours."

"And yours. You've acted as the catalyst in the whole situation, and I think we should be partners."

"No, no! It's *your* talent that got you the offer from Maurice, and your talent that will help you to keep it."

"But I want *you* to get something out of it, too."

"I have the job I want. Publicity and advertising director for Christi's."

"What's so good about that?"

"I'll see you every day!" His grin disappeared. "You know what I'm trying to say, don't you?"

She shrugged helplessly. The conversation had taken an unexpected turn, and she was dismayed by it. It seemed ungrateful to refuse Pierre's love, yet it was equally impossible to pretend she reciprocated it.

"At the moment I can't think of anything except my work," she hedged.

"There's no other man, is there?"

"No."

"Then I'll wait and take my chances."

"You can't mean that," she said uncertainly.

His head tilted quizzically. "I don't think you know *what* I mean, Miranda."

She thought about this at length when, alone in the library that afternoon, she put the final touches to her sketches. For all his warm personality, Pierre had a disregard for other people that showed itself in little, yet revealing ways. His casual teasing of Simone, who made her admiration of him so obvious; his ability to disarm the *comtesse* and pretend the château meant so much to him—when she knew it meant so little; and his changing moods toward Miranda herself—cousinly one moment, loverlike the next, but always with an eye to the main chance. Pierre would not make a good husband, she decided. He would be attentive, loving and unfaithful. Not the partner for her, she knew with certainty, and firmly pushed away more dangerous thoughts about another man.

Pierre did not return for dinner that evening. He telephoned from Nice to say he was still in conference with the lawyers who were drawing up the contract to send to Monsieur Maurice.

"I hope your French is good enough for you to read it," he concluded. "I can't have you signing something you don't understand."

"I'm prepared to rely on you—in business."

He chuckled. "I like your sharpness, Miranda. You'd never bore me."

She was still smiling at the remark when she returned to the table, but hardly had she sat down when the telephone rang again.

"Let Simone take it," the *comtesse* admonished. "We are having dinner, not a running buffet!"

"It might be Monsieur Maurice," Miranda said. "I'd better go."

But the voice on the other end of the line was her father's, announcing his arrival at the Hotel de la Poste in the village.

"I never expected you so soon," she said happily.

"I felt you needed me."

"I do." She found it hard to keep the tears from her voice. "Let me tell grandmother you're here."

"All right. But make it clear I came to see *you*."

"Can I come down to the hotel tonight, or are you too tired?"

"Certainly not. I'll meet you at the gates of the château. I don't like you walking around in the dark."

She returned to the dining room, where the *comtesse*'s sharp eyes immediately noticed her elated expression. "Don't tell me it was Monsieur Maurice who brought the pink to those cheeks?"

"Of course not."

"Alain, then?"

The pink became red. "What a thing to say!"

"A normal remark. He is a handsome young man. Or hadn't you noticed?"

Aware that her fork was trembling, Miranda dug it into a piece of veal. "It was my father on the phone. He's flown over to see me, and he's staying in the village."

This time it was the *comtesse*'s fork that trembled, and seeing it, Miranda hurried to her grandmother's side. "Don't be upset, darling, he won't come here unless you want to see him."

"Naturally, I will see him." The *comtesse*'s voice was quavery. "He should be staying here—not in the village."

"He didn't feel you'd want him to be here."

"He is your father and you love him. His place is in the château."

"I don't think so. It might be too much of a strain for you."

"It is a strain I should have faced a long time ago." Blue-veined lids momentarily lowered over the faded eyes. "I think I will go to my room."

"Aren't you feeling well?" Miranda asked nervously.

"A little upset. It is a shock for me to know your father is in the village again after so many years. The last time he was there, Louise was alive." She stood up, straight but frail. "Please call Simone to help me to my room."

"I'll take you."

"No, I insist you finish your dinner. I will be better once I am in bed."

Having promised to remain in the dining room, Miranda did so. It was strange to dine alone at the long, highly polished table, carefully set with a few pieces of beautiful silverware and delicate lace mats. So must her grandmother have sat alone night after night, accompanied only by anguished memories of the daughter she had lost. How wasted the years had been, she thought somberly and vowed never to let bitterness warp her own judgment the way it had done her grandmother's.

It was with immeasurable relief that she finally hurried

down the driveway to fling herself into her father's embrace. She had forgotten how big and shaggy looking he was, with his thick gray hair and calm smile.

Only as they sat in the lounge of the little hotel did she find a calm to match his and told him of the sequence of events that had led to her meeting with Monsieur Maurice.

"The only thing that worries me is having to live in Paris," she concluded. "I don't suppose you'd give up the apartment and join me?"

"Once you're settled, you won't want your old father hanging around you!"

"What rot! Anyway, you're not old."

"I must say I don't feel it." He waved his unlit pipe around the room. "Coming back here makes me feel thirty again. It seems only yesterday that I met your mother. I was going into the *boulangerie* to buy a *galette*, and she was coming out with a loaf of bread. I bumped into her and knocked it to the floor."

Miranda hid her surpirse. Only rarely had her father talked of her mother, and then there had always been sadness in his voice. But tonight he spoke prosaically, as if the trauma of coming here had finally laid his ghosts to rest.

"Sometimes things are not as bad as you anticipate," he said, verbalizing her thoughts. "The moment I saw the village again I knew I'd been a fool not to have come back before."

"*Grand'mère* feels the same," Miranda said. "She would like to see you."

"I'll call on her in the morning." He indicated the coffeepot, and Miranda poured him another cup. "It's strange the way things have worked out for you," he went on. "I'm glad this Maury chap has agreed to let you market the perfume. It means you're in a stronger position with Maurice."

"That's what Pierre says."

"You don't seem very pleased by all that's happened."

"I will be, later on," she said. "At the moment I'm rather overwhelmed by it all."

"You need time to absorb it."

"Time's one thing I won't have. Pierre wants me to go to Paris to meet the staff at Christi's."

Her father gave her a broad smile. "It will be a far cry from Mr. Joseph's!"

Miranda laughed. "I'd love to see his face when he hears! I'll give him a permanent seat at all my collections."

"So you think you'll last for more than one?"

"Dad!" Miranda exploded and then giggled. "I never knew you had such faith in me!"

"Faith enough to tease you into laughing at yourself. That's one of your best qualities, my dear. As long as you can do that, you'll be able to deal with everything and everybody."

Not everyone, she thought silently; one man—silent and aloof in an ivory tower of his own making—would always elude her.

CHAPTER NINE

MIRANDA FOUND very little to laugh about in the next few days. There was a detailed document of contract between herself and Monsieur Maurice to be read and absorbed; there was her father's meeting with her grandmother—an hour of tension that not even Roger Dixon's quiet humor had been able to lessen appreciably—and a frigid hour at the Maury laboratories in Grasse where she and Pierre had been shown the vial of scent Alain had made from the first perfumed bush of blue roses grown on the Chambray land earlier that year.

"How much will you have ready for Miranda's first collection?" Pierre asked Alain as they left the laboratory and made for the exit.

"If we have a good summer and autumn the supplies should be adequate by January. But if the weather is poor, it would be better to wait until next spring."

"I promised Monsieur Maurice we'd launch the perfume to coincide with Miranda's debut," Pierre said. "That means January."

"Will it make such a difference if you delay the perfume?"

"I've already told you. Without it, Miranda goes into Christi's as a highly paid employee with a bonus dangled in front of her like a carrot! But if she brings Tendresse with her, she gets a partnership."

"I fail to see why a six months' delay with the perfume should affect the situation," Alain said slowly.

"It does so from the publicity angle."

"We will do the best we can. But it really depends on the weather."

"If we're limited in quantity by January," Pierre answered, "we'll still launch it—at double the price. If we make it the most expensive perfume in the world, every woman will want it!"

"Are you the arbiter of what women want?"

"Knowing the female mind has been part of my success!" Pierre smiled slyly at Miranda. "Don't you agree with me, *chérie?*"

"You don't need anyone to agree with you," she replied. "You are your own best audience!"

"On which happy note I will go and get the car."

He moved off, leaving Miranda alone with Alain. Neither of them spoke, and she shifted uneasily, aware of the lean, gray-suited figure beside her.

"Is the entire laboratory used for making perfume?" she asked, for want of anything to say.

"Yes. The cosmetics are made at our factory in Paris."

"It's strange that most cosmetic firms were started by women, yet fashion is predominantly created by men." She hesitated and then added, "Did you always want to work in this particular field?"

"I was originally a research chemist. I became interested in perfume by accident. I suppose you could say my nose led me to it."

She smiled, but there was no response on his face, which remained grave and withdrawn. Guilt tugged at her, but she forced it away. Alain Maury would concoct many other perfumes from the blue rose essence; it would make little difference to him to wait six months before bringing out another new one, whereas for her it would make all the difference in the world.

"I'm glad you let us have Tendresse," she murmured.

"I nearly refused."

"That wouldn't have been very businesslike."

"How do you arrive at that conclusion?"

"It's logical. I mean, you're just selling me the first

cake—you'll be able to make many others to sell under the Adrienne label.''

"What do cakes have to do with it?" he asked in glacial tones. "Or is this some type of English humor?"

"It was Pierre's metaphor," she confessed and hurried through an explanation. "It wasn't until he told me that you'd be able to make several different perfumes from the blue rose that I agreed to let him ask you to sell us Tendresse."

"Wouldn't you have done so otherwise?"

"Of course not." She made her voice as firm as she could. "You haven't produced anything since your—since . . . . That made the blue rose very important to you."

"If you're referring to the fact that I haven't produced a perfume since Lucille died, then for heaven's sake say so! I'm well aware that—like everyone else—you believe me guilty of her death!"

"I d-don't know wh-what to believe," she stammered.

"You astonish me. I thought my guilt was obvious." He flung out his hands. "You mean you don't think I *pushed* Lucille over the mountain ledge?"

"Don't be ridiculous!" Miranda gasped. "Of course you didn't!"

"But if she died because of me—because of what I did—I might just as well have pushed her. It's only a technical difference."

"Please," she cried, "don't say any more."

"Why not? Don't tell me you're tenderhearted about my feelings. If I'm not guilty of *actual* murder, I'm considered to have done it in a more subtle way. Surely the back numbers of *Nice Matin* didn't leave you with any doubts as to my innocence!"

Knowing it was useless to remain silent, she forced herself to look directly at him. "I went to read about the case because I wished to know the *facts* and not the *prejudice* of other people."

"And what did the facts tell you?"

Unwilling to say, she was nonetheless unable to lie. Not that there was need for words; her difficulty in meeting his eyes told him what he wanted to know, and when he spoke again his voice was as icy as the waters into which Lucille had fallen.

"I am not concerned with what people think of me. I am only interested in living the kind of life *I* wish."

"If that's true, why are you so bitter? You don't like being thought guilty, Monsieur Maury."

"Even murderers like to pretend they're innocent!" he said cynically.

"How can you joke about a thing like this?"

"To joke is the only way one can live with tragedy."

"Was it a tragedy for you?"

Before he could answer, light footsteps approached, and they turned to see Madame Maury coming toward them, graceful and serene in a cream silk dress and jacket.

"I didn't expect you here this morning, *maman*," the man greeted her.

The woman smiled and put her hand on his arm before looking in Miranda's direction, her brown eyes dark with hostility. "I did not know *you* would be here, Miss Dixon."

"I've been given a tour of the laboratory," Miranda said quickly. "It was my first visit to a perfume factory."

"I suppose you came to see Tendresse?" The voice, which Miranda had remembered as lilting, was now frigid. "My son has informed me that he is giving it to you."

"We are buying it," Miranda corrected.

Madame Maury shrugged as though the money involved was unimportant. "Tendresse will be yours and not Alain's. That is all that matters. If—"

"Enough, *maman!*" Alain Maury cut into the conversation. "I don't want any more discussion on the subject."

"Why shouldn't Miss Dixon know that—"

"*Maman!*" he said harshly, and Adrienne Maury lapsed into silence.

With immeasurable relief Miranda saw the red sports car approaching, and murmuring goodbye, she ran down the steps and climbed in, looking back only to wave perfunctorily as she and Pierre drove out of the courtyard.

"That was a quick getaway," Pierre commented. "Was Alain being his usual charming self?"

"It was Madame Maury," Miranda admitted. "She's far more upset about giving us Tendresse than he is."

"She's just being mercenary," Pierre shrugged. "She knows she'd make double the money if they launched it themselves." He squeezed Miranda's hand. "You needn't feel guilty about it, dear coz. I agreed to let Alain buy the land at a lower price, so financially they'll be no worse off."

"Oh, Pierre, I'm so glad you did that."

Seeing her pleasure, he smiled. "You're too tenderhearted. It's a good thing you've got me to watch out for your interests."

ONLY LATER, as she sat in the library looking through the large swatch of patterns that had been delivered to her from Monsieur Maurice's factory, did she recall her conversation with Alain, and her mood of pleasure dissolved. He might not have pushed Lucille to her death, but his refusal to marry her had been tantamount to the same thing. As he had admitted!

He had known the girl was expecting his child; had known that her education and character had not given her the capability to cope alone with such a situation. Yet despite this, he had refused to go through with their marriage, and because of it, he would never be able to disclaim guilt for her death. Yet how positively he had stated his unconcern about what people thought of him, even though in the same breath he had admitted that Lucille's death was a tragedy for him. But why was it a tragedy when he did not love her? Or was the tragedy caused by finding himself judged guilty of her death? To an ambitious man, this could indeed by tragic.

She thought of his beautiful house and the huge laboratories in Grasse. Guilt might have temporarily robbed him of his creativity, but it had not stopped him from continuing as a successful businessman. And now the success would be even bigger; the blue rose would see to that. Alain Maury's future was clearly defined: a road strewn with blue petals down which he would walk with Colette Dinard.

"Bother!" she said aloud and flung the swatch of materials on the desk.

"Having trouble with your sketches?" her father inquired, coming in through the French doors.

"A bit."

"Perhaps you're concentrating too hard. Come out for a walk instead."

"Can I take a rain check on that? I really must get on with some more designs."

"As you wish." Her father glanced at his watch. "I'm going back to the hotel. Can I get you anything?"

"Some biscuits. The ones shaped like crescents with nuts on them."

He nodded. "Will you collect them later and have dinner with me? I can recommend Madame Blond's cooking."

"I'd like that. A change of atmosphere will do me good."

Her father went out, and Miranda concentrated on her sketch pad. She was still bent over it when a sudden glow of light made her look up to see Pierre in front of her, his hand on the desk lamp.

"It's bad to strain those beautiful eyes," he said.

"I hadn't realized it was dark."

"How's the work coming?"

"It isn't. I think I'm worrying too much about it."

"Are you surprised? You're bound to be nervous. But you'll worry less once you've seen Christi's for yourself.

I've arranged for us to go to Paris tomorrow,'' he went on casually. ''I hope that's all right with you?''

Her heart started to hammer against her ribs. ''So soon?''

''The sooner the better!''

The prospect excited her, and only when she told her father during dinner did she realize ruefully that he might just as well have remained in London.

''Why don't you come to Paris with us?'' she suggested.

''Can you see me amusing myself in a couturier's?'' he chuckled. ''That's your life, poppet, not mine. No, I'll be perfectly content to stay here till you return.''

''I don't like leaving you.''

''You left me alone in London,'' he teased. ''Anyway, I've been invited out to lunch tomorrow by a very charming woman.''

Uncertain whether she was being teased, Miranda looked at him. ''What's her name?''

''Madame Maury.''

''You're joking! You don't even know her.''

''I do now—thanks to your almond-covered biscuits!''

''What do you mean?''

''We were both in the *boulangerie* at the same time, and we both asked for the last half-kilo they had!''

''I suppose you let Madame Maury take them?''

''Actually we compromised.'' Roger Dixon fished into his pocket and drew out a prettily wrapped package. ''We took half each.''

Miranda laughed. ''I'll really enjoy these now!''

''You sound as if you don't like her.''

''But I do. Unfortunately, I don't think *she* likes me. It's because of the perfume.''

''I see.'' Roger Dixon rubbed the side of his nose. ''Would you prefer me not to see her?''

''What difference will it make?'' Miranda half smiled to herself. ''I just wonder if she would have invited you to lunch if she'd known you were my father.''

"As a matter of fact, we didn't exchange names till we parted. And that was two hours after we met!"

It took a moment for the words to register. "What on earth were you and Madame Maury doing for two hours?"

"Walking and talking. After we'd divided the biscuits, I asked her to direct me to the local museum, and she decided to take me there herself. Then we explored some Roman ruins."

"I can see why you don't want to come to Paris," she laughed. "And here I was, worrying about you being lonely!" She looked down at her fork, and aware that something was troubling her, her father leaned across the table.

"What has this perfume of yours got to do with Madame Maury not liking you anymore?"

"She's angry because we're buying it. Pierre thinks it's a matter of money. If her own company marketed it, they'd make a much bigger profit out of it. But Pierre took that into account when he fixed a price on the land."

"Then you've nothing to feel guilty about. Would you like me to mention the price of the land to Madame Maury if I get the chance?"

Miranda frowned. "I don't think so. I'm probably making more out of her dislike than she meant. It's just that she was so friendly the first time we met, and I liked her so much that . . . ."

"She has a great deal of charm," Roger Dixon agreed and deliberately changed the subject.

IT WAS MIDNIGHT before Miranda returned to the château and, leaving her father at the gate, walked alone down the driveway. In the moonlight the house looked like a fairy-tale palace, and she felt like an enchanted princess caught up in a spell from which there was no escape. But where was she bound? To this lovely house with its centuries of history, or to the glittering, unknown future? Unbidden, her thoughts turned to the dark-haired man who seemed to be constantly in her mind, a man who irritated and annoyed her and, above all, frightened her.

For she was frightened of him, she admitted. Frightened of what he had done to Lucille and what he was now doing to her. She put her hands to her temples, surprised to find them damp. She was crazy to let this Frenchman occupy her mind. There was nothing so special about him that should have made her single him out. Yet she did not even have to close her eyes to see his face in front of her—the thin, straight brows, the firm mouth, the glittering brown stare.

The château door loomed ahead, and she sped up the steps and inserted her key in the lock. Quietly, she let herself into the hall and closed the door. Breathing deeply, she leaned against it to catch her breath. A table lamp illuminated the hall, and in its warm glow her fanciful thoughts evaporated, so that once again she was the determined Miranda Dixon who knew exactly where she was going and with whom.

Mounting the stairs, she firmly resolved to think only of herself and her career.

CHRISTI'S FULFILLED Miranda's greatest expectations. Set in a graceful house a stone's throw from the imposing Georges V Hotel, its opulent interior epitomized elegance and wealth. No woman would dare set foot there if she had to worry about exceeding her budget, nor would buyers come unless they could set down their minimum fifty thousand franc entrance fee, which would entitle them to one *toile*—a linen pattern—from one collection. And the next collection, Miranda thought incredulously, was going to be hers!

The trepidation she had felt during the flight from Nice to Paris had left her the moment she was introduced to the *vendeuses* lined up in the salon to greet her. It was as though her years of training and the startling success she had achieved since leaving college had suddenly come to her aid, giving her the confidence with which to face the supercilious, condescending, curious and occasionally compassionate eyes regarding her.

Only as she went through the workrooms did nervousness return. Here was the hub of her empire; from this great heart would flow the blood to supply the sinews and muscles of this establishment. But looking at the last collection that had been produced, she realized how anemic the blood had become, and how desperately in need of a transfusion the House of Christi was.

"You can see why Monsieur Maurice chose *you*," Pierre whispered to her as the last of a horrendous display of dresses fluttered out of sight.

"Where's the designer now?" she asked.

"He returned to Madrid."

"To bullfighting, I hope!"

Pierre laughed. "He had a good reputation, you know. Perhaps he was overwhelmed by everyone here."

"That happens to many designers. Look what a failure St. Laurent was when he started at Dior. Yet once he was on his own there was no stopping him."

"Don't *you* let anyone here intimidate you," Pierre said quickly.

"They won't. The designs I did for Mr. Joseph would knock spots off the ones I've just seen."

"That's my girl," Pierre laughed and caught her hand to his lips. The gesture, so French, surprised her, for as always he looked more English than Parisian. "Monsieur Maurice is meeting us here at noon. The contract is ready for your signature."

"I never knew lawyers could work so quickly!"

"Maurice doesn't want you to change your mind." Pierre glanced around the salon. "They've never sold perfume here before, so we must decide how to display it. I thought of turning the ground floor into a *parfumerie*."

Miranda shook her head. Until this moment she had not given the subject any thought, but instinct told her that Pierre was wrong.

"I'm going to make Tendresse the theme of my first

collection," she said. "I'll use chiffon and velvet and
sheerest wools. Everything must have movement. Lots
of movement." She pointed to the walls of the salon.
"We'll drape chiffon into the letter T and suspend it all
around. Just the one letter—not the whole word—it will
be *your* job to make women know it stands for Tendresse."

"It *could* work," he said cautiously. "It could indeed." His voice grew more enthusiastic. "I like it. I
know just what you mean. I'd better give *myself* a contract before you decide you can do your own publicity!"

She caught his hand. "I owe you too much to do without you, Pierre."

"Making yourself indispensable?" a cool voice asked,
and they drew apart as Monsieur Maurice and his stepdaughter came in.

"Colette," Pierre said, bowing. "I hadn't expected to
see you here, too."

"Why not? Naturally, I'm anxious to know what's
going to happen to Christi's."

Masking the chill the words brought her, Miranda said
easily, "I'm taking over, Miss Dinard. I thought you
knew?"

"Only some of the details." Hard eyes raked her.
"You surely don't intend to run the entire house?"

"I most certainly do. There can only be one person in
control."

"That's always been Madame Vernier," Colette replied and looked at her stepfather. "Haven't you told
Miss Dixon about her?"

"We were too concerned over the main issue to worry
about details."

"I'd hardly call Madame Vernier a detail," Colette
said dryly and looked at Miranda. "She's been *directrice*
here since Jacques Christi started. She has the loyalty of
the workroom and every *vendeuse* behind her. If *she*
doesn't approve of you, papa will be crazy to bring you
in!"

"Then it's a good thing the contract hasn't been signed yet." Miranda looked at Monsieur Maurice, who stared blandly back at her, unperturbed by his stepdaughter's remarks.

"I suggest we introduce you to Madame Vernier at once," he said. "She wasn't here when you arrived because she came to the airport to meet me." He motioned to a model who had been listening with undisguised interest to the discussion, and she hurried out.

Everyone waited in silence, and Miranda braced herself for a difficult meeting. If Madame Vernier had started here with Christi himself, she would no doubt have a fierce loyalty to the house, that would make her a formidable opponent of anyone whose ability she doubted. *She won't doubt mine,* Miranda thought proudly and tossed back her amber gold hair, the only sign she gave of nerves. "I'm better than the other two men they brought in. I've got to remember that, no matter what happens."

A short, plump woman bustled into the salon, and one look at the shrewd eyes set in the carefully made-up face allayed all Miranda's fears. A martinet the woman might be, but there was no doubting her intelligence, nor her integrity. Miranda held out her hand and felt it taken in a firm grasp.

"Monsieur Maurice told me you were young," the woman said in faultless English, "but not *how* young!"

"Old enough to know my capabilities," Miranda replied with a faint smile, "and young enough to admit my limitations!"

Madame Vernier's chest expanded like a pouter pigeon as she acknowledged the full meaning of this remark. "I am sorry I was not here when you arrived, Miss Dixon."

"Never mind. Perhaps—if it won't inconvenience you—you would show me around?"

"You have already seen everything."

"Only with *my* eyes. I would like to try and see them with yours."

Madame Vernier's eyebrows rose, then abruptly she turned. "Come. I will show you."

Miranda's first introduction to the salon and work-rooms paled into insignificance beside the one she received from Madame Vernier, and for the next three hours she followed the woman from room to room, and person to person, from the newest apprentice to the most experienced seamstress and cutter.

Gradually, the great establishment came to life before her, its past glories reawakened both by the people she met and by the glimpses she was given of the great fashions Jacques Christi had inspired, and which had been photographed and placed in leather-bound volumes in the *directrice*'s office. Patiently, the woman explained how the great man had worked, showing her the mannequins he had used to drape his materials on, the table where he had done his cutting and the desk where he had prepared his sketches.

"Since Jacques's death," Madame Vernier said, "we have existed on his reputation. The two designers Monsieur Maurice brought in were not big enough to wear his mantle, and luckily not big enough to destroy what he had built. But after two bad seasons we are beginning to falter. Another poor collection and we are finished."

"What do you think of *my* work?" Miranda asked bluntly.

"It is good. But putting designs on paper is only half the battle. Seeing that they are interpreted the way you wish—that their final appearance is the way you want them to be—takes determination and strength. This house has its own way of doing things, and if you are not strong enough, it can destroy you."

"I can be strong," Miranda replied, "as long as Christi's is on my side."

"I think it will be," Madame Vernier said and caught Miranda's hands. "We have a great deal of work ahead of us. Will you be ready to design our winter collection? We show at the end of August.''

''I couldn't be ready before January,'' Miranda said regretfully.

''I was afraid of that.''

''Why don't we just have a small show for the winter?'' Miranda ventured. ''We could introduce a few of my clothes perhaps and update some of the Christi coats and suits. After all, they're as famous as the Chanel ones, and *they've* been going for years!''

''An excellent idea. Christi coats and suits are timeless, but Senor Santos refused to put them into his collection.''

''He must have been crazy!'' said Miranda.

''Obstinate and conceited,'' Madame Vernier added.

''I can be obstinate, too!''

Madame Vernier smiled. ''A person is only obstinate if one does not agree with their ideas, but in the main I think I will agree with yours!''

Feeling as though she had come unscathed through the biggest battle of her career, Miranda returned to the salon to find that Monsieur Maurice and Pierre had long since departed, though to her dismay Colette had not gone with them.

''My stepfather has taken Pierre to lunch, but I thought we'd be more relaxed if we went somewhere on our own,'' she explained.

Aware that Colette's decision had not been prompted by liking, Miranda waited for the knife to be unsheathed. She did not have to wait long.

''Do you still feel so confident, now you've met Madame Vernier?'' asked Colette.

''Even more so. She will be of enormous help.''

''You're very young to take on such responsibility.'' Behind the beautiful mask of makeup, the girl's face was sharp. ''Aren't you scared by it?''

''No.''

''Then your imagination must be limited!'' Colette's

scarlet-tipped nails grasped her bag more firmly. "How do you plan to launch Alain's perfume?"

"It's Christi's perfume now."

"It will always be Alain's." Halfway down the stairs Colette paused to look at Miranda. "He hates you for taking it away from him. He'll never forgive you for it."

Miranda was glad she was holding onto the banister, for the impact of the words made her knees tremble. "I'm sure that isn't true. Everything was arranged on a businesslike basis."

"Extremely *good* business on your part," Colette retorted. "If your collection is the biggest flop in the world, you'll still make a fortune out of Tendresse. It was brilliant of Pierre to think of it. There isn't a woman in the world who won't want that perfume."

"Do you know it?" Miranda asked, determined not to comment on anything else Colette said.

"Naturally. Alain gave me a vial. Apart from his mother, I'm the only person who has used it." The hard eyes were mocking. "But now it will be yours—though it won't do you any good."

"You've just said it will be a best-seller."

"Oh, it will bring you money, but it won't bring you Alain—and that's what you really want, isn't it?"

Miranda continued to walk downstairs. "I don't know what you're talking about."

"Yes, you do," Colette said behind her. "You've wanted Alain from the moment you met him."

"I'm not interested in men who jilt their pregnant fiancées," Miranda retorted and could have bitten out her tongue as she heard Colette's laugh.

"I'll have to tell Alain you said that. I'm sure he'll find it interesting."

Blindly, Miranda hurried down to the hall, waiting unseeingly for Colette to catch up with her. "Do you mind if I don't lunch with you?" she said without looking around. "I've been concentrating so much with Madame Vernier that I'd like to go for a walk by myself."

"Of course." The French girl's normally sharp voice was as sweet as saccharine. "But don't forget to come back. My stepfather will be waiting for you."

"I'll be back," Miranda said and set off down the tree-lined road, wishing she need never return; need never see Maurice or Pierre or the House of Christi again; and more particularly, need never see Colette Dinard.

THE COUPLE OF DAYS Miranda had anticipated spending in Paris stretched to ten, and she was once more caught up in the feverish excitement that seemed to go hand in hand with the fashion industry, whether one was in the cheap end of the trade or the most expensive. As Gertrude Stein might have said, she thought wryly on the tenth morning— "A dress is a dress is a dress."

She stepped back from the mannequin on which she had been draping a soft wool georgette, one of several dresses she had designed this past week for the mini-collection that Christi's would be showing in August. With Paris blossoming from late spring into early summer, it seemed ludicrous to be thinking of winter clothes, yet such was the pressure of the industry that one had to work months ahead of each season.

"I like that," Madame Vernier said approvingly, coming into the workroom. "It has a strong line."

"It's wonderful material," Miranda replied. "It drapes itself."

"Everything you design is workable. That's the mark of a couturier. You must know where you're going. If you don't, no one will want to follow you."

Miranda smiled and crossed to the window. It was uncurtained to let in as much light as possible, and though at the top of the building, it was still noisy with the sound of traffic. In the room itself some two dozen *midinettes* were at work, needles flashing in and out of fine materials, and an occasional whirr of a sewing machine punctuated by a burst of laughter or conversation. Not that there was much chattering in Madame Vernier's pres-

ence, for the *directrice* ruled the establishment with an
iron hand that saw no need of a velvet glove.

It was not an attitude that would have succeeded in
London, Miranda knew, but then no one took fashion as
seriously as the French, and any girl lucky enough to be
taken on at a couturier's—even in the lowliest
capacity—repaid the owner by long hours of eye-
straining and back-breaking work.

Madame Vernier came toward her with a look presag-
ing a command, and Miranda braced herself as she wondered what else was required of her. Unexpectedly, it
was a wedding dress.

"It always attracts good press coverage," Madame
Vernier explained, "and I think you should do one."

"Wedding dresses are so banal," sighed Miranda.

"Not to the bride! If you have an idea of the line you
intend to follow for your spring collection, perhaps you
could give a hint of it with the wedding dress."

"That's an excellent idea." Miranda marveled at the
directrice's astuteness. "I'll work something out when I
get back to Provence."

"When are you going?"

"As soon as I can. I had no intention of staying away
so long."

"You should be living in Paris already," Madame
Vernier commented. "You must start to take control
here."

It was a truth Miranda could not deny, and though she
regretted that her stay in Provence must end, she knew it
must if she wished to continue her career. If only it did
not have to be in this most difficult of all cities! Paris
might be gaiety and charm on the surface, but underneath
it was a hard metropolis, much harder than London, yet
with none of that city's efficiency.

"You will need to find an apartment," Madame Vernier said. "If you could give me some idea of what you
want . . . ."

Miranda shrugged away an answer. Until her contrac

had been finalized, she was reluctant to commit herself. Besides, she had no real idea what money she could expect. She would have to discuss it with Pierre. She sighed. She seemed to talk everything over with him. Not an evening passed that she did not dine with him, nor a problem arise that she did not discuss with him. The faint unease he had aroused in her when they had first met no longer disturbed her, and she wondered if she had become used to his worldly cynicism, or found it less noticeable, because she was again living in a commercial atmosphere where achievement of one's ambition was the acme of success.

Yet her turning to Pierre was due, in part, to Colette Dinard. It was as if her awareness of the girl's relationship with Alain had made her conscious of her own barren life. It was not something that had worried her before, and she wondered wryly if it was the so-called magic of Paris that made her feel unfulfilled unless she had an admiring man to dress for and to live for.

Not that she could ever live for Pierre, she decided later that morning as she waited for him to take her out for lunch. He was intelligent and amusing, but not someone with whom she would want to spend the rest of her life. There was no man with whom she could envisage doing that. No man.

She did not realize she had said the last two words aloud until she heard them repeated by Pierre and, turning from the mirror where she had been putting on fresh makeup, saw him framed in the doorway.

"What 'no man' were you referring to?" he quizzed.

"No man in particular! I'm too busy." She covered one side of her hair with a floppy red beret the same shade as the buttons on her navy suit.

"No woman is so busy that she can't enjoy a little flirtation," he replied. "Anyway, I don't want to flirt with you. I'd like something more serious."

"At a quarter to one on a Wednesday afternoon?"

"At any time." The smile left his face and he looked

grave. "You're my sort of girl, Miranda. We would make a wonderful team. You can't tell me you haven't felt that, too?"

She hesitated and then decided to be blunt. "Of course I've felt it. We work marvelously together. Half the time you know what I mean before I've said it, and the other half you've gone and done it before I've even thought of it! But that doesn't mean it's love. In fact, I know it isn't."

"How can you be so sure?"

"Because when I'm away from my work, I'm *not* your sort of girl."

"You can't divorce yourself from your career. It's the very essence of you."

The word "essence" conjured up a narrow, tanned face and a hard, sardonic glance, and she pushed the image fiercely from her mind. "Three months ago I might have agreed with you," she said, forcing herself to concentrate on Pierre, "but now I'm not sure. Living in the château and learning so much more about my mother has made me realize what love can mean between two people."

"Knowing a person is a part of loving them," he retorted, "and you've just said how well I know *you*."

"The business side of me," she reminded him. "You know nothing of the other side."

"Show it to me," he murmured, "or let me find it out for myself."

Before she could stop him, he pulled her into his arms and kissed her. Her resistance was instinctive, but he took no notice and continued to hold her, his grip tightening so that she could not move. Realizing the childishness of trying to fight her way free, she remained quiescent in his arms, but it was like being held by a stranger, so calm and dispassionate did she feel.

The sharp click of a door drew them apart, and Miranda's face burned as she saw Colette and Monsieur Maurice watching them with amusement.

"It would be silly to say we hope we're not intruding," the girl said sardonically, "because we obviously are!"

"Not at all." Pierre sauntered over to the mirror and casually wiped the lipstick from his mouth. "Miranda and I were just going out to lunch."

"Were you having the hors d'oeuvres in the office?" Colette asked.

"I was sampling the sweet!" he said and, coming back to Miranda's side, put his arm across her shoulders, a gesture that had now become second nature with him.

"I suggest we lunch together," Monsieur Maurice interrupted, his brusque tones cooling the emotional tension. "There's a clause in the contract we still have to discuss." He looked at Miranda. "It's about compensation if either of us wishes to end the partnership."

"Do you still doubt Miranda's talent?" Pierre asked.

"*I* believe in it," Monsieur Maurice replied, "but will the public? Only time will tell, and if we are proved wrong . . . ."

"I wouldn't want compensation if you asked me to leave," Miranda said quickly. "Anyway, if I were no good, I'd go without being told."

The pudgy face creased into a smile, though the eyes remained shrewd. "I believe you would, Miranda, but you know what lawyers are—they like everything set down in black and white."

"Add whatever clause you think necessary, and I'll sign it," she said and stared at Pierre, defying him to disagree.

Knowing himself beaten, he shrugged and opened the door.

They lunched at Maxim's, the magnificence of the food suiting the quiet elegance of the decor. Miranda was amused at the intense way Colette and the two men discussed what they were going to eat, though the food, when it came, was worthy of the care taken over its choice: delicious puff pastry cases stuffed with truffles and chicken, followed by sole in champagne sauce.

"I'll never get any work done this afternoon,"
Miranda said as she finally pushed away her plate.
"When I'm working, I rarely have anything more than
coffee."

"That is bad for your health," Monsieur Maurice said.

"Maybe. But it's extremely good for my brain! Right
now I wouldn't be able to tell a dress from a sauce boat!"

"I hope you're not really so sleepy," Colette drawled.
"We're going to Alain's office this afternoon."

Miranda was glad that the folds of the tablecloth hid
her trembling hands, and she looked inquiringly at Monsieur Maurice.

"Alain has brought some vials of Tendresse from
Grasse," he explained. "It seemed a good opportunity to
finalize everything with him."

"You don't need *me* there."

"A couple of points may arise that require your attention. It is better if you come."

He picked up the bill, then set down what seemed to
Miranda an astronomical sum before leading the way out
of the restaurant to his waiting car and chauffeur.

Within minutes they were deposited outside the
double-fronted salon of Adrienne Cosmetics, which occupied a large corner block on the Champs Elysées. The
interior decor was in variegated pastels, which echoed
the floral packaging of all the products, while the furniture was predominantly silver gilt, as was the ornate
elevator that took them to the second floor. There the
colors were strictly functional, and from behind closed
doors came the sound of typewriters and telephones.

Miranda had no time for more than a fleeting impression of bustle and efficiency before Alain Maury came
out of his office to greet them. In a dark, tailored suit he
looked older and more austere than she had remembered, so that it was hard to associate him with the passionate man she had run into on the lawn outside the
château, or the bitter and angry one she had encountered
in Nice.

"A chair," he was saying, and she hurriedly perched on a spindle-legged one and forced herself to listen while Monsieur Maurice drew out some densely typed papers and began to go through them, with Alain making occasional terse interjections and Pierre smoothing over the frequent differences of interpretation that ruffled the conversation.

All the while Miranda surreptitiously looked at Alain. Lines of fatigue had etched themselves on his face, and beneath his tan his skin had a grayish tinge. He looked every one of his thirty years, yet as he rubbed the side of his forehead with a clenched fist—the way a child often does when tired—she was overcome by such tenderness that she ached to reach out and touch him. Appalled by her weakness, she pressed back into her chair. He had only sold them a perfume; he had no right to look as bereft as though he had sold them his child.

His child . . . . The memory of Lucille corroded her thoughts like acid, eating away the tenderness she felt toward him. Tenderness. The name he had given to the first perfume he had created since Lucille's death. How dared he use the word when he did not even know its meaning!

Unable to bear her thoughts, she jumped up and walked over to the window. But nothing could shut out her awareness of the lean figure behind the teak desk, nor the slim, tanned fingers taking out three vials of perfume from a small box.

"This is for you, Miranda." Pierre came toward her with a vial in his hand. Unwillingly, she took it, staring at the bare half-ounce of amber gold liquid, the same color as her hair.

"As there's only so little," she murmured, "I don't think I should keep it. Can't you use it, Pierre? Give it to someone at *Vogue*, perhaps?"

"It's yours," he reiterated. "You said you were going to base your first big collection on Tendresse, so you should at least know what it smells like!" He swung back to the middle of the room. "Miranda has a sensational idea for the design of the bottle."

"So have I," Alain cut in, and from the drawer of his desk he took out a gold-topped container. It was tall and narrow, perfectly plain except for a ripple of glass molded to the front and forming a flowing letter T.

Pierre's mouth dropped open, and he shot Miranda an accusing look. "You told him!"

"I never said a word." Disbelievingly, she moved over and picked up the bottle. "This is the same idea as mine," she said and looked directly into Alain's face.

Dark brown eyes stared at her, but there was nothing to be seen in their depths.

"Great minds think alike," he said coolly.

"It is good that you and Miranda are on the same wave-length," Monsieur Maurice smiled.

The silence was momentary, yet uncomfortable, and was interrupted by Colette. "I adore your perfume, Alain, but I *don't* like the bottle. It's not dramatic enough."

"I prefer subtlety," he replied. "Besides, Tendresse is not a dramatic word. It is romantic."

Colette turned to Pierre. "Do *you* like the name?"

He hesitated. "It's going to be the theme of Miranda's spring collection."

"Christi's has always catered to the sophisticated woman," Colette said sharply and looked at her step-father. "You agree with that, don't you?"

"At the moment Christi's has no image. If Miranda feels the mood is toward romanticism . . . ."

Colette gave an angry toss of her head and subsided into silence. Again Miranda wondered whether it would not be wiser to abandon the idea of working in Paris. What peace of mind would she have if she constantly met Colette and Alain? It would be better to return to London and start up on her own. At least in that way she would be her own mistress.

Was Colette Alain's mistress, she wondered and hastily pushed away the thought, furious at where word association had led her.

In an effort to quell the turmoil inside her, she moved closer to Pierre. "If there's no more need for me to stay, I'd like to go back to Christi's."

"It's far too late for you to work. I'll take you back to your hotel, and we can have a quiet dinner."

"You should find an apartment," Monsieur Maurice advised. "Madame Vernier spoke to me about it this morning."

Miranda could not help smiling. "She said the same to me."

"And me!" said Pierre. "But I've done something about it! There's an apartment available in my building. Three large rooms with a magnificent view of Paris."

Colette gave a sudden meaningful laugh. "It must be wonderful to meet a long-lost cousin and find he's not only handsome, but also so capable of managing your life."

"I wish I'd met him years ago," Miranda replied with commendable calm.

"You'd have still been in your baby carriage," Pierre said tenderly and lifted her hand to his lips.

She suffered his touch with the smile still on her face, but was aware of Alain Maury pushing back his chair and closing the drawer of his desk.

"*I* will drive you back to your hotel, Miranda," he said, startling her not only by the offer but also by the use of her first name.

She opened her mouth to refuse, but the look of fury on Colette's face made her change her mind, and she nodded.

A few moments later she was sitting beside him in a large black Citroën, watching as he weaved skillfully through the crush of cars. He drove with quiet efficiency. No grinding gears or expletives marked his progress, merely a quietness that grew deeper the thicker the traffic became, until finally he gave a long sigh and, turning

the car into a side street, parked it adroitly in what
seemed to Miranda to be a minimum amount of space.

"It's hopeless to drive in rush hour," he said. "Nothing makes me more bad tempered."

"You don't look it."

"The angrier I get the quieter I become."

"You must be very angry now!"

He shrugged and folded his arms across his chest.
"How do you think you will like working in Paris?"

"It will be a challenge."

"Will you cope?"

"Or die in the attempt!"

"You're too young to talk of dying," he said harshly.

"I didn't mean it literally."

"Then don't say such a thing. People talk too lightly of
death."

She knew without being told that he was thinking of
Lucille, and the knowledge was like a sudden stab of
pain. "If you don't like driving in rush hour," she said
quickly, "you shouldn't have offered to drive me back to
the hotel."

"I wanted to talk to you alone."

Her heart began to pound, but she said nothing and
waited for him to continue.

"It's about your father," he began.

She swung around at that. "He isn't ill, is he? I tried to
call him last night, but I couldn't get through. Is that
why . . . ?"

"No, no, it's nothing like that." Seeing her fright,
Alain instinctively put out his hands. They touched her
breasts, and he drew back sharply. "I'm sorry," he
apologized. "I—you—your father's perfectly all right.
There's no need to get alarmed."

"Then what . . . ?"

"It's about his friendship with my mother."

Miranda stared at him. "I don't know what you're
talking about."

"I realize that." For the first time there was a little

humor in Alain Maury's voice. "That's why I wanted to talk to you . . . to explain what has happened." He leaned against the wheel, and the light from a streetlight fell obliquely across his face, catching the gleam of dark hair and the tightly stretched skin over bone. "They met in the village, as you know."

"And shared a half-kilo of biscuits!"

"They now want to share their life," he said. "They've fallen in love."

Miranda was too astonished to speak. For years she had hoped her father would make a new life for himself, but never had she anticipated it being with a woman like Adrienne Maury: not only a successful tycoon but Alain's mother. No, it was impossible.

"Why is it impossible?" Alain's question made her realize she had spoken her final thoughts aloud. "They are old enough to know their own minds, and I believe they are well suited. If you were to see them together, I am sure you would agree. Don't be jealous of my mother, Miranda. She will be good for your father."

Unwilling to have him misunderstand her reaction, she said quickly, "I'm sure they'll be extremely happy together."

"Then why is it impossible?"

"I was thinking about us. Our dislike of each other."

"I do not dislike you," he said slowly.

"But you don't *like* me?"

He hesitated even more noticeably. "That is true."

Depression weighed her down like lead. "Well, then," she murmured, "now you know why I said it was impossible."

"We will have to hide our feelings for our parents' sake."

"Don't you think they'll guess?"

"No. At the moment they're too concerned with each other. And once they're married, we will make sure we visit them at different times."

Again depression made it hard for her to reply, but

knowing he was waiting for her to speak, she forced out the words. "Are you always so capable of settling people's lives?"

"One should do one's best to further a good marriage!"

"Or run away from a bad one?"

His breath hissed between his teeth, and he gripped her arm and shook her. "Don't talk about Lucille!"

"I w-wasn't," she stammered.

"But you were thinking about her. Every time you look at me you think of her!"

"Can you blame me?"

"She's dead," he grated. "Let her rest in peace!" With one powerful movement he pulled her against his chest, his head blotting out the light as he pressed his mouth onto hers.

Miranda's entire body responded to his touch. It was incredible that Pierre's lips left her so cold when Alain's awakened her to such desire, and even as she tried to resist it, her heart played traitor to her head, and her arms crept around his neck to caress the crisp, dark hair. Through the thickness of her jacket she could feel the thudding of his heart, but he spoke no word, merely kept kissing her with a growing intensity that began to frighten her. There was anger beneath his passion, a fury that she was afraid would become uncontrollable, and she pushed against his chest and tried to twist free of him.

"No, you don't!" he muttered thickly, and one of his hands clutched at her hair, twisting several strands around his fingers so that she could not move her head.

She pulled back even harder, the sharp tug at her scalp bringing tears of pain to her eyes. "Must you hurt every woman you want?" she cried. "Isn't it enough that you destroyed Lucille?"

His hands dropped away from her as though she were on fire, and she slid across the seat until the door handle dug into her spine. Beyond the car the traffic droned ceaselessly, but inside it was an oasis of quiet save for the heavy breathing of the man who slumped against the wheel, his head bent over his hands. The anger that had given her the strength to pull away from him dissolved as she looked at him. How guilty he must feel if Lucille's name could still hurt him so much after four years. Yet if justice were to prevail, his conscience should never let him rest.

"I wasn't responsible for Lucille's death," he said suddenly without lifting his head. "I want you to know that."

These were the first words he had ever said in his defense, and she could not hide her surprise.

"Then why did she kill herself?"

"I can't tell you that."

"Can't or *won't?*" He said nothing, and anger rose sharply inside her, made stronger by the knowledge of how much she wanted him to defend himself. "You changed your mind about marrying her," she accused. "That's why she died!"

"I *couldn't* marry her."

"Why not?"

He straightened, his face taut with suffering. "People change their—their minds. Can't you leave it at that?"

"No, I can't! Lucille loved you—she was going to have your child! Or didn't that mean anything to you?"

"Don't!" he burst out. "I don't want to talk about it."

"Because you've no defense!"

He remained silent, and the hope that had stirred in her when he had started to speak died away, leaving behind a bitterness she could taste. "I never despised any man more than you," she said slowly. "My only regret is that we'll have to meet again."

"I'm sorry."

"Is that all you can say?"

He did not reply. Instead he switched on the ignition and edged the car slowly out into the mainstream of traffic.

No word was spoken between them for the rest of the

journey, and in silence they drew up outside her hotel. As the car came to a stop, Pierre hurried from the entrance to greet them.

"You left your perfume in Alain's office," he said, opening the door for her. "So I brought it along for you."

"You shouldn't have bothered." She flashed him her warmest smile, aware of the silent man at the wheel. "But I'll take you up on that dinner after all."

"Wonderful!" he said gaily and helped her out onto the sidewalk.

At once the engine came to life again and with a curt good-night Alain streaked away. Watching the taillights disappear, Miranda felt darkness envelop her, and even as it did, the light of revelation illumined all her past actions and thoughts. No longer did she need to puzzle over her reactions to Alain's behavior or her tormented feelings every time she saw him or heard his name mentioned. She loved him. Had loved him possibly from the first moment she had met his angry brown eyes over a taxi door.

Several passersby jostled against her, and Pierre caught her arm and led her into the hotel.

"You look as if you need a drink." He steered her into the comforting dark of the small bar that lay to one side of the lobby. Leaving her at a corner table, he returned with two glasses and a half-bottle of champagne.

With a determined effort she made her lips curve into a smile. "What are we celebrating?"

"Nothing. That's the best time to drink champagne!"

It was an apt remark, and as the bubbles effervesced beneath her nose, she waited for the lift of spirits that drink would inevitably bring. Better to live with false pleasure than no pleasure at all.

"Drink up," Pierre ordered, "you're already beginning to sparkle."

"I was only feeling tired," she lied. "I'm glad you followed me."

"So I gathered."

She glanced at him beneath her lashes, but the blandness of his expression gave nothing away. Yet to pretend she did not understand him would make both of them look foolish, and she decided to tell him part of the truth.

"I quarreled with Alain," she explained.

"Why?"

"We—we talked about Lucille. He said he wasn't responsible for her death, and I—I didn't believe him."

"I'm not surprised. He must be crazy to think he can fool you."

"I still can't believe he acted so callously," she burst out. "I know he can be overbearing and obstinate, but I don't—I can't believe he's *cruel*."

"He isn't cruel," Pierre said in deliberate tones. "He just isn't capable of feeling love the way other people do."

"But Lucille was expecting his child!"

"I'm sure he'd have taken care of her financially. He wasn't to know she'd do anything so—so—"

"Don't defend him!" Miranda exclaimed. "What he did was despicable."

"I'm not defending him," Pierre said gently. "I'm trying to show you the sort of man he is. Don't be carried away by his looks or behavior. He may be passionate on the surface, but underneath he's ice."

Remembering the way Alain had held her in his arms, Miranda found it difficult to hold her glass steady, and with trembling hands she set it down.

Pierre gave her a sharp look. "Don't tell me *you've* fallen for him?"

"Don't be ridiculous!"

"Then why did you look so shattered when you got out of his car?"

"Because I—" She moistened her lips, clutching hold of her senses in an effort to retain her secret. "Because he—because Madame Maury is going to marry my father!"

Pierre choked on his drink.

"It's true," she went on and, anticipating his questions, quickly told him how it had happened.

"So Alain's going to be your stepbrother," he mused. "No wonder you were upset."

"I've recovered now," she said quickly. "Alain and I have agreed that once our parents are married we'll make sure we visit them at different times."

"You can always take *me* along as a watchdog!"

"I'm not frightened of him." She stood up. "I'll go and change."

"I'll come upstairs with you."

"I *am* frightened of you," she smiled. "Wait for me here."

He smiled back. "Put on something exotic and we'll go dancing."

Only as she left the bar did the smile leave her face. How would she be able to get through the long evening ahead and, more important still, the long lonely days of the future?

She must concentrate on work. That alone would be her salvation. Yet even her work would bring Alain close, for the perfume he had created was going to be an important part of her life.

Tendresse . . . Tenderness.

But *his* tenderness was something she would never know.

CHAPTER TEN

WALKING ACROSS THE TARMAC of the Côte d'Azur Airport at Nice, Miranda was surprised by the sense of homecoming it gave her. Incredible to think she had only seen this coastline a few months ago; it was etched so clearly in her mind that she felt it had always been a part of her life.

Her father was waiting to greet her in the terminal, his hug warm and enveloping as he led her out to a small white Renault.

"I didn't expect to be met," she said as they drove off toward Bayronne.

"It seemed a good opportunity to talk to you. I take it Alain's told you the news?"

"Yes."

"Were you upset? I know it must be a shock for you."

"I'm delighted," she said quickly, "though I must say it seems odd to congratulate your father because he's getting married! It makes me seem *de trop!*"

"You'll never be that." He slowed down and covered her hands with his own. "Nothing that happens to me in the future can alter the past. My love for your mother is something I'll remember all my life. But I've a chance to begin again with Adrienne, and I'd be foolish to turn my back on it. She's a wonderful person. I'm sure you'll agree once you get to know her."

"I like her already. It's only a pity she—" Miranda stopped, unwilling to say more, but she had already said too much, for her father turned his head expectantly.

"What's a pity?"

"That she's Alain Maury's mother," Miranda said slowly. "He and I—we don't get on too well."

"Why not? He seems like an exceptionally nice man."

"It's probably the disharmony of opposites."

"Usually opposites attract!"

"Not in our case," Miranda said with a forced laugh and wished with all her heart that what her father had said was true. Yet even if Alain had reciprocated her feelings, the ghost of Lucille would always have come between them.

"When are you getting married?" She determinedly concentrated on other things.

"In a couple of weeks."

"So soon?"

"There's no point waiting. We won't change our minds."

"Are you that sure?" she asked seriously.

"Adrienne and I knew how we felt within a few days of meeting. It sometimes happens like that. Perhaps one day you'll know what I mean."

Her father's words threatened to play havoc with her self-control, and she stared fixedly at the countryside flashing past.

"Tell me about your visit to Paris," her father asked, and for the rest of the journey she kept up a brisk monologue, painting him a word picture of the House of Christi and the work involved in running it.

"It seems an enormous job," he said. "Do you think you're up to it? You're so young."

"Twenty-two isn't young these days."

"I suppose not. But I'm glad *I'm* giving up the rat race."

"I can't imagine you retiring," she commented.

"Not *complete* retirement. But any future engineering projects will have to be either in England or France. Luckily, Adrienne's reached the stage where she can leave the business any time she wishes."

"Would she like to?" Miranda asked. "Most of her ri

vals died with their boots on—or perhaps I should say their makeup on!''

''Not Adrienne,'' Roger Dixon said firmly. ''She's happy to leave everything to Alain.''

In the distance the red-tiled roofs of Bayronne could be seen nestling against the hillside, while the village clock tower pointed a dark finger into the deep blue sky. She had only been away a short while, yet summer had come to Provence, and there was a languor in the air that had not been there before. The sun was hotter and the shade of the trees cooler as they bowled along the straight, wide village street, past the fountain chattering aimlessly to itself and the gaggle of black-clad women gossiping as they waited for the local bus.

She was relieved when they took the road to the château, though the relief evaporated as she climbed out of the car and saw Adrienne Maury coming along the terrace to greet her.

Resolutely pushing aside her embarrassment, Miranda kissed the woman warmly on both cheeks. The gesture was returned with an aloofness that had not been present the first time they had met. Despite her easygoing manner, it seemed that Madame Maury still resented being thwarted in business. But on the surface all was serene as the three of them went into the salon where the *comtesse* was reclining on her favorite settee.

As though their entry had been a signal, Simone came in with coffee, and Miranda served it and then deliberately went to sit beside her future stepmother.

''I hope you're not upset at my marrying your father?'' Adrienne Maury inquired gently.

''I'm delighted. I'm all for marriage!''

''You should start to think of it for yourself. Success and money can never be a compensation for personal happiness.''

''I never thought they could.''

The sloping shoulders moved as though the woman was about to say more, but evidently she decided against it, for she changed the subject and talked of a new three-star restaurant she had been told about.

Not until her father and Madame Maury left the château did Miranda have time to wonder at the meaning behind the woman's remarks. It was clear that in forcing Alain to let them market Tendresse, she and Pierre had aroused her anger. It was an emotion that did not fit the picture Roger Dixon had built up of her. A woman who was no longer ambitious—who felt she had achieved enough in life to be able to take things easy—should not be so furious at having to forgo the extra profit that would have come to her company had they not sold Tendresse to Christi's.

The hum of a motor interrupted Miranda's thoughts, and she looked toward the horizon.

"It's Alain's men," her grandmother explained. "They are churning up the land as they plant the roses. Half the hillside is already covered. I'm sure you'll have your scent by next January."

"I hope so. Tendresse means a great deal to me."

The *comtesse* smiled. "It's hard for me to think of you as a famous couturier."

Miranda laughed. "Is that wishful thinking, or are you psychic?"

"If one wishes hard enough, one can often make the wish come true."

Miranda bit back a sigh. No amount of wishing could make her own dreams come true; the nightmare of reality made this impossible.

"When do you return to Paris?" her grandmother asked.

"At the end of the month."

"I wish you were a little less ambitious. I would like to see great-grandchildren before I die."

"I haven't found a man yet, darling—and please don't talk about dying."

"Could you not consider Pierre?"

Miranda shook her head. It was one thing to let Alain

Maury think she liked Pierre more than she did, but quite
another to pretend with her grandmother.

"I'm married to my work," she said firmly, "and right
now I've a wedding dress to design."

"How can you think like a bride when you don't want
to be one?"

"That's what being creative is all about!"

MIRANDA REMEMBERED this remark several days later
when, with a pad full of designs she did not like, she finally abandoned the idea of doing a wedding dress at all.
Her failure to produce anything that even approximated
her normal distinctive line made her conclude that the
knowledge that she could never marry the man she loved
was subconsciously preventing her from designing a
dress for another, luckier girl to wear.

She was still musing about this when Adrienne Maury
telephoned to say she was giving a party to introduce her
future husband to her friends and hoped Miranda and the
comtesse would join her.

"I'll be delighted to come," Miranda said, "but I'm
not sure about *grand'mère*."

In this her doubts were proved right, for the *comtesse*
decided she could not cope with the excitement of seeing
so many strange people.

Miranda would have liked to stay away, too, but knowing her father would be hurt if she did so, she put on a
brave face and one of her smartest outfits.

Even so, she was unprepared for the vast throng that
milled around the long buffet tables and spilled over the
lawns down to the rose garden. The majority of people
were French, though a smattering of other tongues could
be heard.

Adrienne Maury looked delightful in soft-hued pink
and made no effort to hide the love in her eyes as she led
her future husband from group to group. Watching the
two of them, Miranda expected to feel a spark of
jealousy, but none came; all she felt was a gladness that

after so many years of loneliness her father had at last found happiness again.

"You are feeling a little left out, perhaps?" a quiet voice murmured in her ear, and without looking around she knew Alain was behind her.

"A little," she admitted, "but I'm very happy for them both."

"Good. So am I."

Knowing she would have to look at Alain sometime, she turned and faced him. Seeing him with eyes of love, she saw much that she had not seen before: the hardness of the jaw and the unexpected softness of the lower lip; the sharpness of glittering brown eyes and the tiredness in the myriad lines fanning out from them; the crispness of black hair and the blue white look of the translucent skin on the temples, where a tiny nerve pulsed erratically. What a strange mixture of toughness and vulnerability he was! No wonder she was so muddled about him, her heart telling her he was one thing and her mind saying he was another.

Before she could speak, Colette appeared beside them, looking unexpectedly feminine in chiffon. "Your mother's looking for you, *chéri*."

With a slight bow he moved away, and Miranda gathered her confidence together to face the onslaught of Colette's dislike.

"Shouldn't you be in Paris working?" Colette demanded.

"I am not starting full time until August."

"I don't see why not. You're getting a big enough profit from Christi's!"

Miranda refused to be drawn, but Colette required no response. "Provence seems to have worked wonders for you and your father. I bet you never expected things to turn out like this when you first came here."

"I didn't expect anything except a few weeks' holiday in the sun." Miranda determinedly accepted the sentence at its face value. It took two to make a quarrel, and though Colette was an eager first party, she had no intention of being the second.

"I'm delighted that my father and Madame Maury met. It makes me believe in fairy tales."

"Have you met *your* Prince Charming yet?"

"I don't see *myself* as a heroine. I'm the Good Fairy and good fairies never get married!"

Colette gave a ripple of laughter that managed to sound unamused. "Thank heavens *I'm* not a good fairy! Life without a Prince Charming would be awfully dull." The gleaming, coiffed head tilted to one side. "Don't tell anyone—Alain doesn't wish it known for the moment—but we're going to be married, too."

It was news Miranda had anticipated, but even so she was unprepared for the shock the words gave her. The noise around her receded and grew louder as the blood rushed to her head. What sort of happiness would Alain find with a hard-faced girl like Colette?

"You don't seem very pleased at my news," Colette said softly. "I hope I haven't shattered your hopes."

"My hopes?"

"About Alain. Women find him so attractive that *they* do the running."

"I could never love a man I didn't trust." Irritation robbed Miranda of discretion. "And I couldn't trust someone who had already jilted another girl. Doesn't his past worry you?"

"I'm only concerned about his future. And I'm not so old-fashioned that I automatically blame the man when a girl becomes pregnant. It takes two to tango, you know!"

With an exclamation Miranda turned away. By showing her anger she had shown her jealousy, too, and she must be careful to say no more in case she showed her love.

The thought of making more lighthearted conversation and pretending a gaiety she was finding increasingly difficult to simulate prompted her to leave at once, and she slipped over to tell her father.

"Adrienne and I would like you to have dinner with us in Cannes," he told her. "We've booked a table for a few friends."

"I've got a headache," she lied. "I wouldn't be very good company."

Her father's gray eyes were searching, but she met them guilelessly as she kissed him goodbye and hurried away. Even if he did not believe her, he was unlikely to do anything about it.

But in this she was wrong, for an hour after she had settled herself in the library, a blank sheet of paper staring her in the face as she again tried to design a wedding dress, the door opened and he came in.

"So much for your headache," he said bluntly. "I knew you were lying."

"I thought it better to do that than to tell you I had work to do."

"That would have been a lie, too. You're only *finding* work to do because you don't want to have dinner with us." He placed both hands on the desk and stared at her squarely. "We've never lied to each other, Miranda, and it would be a pity if we started now. If you're unhappy because I'm marrying Adrienne, I'd rather you said so and gave me your reasons."

Instantly, she jumped up and ran around the side of the desk to stand close to him. "I'm delighted that you're getting married. Honestly. I'm only sorry you didn't meet her years ago."

"Then why did you run away just now? I want the truth—no more excuses."

She knew him too well to prevaricate any longer. Besides, to do so would only make the atmosphere more strained; far better to appear casual about it.

"I've already told you. I don't get on well with Alain, and I—I suppose Adrienne doesn't like me because of it."

"You *suppose?*" her father flared. "Don't you *know?*"

"Know what?"

"Why she doesn't like you?"

"Of course I know!" Miranda was too cross to be careful. "It's the money they're losing over the perfume."

"It's got nothing at all to do with money! In fact, it beats me why Alain bothered to buy the land at all," her father said bluntly. "If I'd been him, I'd have told you to go take a running jump!"

It was a long time since Miranda had seen her father so angry, and she could not understand his reactions.

"Alain's a businessman," she said quietly. "That's why he agreed to the arrangements. He'll make *some* profit out of Tendresse—and a fortuune out of all the other perfumes."

"That's exactly what he can't do!"

"What do you mean?" She peered into her father's face. "What are you trying to tell me?"

"That the blue rose essence can only produce *one* perfume."

Miranda's breath caught in her throat. "Are you sure?"

"Positive. I don't know the technical details, but apparently this essence is so distinctive that it overrides every other scent that's blended with it. You might be able to alter the bouquet a little, but never appreciably enough to make another perfume."

Slowly Miranda absorbed what she had just heard. At last she understood Adrienne Maury's behavior, though it made Alain's totally inexplicable. If he knew the blue rose could only be used for Tendresse, why had he agreed to sell it to her? Certainly, she wouldn't have done so in his position. Better not to grow the blue rose at all than to grow it for someone else.

"Why did he sell me Tendresse?" she asked.

"Beats me. Perhaps just *growing* the rose is important to him. After all, he's spent years perfecting it."

"That still doesn't explain why he let Pierre think he could produce other scents from it."

"*Did* he say that to Pierre?" came the blunt query.

Again Miranda was overcome by shock. What a fool she had been! Loyalty to Pierre fought with honesty, and honesty won.

As though guessing her thoughts, her father said, "Pierre knew you wouldn't take Tendresse if he told you the truth."

"He had no right to lie to me!" She clenched her fists. "How did *you* find out?"

"Adrienne told me. I was upset when you left the party this afternoon, and I tackled her about her attitude to you. She's not a mercenary person, and she had to have a more personal reason than a profit motive. She knows what the blue rose means to Alain, and she was hurt for him."

"I can see why." Miranda's breath came out on a quivering sigh. "I couldn't use Tendresse now."

"There's nothing to stop you."

Miranda looked at her father bleakly. "I mightn't like Alain, but I know what Tendresse means to him— especially if it's the only perfume the blue rose can produce. I'll tell Monsieur Maurice at once."

"What will he do?"

"Alter our contract. But it won't make any difference to my decision."

"Pierre will try to make you change your mind," her father said.

"I'll have a thing or two to say to him!" she said vehemently. "When I think of the lies he told me—"

"He had your interests at heart," her father placated.

She did not answer, uncertain how much of Pierre's behavior stemmed from a desire for her success or from the urge to hurt Alain. And it must have hurt him to have given up all the rights in his beloved blue roses.

"Pierre's flying down from Paris tonight," she said aloud. "He's coming with Monsieur Maurice."

"So you'll be able to tell them both?"

"Yes."

"Are you quite sure you want to?"

"Yes."

Her father came over to her. "Adrienne will be delighted."

"I'm not doing it because of you and Adrienne. I'm doing it because it's the right thing to do—the only thing!"

"I brought you up well," Roger Dixon said lightly.

"Too well, perhaps!" She put her hand on his arm. "Tell Adrienne I'll come and see her tomorrow."

"Why not tonight?"

"I want to talk to Monsieur Maurice."

"And Alain—when will you tell *him?*"

"You can do that for me."

"Oh no, my dear. That's something you'll have to do yourself."

Reaching up, she kissed her father's cheek, then walked with him to the door and watched him leave.

If Monsieur Maurice was unwilling to accept her without Tendresse, she would return to England and continue with her original plans. Perhaps it might even be better if she did, for it would at least put the distance of the Channel between herself and Alain.

CHAPTER ELEVEN

MONSIEUR MAURICE was unable to see Miranda until late that evening, explaining regretfully that he had made dinner arrangements he could not cancel.

"Why don't you and Pierre join me?" he suggested.

"I'd rather see you *after* dinner," she replied.

"You make it sound ominous." He paused as though waiting for her to say something, and when she didn't, he continued, "Let us make it ten o'clock, then."

Agreeing to this, she replaced the receiver. As she did so, she heard Pierre's car and hurried into the hall to confront him before her nerves could play her false.

"I've just been talking to Monsieur Maurice," she said breathlessly. "I'm seeing him this evening."

"Any reason?"

"I'm not going to market Tendresse."

"Is this some sort of joke?"

"The joke was on me," she retorted, "and *you* played it."

"You'd better explain," he commented and led the way into the salon. "Now then," he said as he closed the door "what's it all about?"

"I learned today that only *one* perfume can be made from the blue rose."

"So?"

"So you should have told me. Tendresse belongs to Alain—not us."

"He agreed to let us have it," Pierre responded.

"Under duress! He wants to grow the roses, and that was the only way he could do so."

"Well, he's *doing* so! Where's the problem?"

"It's a moral one."

"Morals mean a lot to Alain, I suppose?" Pierre sneered. "Grow up, Miranda. Selling us Tendresse will put a fortune into his bank account."

The words seemed a logical explanation for Alain's acceptance of Pierre's blackmail, and Miranda's feelings wavered. Was she being quixotic in her decision? Yet, quixotic or not, she would never rest until she had done what she planned.

"I don't believe Alain cares about money to the extent you're suggesting."

"Money's the *only* thing he cares about!" Pierre retorted. "Money and the freedom to do as he wants. He doesn't think the way we do, Miranda. He's obsessed with himself and his own importance."

"Maybe. But I still won't change my mind."

"You must. Everything's settled with Maurice."

"On a false premise. I'll go back to the original offer he made me before he knew I had a perfume to launch. It was a fair one, Pierre."

"It doesn't compare with the one you have now. If you go back to the original offer, you'll just be a dress designer working for Christi's."

"I *am* a dress designer," she reminded him, "and I've got two choices open to me. Either I go it alone—in a small way—or I let Monsieur Maurice launch me in a big way as part of Christi's. And I know what I have to do."

"If you do it," Pierre said tightly, "you can count me out. I was willing to work like hell to promote Christi's so long as I knew you had a decent stake in it, but I won't work my guts out for Maurice!"

He swung away from her, and with a little cry she ran over to him.

"Don't be angry, Pierre. Try to see it from my point of view. Tendresse means so much to Alain. It's like his child."

"That's the last simile you should use," he burst out.

His words stabbed through her, bringing Alain's past vividly close, and she clasped her hands to still their shaking.

"Don't do anything tonight," Pierre pleaded. "Sleep on it, Miranda. In the morning you may feel differently."

"I won't. I've made up my mind. Will you come with me to see Monsieur Maurice?"

"No. If you tell him, you must do it alone. I don't agree with you, and I won't be behind you anymore."

"Is that your last word?"

His eyes were hard and shining. "Is it *your* last word?"

"I must do what I believe to be right."

"So must I." He put his hands in his pockets and teetered slowly backward and forward. "A few weeks ago I had an offer to work in the United States. I think I'll accept it after all. It will be better than watching you throw your future away."

The thought of not having him close at hand increased her feeling of being an alien in a foreign land, and she put her hands out to him. "Why won't you see it my way?" she pleaded.

"I can. I see a great deal. That's why it will be best if I don't work with you. You've fallen for Alain, Miranda. Like most women, you like a scoundrel."

It was safer to say nothing, and she turned away.

"You're crazy," he went on behind her. "Do you think Alain will ever look at a girl like you? A man just has to see you to know you've got wedding bells in mind! And those are the last thing *he* wants to hear!"

"You couldn't be more wrong," she retorted. "He's going to marry Colette."

Pierre's anger changed to amazement. "Doesn't knowing about Colette make you realize how stupid you're being over Tendresse?"

"What Alain does with his personal life doesn't affect what I decide to do with my business life."

For a long moment he stared at her, one strange expression after another flitting across his face.

"You're a fool," he said finally, his voice flat and bitter, "and Alain's a bigger one!"

"Why do you hate him so much? Is it because of Lucille?"

"I always disliked him!" came the retort. "Lucille was just the final reason."

Miranda remembered these words as she sat in the back of the local taxi speeding down to Antibes. She had a vivid picture of Pierre as an impecunious young man living with his widowed mother in a beautiful château that was slowly crumbling into decay, while close by another boy—several years his junior, but fatherless like himself—was facing a glittering future. Pierre's envy must indeed have been deep for it to have lasted from youth through to maturity. How much this dislike had been increased by Alain's behavior toward Lucille, she did not know, nor was she ever likely to find out, for Pierre would no longer confide in her nor help her. She frowned. He never *had* confided in her. Thinking over their many conversations, she realized how little she knew of him. What would have happened if she had agreed to marry him? Would he have broken their engagement today? Somehow she knew that he would; knew, too, that his proposal had been born of expediency, rather than love. But she could not find it in her heart to condemn him; rather she felt a deep sadness that her idea of what was right should be so different from his.

ANTICIPATING A DIFFICULT MEETING with Monsieur Maurice, she was agreeably surprised that though his reaction was one of regret that they could not market Tendresse, he nonetheless understood and appreciated her decision.

"You had no choice," he agreed. "Every perfume Alain blends is part of himself, and with Tendresse it is even more so."

If only Pierre could have seen it this way, she thought and said aloud, "I realize our contract will have to be revised, and I'll understand if you decide not to go ahead with it at all."

"And lose you completely?" Pudgy hands shot up in consternation. "Madame Vernier would walk out with you! She is so convinced of your talent she would even follow you to London! No, my dear, we will leave the contract the way it is."

"But without a perfume."

"Forget it," he interrupted. "By keeping the contract the way it is I am being clever—not generous. If Madame Vernier sings your praises so loudly, then you are the right person to wear Jacques Christi's mantle. And once you make that mantle your own, you won't stay with me unless you are happy with your contract."

"I wouldn't go back on my word," she protested. "Money isn't that important to me."

"I realize that, my dear. And tonight, you have made it unimportant to me. The arrangements remain as they are—perfume or no perfume."

Pleasure warmed her; pleasure at having Monsieur Maurice behave so unexpectedly; and pleasure at being able to tell Pierre how wrong he had been. With her position remaining the same he would have no need to go to the United States. Yet even as she thought this, she knew it was not to be. Certain things could be forgotten, but some things—once said—could never be erased, and her horror at his implacable hatred of Alain was one of them.

Not that she herself would ever be able to hear the name Lucille without feeling pain at what he had done, but this did not give one the right to extract one's own vengeance.

She held out her hand to Monsieur Maurice. "Suddenly, I'm not afraid of the future."

"I never have been." A door clicked and the man's eyes moved to it, his face creasing in a smile. "Alain," he welcomed, and Miranda turned to see him and Colette in the doorway.

"Don't you ever stop working?" Colette said, coming over to her stepfather. "Your weekends here are supposed to be for relaxation."

"It is not working to talk to Miss Dixon." He turned to Alain. "You must be delighted about Tendresse?"

Alain's brows drew together in a frown. "I beg your pardon?"

"You are obviously not on the scent!" Monsieur Maurice chuckled at his own joke, and then seeing Miranda's consternation, realized his indiscretion. "*Hélas!*" he said. "I have, as the English say, put my shoe in it!"

"Foot," Colette corrected. "But what are you talking about, *papa?*"

"About Tendresse, my dear." He began to explain, and Miranda edged toward the door, wishing she could disappear through it without having to say good-night.

With an effort she fought against her embarrassment and felt the swift racing of her pulses subside, so that she was able to hear what he was saying.

"Why have you done it, Miranda?" Alain was speaking to her, a look of disbelief on his face. "I agreed to let you market Tendresse."

"I can't—not now. The blue rose means a lot to you. We both know that." She backed away from him and looked at Monsieur Maurice. "I'll see you again in Paris."

He nodded jovially and glanced at Alain. "You will surely offer Miranda a lift home? She came down by taxi."

"Of course," Alain said jerkily and went to the door.

"There's no need to spoil your evening," she protested.

"It isn't spoiled. I am returning home anyway."

Within a moment good-nights were said, and Miranda found herself sitting beside Alain in his car. It was the first time she had been completely alone with him since the night in Paris when he had driven her back to her hotel, and she could not help remembering the way he had pulled her into his arms and kissed her. She glanced at him, but he appeared oblivious to her presence, his eyes fixed on the road, his hands gripping the wheel so tightly his knuckles gleamed white.

She wished she need not make any further reference to the perfume, but her father's marriage to Adrienne—which would make her meetings with Alain at least occasional, if not frequent—decided her to try to clarify the position completely. In that way there would be no more room for misunderstanding.

"I had no idea you could only produce one perfume from the blue rose."

"Pierre knew," Alain said coldly, not looking at her.

"*I* didn't."

The car engine raced as though the accelerator had been pressed harder.

"I didn't know," she persisted, "until my father told me."

"It needn't have affected your decision."

"Don't be ridiculous. Tendresse is yours."

"You knew that when you agreed to take it!"

"I didn't know it was the *only* perfume you'd be able to make. . . . I know what the rose means to you. That's why I couldn't take it."

The engine raced again, but the man at her side said nothing. Finally she could bear the silence no longer, and she turned to look at him. "Aren't you even a bit pleased?"

"Why should I be pleased to get back something that is rightfully mine?"

"You should at least be grateful I'm—"

"Grateful!" He stopped the car so suddenly that her head banged against the windshield, and the sharp pain of it broke the final control she was holding on her temper.

"Yes, grateful!" she stormed. "If it hadn't been for Chambray land you wouldn't have grown your beastly roses in the first place!"

"You'd have liked that, wouldn't you?"

"Yes! You don't deserve to create anything beautiful. You're too evil and vicious!"

"I thought you'd soon start on my qualities! It's your favorite subject." He was angry as she had never seen him angry before, his eyes glittering like jet in a face that was bloodless. "How dare you set yourself up in judgment over me?"

"Why shouldn't I? I know the sort of person you are!"

"You know nothing!" he raged. "All you know is how to destroy a person!"

"You're the one who destroys!" she cried, and thought of the mountain ledge and the long rocky fall down to the ice-cold waters of the *vallon*.

"Leave Lucille out of it," he said in a deep, grating voice. "If you ever mention her again I'll kill you!"

"What's a murder to a man like you?"

"How dare you say that!" He lunged forward and gripped her throat.

She tried to struggle free, but she was powerless against his hold, and his nails dug into her skin.

"Save your energy," he rasped. "I'm not letting you go. Ever since I met you, you've been in the way. You've stopped me from thinking—from doing what I had to do!" He pulled her sharply forward, the rest of his words muffled against her mouth.

With all her strength she fought to push him away, but he pulled her closer still, his lips bruising in their intensity, his teeth drawing blood. She tried to stop the desire mounting inside her, to combat the fierce urge to respond; but she was powerless against the touch of his hands, against the pressure of his chest and the hard throbbing in the sinewy thighs that lay upon her own.

This was not the sort of love she wanted, this momentary flaring of the senses that would die out as quickly as it had erupted. Yet it was all Alain was capable of giving, all he *wanted* to give. Not for him a lasting relationship that would grow stronger with the years, but a few mean-

ingless caresses from meaningless women who could be
forgotten the moment they were out of sight. Or Colette,
who was as tough and cruel as himself.

The thought of Colette was like a barricade against her
senses, preventing her final surrender, and she struggled
in his hold, hearing the rasp of tearing silk as she fought
her way out of his arms.

"Leave me alone!" she cried. "I hate you!"

"You want me!" he mocked. "I felt the way you
trembled."

"With hatred!" she cried. "Go back to Colette. She's
the only woman you deserve!"

"You've a cruel tongue, Miranda. It's your best
weapon."

"Because I tell you what you are?"

"How do you know what I am?" His voice was bitter.
"It's a good thing you're not a judge. You'd never bother
with prison sentences. As far as you're concerned no one
could expiate their guilt even if they spent a lifetime behind bars!"

"You're right," she panted. "I could never forgive a
murderer!"

He drew away from her, the fury draining from his
face. "A murderer," he echoed softly. "Yes, you have
made me feel more like one than any woman I've ever
known."

There was a desolation in the words that made her
ache with pity for him. But she mustn't pity him. She
must despise him; it was her only salvation.

"You feel what you *are*," she told him, "and I'm sorry
for you."

Silently, he switched on the ignition and concentrated
on the ribbon of road unwinding in front of them. His profile was forbidding, his brows drawn together in a scowl.
No need to ask if he ever sat in judgment on himself. The
lines on either side of his mouth were a sure indication
that he had, as were the years when he had struggled—
and failed—to produce his perfume. Remembering the

viciousness of her words she was appalled, but knew that to attempt an apology would be worse than useless. Some things, once said, could never be forgotten.

Only when they reached the château did he speak to her.

"Even for my mother's sake I can't face the prospect of seeing you again," he said. "We'll have to meet on the day of the wedding, but after that, make sure you keep away from the house when I'm at home."

"Don't worry," she retorted. "I don't want to see you, either!"

"Not even to call me a murderer again?"

"Now *you're* talking about Lucille," she pointed out, jumping from the car.

"Only as an epilogue. Believe me, I felt far more like killing you than I ever did her!"

Before she could think of a suitable retort, he shot down the driveway as if all the demons of hell were after him.

As they deserved to be, she thought and closed the door of the château, wishing she could just as easily close Alain from her mind.

CHAPTER TWELVE

IT WAS MIDMORNING before Miranda awoke. Her aleep had been heavy and dreamless, and she lay for a long while in the large bed, hearing the creak of the shutters and wishing that the hills outside were the hills of Hampstead and not Provence.

Memory of the night before washed over her and, like a sea of sand, scratched against her consciousness, so that she sat up irritably and reached for her dressing gown.

By the time she had made her way downstairs, it was well after eleven, and deciding not to bother with breakfast, she went into the kitchen to make herself some orange juice. Simone greeted her with a dourness reminiscent of her earlier unfriendly attitude, and Miranda, wondering what had caused it, soon learned the reason.

"Monsieur Chambray has gone."

"To Grasse?"

"To Paris."

Miranda concentrated on the thick yellow juice she was pouring into her glass. "Did he leave a message for me?"

"He said nothing. He spoke to the *comtesse*, though."

Glass in hand, Miranda went in search of her grandmother, whom she found on the terrace. As always the old lady had made no concession to the weather, and a mohair stole covered her head and shoulders.

"I understand Pierre's gone back to Paris," Miranda said, kissing her good-morning. "Did he say why?"

"He gave me a reason, but I do not believe it was the real one."

The words were an indication of the *comtesse*'s intelligence, and Miranda abandoned the idea of lying to any questions that might be asked.

"He said he had only come down to say goodbye to me before going to the United States," the *comtesse* continued. "He is thinking of accepting a job there."

"He told me the same thing."

"Does that mean he won't be working with you at Christi's?" And at Miranda's nod she asked, "What about you? Are you leaving France, too?"

"Of course not. My plans are unchanged."

"Then why did Pierre's plans alter?"

"We had a quarrel. Pierre lied to me about Tendresse." Perched on the edge of a bamboo chair, Miranda recited a carefully monitored account of the events of the night before, omitting entirely her final scene in the car with Alain.

"You did the only thing possible," the *comtesse* said at last, her voice a breath of sound no stronger than the faint breeze stirring the clematis that climbed the stone pillars of the terrace. "I am sure Alain can create another perfume for you to launch—if you wish him to do so. It won't have the exceptional properties of Tendresse, but at least you need have no guilt at selling it as your own."

"If Christi's launches a perfume," Miranda replied, "it won't be Alain's. My one aim in life is never to see him again!"

"The young are so positive in their assertions," the *comtesse* sighed. "I suppose when blood runs hot, the feelings run high!"

"Alain makes my blood run cold," Miranda said crisply.

"Don't sit in judgment on anyone, my child."

The words were so similar to Alain's that Miranda jumped up, knocking over the glass of juice as she did so. "Now look what I've done!" she cried, and tears of exasperation rushed into her eyes, telling her more clearly than words how on edge she was.

The day stretched unendingly ahead of her, and had it not been for upsetting her grandmother, she would have returned to Paris immediately. Memory of all she had said to Alain kept reverberating in her brain, while her mind's eye pictured him with Colette. Was the French girl able to rouse him the way she herself had done? It was difficult to imagine Colette abandoning herself to love, though there was no doubting her possessive attitude. Poor Alain! She could almost pity him being married to such a woman.

The thought of Colette as a bride made Miranda realize she might be asked to design the wedding dress. Though the girl normally patronized other couture houses, Miranda was convinced that spite would bring her to Christi's. What torture it would be to make the dress that would also make her Alain's wife.

"Is anything wrong, child?" the *comtesse* asked. "You didn't cut your hand on the glass, did you?"

Miranda stared at the empty tumbler in her hand, realizing that her silence of the past few moments had been misunderstood.

"I'm fine," she said hastily. "I was just daydreaming."

"Are you very upset at Pierre's departure? I know you were fond of him."

"I'm glad he's gone. He behaved badly, *grand'mère*. There's no point pretending he didn't."

"He did it because he wanted the best for you."

"He wanted the best for himself."

Even as she spoke, Miranda felt there was something she did not understand about Pierre. If he had been solely concerned for his own advancement, he would have accepted her offer of financial participation in her arrangements with Monsieur Maurice. Yet he had refused to do so point-blank, expressing himself perfectly with position of publicity director for the company. But somehow she was convinced there *had* been an underlying reason behind his determination to get her the best deal possible, even though it had meant lying to her about Tendresse.

This brought her back to Alain. In his place she would rather have abandoned the entire rose project than let someone else market the single perfume it could produce.

With a sigh she took the empty glass back to the kitchen. She was thinking in circles; it would be as well to concentrate on something else. She glanced at Simone, who was standing by the stove stirring the contents of a large black pot from which emanated a delicious smell of hare and wine.

"Lovely," Miranda said, sniffing. "Is it one of your own recipes?"

The woman grunted. "It is Monsieur Pierre's favorite. I wouldn't have done it if I had known he was leaving."

"I'm sure my grandmother and I will enjoy it just as much." She set her glass down on the drain board. "Monsieur Pierre's going to the United States, Simone, so he may not be back for quite a while."

The woman said nothing, though her face had a pitifully mottled look that roused Miranda's compassion. "But I'm sure he'll come back for holidays and to see *grand'mère*."

"I'm used to his being away," Simone said staunchly, the wooden spoon in her hand moving vigorously in the pot. "After Mademoiselle Lucille died, he was afraid to come back for more than a year."

For a long while Miranda stared at the casserole, her own thoughts quietly simmering. "Why was he afraid to come back?" she asked finally.

"I don't know what you mean."

"You said he was afraid to come back for more than a year after Lucille died."

The thickset shoulders lifted. "I did not mean anything by it."

"You must have meant something," Miranda persisted. "Why did Monsieur Pierre stay away?"

"He was upset because of the tragedy," Simone said stonily. "We all were."

With a flash of inspiration Miranda felt she was glimpsing the truth. "Was Monsieur Pierre in love with Lucille?"

"What if he was? It's all over with now. The past is finished. Dead."

"I was only curious." Miranda made an effort to be casual. "As you say, it doesn't matter anymore."

There was a flash in the dark eyes before the veined lids rolled over them. "Yes, he loved her. That's why he stayed away afterward." Clanging the lid back on the casserole, Simone moved over to the table and began to roll out some dough that had been resting in a bowl; her elbows moved as she kneaded and pummeled, and watching the continuing rhythm and the shuttered face, Miranda knew she would learn no more.

As always when she felt troubled, she went to the library. The sunlight streamed in through the windows, warming her shoulders, and she relaxed in it, feeling some of her tension ebb. It had been stupid of her not to have guessed that Pierre had loved Lucille. It explained his animosity toward Alain and why he had driven such a hard bargain over the land and the perfume.

She wondered why he had hidden his feelings for Lucille. Had he told her, it would have made her much more understanding of his behavior. She glanced at the telephone. Perhaps she would call him in Paris. Yet if she did so, he might decide to come back—especially once he learned that Monsieur Maurice had left her contract untouched.

She shook her head and wandered aimlessly around the room. She did not want to work with Pierre. His hatred of Alain went too deep, would keep Alain vivid in her own mind, too.

Stopping by a bookshelf, she picked out a hand-tooled leather book depicting eighteenth-century costume that she was using as a reference. Forcing her mind back to her work, she rummaged through the pages of the book. The delicate drawings were a joy to see, and she studied the details of the costumes carefully, making copious notes and redesigning some of the accessories and embroideries to be more evocative of the twentieth century. She was still absorbed in her task when the gong sounded for lunch, and she hurried to wash her hands before going to the dining room.

At the table she forced herself to make conversation, and though she did not have much appetite, the hare casserole was so delicious she ate a normal serving.

"You look flushed, Miranda," her grandmother commented.

"I've been concentrating," Miranda smiled. "You've some wonderful old books in the library, *grand'mère*. Some of them must be valuable."

"A few of them were printed especially for the family."

"I had no idea."

The *comtesse* smiled. "If you come across any marked Editions Dauphin, they were printed for us in Paris in 1810, when the Chambrays still had money."

"I think I'm working with one of those books now," Miranda said and ran into the library to fetch it. "Yes, it is," she said, coming back with it in her hand. "How exciting to think it's one of our own."

"You'll find several more if you look. There were three different ones of that edition you're holding."

"I've only found one."

"The others are definitely there. Three years ago a couple of students stayed here for a holiday and repaid me by cataloguing the books. If any had been missing, they'd have mentioned it. You have no idea what a state the library was in before they tidied it. Books everywhere. Pierre was always promising to put them away, but he never did, and Simone just dusted them and put them back in the same old piles. Now, of course, it's as tidy as a public library!"

"I'll look for those other two books later. If they're fashion ones, I'd love to find them."

Returning to the library at the meal's end, Miranda started to sketch again, but the lunch she had eaten coupled with the warmth of the room made her drowsy, and she closed the book and pushed back her chair. If she went on sitting here, she would fall asleep. Determined not to get into the siesta habit, she decided to look for the other two books right away.

Methodically, she began to scan the shelves. It became clear to her why the books were in such disorder; the students might well have catalogued them, but they had not put them back in any order. If she wanted to find the two she was looking for, it would require more than a casual glance along the shelves. Deciding to do it systematically, she carried over some small antique library steps to the farthest corner of the room and began her search from there.

It was slow work, enlivened by the occasional discovery of an interesting book either beautifully bound or with unusual illustrations. Soon the rows of shelves opposite the window had been examined and left, and she concentrated on the ones facing the door. There were no signs of any books from the Dauphin Press, and she climbed the ladder to complete her search of the topmost shelf. One ponderous title after another passed before her eyes, but there were no books on fashion. She had better settle for the one she already had.

Even as she decided to end the search, her hand came to rest on dark brown calf, and with trembling fingers she drew out two books of equal size and shape to the one on her desk. With an exclamation of pleasure she flipped through the first few pages. She had come to the end of her search.

Clasping the books to her, she descended the ladder. As she reached the last step her heel caught in the rung, and she lurched forward. Afraid of hitting her head, she put out her hands to save herself. The books thudded to the floor, and she fell on top of them, the breath knocked out of her body.

For a moment she remained on the carpet, then quickly scrambled to her feet. She bent down and picked up the books, examining them carefully to make sure they were not damaged. Apart from one page being crumpled, they seemed intact, and she gave a sigh of relief and closed them.

As she did so she noticed one of the pages sticking out at an angle. Hurriedly she opened the book again, stopping in surprise as she saw it wasn't a page jutting out but a separate sheet of paper in the same gray parchment color. It was a handwritten page with delicate flowing writing. And not written in the nineteenth century, either, but in the twentieth.

From four years ago, to be precise . . . from Lucille.

Miranda's knees gave way and she sat down abruptly, surprised at the emotion engulfing her as she held the letter in her hands. The writing was large like that of a child, the script unmistakably French and a replica of the one she had seen in the yellowing pages of *Nice Matin*.

Without being aware of doing so, she read a few words and only then realized that the letter was addressed to Pierre. But what was a letter from Lucille doing in this book? He had obviously received it and slipped it between the pages for safe-keeping until he could either file it or throw it away. It was odd he should have left it here, though. Suddenly she smiled. He must have put the letter in the book and then gone off for the day, a habit she had noticed he had during his stay here. During his absence the students had obviously started tidying the library and had tidied away the letter at the same time.

Pleased by her logical deduction, Miranda looked at the letter again. The last L and E were blurred, as though the ink had been rubbed by water, and with a sudden stab of pity she realized the blob was a tear stain.

She knew she should put the letter away unread, but curiosity was too strong to be denied, and despite a feeling of guilt she started to read it.

Quickly she scanned the lines, and as their meaning
became clear the page shook so hard in her hand that she
had to rest it on the desk. More slowly, she read it a second time. The writing was scrawled, and some of the sentences were unfinished, but despite this the plea came
through with heartrending clarity; a plea for a man's love
and help—as she had expected—but Pierre's.

Pierre . . . .

It couldn't be true. Yet there was no denying it. It was
here for her to see in black and white. Lucille and Pierre
had been in love. Or at least he had pretended to be, for
he had obviously changed his mind, and Lucille's letter
begged him to tell her he did not mean it:

> You can't have stopped loving me. Not after all you
> said—the things we did. . . . It's useless to pretend
> nothing has happened. Alain doesn't know the
> truth, but I'm sure he suspects, and I'm going to tell
> him he's right. A few weeks ago you might have
> convinced me I should keep silent, but I can't do so
> any longer. Adrienne has been like a mother to me,
> and for her sake I must tell Alain the truth. I can't
> become his wife when I'm carrying your child! It's
> too much to ask of me.

Several words were too blurred to be deciphered, as
though tears had fallen faster at this point, and Miranda
skipped them and read on:

> I'll be at the usual place this afternoon, and I'll wait
> there till you come, no matter how late it is. You
> mustn't leave me, Pierre. If you do, I can't face this
> alone. Nor can I ever do as you suggest. If the child
> dies, I will die with it.

The name Lucille marked the end of the letter, as it
marked the end of everything Miranda had believed
about Alain.

The truth was so staggering that it made coherent thought difficult, and for a long while she sat without any clear awareness of the passing of time.

No wonder Pierre had left the château after Lucille's death and had not come back for more than a year! And how clever of him to accuse Alain and foster the accusation so that it remained as strong in people's minds today as it had been four years ago.

Fury brought her to her feet. Why hadn't Alain defended himself? How could he have let the scandalmongers go on crucifying him? Slowly, inexorably, the answer came to her, as it would have come a long time ago if she had had any sense. Loving Lucille the way he had—and she was prepared to believe that now—he had guessed her feelings for Pierre, and after her death and the discovery that she had been pregnant, he had known that to assert his own innocence would mean besmirching her memory even more, and regardless of the consequences he had remained silent.

In a large city the pregnancy and death of an unmarried girl—whether it was accident or suicide—would have aroused comment for a few days and then been forgotten. But in a village like Bayronne the story had lived and flourished, reaching out evil tentacles to stifle Alain's life for years, making it impossible for him to continue with the work he loved. It was not the stench of his own guilt—as she had so cruelly said—that had prevented him from creating other perfumes, but the bitter knowledge that he had been let down by the woman he loved and the man he had hero worshiped as a boy. It was amazing how she was remembering all the things Alain had said to her on the subject, and how—since the discovery of this letter—they cast such a different light on it. The light of truth.

Holding the letter in her hand, she went upstairs to her room and put on a pair of flat-heeled shoes. She had to give this letter to Alain and apologize for everything she had said to him. Nothing less would do. The thought of what he might say to her was daunting, but she refused to be put off by it.

Slipping a cardigan over her shoulders, she hurried out of the house. She was halfway down the driveway when she chided herself for not having telephoned first to make sure he was at home. Yet to have called and told him she was coming might have caused comment and forced her into an explanation. No, it was better to go unheralded and talk to him face to face. The letter crackled in the pocket of her dress, and she began to run.

She was breathless by the time she reached the village, but here luck was with her, for she recognized the young man coming out of the *boulangerie* as one of the servants from the villa.

Obligingly, he let her ride on the back of his motorcycle, depositing her outside the front door in the time it would have taken her to walk twenty yards.

"Is Monsieur Maury at home?" she asked breathlessly as she climbed off the bike.

"Yes, *mademoiselle*."

Another thought struck Miranda. "And Miss Dinard?"

If Colette was here, she would be unable to talk to Alain. It was impossible to make her apologies in front of that ice-cold woman. Yet ice-cold or not, Colette had shown greater loyalty to Alain than she had herself. The thought smarted, and she burned with the shame of it.

"Miss Dinard is not here," the man said. "Only the family. But if you want Monsieur Alain, you will find him in the conservatory. He is always there at this hour."

Miranda sped around the side of the house and found herself facing a glass door. Nervously, she turned the handle and went in. Despite the warmth outside she was struck by the moist heat billowing around her. The heavy scent of exotic blooms hung in the air, and her eyes ranged from one colorful plant to another. A huge cactus masked part of her view, and she edged past it and down the narrow aisle. This was more like a glassed-in ballroom than a conservatory, she thought, and stared in bewilderment at a never-ending vista of greenery.

She came to an intersection and paused. A trickle of water sounded in her ears, and she moved in the direction it came from, her steps faltering as she skirted some dangerous-looking spiky leaves and saw the slim, dark-haired man bent over a small pot. In it was a straggle of wispy leaves and an amber gold flower that reminded her of a columbine.

Unaware of anyone watching him, Alain was not monitoring his expression, and it was half sad, half tender as he bent over the tiny plant, his fingers exploring the leaves as gently as they had explored her last night. Emotion flooded through her, and she must have given a gasp, for he started and turned, his expression hardening as he saw her.

"What are *you* doing here?"

"I came to see you—to say how sorry I—"

"Forget it," he said harshly. "We both said more than we should have last night."

"I shouldn't have said *any* of it!"

"There's no need to abject yourself," he said wearily. "Let's be civil about it and go back to our original plan of pretending some form of friendship for our parents' sake."

"I can't," she blurted out and stopped, digging her hands into the pockets of her dress. It was going to be hard enough to tell Alain the truth without completely losing face and letting him know she loved him. Paper crackled beneath her fingers, and she took out the letter.

"Read it," she said in a ragged voice. "It's from Lucille."

"For God's sake!" he exclaimed. "I thought we weren't going to talk about her anymore."

Ignoring his remark, she thrust the letter into his face, and with a slow, almost reluctant gesture he took it from her and began to read.

Watching him, Miranda saw the color ebb from his

face, leaving it as gray as a corpse. Unable to bear the sight of it, she turned away and stared at a group of plants, counting the leaves and then, when she had reached one hundred, counting them again.

"Where did you find this?" His voice was devoid of expression. He might have been asking her what time it was.

Equally coolly she gave him the answer, telling him also how she thought it had come to be in the book.

"You're probably right," he replied. "Pierre must have received the letter and then shot off to Cannes. I know he was there at midmorning and didn't leave till midnight . . . by which time Lucille was dead."

"How could he have run away like that?" Miranda whispered. "He knew what she'd do. She couldn't have put it more clearly."

"He wanted her to do it. It was the best way out for him."

Miranda shuddered. "*He's* the murderer! When I think of the things I said to you . . . . How can I apologize?"

"There's no need. You were not alone in thinking me guilty."

"Why did you *let* people think it?"

"I had a duty to Lucille."

"I knew you'd say that!" she exclaimed. "But what duty did you have to a girl who let you down the way she did?"

"Because I let *her* down." He averted his head so that she could only see his profile, with a lock of dark hair falling over his forehead and a muscle twitching in his cheek like a pulse. "I became engaged to Lucille without loving her. I did love her, of course, but as a member of the family—as my mother's goddaughter who had grown up with me—not the love a man should have for the woman he's going to marry."

"And Lucille knew this?"

"Yes. Her feelings for me were the same. Our mar

riage would have been one of convenience. A happy one, I am sure, but without the *grande passion*." He glanced at her momentarily. "It is hard for you to understand our French customs, I suppose, but such a marriage is not unusual even in this day and age."

"I know that," she said stiffly, "but I wouldn't have thought you'd have wanted that kind of marriage!"

"Wouldn't you?" Again he glanced at her. "Last night you seemed very sure I had no love to give anyone."

"I merely meant that I didn't see—still don't see—as loving anything except your work."

"I didn't at that time. That's why marriage to Lucille seemed a satisfactory solution. Neither of us would have made great demands on the other." He paused and looked down at the gold plant in front of him. "Then gradually, I sensed a change in her. I was certain she had fallen in love with Pierre, and I waited for her to tell me. When she didn't, *I* decided to tell *her*. It seemed foolish for us to pretend. Pierre was single, and if they loved each other . . . ."

"He didn't," Miranda whispered.

"I realized that when she denied the whole thing. She swore I was imagining it."

"When did you find out it was true?"

"On the morning of the day she died." Alain rubbed the side of his face wearily. "She had discovered she was pregnant, and she told me the whole story and gave me back my ring. I was very bitter—as you can imagine—and we had a row. I went off to Grasse and left her. She wrote me a letter then—the letter that was found in her pocket after she killed herself. It was the letter you read in *Nice Matin*."

Remembering the interpretation she had put on it—that everyone had put on it—Miranda's cheeks burned with shame.

"Why did you take the blame for her death?" she whispered.

"Because if I'd really loved her she mightn't have turned to Pierre."

"That's nonsense. A moment ago you said your marriage would have been one of convenience."

"Lucille was an impressionable girl. If I'd spent more time with her—if I'd cared for her—she might have fallen in love with me."

"And perhaps she mightn't," Miranda said crisply, compassion giving way to anger that he should have allowed his good name to be usurped so quixotically. "It was crazy to think like that. Pierre behaved like a swine, and you took the blame for it! Surely for your mother's sake you could—"

"My mother knew the truth."

Miranda was astounded. "And she let you go on with the pretense?"

"She felt I should do what I wanted."

"*I* wouldn't have let you do it," Miranda said fiercely. "You were a fool!" Tears blurred her eyes, and she rubbed them away with the back of her hand. "I'm not going to apologize to you after all! Why should I blame myself for believing the worst of you when you encouraged everyone to think so?"

"The people who knew me," he said softly, "knew I wasn't guilty."

"But you never told them?"

"No."

Miranda lowered her eyes. Implicit in his words was Colette's belief in his innocence, or perhaps Colette had not cared either way.

"It was kind of you to bring me the letter," he said suddenly. "It at least confirms that Pierre knew what she intended doing."

"That's the worst part of it all. I'm glad he isn't here now," she said savagely. "If he has the gall to come back to the château, I'll throw him out!" She tilted her head. "I'm going to tell my grandmother the truth."

"Why bother? She is old, and the shock could be harmful."

"She's a Chambray," Miranda said fiercely, "and she wouldn't thank me if I kept her in ignorance. Pierre acted despicably, and the facts should be known."

"You must tell no one else. I've protected Lucille's name for four years, and I intend to go on doing so."

"At least you love her now," Miranda said shakily.

"I know what love means," he corrected, "and because of that, I know what she missed."

She absorbed his words slowly, finding the message they bore to be a painful one. His marriage to Colette was obviously not one of convenience, but the *grande passion* he had never felt for Lucille.

"So you're in love at last?" she whispered.

"Does that surprise you?"

"Not really. I don't suppose you'd get married otherwise. Not that I like your choice." She bit her lip. "I'm sorry, I shouldn't have said that."

His brows rose. "What's wrong with my choice?"

"You know without my telling you."

"I'm afraid I don't. Please go on."

"I have no actual reason," she shrugged. "You could call it mutual antipathy. It's the way *we* felt about each other the moment we met."

"We did?"

"You know we did!" she said sharply. "And that's what I feel for Colette. So don't let her ask me to design her wedding dress, because I won't."

A strange light glittered in Alain's eyes. "Won't you do it even for me?"

"No."

"Not even if I begged you to do so?" He came a step closer. "Not even if I told you that unless my bride wore your dress, I wouldn't marry her?"

"Don't!" she cried. "Don't be cruel!"

"Cruel?" he repeated, looking astonished.

"Yes," she said and burst into tears. "You know I

love you. You must know, or you wouldn't be so heartless."

"I'm certainly heartless," he groaned and pulled her
violently into his arms. "You took my heart the moment
we met."

"No! You don't mean it!"

"Don't I?" he said against her mouth. "I loved you
from the moment I saw you at the château."

"No," she said again. "Not after the way I
behaved . . . the things I said . . . ." She pulled slightly
back from his hold. "What about Colette? You're going
to marry her—she said so!"

"Wishful thinking, I'm afraid. I have never proposed
to her. Never!" he affirmed. "Not even when I was furious with you."

Tears blinded Miranda's eyes. "When I think of all the
awful things I said to you . . . . I must have hurt you so
much."

"You did. And I was sorely tempted to hurt you
back."

"Then why did you agree to Pierre's blackmail over
the perfume? You should have refused to buy the land—
refused to grow the roses."

"I grew them for you. I knew of your arrangements
with Maurice and what the perfume meant to you."

"I didn't deserve it." Her tears fell fast. "You make
me feel so small . . . so mean."

"Don't talk like that about the woman I love!" He
wiped her tears away with his hand. "You will take Tendresse back—"

"No! It's yours."

"It's *ours*. Your success will be mine."

"Oh, Alain!" Her tears flowed again. "I don't know
what to say."

"Thank heaven for that," he said and gently moved
his lips against hers.

"Alain, I—"

"No more words," he whispered. "We've a lifetime

ahead for explanations. Right now there's only one thing I want to do.''

"What's that?" she asked, starry eyed.

"I'll show you," he replied.

And did.

THE DREAM ON THE HILL

The
Dream
on the Hill
Lilian Peake

Nicola Dean disliked Dr. Connor Mitchell at first sight. Not only was the man abominably rude, he treated her like the village idiot. He was unaware, of course, that like himself, she had given up a promising career to aid a parent—but that didn't excuse his insolence....

Nicola's distress at the situation intensified when she found herself actually falling in love with the arrogant man—for not only had he openly admitted his dislike of her, he had declared his love for another woman.

And besides, he had compared their reaction to one another to that of two dangerous chemicals—chemicals that when combined produced disastrous results!

CHAPTER ONE

EVER SINCE NICOLA had boarded the train that morning she had been asking herself the same question. Had she done the right thing in leaving behind her friends and a job she had loved?

She had turned her back on a promising career and virtually thrown away years of study and training because her mother had begged her to come home. She searched in her handbag and found her mother's letter. It was more than two months old.

> I haven't been well—I didn't want to worry you by telling you before. But the doctor has advised me to give up the responsibility of running the store and take life more easy. He says I need looking after, too. I know it's asking a lot of you, Nicola, but there's no one else I can turn to. I don't want to sell the business because, as you know, it's my only source of income. Would you come home, dear, and take over from me?

Such an appeal would have been difficult to resist from a friend, let alone a mother. Nicola put the letter away and stared out of the window, watching the great sweep of countryside through which the train was passing on its way from the northeast of England to Shropshire, with its pleasant hills and green fertile valleys.

She would miss the girls at school, not to mention her needlework classes. And Terence, in his hesitant way, had told her he would miss her, too. She did not know whether she could repay the compliment.

In a way, this parting would be a test. She liked him very much but doubted that her feelings for him went much deeper than that.

She had been on the staff of the school for four years. It had been her first and only appointment. And now she had said her goodbyes, both to her colleagues and her career.

At Birmingham she changed—it was not easy because she had so much luggage—to the train that would take her on the final stage of her journey. After a late lunch of sandwiches and coffee, she found a magazine and read the rest of the time away. Later, she took out her compact, added a touch of powder, renewed her lipstick and flicked a comb through her hair.

Auburn it might be, she had often thought, but its curls seemed to have minds of their own. They refused to allow her to conform to fashion, no matter what the current hairstyle might be. The compact snapped shut, cutting off her reflection. She looked travel weary and bored. *And bored I'll remain*, she told herself with a touch of fear, *for years to come*. Serving behind a counter was hardly an intellectual challenge.

When the train pulled into the station, her exit was almost as undignified as her entrance had been. She struggled with her suitcases and a gallant and smiling middle-aged man, seeing her distress, helped her down to the platform, then, as she thanked him, climbed back into the train.

She was left planted firmly amid her luggage, and decided that if she were not to take root where she stood, she would have to find a porter. But it had taken her so long to unload herself from the train, there was not a porter to be seen. So she swung her knapsack over her shoulder, picked up her tote and tucked it under an arm, leaving two hands free for three suitcases.

While she gazed down helplessly at the third suitcase another middle-aged man materialized from nowhere and, with a gallantry equaling that of his predecessor, picked up and carried the remaining suitcase. He stopped obligingly at the gate while Nicola found her ticket and walked with her to the taxi stand, where he put the bag down. Followed by her effusive thanks, he went smilingly on his way.

It was not long before an empty taxi stopped a few yards ahead. Nicola picked up all the luggage she could manage and ran, leaving the third suitcase on the pavement. As she reached the driver, intending to ask him to wait until she retrieved the other suitcase, someone else strode toward the vehicle, put a proprietorial hand on the door handle, told the driver his destination and got in.

Nicola could not believe her eyes. She was so incensed by the man's inconsiderate behavior that she directed an accusing, belligerent and—she couldn't help it, she was so tired—half-tearful stare through the taxi window. But, she told herself furiously, this man was young, unlike the other two who had helped her, so what could she expect.

She gazed resentfully at the retreating vehicle, then watched, unbelieving, as it slowed to a stop and backed up until it was level with her again. The driver leaned across and said, "The gentleman wants to know which direction you're going in, miss, because if it's in his he's willing to share."

"Roydon Kingsley," said Nicola eagerly.

The driver passed the information to the passenger, who gave a curt nod. "He says hop in," said the driver. Nicola did not think the passenger, whose expression was decidedly caustic, had said anything so glib, but the invitation was too attractive to refuse.

The driver got out and fixed the bags into position in the front seat, while Nicola ran back for the third suitcase, and took it with the knapsack into the taxi.

All the time the passenger had been watching the proceedings with an odd expression. She turned on a grateful smile and began to thank him for his kindness, but when she saw how coldly he was accepting her gratitude—he had not even looked her way while she had been talking—she became as surly as he was. She did not speak again until they were on the approach road to the village.

"You can drop me anywhere," Nicola said. "I don't want to take you out of your way."

"You are not taking me out of my way." The answer was crisp and to the point. And it ended the conversation. His head had been resolutely turned away and he had spoken to the passing hedgerows. Nicola hoped the hedgerows had realized how honored they had been.

Her resentment returned, and she stared reproachfully at his implacable profile, seeing the regularity of his features, the jutting chin, the uncompromising mouth with an unmistakable touch of ruthlessness lurking in its corners. His hair was thick and dark, the rest of him substantially and endurably built.

Reluctantly, and in the deepest valleys of her mind where her resentment had not yet had time to descend, she had to concede that in times of crisis, this was undoubtedly a man to whom one could turn for protection and support; and who, despite his distant and apparently impenetrable exterior, would give it in abundance.

But there was apparently no such crisis at the moment to bring out the better side of his nature—if indeed he had one and it wasn't simply imagination on her part—and in the few moments in which her eyes were carrying out their examination in depth of his person, he turned. She was subjected to the low temperature of his eyes and felt a strong desire to take refuge inside her coat collar.

Ironically, the tables were turned and it seemed that, judging by his expression, he now bore a grudge against her for the impudence of her scrutiny, of which he must have been aware all the time. Despite the ice in his eyes, her cheeks burned and she almost felt the need to apologize. As the driver signaled and turned left into the main street of the village, her relief knew no bounds. She was beginning to grow rather tired of the human refrigerator beside her.

The driver asked, his attention still on the road, "Where d'you want to go, miss?" .

Nicola glanced at her fellow passenger—the address she was about to give would, she was sure, push her even farther down his social scale than the lowly place to which he seemed already to have assigned her, and said, "Dean's store, please. Do you know it? It's the grocers'."

"Yes, I know it all right, miss. It's the village store. I know the old lady." Nicola held her breath. What else was he going to say? "Nice old dear." She let out her breath. *All the same*, her mind objected, *my mother's not old*. He drew up outside the store. "You going to work there, miss?"

She shot another glance at the superior, silent passenger. "Yes, I'm going to work there."

The man's eyes detached themselves from the window and swung around to inspect the girl beside him. There was no flattery in his look and there was no mistaking his dismissal of her mental furniture. Secondhand, it said, unreliable and unstable, like a rickety chair. Contents, put up for auction, would realize a mere pittance, or even a loss.

But his eyes strayed somewhat from their apparent estimation of the capacity of her brain. Instead they engaged in an assessment of her physical attributes—they were, Nicola knew, too conspicuous to be overlooked—and in doing so became essentially masculine and almost as insulting. Their eyes clashed and for the second time Nicola colored furiously. Now it was not with embarrassment, it was with anger.

Even so, he continued to look at her. To hide her confusion, she searched in her bag for her purse, but the passenger said shortly, "I'll pay."

"No, thank you." She wanted no charity from him. "You can pay your own. I'll pay my share. Driver—" she leaned forward "—however much that was, I'll pay half." He told her and she handed over the money, offering him something extra, but he waved it away.

"That's all right, miss."

Nicola got out, shouldering her knapsack and holding her suitcase.

The driver relieved her of most of her burdens and she picked up the third suitcase. Without another glance at the silent passenger—she hoped she would never meet him again—she led the obliging driver to the store doorway, where he put the bags down and left with a cheerful wave.

Her mother was behind the counter tidying the shelves. She turned, expecting a customer, and saw Nicola. Arms outstretched, she went toward her. They embraced and there were tears in Nicola's eyes. There was something more than welcome in her mother's greeting. Nicola clung for a few moments and her mother murmured, "You're so good, love, to do what you've done. I know how much you've given up. Don't think I don't appreciate it."

Nicola held her away and said, "It's you I'm worried about, mom. What's wrong?"

"We can't talk here. A customer might come in. Let's go through into the house."

Nicola followed asking, "Where's Mrs. Bailey?"

"Left to have a baby. I've got Joy now, Joy Atkins. She's only seventeen, but a nice kid. She's just had a quick cup of tea."

Joy was at the sink washing her cup. Mrs. Dean introduced them and Joy, plump and pretty, returned to the shop.

No wonder, Nicola thought, looking at her mother, the taxi driver had called her "old." Her hair was white, her face pale and lined. She had aged alarmingly since Christmas.

"You haven't been looking after yourself, have you?" Nicola said, half affectionately, half accusingly. "Is it your old trouble?"

"Yes, bronchitis." A hand went to her chest. "I've had it twice in the last four months. Twice too many, the doctor said. Each time it's a bit more difficult to throw off."

"In that case, I'm glad I came home."

"Are you really, dear? No regrets?"

Nicola shrugged, although with her mother she had to be honest. "A few, perhaps. But I'll get over it."

"It's strange," said Enid Dean, sitting down wearily, "how you and Dr. Mitchell are in the same boat."

"Dr. Mitchell? But how can we be? Isn't he nearing retirement?"

"He was, dear. He died over three months ago. His son, Connor, has taken over his father's share of the practice. He had a good hospital job, but gave it up to please his mother. She didn't want the practice to go to someone else—you know old Dr. Mitchell was the senior partner? So, like you, the young man's had to make a sacrifice."

"What's he like?"

"Oh, nice enough, but a bit abrupt. Not a bit like his father. All you young people have so many new ideas." She smiled. "Old ladies like me prefer the old ways best."

"You're not old," Nicola protested, although she knew it was only a half-truth. Her mother was certainly not young, having besides herself a son of thirty-two and a daughter of twenty-nine, both of whom had made her into a grandmother five times over. Nicola was four years younger than Lucille, her sister, but they rarely met. Lucille lived in Geneva with her husband and family, and Leslie, Nicola's brother, lived and worked in Canada, with his wife and family.

"Talking of abrupt," Nicola remarked, "I was given a lift by a very rude man." She explained how he had snatched the taxi from her, had had a stab of conscience and offered her a lift in it. Oddly enough, Nicola added, he had come this way and had dropped her outside.

"Well," Enid said laughingly, "I don't know about his manners, but I don't think you can complain. He didn't have to let you share his taxi, did he? He was kind enough to do that, after all."

Only grudgingly did Nicola concede that perhaps her mother might be right.

DESPITE THE FACT that it looked like rain, Nicola pulled a jacket over her striped top and went for a walk. As she left the village and felt the pull of the increasing gradient, she realized how much she had missed the Shropshire hills.

But only when she reached the summit did she allow herself to turn and look at the view she loved. Great billowing clouds hung over the land and the atmosphere was so clear, threatening rain, it was possible to see across to the Welsh mountains many miles away. Down below and in the distance was the river; to the south were cultivated fields, steep, tree-lined slopes and sheltered valleys.

No wonder, Nicola thought, such countryside inspired poets and musicians to record its beauties in words and song. This hill had been her favorite haunt since childhood. Up here she could count on being alone, although there were times, of course, in the summer when she had had to share the place with visitors.

It was growing colder and the clouds had begun to shake their drops over the landscape like a sprinkler on a garden hose. She decided, reluctantly, to make her way back and turned to see, with a profound shock, that she was not, after all, alone.

A man was standing some yards away. In the twilight caused by the rain clouds adding their shadows to the darkening evening, it was difficult to see his face. As she studied his broad shoulders, he turned, as if he had felt her regard. It was the man who had allowed her to share his taxi, and once again he had caught her examining him. He appeared to like it no more now than he had earlier in the day.

With all her being she resented his intrusion into her solitude, his invasion of her favorite hill at such a—well, a private time of day. He had been looking at the view as though he, too, appreciated its beauty. Although in her heart she had to acknowledge that he had a perfect right to enjoy it as much as anyone else, nevertheless she took unreasonable exception to the presence of such a disagreeable, abrasive creature as this man appeared to be. While she had been staring at him, and he at her, the rain had begun to fall in earnest, so she made for the shelter of the nearest tree.

The shelter was meager, although it was officially spring, the trees seemed hardly aware of the fact, offering only the minutest of buds as a covering, buds that obviously had no intention of turning into full-blown leaves for a long time yet.

She turned up the collar of her jacket and wished she had come better prepared for the weather. *I should have taken more notice of the lowering clouds*, she reproached herself. To her annoyance, the man made for the same tree and they stood only a few yards from each other, in complete silence, each trying to pretend the other was not there.

He was wearing a thick waterproof jacket and stout shoes. Nicola found herself detesting his common sense in coming for the walk so well prepared. She started to shiver, and he seemed to know it—did the man possess some kind of sixth sense that enabled him to know so many things without being told?

He turned, giving her a scathing up and down stare that knocked twenty years off her age. *Well*, she thought, *I'm no five-year-old*, so she returned his stare in full measure. But a tree would have shown more response. She was so provoked by his unspoken criticism of the way she was dressed, and by his supercilious manner, she refused to stay under that tree another minute. Shrinking an inch or two deeper into her jacket, she turned toward the downward slope of the hill.

He broke the twilight silence. "I wouldn't if I were you."

She asked, in her most frigid manner, "I beg your pardon?"

"I said I wouldn't if I were you." He nodded at her feet. "Go out into this downpour in those flimsy shoes."

She followed his eyes and dwelt, as he was doing, on the lightweight summer sandals she was wearing.

He raised his eyes and contemplated her jacket and skirt. "Or in that inadequate clothing. It's plain you're new to these parts. No local inhabitant would dream of coming out in this inclement weather so inappropriately dressed. From the health point of view it's asking for trouble."

New to these parts, indeed! she thought. *I, who was born and brought up here!* "Thank you for your concern," she replied icily, "but my state of health is my business."

And she stepped boldly into the heavy rain, lifting her face to meet it, and almost choking under the impact. Feeling a little foolish, she made for the path, now squelching wet and slippery, that led down the hill.

His amused voice followed her. "Next time," the man called, "bring a bath towel. And some soap. Then you can really do the job properly!"

IN THE MORNING Nicola joined Joy, the young assistant, behind the counter. She had helped many times in the past during vacations and was no stranger to the work. The store was known locally as "Dean's the grocers'", but it stocked many items besides groceries. Enid Dean had widened its scope to such an extent that she had often looked longingly at the blank window space of the empty store next door.

The owner had closed the business after the death of her husband, and had gone abroad, leaving it unoccupied and neglected. But Enid had never seemed to possess the necessary capital to indulge her desire to expand. Instead, she had compromised by adding more and more shelves to her existing store. Some of them stretched almost to the ceiling, this being the only way she knew of making more room for her ever increasing stock.

The doorbell clanged and a small boy came in. Nicola recognized him as the son of an old school friend. He was nearly six years old and knew Nicola well. He pushed himself to the front of the line, and the other customers good-naturedly moved back to allow him in. Joy moved to serve him, but he demanded that "Nicola" should serve him.

Having been taught by her mother that the customer, however small, was always right, Nicola indicated to Joy that she would take over. It was his mother's birthday soon, Barry said, and he wanted to buy her a present. Nicola waited on him cheerfully, bringing out of glass cases and off shelves everything he thought he fancied. His choice ranged from pincushions to dishcloths, from handkerchiefs to cleaning powder—all the things he had seen his mother use at home.

"Don't you think, pet," said Nicola, crouching down to his height, "she might like something that would make her smell nice?"

Offended, he said his mother smelled nice now. The other customers laughed, and Nicola had to explain hastily that she really meant "extra nice." She pointed toward a shelf that met the ceiling.

"Up there, I've got something that goes all frothy when you pour it into the bathwater. If you swish it around it makes lovely big bubbles. Think she'd like that?"

Barry said yes, she would like that, and had he got enough money? Nicola counted the coins on the small moist palm and knew that he was quite a bit short of the necessary amount.

"Yes," she told him, "you've got enough there. I'll

get the stepladder and climb up and bring some bottles
down. Then you can choose.''

She lifted it from its corner and opened it out. As she
climbed to the top it swayed and a customer warned,
''Careful, dear.''

Nicola stretched out to reach a particularly attractive
bottle of bubble bath, but as she moved one way, the
steps moved the other. There was nothing stable for her
to grasp and she lost her footing. The steps overbalanced
and the onlookers gasped as she plunged helplessly
down. But someone must have moved with the speed of
light because she was caught, incredibly, by two tough,
muscular arms and held for a few steadying seconds in an
almost brutal grip.

''You're determined,'' the familiar, maddening voice
said, ''to do yourself an injury. What with a drenching
last night and overreaching yourself this morning like a
clumsy, inexperienced rock climber . . . .''

She was face down in his arms and if it had not been so
undignified she would have started kicking her legs and
shrieking, ''Put me down!''

Instead, she went scarlet and held herself stiff until he
lowered her to the ground. She straightened her overall
and quite unjustifiably gave the man a withering look.
Then she turned to the steps again, but Joy said, ''I'll
take over, Miss Dean, while you get your breath back.''

Joy moved the steps into a better position, an act that
obviously received the approval of the owner of the
tough, muscular arms, and proceeded to satisfy Barry's
requirements.

Nicola turned a pink, defiant face toward her rescuer,
but the words she spoke were prim and correct enough.
''Can I help you?''

''I hope so,'' said the man. ''It would make a nice
change if *you* helped *me* for once. I want some envelopes.''

''Oh, envelopes,'' Nicola repeated, and looked inquiringly at Joy, who was taking Barry's money and counting

it with a puzzled expression. She had realized it was not sufficient to cover the cost of the bubble bath. "Er—Joy," Nicola whispered, "I know, but it doesn't matter."

Joy nodded understandingly and wrapped the precious gift in a specially bright wrapper.

"All right, Barry?" Nicola asked, smiling at him. Barry nodded vigorously and ran out of the shop.

The tall, dark, muscular customer, who had been watching the proceedings, was leaning languidly on his elbow on the counter. He murmured to himself and it sounded suspiciously like "Lucky Barry. What's he got that I haven't?"

Nicola said frigidly, "I beg your pardon?"

"Envelopes," said the man.

"Oh, yes, envelopes," she repeated again, wishing the man did not always manage to make her appear so brainless and inefficient. "Joy?"

Joy, who was serving another customer, pointed to the display of stationery near the window.

"You should promote your assistant, Miss Dean," said the man, with a lazy smile. "She has her wits about her."

Nicola drew in her lips. Arrogant the man might be, but he was certainly neither obtuse nor deaf. Miss Dean, indeed!

"The envelopes," said Miss Dean, pointing, "are over there."

"I am aware of that," the man answered with exaggerated patience. Nicola closed her eyes. "The customer," she told herself, "is always right." She opened them again and he had straightened himself to his intimidatingly full height. "Unfortunately, they are the wrong envelopes. I want a large size, large enough to take a detailed report, consisting of a dozen or so pages."

"Then I'm sorry," Nicola said icily, with a flick of pleasure that he was not going to get what he wanted, "we have none in stock."

The man tapped inpatiently on the counter. "Could you order a supply for me?"

Again she had to ask, "Joy?"

"Yes," said Joy. "Just give me the measurements, sir, and I'll ask Mrs. Dean to get them specially."

"I'm obliged," said the man. "Any time you need a reference as to your competence, Joy, just give my name. I shall be delighted to supply it." He lifted a challenging eyebrow at Nicola, smiled to himself and wrote the required dimensions on a piece of paper, which he then held out to her. As she was about to take it, he changed his mind and handed it to Joy. He smiled again, this time at Nicola's indignation. "I always go," he murmured, turning away, "where my custom is most appreciated."

Another customer claimed Nicola's attention and she had instantly to substitute her glower for a welcoming smile. As she collected the requested groceries, Nicola heard an elderly lady say, "Hello, doctor. Surprised to see you in here at this time of day. You're usually on your rounds, aren't you?"

The man she had called "doctor" nodded. "Morning, Mrs. Rowley."

"I saw you catch that young lady, doctor. Good thing you moved so fast."

"It was, wasn't it?" said the dry voice. "Otherwise I would have had another patient on my hands."

The woman laughed and he moved away. Nicola said to the customer she was serving, "Who is that man? Do you know him?"

"Everyone knows him, dear," she answered.

"He's the new doctor," Mrs. Rowley supplied from the end of the line. "Took his father's place. Practices with three other doctors in the town, but holds office hours in the village three afternoons a week."

"Dr. Mitchell, that's who it is," said Nicola's customer. "He's a good doctor. I know, because I've been to see him, but he takes a bit of getting used to."

"A bit short with you sometimes," said Mrs. Rowley. "Not like his old father. Had the patience of an angel, he did."

"Yes, well," said Nicola's customer, "his son's young, believes in the new ways. And that's into the office, say your piece, watch him write a prescription and out you go."

"I wouldn't have him as *my* doctor," Nicola said, her pride still injured and raw, "not for the whole world. Not even if I were dying."

Someone cleared his throat loudly and Mrs. Rowley put her finger to her lips. The doctor of whom they were talking came round the corner from the rear of the shop. He must have been inspecting the birthday cards.

Now he was inspecting Nicola. Narrowly and minutely, like a biologist examining an unpleasant specimen, he assessed her, taking in her unruly hair, her startled eyes and her parted, shocked lips. He did not appear to like what he saw.

"I'm s-sorry," Nicola stammered, but she might not have spoken. He turned coldly from the apology and left the shop. She felt as small as the biscuit crumb she flicked off the counter. He had, after all, just saved her from a nasty injury, and she hadn't even thanked him.

IT TOOK NICOLA a few days to become acclimatized to her new environment. Apart from college vacations and, after taking up her teaching job, school holidays, she had not lived at home for long periods for some years. Seeing her mother now at close quarters, it was plain that her health was not good. Once a month she visited the doctor for a checkup.

"It's his particular line," Enid said one day. "At the hospital he specialized in respiratory diseases. He's a very good doctor, Nicola."

But despite her praise, something stopped Nicola from putting herself on Dr. Mitchell's list as a patient. There was a quality in the man that grated. She could not visualize herself ever pouring out her health troubles to him. So she had become the patient of one of his partners, Dr. Muirson, an older man who, even if he was a little old-fashioned in his methods, was more paternal and sympathetic.

Later, Nicola went for a walk to the top of her hill. The evening sun lingered as if loath to set and make way for the darkness. Although it was early April, there was a stiff breeze and this time she was determined to dress appropriately. If by any mischance, she told herself, she were to meet that irritating doctor, she would give him no further cause for criticism on that score.

Her blue tweed jacket had a hood attached and her scarlet slacks were close fitting and warm. A sense of elation carried her easily up the incline and she sat on the trunk of a fallen tree. She gazed across the landscape, but she was not seeing it. Nor was she listening to the restless swooping and crying of the birds or hearing the sound of a distant tractor.

She was telling herself that somehow she would have to get used to the idea of being a business woman instead of a teacher. She did not take gladly to the thought. She had been trained to use her brain. Would she, for an unspecified number of years, have to stand back and watch it rust away, like an abandoned piece of machinery in a junk yard?

She wondered what she could do with her spare time. She rarely watched television and she supposed she was, in essence, antisocial, so parties had no appeal. Her hands . . . she looked at them. She must find something to do with her hands. Make a dress for her mother, and then perhaps an outfit for herself? And then . . . ? Couldn't she make some children's clothes, she wondered, and sell them in the shop? Baby clothes, suits for small boys, dresses for little girls?

Her depression lifted and she gazed around rapturously, seeing, feeling and hearing again. And the first thing she heard was footsteps, and a new emotion stumped its way into her with each crunch of shoe on grit and undergrowth—fear. Fear that it would be the man who seemed to have haunted her since her return.

It *was* that man, of course, standing only a few yards away. The hunch of his shoulders betrayed that he was as resentful as she was at having his secret retreat invaded yet again by an alien creature, and what was more, his frown said, by the same irritating woman as last time.

Their eyes met only a fraction of a second before the light in Nicola's died out. The doctor nodded and turned his back on her. His hands found his pockets and he scanned the landscape as Nicola had done, his desire to be alone evident in every line of his body.

Well, she thought indignantly, *I want to be alone, too, so I'll leave the place to him.* It had lost its attraction anyway, now he had come. She stood up and he turned at once. He seemed to be sensitive to every movement, every thought, anticipating every action and on his guard to remedy the effects of such action should the necessity arise. She remembered his unbelievably quick reaction to her fall in the store.

As she started down the hill, it occurred to her that it might be a good opportunity to thank him for breaking that fall. She checked her steps and climbed back until she was within talking distance. He was staring at her and although his expression could hardly be called encouraging, she said, "I must apologize, Dr. Mitchell, for forgetting to thank you for catching me when I fell from the stepladder."

His shrug dismissed the apology. "All part of my job, preventing accidents. Then I don't have to deal with their consequences. A kind of paradox, I suppose, where a 'lazy' doctor could be said to make a good doctor."

If he was being serious it was, she thought, an odd statement for a reputedly conscientious physician to make. "But," she said, "I always thought preventive medicine—isn't that what you're talking about—was good medicine."

"Perhaps." He was still staring at her as though he was only half listening to what she was saying. She grew uncomfortable. Why had she been so stupid as to turn back and speak to him? It was obvious he wanted to get rid of her. The wind was blowing her hair about and she drew her hood over it.

"I'm afraid," she persisted, against her better judgment, "I didn't thank you for sharing your taxi with me the other day." She reasoned with herself that she might as well get it all over at once.

He turned away, but only for a moment. Back his eyes came and focused on her face. "I owe you an apology, too." *This* man was about to apologize to *her?* "That day I was late for my afternoon office hours. I had attended a conference in Birmingham. It was essential that I take the first available taxi. It must have looked rude on my part."

"It did," she answered, but softened her frankness by saying, "all the same, thank you for explaining."

Then she turned and ran down the hill, through the trees and home.

NICOLA told her mother about her new idea. Enid was enthusiastic, and they began to plan a fresh layout for the store and to find a way of making space in one of the two display windows.

Nicola took the morning off and went to town. She returned home with her arms full of material and her head full of ideas. Her mother told her that Connor Mitchell's mother, Barbara Mitchell, with whom she was friendly, had called for morning coffee.

"I explained your plans to her and she was so interested to hear you were an accomplished needlewoman." She watched her daughter unburdening herself all over the dining-room table, spreading out the delicate fabrics, the softly colored embroidery silks and the paper patterns. Then she said, a little uncertainly, "Barbara asked a favor of you, dear."

Nicola smiled. "Don't tell me, would I make a dress for her?"

Enid seemed relieved at the good-tempered response. "I hope you didn't mind my telling her. She said she'd be willing to pay you well for your efforts. She had invited you to call this evening and see her."

Nicola nodded. "I'll need to take her measurements, of course, and discuss details. What time shall I go?"

"About eight o'clock. Her son finishes his office hours in the town about seven-fifteen, then she gives him an evening meal. He usually goes out after that, so the two of you will be able to talk in peace."

At that information Nicola rejoiced. She had no wish to spend even part of the evening in Connor Mitchell's company. The envelopes he had ordered had arrived, so she decided to take them and leave them with his mother.

As she approached the house, she heard mother and son talking. The front room window was open and their voices carried.

"Why is she coming here?" Connor Mitchell's voice demanded.

"Because I hope she'll be kind enough to agree to make me a new outfit." His mother's tone was kindly and reasonable, showing up the abrasiveness of her son's.

"Why don't you patronize one of the department stores in the town or, if you must have a personal dress-maker, get an expert to make your clothes instead of some semi educated, untrained village woman?"

Nicola reacted violently. Village woman! She lifted her hand to raise the heavy black knocker, intending to let it fall with a resounding crash, when she heard his mother reply in a shocked voice, "She's neither half-educated nor untrained. She's a needlework teacher, or rather, she was until she gave up the job to come home and help her mother."

There was a brief silence, followed by a thoughtful, "Did she now?" Then, in a louder voice, as though he was growing annoyed, "You're asking for trouble if you employ an ex-schoolteacher to make a dress for you. No doubt her only experience has been to teach kids how to embroider dainty doilies and cushion covers and useless objects like nightgown cases. You'll be wasting your money. The result of the exercise will probably be something resembling a sack presented to you lovingly in tissue paper concealing a large bill."

Nicola drew a strangled breath. The voice went on. "A teacher she may be, but in the dealings I've had with the girl so far, and that's a darned sight too many—wherever I go, sure enough she turns up—she's given me the impression that she's anything but bright and endowed with only a modicum of intelligence. So for heaven's sake, take my advice and send the girl away before we get too involved with her, and before it's too late."

CHAPTER TWO

NICOLA HAD HEARD enough. She lifted the knocker and thrust it down so hard it must have awakened all the sleeping children in the neighborhood. By the time the door opened, she had managed to control her expression, if not her temper.

She fixed a smile to her face, but when she saw the person who was inviting her into the house, the smile fell away, revealing the scowl beneath.

"I think," she said, holding her head high, "it's only fair to tell you that I heard what you said about me."

Connor Mitchell closed the door. "Yes, I know you did. I saw you come along the path." Did the man miss nothing? "As a matter of fact, I was wondering how long you would let me go on talking about you and abusing you before you stopped eavesdropping and made your presence known."

The man was impossible. No doubt he was taking his revenge for her comment about him in the shop. She held out the envelopes. "They arrived today. I thought you might be wanting them urgently."

He took them without ceremony and scant gratitude. "Thanks. I was. How much?"

"It doesn't matter."

He eyed her suspiciously. "What do you mean, 'it doesn't matter'?"

So he even managed to turn her generosity into something evil. "They only cost a few cents."

"Then it won't break me to pay for them, will it? This is a business transaction, not a favor." She was taken

aback by his abruptness—but hadn't she been warned
about it by her mother? "I notice," he went on, "that
you insist on paying your debts. The taxi, remember? So
how much do I owe you?"

She told him and he gave her some money. "Sorry I
haven't the exact amount."

She opened her handbag and found her purse, expecting any moment that he would insult her further by telling
her to keep the change. As she handed him the necessary
coins, he smiled as if he had guessed what had been in her
mind. She swung away from him to meet the gentle smiling face of his mother, who had emerged from the front
room.

"Miss Dean?" Their hands met. "My word, you *are*
like your mother!" They laughed and Nicola felt that she
liked her mother's friend.

Barbara Mitchell was of average height, tending to
stoutness, her hair carefully tended to keep the gray at
bay. Although she had, like Enid Dean, been widowed at
a relatively early age, she was better preserved, having
led a more sheltered, less financially troubled life.

"How kind of you to come," Mrs. Mitchell said. "I
hear from my son that you two already know each
other."

"It's our misfortune," said her son, with a bland smile
"to have met before."

Nicola presented him eloquently with her back and followed his mother into the spacious living room.

It was furnished comfortably and unpretentiously in
country style, the floor-to-ceiling curtains matching the
fabric of the loose covers on the deep armchairs and
couch. The well-polished parquet floor was partially covered by oval-shaped rugs, the long coffee table was
glass topped, the sideboard exhibited, with the gracious-
ness of a country house, shining silverware and crystal
glasses.

Nicola was invited to sit down in one of the armchairs
The son selected another on the other side of the fire
place.

To Nicola's annoyance, he continued to look at her as though she were an absorbing and unique medical puzzle that he had never come across before.

But she concentrated her gaze on his mother, who remarked, "I've heard so much about you. Your mother has told me how clever you are with your dressmaking and embroidery."

"Mothers the world over," the son told the end of his tie, which he was idly flicking up and down, "are notoriously prejudiced in favor of their offspring."

"Be quiet, Connor," his mother reprimanded mildly. "Pretend he's not here, Miss Dean."

As if, Nicola thought, *I could pretend that such a solidly built, six-foot-plus, objectionable specimen of humanity was invisible!* But she took his mother's advice and kept her face resolutely turned away from him, talking dressmaking and needlework with her for some time. The son picked up a book and appeared to be absorbed in it.

Mrs. Mitchell told Nicola she had seen a dress in a magazine and asked if she would be able to copy it without a pattern. Nicola told her a pattern could be dispensed with. "I've made a number of dresses just by looking at the picture."

"You must be very gifted," she said.

Nicola shrugged. "Once you know how, it's reasonably straightforward."

"I think you're being very modest," Mrs. Mitchell said, getting up and searching through the magazine rack. "It must be upstairs. I won't be a moment, Miss Dean." She glanced at her son. "Connor will entertain you while I'm gone."

"It all depends," said her son lazily, sliding farther down in his armchair and stretching out his long legs, "what you mean by 'entertain.' Alas, I'm no actor."

You're right there, Nicola thought, as his mother left them. *You certainly don't bother to hide your aversion to someone you dislike.*

"So—" his head was resting on the upholstery and

only his eyes moved—all over her "—you're not a new-comer to the area or to the local climate as I assumed the other evening. Which means you should surely have known better than to have dressed so inappropriately." She was silent, knowing by the roving appraisal in his eyes that he intended to continue. "So," he repeated, "you are Miss Dean, daughter of the owner of the village store."

Which, Nicola fumed, *puts me right in my place*.

"You have, I assume, another name by which people address you more familiarly?"

"Yes, of course. It's Nicola."

"Ah, yes. Ni-co-la." He rolled it around his tongue as if trying it for size. It obviously did not fit, because he went on, "It's odd, Miss Dean, how you and I seem to react on each other, no matter what the circumstances or situation, as if we were two dangerous chemicals that, when combined, produce disastrous results." He pulled himself into a more correct sitting position. "Whenever I talk to you—look at the way you're responding to me now—it's like stroking a cat's back in the wrong direction. Your fur stands on end!"

"I'm sorry," she said stiffly.

"You're not sorry, Miss Dean, so don't lie. It's out of character."

"What," Nicola said waspishly, "do you know about my character? You know nothing about me."

"Now that's where you're wrong. I know a lot about you. I know, for instance, that you're precipitate. How do I know?" He sat forward, clasping his hands loosely. "The other evening, the first time we met on the hill when you rushed out of the house—I'm right, aren't I—unsuitably dressed. Also when you stretched too far while perched at the top of the stepladder and I caught you as you fell. Correct?"

Nicola hoped her nod would bring his lecture to an end, but instead it encouraged him to elaborate on his theme. "Also," he went on, "you're kindly, unselfish and anxious to please.'' Praise from him? Where was the catch? ''Which is why you're annoyed with me. I refuse to be pleased by you.'' *Now I have it*, Nicola thought. It was his rather subtle way of saying he didn't like her. ''You want, in fact, to please others at no matter what cost to yourself.''

Which was true again. Hadn't she left a job she loved for her mother's sake? She heard his mother walking around overhead and wished she would find her magazine and join them downstairs. Otherwise it wouldn't be long, Nicola fumed, before her doctor son changed medical roles, turned psychiatrist and had her stretched out on the couch so that he could continue his psychoanalytical dissection of her character.

''You like children,'' he continued remorselessly, ''and have a great deal of patience with them. How do I know? That small boy in the store. Also, you struggle against impossible odds; for instance, three suitcases, two hands. And, er, you're either amazingly generous, or you can't add up money correctly. That small boy, again.''

''You,'' she muttered, exasperated, ''see far too much.''

He smiled and leaned back. ''I do, don't I? But observation is part of my stock-in-trade as a doctor. To treat people successfully, I have to use my eyes as well as my hands. I can tell at a glance just how ill somebody is. Accurate observation is a great asset to a physician.'' He grinned. ''Shall I continue with my character analysis?''

''No, thank you.''

''All right, I will. You see, I can be obstinate, too. I know, for example, that it's your nature to attempt just a little more than you can reasonably achieve, possibly to prove to yourself that you can do it—those suitcases again, and that stepladder. I know you dislike being under an obligation to anyone—the taxi. And I know you love the beauty of the hills. Oddly enough—'' softly, reflectively ''—so do I. You also enjoy your own company, again as I do." He paused. "I also know that you can't stand me at any price."

"Is it any wonder?" she asked a little wildly.

"Oh, I'm not complaining. I'm just stating a fact." He stood in front of the empty grate, his hands behind his back. "It's time I went for my evening walk. I can be sure of one thing. I won't find you on my particular hill this evening." He didn't add, "Thank goodness," but the words were implied.

"It's *my* hill, too," she murmured childishly.

"So I gathered." He thought a moment, then he said, "I'll strike a bargain with you, Miss Dean. If you're agreeable, whenever we meet up there, let's pretend we're really alone. What I mean is, I'm willing to ignore you if you promise to ignore me." Nicola frowned. "There's no other way, Miss Dean. I can't say to you, 'you mustn't come here,' any more than you can say the place is out of bounds to me. Do you agree?"

Nicola said she supposed she had no alternative. "I love the view too much to deny myself the pleasure of seeing it whenever I feel the urge."

"I echo that. You need never be afraid I'll invade your privacy. I value mine too much to want to intrude upon another's. I'll keep rigidly to my side of the bargain."

"So shall I," she said indignantly, because his words implied that she might not. "If we find ourselves up there together, I wouldn't speak to you even if I were drawing my last breath."

"You wouldn't be able to," he answered dryly.

The telephone rang. Mrs. Mitchell, who was coming down the stairs, answered it. "For you, Connor. Your ladylove."

He went into the hall. "Velma?" Nicola heard him say, just before his mother closed the door. "I wondered if you'd call . . . ."

"His young lady," she explained, turning the pages of the magazine. "She's a nurse at the hospital."

"Are they engaged?" Nicola asked.

"He hasn't actually said so, but I really think they must be unofficially." She laughed. "Whenever I try to get the truth out of him about their friendship, he puts up the shutters. I'm told politely but firmly to keep out!" She sat down and continued turning the pages. "What about you, Miss Dean? An attractive young woman like you must surely have a devoted young man in the offing?"

"Well, there's—" The door opened and Connor put his head around it. Nicola would have preferred to have stopped there, but Mrs. Mitchell was looking at her with such interest she had to continue. "There's Terence, Terence Stevens. He's—" she glanced at the son wishing he would go away, but he had come into the room and obviously had every intention of hearing her out. "He's a history teacher at the school I used to work in."

"And," said Mrs. Mitchell, "are you going to marry him?"

Nicola grew confused by that concentrated male stare. "Well, I—we—I don't know, really. We've been going around together for quite a while now, but—" This time she did stop, because there was nothing more to say.

Barbara Mitchell laughed. "It's as difficult getting information from you about your love life as it is from my son! But then I have no right to pry into yours!"

"Implying, you'll notice," Connor Mitchell said to Nicola with a smile, "that she has a right to pry into mine. Which she hasn't, of course. Take my advice, Miss Dean. Keep your love affairs to yourself."

His tone had been almost friendly, but his automatic assumption that her friendship with Terence had a deeper, even sordid side to it irritated her and she brushed aside indignantly what might well have been the offer of an olive branch. "*I* have no 'love affairs' to keep to myself, Dr. Mitchell." As soon as she had spoken she realized how prim and self-righteous she had sounded. A fact which, of course, did not fail to register with Dr. Connor Mitchell.

"Then it's high time," he said softly, insinuatingly, "someone knocked you off your pedestal and brought you down to earth. In the literal as well as the metaphorical sense, Miss Dean." Her heightened color gave her away and he watched with unmistakable satisfaction as his message went home. Then he withdrew his attention from her as though she had melted away like a snowflake on a warm hand.

"I'm meeting Velma in town, mother."

Mrs. Mitchell raised her eyes from the magazine. "But, dear, I thought you were going for a walk."

"Velma doesn't take kindly to walking in the great outdoors. She does so much indoors, walking the wards. So I've changed my mind. Just for once I've decided that looking at a beautiful woman will be more rewarding than looking at a beautiful view. And—" he flicked Nicola a malicious glance "—I don't suppose we shall be doing much—walking."

He slammed the door behind him.

As his car revved up and roared away down the road, Nicola wished she had accepted his olive branch—and thrown it back in his face.

His mother sighed with relief. "At last we can get down to business without fear of interruption."

By the end of the visit, all the details had been decided on. Mrs. Mitchell promised to go to town to buy the material and would bring it to the house herself.

"You'll need a couple of fittings, at least," Nicola told her.

"Call me anytime, dear. I'm in most evenings."

Nicola left with as much speed as politeness would allow. She certainly didn't want Connor Mitchell to find her there if he brought his "ladylove" back to the house.

DESPITE her good resolution to make Mrs. Mitchell's dress before anything else, Nicola could not resist starting on at least one small garment in her spare time. It was a baby girl's dress with multicolored smocking across the yoke.

But as soon as Mrs. Mitchell brought the material, Nicola made a pattern and cut out the dress. She worked fast and it was not long before she was able to fix a time for the first fitting.

Within an hour after the baby's dress was put in the store window, it had been sold. But it had been on display long enough to be noticed and for mothers to ask if there were others in stock.

So Nicola began to take orders and as they grew she started to worry about her ability to fill them. She sat up into the early hours cutting and sewing and embroidering and still the orders came in. Her mother asked, hadn't she taken on too much? Nicola disagreed strongly, unwilling to admit that she might be right.

She had received two or three letters from Terence that she had not had time to answer and one evening he phoned, demanding a reason for her silence. He was coming to see her, he warned, but she told him he mustn't because she was too busy to entertain.

SHE WENT to the Mitchells' house for the fitting and hoped that Connor Mitchell would be out. He was in. As she entered the living room he looked up from his book, nodded and continued to read. He was plainly in an uncommunicative mood.

Mrs. Mitchell took Nicola upstairs to try on the dress. It was an excellent fit. "You have good judgment," she said, eyeing her ample proportions a little ruefully. She slipped the dress off over her head and Nicola folded it carefully, putting it back into the paper bag. "Do come down and have a coffee."

Nicola was in the middle of protesting that she really should go home and get back to her sewing when Barbara Mitchell said, almost pleadingly, "Your mother told me how hard you've been working, so it would do you good to take a break. Do stay, please. My son's in one of his moods. Sometimes he withdraws into a world of his own and since I know nothing about medicine, I can't follow him there. So I have to be as silent as he is, even when I'm longing to talk.''

After such an appeal, Nicola felt she had to agree. Mrs. Mitchell told her to join Connor while she made the coffee. Nicola knew a moment of panic. Go in there and sit silent while the son brooded and meditated and ignored her as though she was of less importance than the hearthrug his highly polished shoes rested on?

"Can't I help you, Mrs. Mitchell?" It was Nicola's turn now to plead.

But Barbara would not hear of it. "Take a rest, Miss Dean. You look as though you could do with it!"

"Oh, dear. Does it show that much? My mother keeps telling me I look tired."

She crept into the living room, not wishing to distract the doctor in the house from his private world. But as she glanced at him secretly and a little fearfully, he looked up. His eyes scanned her face.

"Yes, you do," he commented, and returned at once to his book. "Look tired," he enlarged, as if she had asked for an explanation. "Why?"

"She's working too hard," his mother called from the kitchen, "making baby clothes."

Nicola explained, "I'm making children's clothes for sale in the shop."

He did not look up. Instead he asked the printed words in front of his eyes, "And why should that make you tired?"

"Well," she said running a hand over her hair, smoothing out the curls which would keep springing up over her head no matter how hard she tried to flatten them, "I made a baby's dress and sold it at once, and now I've got so many orders for similar ones I can hardly keep up with the demand."

He nodded. "In character, attempting more than you could reasonably expect to achieve." He looked up.

"Precipitate, too, failing to look intelligently into the future before you leap." His eyes glinted. "Wasn't I right?"

Nicola refused to concede victory. "It's keeping me busy."

"Too busy, if it's tiring you." There was a pause. "I wondered why you hadn't been up to the hill lately." Another pause. "I did think I might have frightened you away."

She said untruthfully, "I haven't even thought about you."

He looked up, this time with eyebrows skeptically high and Nicola colored, giving herself away. The silence grew so long she began to fidget. No wonder his mother craved company if this was what she had to put up with whenever he was at home.

She inhaled the pleasant aroma of coffee creeping along the hall, studied her hands as closely as if they were ancient stone tablets inscribed with hieroglyphics, inspected her nails, stared at the lines on her palms, turned them over and tested the backs of them for smoothness. Why did the man reduce her to such a state of nerves, she asked herself desperately. No other man had that effect on her.

She looked up involuntarily and caught his derisive smile. Through her agitation he was, of course, able to interpret her state of mind. Suddenly she hated everything about him, his supreme self-control, his coolness and self-possession that amounted almost to indolence. She detested his perspicacity, his insight, his ability to "read" her every action.

The cups rattled along the hallway. Activated by relief, she stood up and helped Mrs. Mitchell pour the coffee. "That's for my son," she directed. "He doesn't take sugar. I wish he did. It might help to sweeten him a little!"

He took the coffee and as Nicola bent over him, he gave a swift, mocking smile. "You haven't added an odd grain or two of arsenic?'' he murmured so that his mother could not hear. Nicola did not deign to reply. He subsided into his book, which seemed to be on some aspect of medicine.

Mrs. Mitchell stirred her coffee thoughtfully. "I don't know whether you and your mother have heard," she said, a little anxiously, "but there's a rumor going around that a supermarket chain is interested in establishing a branch in the village."

Nicola frowned and put down her cup. "No, we hadn't heard. Oh, dear! That could present quite a problem."

"Personally," said Connor, sipping his coffee, "I think it's an excellent idea."

Nicola said frigidly, "It's our livelihood at stake, Dr. Mitchell. It would ruin our trade."

"Make the first move. Offer your premises to the firm, do a deal and you might make yourselves a bundle of money." He closed the book and drank his cup dry, banging it down on the saucer. "Let me see, isn't the shop next door to yours empty?"

"What if it is? We'll never sell!" she declared, conscious of an element of melodrama in her tone. She drank some coffee, feeling she needed its strength to pursue the argument.

"Brave words," the doctor jeered, "but the time will come when you'll be forced to. Ye olde family businesses such as yours are doomed. A self-service store is long overdue in this village. It's about time it plunged into the twentieth century."

"I hate the twentieth century!" The man was a traitor, but she reacted violently because she knew in her heart that he spoke the truth, and that particular truth both hurt and worried her.

"Too bad," he said unfeelingly, opening his book again "You were born into it, so you have to make the best of it. Anyway, what's wrong with it? It's a century of what people hundreds of years ago would have called miracles."

"You can keep your miracles, your new inventions!" Nicola answered furiously, but secretly surprised by the way she was overreacting again. What was it about the man that brought out the worst in her? "And your new ideas. Everything is changing and there seems to be some odd law that dictates that nothing ever changes for the better!"

He closed his book with a thump. "You're talking the most arrant nonsense. And spoken with such passion, too." He looked her over derisively. "You must fit in so well with your boyfriend. Teacher of history, you said? Do you honestly believe the past has more to offer modern man than the present? What is it you're running away from, Miss Dean?" He folded his arms and watched her with a clinically detached gaze. "Psychologically speaking, you'd make an interesting case."

Conscious of his mother's lively interest in their argument, she shot at him, "Why have you suddenly turned personal? I thought it was a woman's prerogative—it's an accusation always being thrown at her—to divert the course of a discussion toward herself?"

He grinned. "You have me there, Miss Dean. So we're having a 'discussion,' are we? I'm relieved. I really thought it was a quarrel. You'll have to calm down, you know. You're doing your blood pressure no good at all."

"Then stop provoking her, son," came his mother's soft, urgent voice.

But his calculated coolness goaded Nicola still more. "New ideas equal change and change equals evil," she declared, aware even in her anger that she was overstating the case. But something inside her drove her to try to get even with the man, to arouse him from his smugness, his reasoned equanimity. "All the change going on around us is affecting people adversely. It's lowering their standards and destroying their moral codes." She knew she was back to her primness and he took her up derisively.

"Behold, a fugitive from the Victorian era!" Then he

put aside his book and became serious. "I disagree with you absolutely. The evidence all points to ideology affecting the environment, not the other way around. It's the new ideas that are giving rise to new technologies and it's these that are changing our surroundings. And you can play the ostrich and oppose the fact as much as you like, but the rate of change will accelerate. Everything is moving faster, even—" he grinned suddenly "—my heart when you're around!"

His mother laughed and Nicola, turning away from the very masculine look in his eyes said, "If it's true, then it's only because I annoy you, nothing else." He did not deny the statement. "All the same," she went on, "the fact that these changes are taking place doesn't necessarily make them good. There's a lot to be said for the old ways."

"Good God," he interrupted with disgust, "you talk like an octogenarian instead of . . . let me see," he said studying her, "how old are you? Middle twenties?"

"Twenty-five."

"So I'm ten years older than you, yet my ideas are more progressive. Odd, isn't it? If I, as a doctor, had your outlook, I'd still be dosing people with ancient remedies, using leeches and advising them to 'take the waters.' "

He had had the last word. He had won on points. He subsided into his book and Nicola took this as an inference that her presence was no longer welcome. Nor, she could have told him, was his.

She took the half-finished dress with her, and went to the door saying, "There will have to be one more fitting at least, Mrs. Mitchell."

"You're being so quick with it, dear. I suppose it was because you were so accurate with your original measurements."

Nicola shrugged off the praise. "It was all part of my training."

"You should see it, Connor," his mother said, "it really has the professional touch."

"Has it?" He displayed the minimum of interest, not even raising his eyes. "When the supermarket gets its foot in the door, Miss Dean will have to earn her living by setting up a *haute couture* business in the village, won't she?"

The sarcasm stung. "I was a teacher of needlework, Dr. Mitchell," Nicola said quietly, so quietly he looked at her. "And if a teacher can't do a good job, how can she teach her pupils properly? How can she in all honesty justify her position as an instructor and guide?"

He gave her a curiously probing look. When she said, "Good night, Dr. Mitchell," he merely nodded.

A FEW DAYS later, Connor Mitchell patronized the store again. Joy was busy serving a line of customers and Nicola was talking to a young man near the door. As soon as the doctor walked in, she ended her conversation. "I'll call around this evening and have a look at the van."

The young man, wearing soiled overalls, raised his hand and left.

She took her place behind the counter and assumed a blank expression to hide the odd disorder of emotions the appearance of Barbara Mitchell's son always seemed to create inside her.

"Can I help you, Dr. Mitchell?"

"No," he said tersely, "but you can help my mother." He threw a list onto the counter. "Her grocery order. Unfortunately her car's being serviced so she can't pick it up as she usually does, but she would like it delivered this evening."

Nicola nodded, picking up the list. He leaned on the counter and the action brought his face uncomfortably near, but she stood her ground and met his eyes unflinchingly. "Forgive the question, but are you able to make deliveries?"

"We have a boy who delivers orders after school. Why?"

Something in her face seemed to catch his attention and he did not reply at once. Confused, she pushed back a stray piece of hair from her cheek. She wondered if there was something wrong with her.

He straightened abruptly and said, "I heard you say something just now about a van."

Did nothing pass by him? "I'm thinking of buying it. I miss the car I used to share with my boyfriend. The van's secondhand, of course. I'm going to see it this evening."

"I assume you'll get an expert to look it over before you part with your money?"

"I don't know an expert. The young man who owns it is a mechanic."

"Is it his job?"

"No, it's his hobby. I'll just have to trust him and take a chance that the van's roadworthy."

"And end up in hospital."

"It's cheap. I can't afford anything better at the moment."

"I'm surprised at you, Miss Dean. I credited you with more sense."

Nicola smiled down at his mother's grocery list. "It's something to know that you credit me with *some* sense, Dr. Mitchell. I thought you'd written me off as dim-witted and stupid beyond words."

He leaned forward and she could feel his breath on her mouth as he said, in a falsely confiding tone, "I haven't even written you *down*, Miss Dean, so how could I have written you *off*?"

After that crushing reply he removed himself from the store.

Nicola kept her promise and looked over the van. It was rusting here and there, but after taking it for a short test run she decided to buy it. The young man took the check and said the van should "do her all right." He'd spent some time on it and got it into working order. "If you ever want it serviced," he offered, "I'll do it for you cheap."

She drove away with a wave of the hand. She bumped over the level crossing that cut across the village street.

It had been converted into a continental crossing and the barriers were raised, implying that there was no train coming and it was therefore safe to drive across it.

On her way home, she approached the doctor's house. Connor Mitchell was getting out of his car in the driveway. The van was noisy and he looked around. When he saw who was driving it, he came to the curb and signaled to Nicola to stop.

She could have ignored the imperious gesture, but she pulled up beside him. He leaned on his arms against the door, gazing at her through the window. "I see from your self-satisfied grin that you're pleased with your new toy." He stood back and inspected the bodywork, shaking his head. "I know what they say about fools and their money. I didn't appreciate the truth of it until now. You've just purchased a potential suicide weapon, Miss Dean. When you come to grief in it—as you will—don't come to me to patch you up."

She revved the engine noisily. "I wouldn't dream of it, Dr. Mitchell. I would go to my own doctor." She let out the clutch, preparatory to driving away. The gears ground and he flinched exaggeratedly. "I'm not one of your patients."

"Quite right, you aren't. For that at least I must be thankful. If you were to walk into my office, the air would turn electric and we would both receive fatal shocks!"

"Then you haven't got to worry, have you, if I were to *kill* myself in this?"

"In my profession, Miss Dean," he said, with a faint smile, "human life is regarded as precious and to be preserved at all costs, even if the one who possesses that life is an aggravating, exasperating woman!"

Nicola drove away, making as much noise as she could produce with the pressure of her foot on the accelerator.

A FEW EVENINGS later, Nicola put aside Mrs. Mitchell's dress, pushed to the back of her mind the orders for baby clothes that were clamoring for attention like the children who would one day wear them, and decided to become reacquainted with her hill. It was some time since she had been there. She refused to admit that the fear of meeting Connor Mitchell had kept her away.

Enid had gone to bed early. She was reading and Nicola was worried by her paleness, wondering if she should have a word with her doctor. If the doctor in question had been anyone but who it was, Nicola would not have hesitated. But she could not imagine herself having a confidential chat of any description with that particular doctor.

She crossed the railway track and strode up the path that led to the hilltop, her elation at her sudden freedom increasing with the steepening slope of the land. As she reached the summit, hands in pockets, her hair bouncing in the wind, she was panting and exhilarated with effort—and her heart somersaulted under her ribs. Someone was up there before her, hands in his pockets, too, standing, easy, relaxed, lost to his surroundings, contemplating the view.

But he was not so "lost" that he was not immediately aware of a stranger's presence. He turned at once and looked, not at, but through her. They might indeed have been perfect strangers, as though he did not know her name was Nicola Dean, who made clothes for his mother. The dull nonrecognition in his eyes brought her to a shocked standstill, until she remembered their pact, their promise to ignore each other if they ever met up there.

Not a smile passed between them, not even the briefest of nods that sometimes passes between true strangers. She stood a few yards from him wondering what to do. She had never considered having to share her hill. Should she make a quick retreat, leaving him in possession? The thought of conceding victory to such an arrogant, discourteous man brought her fighting spirit into play. She sat herself firmly on the fallen tree, rested her elbows on her knees and her chin in her hand. Although her eyes roamed the landscape, her mind was busy growling over the man standing a few yards from her.

But was he really being discourteous? Wasn't he honoring their pact? All the same, she argued perversely, he might have given some sign that he knew who she was. She heard a movement and looked at him covertly. He was sitting, knees drawn up, arms resting loosely on them, hands linked, still staring into the far distance.

She tried focusing her attention on the far distance, too, but the bulk of a man kept coming between her and the beauties of the countryside, the assured way he held his head, the confidence of his manner, his remote, off-putting expression, the watchfulness not only of his dissecting glance, but of his penetrating mind.

She grew angry with herself for her inability to switch him off, like a television picture. Closing her eyes didn't shut him out, because she tried. She moved to sit on the ground, fidgeted with twigs, pulled at leaves and grass. She simply could not keep still.

Apprehensively, she looked at him, wondering if he was aware of her restlessness. He was not looking at her, of course, but she was certain he was conscious of her agitation.

She bent her knees and clasped her fingers around them, copying him. *There are the hills*, she told herself, *there are the Welsh mountains, distant and grand. Wouldn't you like to be climbing them, going higher and higher until you reached the clouds?*

He moved again and she saw that he was lying full length. She changed her position and he turned his back on her. A few minutes later she glanced at him again. He was so still it was unbelievable. He was not worried by her presence, so why should she be by his?

One by one her muscles relaxed until she felt a compulsion to lie down as he was doing. His serenity had at last communicated itself to her. She put a hand under her head and listened to the country sounds, the neighing of a horse in the valley, the birds twittering, a barking dog, the hiss of the wind through the trees like the sea ebbing and flowing over shingle. . . .

In her dream a man was standing in front of her. Her heart was pounding and she was in distress. She couldn't see his face, but he was tall and broad and his arms were a refuge. He was holding her and comforting her and trying to calm her, but she would not be calmed . . . she looked up at him, desperate to discover his identity . . . his head came down . . . and she woke up, so out of breath she felt she was suffocating. She remembered where she was and sat up in a panic. Connor Mitchell was there and he would be watching her, laughing at her. . . .

She looked around, all around the summit of the hill. She was alone. He had gone.

CHAPTER THREE

ONE EVENING Enid invited her friend Barbara Mitchell for a visit and told her that the dress would be ready for another fitting.

Connor gave his mother a lift. Nicola looked out of the bedroom window as her mother opened the door to let Mrs. Mitchell in. Sitting beside the driver was a young woman, her hair the deepest red Nicola had ever seen. It made her own hair, a delicate auburn, look as faded as fabric bleached by the sun. She supposed his companion was Velma, his girlfriend.

The red-haired girl raised her eyes at Connor's bidding and gave a self-satisfied smile. Connor gazed up at the window, too. Nicola knew he must have seen her blank face and staring eyes. He waved a careless hand and, as soon as his mother was admitted into the house, drove away quickly.

Nicola had tried so often to fit the many aspects of the man together: the side of him that liked the loneliness and solitude of a hilltop, the dedicated doctor, the abrupt withdrawn side he so often presented to the world. There was the man in him who liked driving fast, who appreciated the attractions of the city and those of a beautiful woman. Yet he had never married.

It was about a week later that Enid decided one morning not to get up. "My chest is bad," she told her daughter. "I've coughed away half the night. You can cope in the shop, dear, can't you? If any salesmen call, Joy will take over while you see them. I may get up later if I feel like it."

But as the day passed, Enid did not feel like it. Just before six o'clock Nicola told her, "You can say what you like. I'm sending for the doctor." When she made no objection, Nicola grew even more worried.

So, disregarding the unreasonable increase in her own heartbeats, she dialed Connor Mitchell's number. His mother answered. She was sympathetic and anxious and said, "Just a moment, Nicola—you don't mind if I call you that, do you? Miss Dean is so formal. I'll get my son."

A terse "Yes, Miss Dean?" came crackling out of the receiver.

His curtness threw Nicola for a moment, but she recovered and explained, "It's my mother, doctor. She's—she's—"

"You want me to call?"

His swift grasping of the situation made her unusually effusive. "Oh, yes, please, Dr. Mitchell. I'd be so pleased if you—"

The receiver at his end was slammed down and Nicola was left feeling a stupid, overanxious nuisance. It took him only a few minutes to reach the house. She was looking out for him and had the door open before he could ring the bell. His frown should have alerted her, but in her anxiety over her mother's condition his latent ill-humor did not register—until he spoke.

"Why didn't you call me earlier? Why did you leave it so late in the day? I have office hours in the town starting in fifteen minutes."

His unwarranted attack made her heart slip like a climber losing a vital foothold. "I'm sorry if I broke the rules," she said miserably, following him up the stairs and speaking to his back, "but my mother didn't seem ill enough this morning, so I waited before troubling you and—"

He was not listening. When he greeted the patient, his manner underwent a transformation. He became understanding and kindly, gentle in his examination and considerate in his explanations. He wrote out a prescription and handed it to Nicola.

"You'll have to look after your mother. Can you cope? What about the store?"

"It's all right, doctor," Enid answered. "We've got Joy. She may be young, but she's capable and trustworthy. But I'm not so ill I can't look after myself a little bit."

He smiled. "The last three words are the most important."

"All right, doctor, I'll remember that. But I can't trouble my daughter too much. She's got so much work on hand, what with having to keep up with the orders for kiddies' clothes." She looked at the alarm clock ticking loudly beside her bed. "We mustn't keep you. You're busy, I expect."

He went to the door. "I'll call again in a couple of days." To Nicola he said, "If you need me before that, give me a call. But don't—repeat, don't—leave it as late in the day as you did this time."

He must have seen the rebellion stirring in her eyes because he watched her narrowly, as if wondering which way she would jump. But like a cat with a dog on both sides of the fence, she stayed where she was. Would he, Nicola wondered as they went downstairs, speak to any other anxious relative in that offensive tone? No, she answered herself, he would not! He was taking unfair advantage of their acquaintance. She had already apologized. She was not going to prostrate herself for calling him at such an inappropriate time.

She was so irritated by his high-handed manner and so anxious about her mother that she became angry—and recklessly blunt. It was time, she decided, someone told him a few home truths about how the other half—the patients and their relatives—lived. So she leaped from her fence and landed slap on his head.

"The trouble with doctors," she fumed as they reached the hall, "is that they're never ill, so they don't know what it's like to suffer." He opened the door and rested his hand on it. "And it's not only the patient who suffers," she raged, regardless of his hardening expression. "The one who's looking after the patient suffers, too, especially when they see someone they love so ill they feel helpless and don't know what to do. And by that I mean whether or not to "bother" the doctor, as my mother calls it."

"Point taken, Miss Dean." His tone was brisk. "But I'm no student. I've passed all my exams. I've been in the medical game for some years now. Not to mention that I have ten more years of living to my credit than you have. You're telling me something I learned long ago." He stepped outside.

His cool, matter-of-fact manner so goaded her she dug in her claws. "The trouble with you, Dr. Mitchell, is that you're such a bighead you think you know everything!"

He deflected her anger with a smile, but this only increased it because it made her feel the size of an insect. And she wasn't going to be ground into oblivion by the heel of his ruthless foot. She banged the door in his face so hard it echoed up and down the street.

Then she leaned against it, horrified because she had been so rude. Would I, she asked herself, have done that to any other doctor? She was forced to admit that under no circumstances would she have done so. She wrenched the door open to apologize, but his car had gone.

THAT EVENING Nicola finished Mrs. Mitchell's dress. She took it upstairs for her mother to admire. She praised it as Nicola had hoped she might.

"Why don't you give Barbara a surprise and take it over straight away? I'll be all right on my own for a while, dear. She'll be so pleased with it she'll want you to make something else for her." She put out a warning hand. "But go easy about taking on anything at the moment. You're swamped with orders for kiddies' things, as it is, and what with me and the store . . . .''

Nicola shrugged off the caution. "I'm enjoying myself. It's what I was trained for, wasn't it?"

"My dear," for a passing moment Enid looked stricken, "when you say that, you make me feel terrible because I took you away from your teaching. And you loved that, didn't you?"

Nicola bent down and hugged her. "That isn't what I meant. I didn't realize you'd take it that way." She folded the dress carefully. "Not to worry. I'll cope." But she sounded more confident than she felt.

As she approached the Mitchells' residence with its attractive red brickwork and its diamond-patterned windows gleaming in the evening sun, she regretted having agreed to her mother's suggestion. It seemed the Mitchells already had a visitor.

She pulled up to the curb behind another car parked outside. Next to it her dark blue van looked ordinary and ready for the local junk yard. The other vehicle was small, red and shiningly efficient. A filmy green scarf had been flung carelessly over the driving seat and as Nicola walked past, a heavy perfume drifted from the interior. A feminine aura still hung about the vehicle. It must, Nicola decided, belong to Connor's girl friend.

It wouldn't take a moment, she consoled herself, to hand in the dress. She lifted the knocker and as it sounded, Mrs. Mitchell's head appeared at a bedroom window.

"Let yourself in, dear," she called. "Just push the door. I'll be down in a moment. Go into the living room and make yourself at home."

Nicola lingered uncertainly in the hall. The strong sweet smell had followed its owner into the house, but there was not a sound from any of the rooms. If Connor and his lady friend were anywhere, they must be in the garden. Slowly, hesitantly, she opened the living-room door—and was immobilized with embarrassment.

A slender, shapely young woman was clinging to Connor's neck. Her lips were pressed against his, his hands were resting just above her waist and if her body could have spoken it would have shouted, "I've been here—many times—before."

The kiss the girl was giving him did not seem to be at all unwelcome. The silent but not unresponsive recipient of the embrace must, with his uncanny inbuilt radar system, have become aware of a stranger in the room. He pushed the girl away and as his eyes swung toward Nicola, they narrowed into a knife edge.

He walked toward her with a thrusting anger out of all proportion to the crime she had accidentally committed. "What do you want, Miss Dean?" he rasped. "And what do you mean by bursting in here uninvited?"

His guest, unperturbed, pushed a few wisps of hair into place and watched the proceedings with considerable amusement. Her slanting eyes, the high cheekbones, the pale, slightly freckled skin that so often seemed to go with such intensely red hair, the sophistication; all combined to expose Nicola's timorous, self-effacing presence like the merciless beam of a spotlight on an actor.

But Connor was at that moment plainly in no mood to appreciate drama of any sort. He bore down on the intruder, but she stood her ground, even when he faced her squarely and said, "Well?"

It was no good. With that fabulous female hovering theatrically upstage, Nicola could not stand up to the belligerence of the leading man. She began to retreat backward out of the door, looking up at the male lead with a timidity that annoyed her but which was not merely part of the act. She was genuinely scared.

"I'm—I'm sorry, Dr. Mitchell, I'll wait in the hall." She backed outside and, as she thought, offstage and out of reach, but he followed, so she tried to explain. "I—I wasn't really uninvited. Your mother told me to go into the living room, and as I didn't know it was already occupied, I obeyed instructions and went into the living room."

"Then for heaven's sake *come* into the living room." His hand came out, fastened onto her wrist and jerked her into the room. The remnants of his anger still clung to him and Nicola's placatory words had done nothing to brush him free of them.

Clutching her parcel, she stayed near the door. Off-handedly the host performed the introductions. "Miss Dean, Velma Westlake, a friend of mine. Velma, Nicola Dean, a girl from the village."

The insult implicit in the description set Nicola's nerves on edge. For a few reluctant seconds, Velma Westlake allowed her hand to rest in Nicola's. "Didn't I see you," she purred, "at an upstairs window over the village store the other evening? I remember thinking how odd it was that we had the same—" her gaze lifted to Nicola's curls "—well, almost the same color hair."

Connor had thrown himself into an armchair. His eyes carried out a thorough examination of the two heads. He said lazily, "My dear Velma, it's almost an insult to put the color of your hair into the same category as that of Miss Dean's." He did not specify which of the two heads of hair was being insulted, but Nicola guessed it was not Velma's.

Velma must have guessed it, too, because her hand fingered a few strands of her enviably smooth, fiery red locks and she murmured, "How sweet of you, darling, to like the color of my hair so much."

Connor did not reply, but continued to look at them both as if the comparison afforded him unending amuse-ment. Velma sat on the arm of his chair and closed her fingers possessively over his two broad shoulders. He did not object to being thus possessed.

As Nicola watched them, an extraordinary pain gripped her inside. It tugged at her unbearably like two hands on a bell rope, two inexperienced hands ringing discordantly and painfully out of turn.

"Why have you come, Miss Dean?" He shot the ques-tion at her so suddenly she jumped.

"To—to give your mother her dress. I've finished it."

"My dear Nicola," Mrs. Mitchell said, coming into

the room, "you really are wonderful to have got it done so quickly. And to bring it to me, too! I would have collected it."

Nicola turned to her as gratefully as a sunflower to the rays of the sun. "I wanted to give you a surprise. But if I'd known you had company . . . ."

"Miss Westlake is my son's company, not mine," Mrs. Mitchell said gently. "Show me the dress, dear."

With care Nicola removed it from the packing and held it up by the shoulders, allowing it to fall loosely into folds. "It will look better on," she said apologetically. "It always does."

"You dabble in dressmaking, Miss Dean?" Velma asked, her tone unmistakably contemptuous.

"She's an expert, Velma," Mrs. Mitchell answered quietly.

"The *village* expert, of course," laughed Velma.

"Which," the son of the house said languidly, "is not saying much, is it?"

Nicola swung around, only to encounter his smile. She had fallen into his trap again, acted in character, risen to his bait. *Call it what you will*, she thought bitterly, *he's only demonstrating how well he thinks he knows me, and because of that knowledge, what a command he has over my responses*.

"Now, how much do I owe you, Nicola?" Mrs. Mitchell reached for her handbag. "I'll write you a check."

"No, no, please don't, Mrs. Mitchell. You owe me nothing. You're a friend of my mother's, so I wouldn't dream of charging you. I enjoyed doing it."

"But, my dear, I wouldn't have dreamed of asking you to make it if I'd known that. Of *course* I must pay you for the work. You see, I have another outfit in mind—"

Nicola responded eagerly, "I'll do it, Mrs. Mitchell."

"A suit?" she asked. "Could you manage a two-piece suit? Summer weight?"

"Of course."

"Right, now we must talk business. And no nonsense about doing it for nothing."

"Oh, but I—"

Her son, who had been listening as intently as a judge at a trial, gave his verdict. "Miss Dean is a fool, if I may say so."

Nicola reacted violently to the laconic remark, but his mother said, with her customary mildness, "I simply can't allow you to insult my guest in such terms, son."

He stood slowly and clasped his hands behind his back. "It was not an insult. It was intended as a corrective. I know for certain that she already has too much work on hand, more than she can cope with. Taking on yet another sewing job is asking for trouble, health trouble."

"Trying to save yourself work, darling?" Velma asked, stretching out a hand to him. It was ignored.

"She's not my patient, for which I must be truly thankful." The half smile that lifted the corners of his mouth was not meant to reflect amusement. "She's so rude to me that if I got her at my mercy in my office, I'd be so rude back I'd be in danger of being struck off the medical register." Under the sardonic note there was no mistaking the suppressed anger.

"That's a little harsh, Connor," his mother commented.

Nicola cut in defensively, "If you're referring to earlier this evening, Dr. Mitchell, when you called on my mother, I tried to apologize, but you'd gone." She took a breath because having to do just that in front of an audience—and such an audience—was the height of humiliation. "May I—may I say how sorry I am for what I said—and did?"

Velma, plainly feeling the tension, said placatingly, "Darling, it must have been pretty terrible for you to take her to task like this."

"It was not so much what she said," he persisted, talking to his girl friend, but looking at Nicola, "as her whole attitude I took exception to."

Nicola pressed her lips together and turned away. Why was he pursuing the subject? She thought miserably, she had apologized, hadn't she? Couldn't he accept it and let the matter rest? Even his mother must have felt his unfairness.

"What's come over you, Connor?" she asked, seeing the tears Nicola was trying to hide. "Let it go, son. You've upset her, and that I won't allow." She put a hand on Nicola's shoulder. "Come into the dining room, my dear. We can talk there undisturbed." Together they went to the door. "I must tell you how much I, at least, appreciate all you've done, and for bringing the dress as a surprise."

When she showed Nicola out twenty minutes later, it had been agreed that she would make Mrs. Mitchell a suit and that she would do it for payment. There would be no time limit and she would have to promise to fit in the work with all her other commitments. It was a promise she had gladly given.

NICOLA WAS BUSY in the kitchen next morning when the doctor called to see her mother. She opened the door and the face she presented to him was as blank as an empty television screen.

"Good morning, Dr. Mitchell." She gave herself full marks for her exemplary politeness. She was determined to give him no further reason for castigating her for lack of manners.

However, her impeccable civility passed over him. He merely nodded and sprinted up the stairs. Now who's being rude, she crowed, assuring herself that her rudeness the day before had been almost vindicated by this this morning.

When she reached the bedroom he was examining her mother's chest, his stethoscope to his ears, listening intently. Nicola stood quietly in the background, waiting until he had finished. He put away the stethoscope and glanced around.

"Still here? My word, you're as submissive and obedient as a well-trained nurse this morning." An eyebrow flicked upward. "Sure you're well, Miss Dean?"

She laughed and her mother said, "She's a good nurse, doctor. What with working the store and running up and down to see if I want anything, she must be wearing herself out."

He was writing on his prescription pad and asked, without looking up, "Is there no one else you could get to take your place behind the counter, Miss Dean?"

"No, Dr. Mitchell. We have Joy. She's all we can afford."

"I see." He ripped the prescription form from the pad, held it out and said, "Give your mother two of these tablets three times a day."

"Yes, doctor." She was determined to show him how polite she could be if she really tried so she added, suppressing a smile, "Thank you, doctor."

He looked at her quizzically. "Good God, I feel I'm back in the wards, doing the rounds. Are you *sure* you're not training to be a nurse?"

She laughed again and their eyes met. Something in his made her look away quickly. "I will, if you insist. That is, if you think I'm made of the right stuff."

He studied her for a moment. "No, on second thoughts, you'd better stay as you are. With your love of the past, you might revert and do a Florence Nightingale, walking the wards with a candle instead of a flashlight!"

They all laughed, then Nicola caught her breath. "My jam," she shrieked, "it's boiling over! I can smell it!" She dived down the stairs.

"Your *what?*" followed her from the landing.

"She's making jam," she heard her mother explain.

Moments later Connor came down the stairs. Nicola put aside the cloth with which she had been mopping up the spilled jam and went into the hall intending to show him out, but he was coming toward the kitchen.

"Smells good," he commented, "so good I can almost taste it. Apricot?"

"Yes. Dried. We stock them in the shop. These are all for sale."

"You're making jam for sale?"

"Why not?"

"I suppose you'll tell me in a moment that you make cakes for sale, too?"

"Yes. And candy. And biscuits."

"You're not serious?" He put his medical bag on the floor. "You're crazy, girl! Are you trying to kill yourself with work?"

"Well," she smiled at the jam she was stirring, "I'm not actually aiming to commit suicide by working myself to death." She glanced at him. "I look fit enough, don't I?"

He leaned against the draining board and looked her over. "If I were to tell you how you looked, I'd still be here two hours from now."

"I didn't realize," she muttered into the steam rising from the boiling amber liquid, "you thought so badly of me. I really must look awful." Silence, while he watched the rotating movement of the wooden spoon. "Aren't you busy this morning?" she asked, taking a test sample of jam and dripping it onto a saucer. She cooled it by fanning it with a cookbook.

"Is that a subtle hint that you want me to go?" She wanted him to stay so much she dared not answer. "As a matter of fact," he went on, showing every sign of remaining where he was, "there haven't been as many calls as usual. Just as well, because I was up half the night bringing an infant into the world. Difficult birth."

"Oh." It was the first time he had spoken about his work. "You must be tired, then."

"My head feels like lead, my eyelids keep slamming shut as though they're on spring hinges and I can't stop yawning," which he proceeded to do, widely, behind his hand, "but, no, I'm not tired!"

They laughed together. Nicola decided that the jam was ready and put it aside. "Would you like a cup of coffee?"

"If you're making one."

"Won't you go into the dining room, Dr. Mitchell, while I make it?"

He pulled out a chair. "The kitchen's good enough for me."

With her back to him she asked, "Dr. Mitchell?"

"Yes, Miss Dean?"

It sounded as if he was smiling. "My mother—is she very ill?"

He took a few moments to reply. "She has bouts of illness. But you know that." Nicola nodded. "She suffers periodically from acute bronchitis. We can give palliatives. They won't cure, but they ease the suffering." He paused. "She will almost certainly continue to have attacks of the trouble. Their frequency will depend upon how well she looks after herself." He stood up. "I'll take a cup to your mother."

"*You* can't take it!"

"I don't see why not. I have two legs, like most people." He looked down. "Nothing like as shapely as yours, but anatomically they serve the same purpose."

"But a doctor can't wait on a patient."

He smiled and took the cup. It was a warm, friendly smile, sincere, free from impurities, without the slightest stain of cynicism—the first genuine smile he had ever given her. If, Nicola told herself, he took my pulse now, he would have a shock. "This doctor can. Your legs must be tired with all that jam making."

They were not only tired, they felt oddly weak. "You're very kind," she murmured as he went along the hall. By the time he returned she had arranged some cookies on a plate.

"I'll take the tray into the dining room," she said.

"What's wrong with the kitchen?"

"I can't give a doctor morning coffee in the kitchen! What on earth would people think?"

"Can't you? You can this one. What odd ideas you have about doctors. Why do people think they have to treat us in such an exalted way? Granted we know all about the working of the human body, but so do motor mechanics and automobile engineers know about the internal workings of cars, yet they're not treated as though they're royalty.''

Nicola smiled, sitting opposite him at the kitchen table. "You won't get anyone to agree with you. Doctors save lives, automobile engineers don't."

"That's where you're wrong. Car mechanics, by their timely intervention, must have saved countless lives. Try again."

"Well," she groped for a suitable reply, "there's a—a remoteness, a mystique, an aura of untouchability about a doctor. . . ."

He laughed out loud at her struggles to express her thoughts clearly and remained unconvinced by her feeble arguments. "No doctor can afford to be 'remote' from his patients, Miss Dean. He has to try to understand human nature and to appreciate human failings. A medical student learns, for his own good, not to become emotionally involved with his patients, but that doesn't mean that doctors aren't human beings too, with faults and weaknesses like anyone else. You have to be aware of this all the time."

He smiled at her, intending to tantalize her and succeeding. "Of course you won't agree with me, but I am speaking from experience, Miss Dean."

His grin tormented her and she struggled to pour oil on the rough seas of her emotions. She accused, "You're sidetracking. *I* talk from experience when I say that people in general regard doctors as demigods, quite without any of the baser human weaknesses."

Item by item he contemplated the hills and valleys of her figure—which, in her tight trousers and even tighter top were only too conspicuous—and she steeled herself not to squirm under his scrutiny. He commented with a grin, "If you knew just how many of the 'baser human weaknesses' doctors do suffer from, Miss Dean . . . ."

He stirred his coffee and helped himself to a biscuit. It was a surprisingly intimate scene for two people who usually spent their time together quarreling. He must have sensed it, too, because he looked at her with a quick, sarcastic smile. "Peaceful, isn't it?"

She laughed again. She seemed to be laughing a lot that morning. His eyes lingered on her face, and his expression was oddly similar to that with which he contemplated the view from the hill.

He asked after a while, "Is your life all work? Don't you ever relax, go out anywhere, have fun, go to dances?"

"I'm not a very social animal."

"So I've gathered. Your boyfriend, the history teacher—what's his name, Terence?" He had a good memory. "Don't you miss him?"

Nicola said she supposed she did. "We phone each other. We write sometimes."

"And is that sufficient?"

"It has to be. He's a good many miles—and hours—away, in the northeast of England. I can't get up there to see him, and in term time he can't get here to see me."

"Are you engaged to him?"

Why the cross-examination she wondered. "No. We have what I suppose is called an 'understanding.' "

He drank some coffee and lowered the cup thoughtfully. "Why did you leave teaching?"

"Because my mother needed me."

"And you always go where you're most needed?" She shrugged. "Doesn't your boyfriend need you?" She looked puzzled. "If he's in love with you, as presumably he is, he must want you with him, surely? And if you love him, you must feel likewise?"

He was probing too deeply, like a dentist into a sensitive, decayed tooth. "I don't see where all this is leading."

He did not enlighten her. Instead, he drained his cup and stood up. "Don't bother to see me to the door.

Thanks for the coffee." He took his medical beg and let himself out.

IT WAS EARLY closing day and Nicola spent the afternoon working. Over the noise of the sewing machine, she heard a gentle tap on the front door. It sounded so furtive she was puzzled. Was it, she wondered, Mrs. Mitchell with her material, afraid, perhaps of waking her mother?

It was nothing so straightforward. Standing on the pavement was a woman Nicola recognized as a regular customer. She was short, shabbily dressed and so obese her shape was almost spherical. In her mouth was a cigarette which she removed in order to speak.

"May I come in, dear?" she whispered. Nicola let her in. "Just wanted to ask a favor. Is your mother in?"

"She's ill, Mrs. Henderton." Nicola nodded toward the stairs.

"Oh. Sorry to hear that, dear, but perhaps you can help me instead." She lowered her voice to a whisper and Nicola had to strain to hear. "I've run out of cheeses—you know, those little round boxes, and my boy's got a friend to tea. Would you be a love and slip me one?" She held out her hand. "I've got the money." While she waited for the answer, she drew on the cigarette, inhaled and released the smoke through her nostrils like the mythical dragon.

Nicola was taken aback by the request, recoiling at the same time from the dual streams of smoke. "I'm sorry, Mrs. Henderton, but it's against the law to serve the public on early closing day. I wouldn't want to get my mother into trouble."

The hall was filling with a swirling, pungent mist. "I won't tell anyone, dear. Your mother's often obliged. You just slip up and ask. I'm sure she'll say yes."

Nicola began to worry in case the smoke reached her mother's bedroom. She had been coughing enough, without an extra irritant to aggravate her trouble. "Well," she hesitated, "she might be asleep, but—"

Anything to get rid of the woman. She ran up the stairs and put her head round her mother's door. "Are you awake?"

Enid was reading. "Who is it, dear, that Mrs. Henderton? I can smell the smoke. It's her hallmark."

"She wants a box of cheeses, but I told her it's against the law."

"Quite right, dear, but she won't take 'no.' She's done this before. Sometimes she calls at bedtime." She eased herself upright. "What I usually do is let her have the stuff and tell her to pay next morning."

Nicola said she thought it was wrong to give in to the woman, but Enid said, "Tell her it's absolutely the last time. We've got to try to stop her, otherwise the whole village will hear of it and line up at the door."

The woman took the cheeses, her cigarette smoke and her rotund self away, saying she wouldn't do it again. When Nicola told her mother, she laughed. "She's said that before."

Nicola took her mother's cup of tea upstairs and drank her own. As she settled down to work again, the doorbell rang, once, twice, three times. No timid, illicit caller, this. There was no mistaking the decision and confidence behind the impatient, pushing finger.

A man stood on the doorstep, manners assured, dress immaculate, smile breezy and brash. A bulging briefcase added status and importance and by the way he was holding it, it was carried not merely for convenience but to impress and even, perhaps, to intimidate? He looked that sort of man.

He was, he said, a representative of a nationally-known supermarket chain. Nicola let him in—she had no choice—and he put himself inside the hall. The sudden, although half-expected materialization—as if a malicious genie had rubbed a lamp—of the man whose coming she had dreaded disturbed her inordinately.

Could he, he asked, see the proprietor of the business, the gentleman who owned it?

"My mother's the owner," Nicola answered shortly.

"Then may I see her? It's a matter of some importance."

"I'm sorry. She's ill in bed."

"Oh." For a moment he was stumped, then he brightened. "Ah, then I can talk to you, can't I?" His hand shot out. "Goodman's the name. I've come with a business proposition that I'm sure you and your mother will find impossible to resist. It would without doubt be worth your while to listen."

Nicola smiled. "I'm afraid you're wasting your time, Mr. Goodman. You see, I can guess what you're going to say. A rumor's been going around for some time about a supermarket coming to the village."

"Since you're so blunt, Miss, er—" he consulted a sheet of paper "—Miss Dean, I'll return the compliment. My company is interested—very interested—in your store. We know the adjoining shop is empty and this site—the two shops together—would be ideal for our purposes." Nicola began to protest, but the man held up his hand. "We recognize the financial value and we're prepared to pay a high figure."

She had been shaking her head while the man had been speaking. He seemed to grow impatient. "If I could see your mother, if only for a few minutes, perhaps I could begin to do business."

Nicola's manner iced over. "My mother and I think alike on this matter, Mr. Goodman, my mother, perhaps, being even more determined than I. We are not selling. I'm afraid that's all there is to say."

He named a sum which raised Nicola's eyebrows. But she still shook her head. "At least," the man said, "convey what I've said to your mother. She is, after all, the owner, isn't she?"

That Nicola could not deny. She showed him into the sitting room and he eased his long, large frame into an upright chair, putting his briefcase, his daunting briefcase, on the coffee table.

Her mother, as she had predicted, was adamant. "Don't budge. We're not selling, not even for a fortune."

Which sentiments Nicola expressed to Mr. Goodman.

"She'll regret it, Miss Dean. We're coming to this village, even if we have to buy a plot of land and develop it ourselves. The whole area's ripe for development. As I drove in from town I noticed the estates growing up on the outskirts. There's even room for light industry to establish itself before long. No doubt some farmer will be persuaded to part with a plot of land for the price we're willing to pay."

"Still no go, Mr. Goodman."

He became bellicose. "We'll set up in opposition, Miss Dean. You'll lose your business. It's the way of things these days. More and more self-service, which means more and more supermarkets. We're giants in the field. You can't fight us, you'd be trodden underfoot, we would bleed you of customers." His choice of metaphors was so gruesome Nicola found a chair.

He watched her closely and must have seen the fear flicker behind her eyes, and knew he had scored a point, a vital point. He smiled and, satisfied by what he considered a partial victory, abandoned his threatening manner like an actor changing roles.

His hand came out, which Nicola found herself shaking. "Think about it, Miss Dean, you and your mother." He felt in his pocket. "My card. If you have a change of heart—and I do advise it for your own sakes—contact me at my Birmingham office. Ask for me personally, and you will, I assure you, get VIP treatment. Good day, Miss Dean."

Accompanied by his briefcase, he swept out. Nicola sat on the stairs and mopped her brow.

Connor Mitchell called once more to see Enid. Nicola was serving in the store so he let himself into the house. Her mother told her later that he had said she could get up next day. "But I mustn't go back to work. He said I had an able, if fanatically overconscientious, daughter, so I must sit back and let her get on with it!"

That evening, over their late-night drink, Enid told Nicola she had decided to go away for a while. Sheila, her sister, and her husband, Will, would have her to stay. They had often invited her, but she had never had the time to go. "I feel you've got enough work, dear, without my adding to it."

Nicola protested that it wasn't "work," but felt it would do her mother good to spend a few weeks in the bracing air of the North Wales coast. It took a few days to arrange the visit and for Enid to get herself fit enough to travel. Nicola said she wished she could drive her there herself one Sunday, but she honestly didn't think the van would stand up to the journey.

"It keeps stalling, and the clutch needs attention. I suppose it's getting old."

"It wasn't exactly 'young' when you bought it," her mother commented, smiling.

Nicola took her to the station. When her mother had withdrawn tearfully from the window, Nicola wandered lonely and depressed back to the van. She drove slowly through the town, enduring the traffic jams with a dull acceptance. She passed the Medical Center on the main street. It was closed and she supposed Connor was making his morning calls.

The Tudor-style café she usually patronized looked inviting. There was a parking place empty and she reversed into it. As she entered the café, she caught sight of a man at one of the tables. His substantial shape gave away his identity and her first instinct was to turn and run. But he lowered his newspaper as the door bell jangled and saw her. He nodded and Nicola smiled faintly, faintly enough, she hoped, to let him know that she had no intention of joining him. But the hint must have been too subtle.

He called, "There are three empty seats at this table, Miss Dean. Try one for size."

She could, of course, have pretended to be deaf, but he

was folding his newspaper and putting it aside in the expectation of her joining him.

"Good morning, Dr. Mitchell," she said formally, removing her jacket and draping it across the back of the chair.

He looked at the ancient pendulum clock on the wall. "How come the superefficient Miss Nicola Dean is in town at this time of day? Surely you're not *slacking*, Miss Dean? Shouldn't you be busy in your store, or sewing your baby clothes or standing over your cauldron of boiling jam?"

The waitress approached and Connor ordered a coffee for Nicola and another for himself. Nicola explained that she had seen her mother onto the train to North Wales.

"Glad to hear it. A holiday should do her good. And take some of the burden off your back." The coffee arrived. "So you're on your own now? Won't you find it lonely?"

"I doubt it. I never mind being alone."

An eyebrow lifted. "Thoughts of the boyfriend to keep you company?"

She did not answer the question directly. "I'll probably phone him this evening and have a chat."

"My mother would be pleased to see you anytime." He caught her eye and smiled. "I'm out so often you need not worry about finding me there."

She smiled back. "I suppose I could telephone first anonymously and ask to speak to 'the doctor' to discover if you're in, and if you are, stay away."

He laughed. "You tempt me to sit at home every evening just to annoy you." He picked up a knife and pushed some scattered biscuit crumbs into a neat pile on his plate. "It's so easy for me to annoy you, isn't it, Miss Dean?"

She watched his hand, his capable doctor's hand, as it pursued its pointless sweeping-up operation with the crumbs. What would it feel like, she wondered, to be touched by that hand. . . ? She jerked her thoughts away as if they had ventured too near a roaring fire, then looked up, panicking, and found his quizzical eyes on her. She colored and stared out of the window. "Yes," she said, mechanically answering his question.

A moment passed and he hazarded, "I sense you're worried about something. Are you?"

I am, she wanted to say, *about the devastating effect you have on me every time we meet.* She had to think quickly to find an explanation for her anxiety, so she told him about the visit from the supermarket representative. "But we're not selling."

"Whether you do or not, they'll get to the village somehow. It's a good offer. Why are you being so obstinate? If you sold, you'd be free to return to your teaching and your mother would be well provided for for the rest of her life."

She twisted around the empty plate as if it were a steering wheel. She was trying to swerve away from the undoubted truth in his words. "Far from selling, Dr. Mitchell, I should like to expand. If I had the money, I'd buy the store next door and use it to sell the clothes I make."

"Not to mention the homemade jam, cakes and candy?"

She looked up eagerly. Was he encouraging her? He was smiling, but it was full of indulgence, as if she were a child wanting the impossible. Her dream faded and her eagerness with it. "But I haven't the capital, so it's out of the question."

He looked for the waitress and asked for the bill. It was placed on the table. Nicola felt in her bag. "I'll pay my share."

His hand came down and covered hers, holding it still. "Sometimes you take your bid for independence too far. I don't want your money. Keep it, to buy your store."

Now she knew what the touch of his hand was like. It was heaven. She looked at him and he was laughing at her again. She pulled her hand from under his as though the feel of it repelled her. He frowned and stood up. She shrugged on her jacket and her formality with it.

"Thank you for the coffee, Dr. Mitchell."

He paid the bill and followed her out. He did not speak again but nodded and went on his way.

JOY GREETED NICOLA when she returned with the news that Brian, the delivery boy, was ill. "His mother said she's sorry, but he won't be able to take the orders around tonight."

Nicola sighed. "I suppose I'll have to do it. At least I've got the van."

"Some of those boxes are heavy, Miss Dean. I'll come out with you. I can put my boyfriend off."

"Thanks, Joy, but I'll manage. You keep your date."

When the shutters came down and Nicola turned the Open sign to Closed, she had her tea. Then she loaded the van with groceries. The engine did not start first and her heart sank. But after the third attempt there was an ear-shattering roar. As she was about to pull away, the engine stalled. She tried again. This time it took six attempts to get it going. It moved off a little jerkily, but seemed to settle down.

With four deliveries behind her, she approached the level crossing. She had never reconciled herself to its conversion from old-style gates to automatic barriers. It was, in her opinion, a perfect example of her theory that nothing ever changed for the better. It always worried her to have to cross the track there. Her imagination, colored by newspaper stories of hair-raising accidents in such places, played tricks.

As she drove toward the railway track, the barriers were raised, open and as guileless as an angelic-looking child. But, Nicola told herself, she never had trusted angelic-looking children. They were usually young devils in disguise. With exaggerated caution she approached the crossing and in her wing mirror she saw reflected a familiar yellow car. Connor, she supposed, must be out on a call, or on his way to visit his lady friend.

The van bumped, complained and rattled over the

track, but she was going so slowly that the engine, having already demonstrated that it had an evil mind of its own, stalled. It would not budge. It was not her imagination tricking her now, it was the real thing, happening to her, Nicola Dean. Her van had stalled in the middle of the crossing, and no matter how hard she tried to restart it, it would not respond.

With a superhuman effort, she held down her panic. She tried again. Drivers began to hoot. Were they angry at the delay? Her heart pounded, she came out in a cold sweat. The warning bells rang and the lights flashed. The barriers fell and she was caught. Her mouth dried up, her breathing stopped.

A train was coming. Her staring, terrified eyes saw it racing toward her and she was paralyzed. Not a muscle would move, not a finger could she lift to save herself. In an almost detached, disembodied way, she heard the shouts behind and in front. It was her life coming to an end, death was hurtling toward her and there was nothing—absolutely nothing—she could do to hold it off.

CHAPTER FOUR

THROUGH THE ROARING in her head she heard her name being shouted. "Nicola!" It came over and over again. "Nicola! *Nicola!* Get *out!* For God's sake, girl, *get yourself out!*"

But the man didn't understand. She couldn't move, she simply could not move. The van door was wrenched almost off its hinges; violent, clawing fingers dug into her arm. She was dragged, by her clothes, her legs, her hair, out onto the track. Her limp body was hurled across the barrier and she came to rest, sprawled full length, face down on the earth. The thunder grew, the vibration shook, the roar deafened. There was a reverberating crash, a smashing of glass, a rupture of twisting metal, and a screeching of brakes applied with desperation.

Consciousness slipped away. But only for a few moments. A man was bending over her, his fingers on her wrist. As her eyes fluttered open she saw with surprise how pale he was. She wondered why.

His hands were feeling her body, with gentleness and with skill. All over her they moved, searching— searching for what? Physical damage? Broken bones? He seemed to be shaking.

"My God, Nicola," he whispered, "that was nearly the end. So nearly the end of your life."

The voices around grew louder. "The van," someone said, "it's had it all right. Bits all over, down the track, on the bank. . . ."

There were pounding footsteps and someone else said, "That was a near thing! You saved her life, sir, no doubt about that. Best get a doctor."

"I am a doctor, guard, so all's well. I also know this young woman. I'll handle her affairs. Here's my card."

She heard the words "insurance," "liability," "claim," and they meant nothing, nothing at all. She thought she was going to faint and reached out to the man who was being so gentle with her. Whatever happened, he mustn't leave her now.

"It's all right, Nicola," he murmured, bending down beside her again, "I'll take care of you. Bear with me while I lift you."

"Connor," she whispered, "what happened?"

She was floating through the air and she held onto the solidity of him as he carried her. It was like reaching harbor after a stormy crossing. She was lowered into the backseat of a car and covered with a blanket. The drive was slow and at the end of it she was lifted again and put on a couch.

"Mother," he called, "emergency!"

Footsteps came quickly down the stairs and there was a gasp. "It's not Nicola? What happened, son?"

He explained, and Nicola thought he was talking about another girl. Blankets were wrapped around her and yet more blankets. She had begun to shake.

"Nicola, my dear." Her hand was taken and rubbed, her hair smoothed. She opened her eyes.

"M-Mrs. Mitchell," she whispered, "w-what h-happened?"

"Connor will will tell you later. Don't tire yourself by talking. He'll attend to your cuts and bruises, then you can sleep."

"No, no," Nicola started up, "n-no time for sleep. I still have some orders to d-deliver. . . ." She turned her wide-open eyes toward the two people looking down at her. "The groceries, the van! It's gone, all of it!" She struggled to get up, but Connor held her still.

In his hold she became calmer and sank back, defeated, as memories of the event battered down the door she had bolted and barred to them. "You saved my life,

Dr. Mitchell," she said dully. "At least I must thank you for that."

"It's a doctor's job to save lives, Nicola." "Nicola," he'd called her. A slip of the tongue.

"Tea, son?" his mother asked.

"Please, and plenty of it. Good and sweet. Warm water, towels, my medical bag from the car."

"I know the drill, dear," his mother said, and left them.

Nicola thought he would start talking, but instead he smoothed back her hair—it still hurt where he had tugged at it—and moved experienced fingers over the side of her face that had hit the ground.

"Will I be bruised?" she murmured, wincing at his touch, gentle though it was.

"Yes. Sorry I had to be so rough with you, Nicola, but it was either that or—we both died together." He paused. "I only just made it myself."

It was the thought of his being prepared to die for her sake that started the tears. They didn't burst out, they trickled down her cheeks. "It's terrible," she muttered, "what doctors are ready to do for their patients. They would even die if that was the only way to save them."

He watched her tears, doing nothing to stop them. Mrs. Mitchell came in and china rattled.

"When you've had some tea," Connor said, "I'll have to examine you and treat any lacerations. They should only be superficial, but I've got to make sure." He stood, hands in pockets, looking down at her. "Do you mind? My mother will be here."

She said she didn't mind, and that her trust in him was absolute, and he smiled. He helped her drink the tea, and the sweetness was pleasing. The warmth returned to her cheeks, the blood flowed more swiftly through her veins. Connor was gentleness itself as he examined her, swabbed her cuts and covered them.

"You'll feel worse tomorrow, when the bruises start coming out," he warned as his mother went from the

room. "I think you've got over the emotional shock, but
even so it could still catch up with you." He moved her
feet to one side and sat at the other end of the couch. "I
should like you to stay the night here." He cut through
her protests. "You can't sleep alone in an empty house.
Tomorrow you may feel pretty bad and—"

"But the store, Dr. Mitchell—I can't take the day off.
There's only Joy, and she won't be able to cope on her
own."

"First, let's get one thing sorted out. My name is Connor, as you well know. So drop the formality. You did
earlier."

"I'm sorry, I didn't realize that."

"Why be sorry? You're a friend—of the family." She
noticed the qualification of the statement. "Now, having
got that settled, we'll discuss your fitness for work. I
know I'm not your doctor, but because of the circumstances, I'm treating you at the moment. As your—
temporary—medical adviser," he was emphatic on
this point, "I think you should take at least one day off. Is
there anyone who could help out in the store—a neighbor, for instance?"

"Well, there's Joy's mother."

He stood. "Does she have a phone? Tell me the surname and I'll contact her at once."

When he returned, he was smiling. "All settled. Mrs.
Atkins is only too willing to oblige. She was horrified to
hear what happened and hopes you'll soon be fit again.
She asks if you'd delivered all the orders before the accident."

Nicola shook her head and discovered how stiff her
neck muscles had become. "There were three more customers to call on."

"In that case, if you'll tell her where the order book is,
she says she'll make them up again and get them delivered."

She told him and he passed the message on.

When he returned, he said, "You can have the guest
room. My mother's making up the bed."

"But, Connor, I can't—"

He stood over her and said in a voice that allowed no arguments, "But you can. And will."

The phone rang and his hand slapped against his forehead. "Velma. I was on my way to a date with her."

He went into the hall, leaving the door open. "Sorry, sweet," he said, "emergency—can you hang on where you are, say, another half hour? I meant to call. . . ."

"That," he said, coming back and fingering his collar as if it was choking him, "was a blatant lie. I'd completely forgotten her, and only just prevented myself from telling her so!"

"Don't let me delay you any longer," Nicola said, avoiding his eyes. "I'm quite all right now."

There was a brief silence and she looked up at him, meeting his "I know better than you" smile. "Are you? When I don't say something to bring the color to your cheeks you're deathly pale."

"Connor, bed's ready," his mother called.

"Come on, young woman. Get up them stairs—fast!"

She pushed aside the blankets and tried to stand, but he stopped her. "Now, now, wait for the transport."

His arms came out and she saw his intention. "No, thank you, I'm quite capable of walking."

"Prove it. Go on, try to walk."

She did try, taking a few uncertain steps, but lurched against him in a most undignified manner and he laughed, catching her under the armpits and holding her close. The thought did flit through her mind that it was not usually the way a doctor held a patient, but she dismissed it as a trick of her fevered imagination.

"You're hardly in a condition," he said, swinging her up and into his arms, "to argue with someone so much bigger than yourself. Or to refuse a lift when it's offered."

His face, so near, did not deter her from saying, with a grin, "Even when it's from a strange man?"

He looked into her face. "Impudent, too! You're recovering fast. Put your arm around my neck and stop

asking for trouble. You're not fit at this moment to be
spanked, but when you've recovered . . . ." She put her
arm around his neck. She did more, she rested her head
against him. It had suddenly become too heavy for her
neck to carry. He strode up the stairs, murmuring,
"You're much too light. I told you your were working
yourself to death. You nearly achieved it this evening.
You, out delivering groceries and at that hour! I thought
you had a delivery boy."

"He's ill. There was no one else."

He shook his head. "Will you never slow down?"

His mother stood back while he lowered Nicola onto
the bed. Her eyelids, as she lifted them, felt as heavy as
sash windows grown stiff with age. She smiled, discovering now that her facial muscles were stiffening up.
"You're being so kind, both of you."

"Nonsense," said Mrs. Mitchell. "It's my son's job,
and it's mine to look after my dear friend's daughter
when she's in need and there's no one else to do it."

Yes, Nicola thought wearily, *it's her son's job.
Nothing else. However much he might mean to me, I
mean no more to him than just another patient. And I
mustn't ever forget it.*

"Right," said Connor, going to the door. "My mother
takes over from here."

"Are you off to meet your lady friend, dear? Will she
understand? Being a nurse herself, she should."

"A nurse Velma may be," said her son dryly, "but
when she's off duty, she's a woman like every other
woman. I'll have to do some fast talking to explain this
little delay. I'll have to pacify her somehow."

"Give her an extra kiss, Connor," she said, laughing.

"Yes." His eyes rested on Nicola in a curious, tor
menting way. "Kisses are cheap. They're so easy to give
and they cost nothing."

HOWEVER MUCH NICOLA tried to coax sleep to make :
take-over bid for her mind and body, it was no use, th
deal kept falling through. The shareholders wouldn'

budge. The clock downstairs chimed midnight. She hated it. It was pompous and stentorian and had an inflated sense of its own importance. As the last note sounded, the front door opened and closed.

Footsteps climbed the staircase and the fever in her cheeks burned through to the pillowcase. The footsteps stopped outside her door and she held herself rigid until they went away. They did not go away. The door opened and she blinked at the light from the landing.

Connor stood at her bedside.

"Don't say it," she said irritably. "I've tried. It just won't come."

"Imagination playing tricks? Reliving the nightmare?"

"How did you guess?"

"Any aches and pains?"

"All over. I keep twisting and turning and it hurts. And I'm so hot."

His hand rested on her forehead. "I'll give you something." He left the room and returned quickly. "Close your eyes. I'm switching on the bedside lamp." In his hand was a hypodermic syringe. "Don't look so scared. My intentions are strictly professional."

"I don't want an injection. I thought you meant a sleeping pill."

"Don't argue with your superiors. This will act faster and be more effective. Give me your arm." He bent down and his fingers closed softly around her flesh. Momentarily their eyes met. In hers was complete trust, in his, nothing. She hoped frantically that he would not take her pulse.

"This won't hurt." He rubbed her upper arm with a piece of moistened cotton wool and gave the injection. "It didn't, did it?"

"No. You're so gentle."

"Am I?" He put aside the syringe. "You haven't seen me when I'm ar-roused." His throat growled, drawing out the final word.

She remembered when he had censured her for rudeness, "I have," she reminded him. "You tore me into little bits."

"That, I assure you, was nothing."

She felt calmer and looked at him speculatively. He smiled as if her inspection amused him. "What now?" He sat on the bed and his fingers rested idly against her wrist. Her pulse was racing, his nearness excited her, his touch made her want to reach out and touch him. But she had to lie there passively, registering no outward emotion. She knew he must be able to feel the thump of her heartbeats, but his expression did not alter even by the flicker of an eyebrow.

"Tell me what you're thinking."

She complied, but with a half-truth. "How surprised I am that you possess a bedside manner. When I first met you you were so brusque—"

"I reminded you of a bear?"

She laughed. "Perhaps."

"My manner depends on the circumstances—and the patient."

"The patient" again. Despite his hand, which was almost caressing her wrist, that was all she was. But it didn't stop her talking.

"You're so difficult to get to know." She supposed she shouldn't be lying there saying such things, but somehow she didn't care any more. Her barriers were down. It was probably the effect of the drug he had pumped into her.

His voice came softly, as if through a mist. "Do you want to get to know me?"

"Yes." Her head fell to one side, but she pulled it back, resisting the sleep that, earlier, she had wooed so eagerly. "But it's not easy to know where to start. You're so many people in one."

"Aren't we all? You, for instance."

Her lips would hardly form the words. "You said once you knew a lot about me."

"A lot, yes, but not everything. One day you might surprise me."

She was drifting off. "Or shock you."

"As you say, or shock me."

She turned her cheek against the pillow and he tucked her hand inside the covers.

"Good night, Connor. Thank you for—" For what? She had to remember. It was very important. "For saving my life."

"All part of the service, madam." His face seemed very large and very close, like looking at one's reflection in a magnifying mirror. "All part of the service." His voice was fading. "Good night, Nicola."

Something touched her cheek. A wisp of hair, probably. She was too tired to bother—or care.

WHEN SHE AWOKE next morning, the sun was streaming in and the breeze ballooning the flowered curtains, which had been pulled apart. Connor was standing beside the bed.

"Oh, dear," Nicola murmured, stirring and stretching, "have I slept in?"

"You have, but it's what I intended. It's almost noon."

She started to sit up, but winced at the pain from her bruises.

"I did warn you," he said.

"Are you going to work now?" she asked for something to say.

"I've been and returned. Morning office hours were over an hour ago. I've called in for coffee before going out on my calls. You're the first."

She smiled up at him. "So this is a doctor's visit?"

"Strictly professional. What else could it be?"

It was a reasonable question and it made her want to slide under the bedclothes with embarrassment.

"Did you," she asked to divert his contemplative eyes from her, "manage to placate your girl friend last night?"

He gave a short, reminiscent laugh. "I didn't set out to. She fretted so much at what she called my 'neglect' of her—she said I should have passed the 'emergency' to one of my partners in the practice—do you know what I told her? I said I'd entertained another woman for an hour and a half, and then I took her up to bed!''

They laughed together. ''That was rather bad of you.''

''It did her good. Made her realize she wasn't the only pebble on my beach. Anyway, it's true, isn't it?''

Nicola went pink and looked away. ''In essence, yes, but in the way you presented it, it was quite false.'' She looked up at him. ''What was her reaction?''

''She sulked.''

''Which spoiled your evening.''

''Not really. I was somewhat preoccupied. I had just saved two lives, remember, yours—and mine. So I had plenty to think about. Doctors are only human. It was a bit of a shock to my system, too.''

''I'm sorry. Patients never think of that.''

''They're not meant to. By the way, my mother's bringing your breakfast to you.''

''There's no need.'' She maneuvered herself into a more upright position. ''I'll get up and save her the trouble.''

''When you're given the chance to be waited on, woman, seize it. It's probably a luxury that rarely comes your way, so enjoy it while you can. Incidentally, there's no need for you to worry yourself about yesterday's accident and all the legal business it will involve. If you've no objection, I'll contact my solicitor and I'm sure he'll be willing to look after your affairs.''

''Well, to be honest, it was worrying me—''

''Then it's all settled. I suppose you insist on going home today?''

''Of course. It's not right that I should stay here accepting your hospitality indefinitely. I'm just a patient—''

''A friend of the family,'' he corrected. His tone softened. ''And in spite of my mother's unfashionable night attire you're wearing, a very attractive friend of the family.''

She colored and reached for the neckline, which, cut to fit a much larger figure, had slipped off her shoulder. He grinned and his hand reached for her pulse, but she snatched it away. He was not going to learn all her secrets that way. Every time he came near she felt the pull of him, and her pulse rate responded accordingly. She looked up a little fearfully, but he was not annoyed.

Instead, he laughed as if her action amused him deeply. "It's the first time a patient has ever done that to me."

She said, part shyly, part provocatively, "There has to be a first time for everything, hasn't there?"

"You're so right." He looked her over and for the merest second his eyes lost their professional detachment. Then the mask came down again. "I'll drop in at your house this evening to check up on how you are."

When he left a moment later, she felt as dazzled as if the sun had forsaken its usual place in the sky and had embedded itself in the ceiling of the bedroom.

Joy and her mother had the shop running so smoothly, Nicola was able to relax at home for the rest of the day. She chafed at the way the hours dragged, fretted that the evening—and Connor—never seemed to come.

After supper she changed into a sleeveless dress and used makeup to hide her pale cheeks, and to cover the bruise that was turning blue where her face had hit the ground. Then, for want of something better to do, she took up her sewing. Time passed and she began to fidget.

The phone rang and she ran to answer it. "Nicola?" Connor said. "Sorry I couldn't make it." Her heart plunged. "How are you?"

She answered stiffly, "Better, thank you."

"Aches and pains improving?"

"Yes, thank you."

There was a short, unexplained pause, then, "I'm handing over your case to Jim Muirson, your own doctor. If you have any further trouble, which is unlikely, contact him, will you?''

She could have cried. ''Yes. Thank you for all you've done.''

''That's all right. Good night, now.'' He hung up.

Well, she told herself, *hadn't I once said, in his hearing, that I wouldn't have him as my doctor even if I were dying?* To fight off the tears of disappointment and to fill the empty evening ahead, she dialed Terence's number and talked to him for some time. He said he was longing to see her again, and would make every effort to do so as soon as the opportunity arose.

Mrs. Mitchell delivered the material for her new outfit a few days later. ''I won't come in. Connor's waiting outside. My car's having a new set of tires put on.''

Connor beckoned and Nicola followed his mother across the pavement. He said, ''I take it you're now on the lookout for a new car?''

''Yes, preferably a van.''

''Not a van. I've had enough of you and vans.''

''It's my business, isn't it, what kind of vehicle I buy?''

''Not when it involves the lives of others it isn't. I don't want to have to rescue any more maidens in distress from oncoming trains. What I really wanted to say was that I think I'm on the trail of a secondhand car.''

''It's very kind of you, but I hope you realize I haven't an inexhaustible supply of money in the bank.''

He answered somewhat acidly, ''I do realize, I do possess a reasonable—if limited—quota of judgment and common sense.''

''Son!'' his mother cautioned him from the passenger seat.

But he went on in the same curt tone, ''The wife of a doctor friend of mine is selling it. As soon as it's available for viewing, I'll tell you.''

Nicola said thank-you in a strained, distant voice and returned his mother's wave as they drove away.

She wandered back into the house. His change of manner tormented her. But was it a change? Wasn't it just that he had reverted to his habitual brusqueness? The incident with the van had jolted him out of it. Now she was back to normal, he need never be gentle and considerate to her again. A friend of the family, he'd called her. She must never forget that, as far as he was concerned, that was all she was, or ever could be.

CHAPTER FIVE

ONE evening Nicola took her embroidery to the hilltop.
It was late May, unusually warm for the time of year, and
the distant countryside was rich with pink and white
blossom.

She hoped fervently that she would be alone. Her wish
was granted. If Connor had been there, she would not
have known whether to ignore him as they had agreed,
or, because they knew each other better now, whether
out of politeness to speak to him. It would not be easy to
find a subject of common interest. They were so much at
odds with each other that any subject she might choose
probably would lead to an argument.

The trunk of a fallen tree proved useful as a back
rest, and she spread her materials around her on the jacket that she was sitting on. If there had been even the beginnings of a breeze, it would have been difficult to
anchor her belongings to the ground, but the air was still
and a little humid, with great clouds massing overhead.
Yet the sun shone undaunted, escaping whenever it
could from the huge black formations that strove to keep
it prisoner.

Someone was climbing the hill. Nicola hoped it was
not, yet longed for it to be Connor. She glanced around
and saw that Connor had come, but judging by the expression on his face it seemed that he had hoped to be
alone, too. He was frowning and Nicola decided it would
be wise to keep to their pact and ignore him.

She could not believe it when he strolled toward her
and stood only a short distance away. He did not ac-

knowledge her, but the silence between them was in itself a kind of greeting. Her eyes slid upward from his legs. His hands were in his pockets, his shoulders were pushed forward and he was frowning. After scanning the view and watching the cloud shadows chase the sunshine patches from field to field, Connor lowered himself to the ground. He moved as if he were in pain, but it was the pain of someone in mental, not physical, distress. His eyes stared about him, but they might have been sightless for all that he saw. He was so pale Nicola was shocked.

"Connor?" she ventured, willing to take the consequences of her audacity.

"Yes?" His voice was leaden and he did not look at her.

"Something wrong?"

He did not answer, which was in itself a reprimand.

"I'm sorry."

He made a brief movement with his hand, telling her she need not have apologized. He threw himself back full-length, shielding his eyes from the sun that streamed through the trees whenever it could. He murmured, "I was up most of the night." There was a long pause and he was so still—she envied him his ability to stay immobile—she thought he must be asleep. But he moved a hand to cushion his head. "The patient died."

To have said she was sorry would have been ineffectual and pointless, so she left it to him to explain if he wanted. It seemed he did.

"A girl, about your age—" he moved his hand momentarily from his eyes "—your color of hair, too. Drove into a tree at high speed. So badly injured she never recovered."

"It upsets you, although you didn't know her?"

"No doctor likes to lose a patient, any patient. Whether you know them or not is irrelevant. To watch a human life slip away, especially a young life, out of the reach of your skill, beyond your powers of healing, is terrible." After a pause, he went on, "I told you, although you wouldn't believe me, doctors are human, too."

There was such compassion in his voice that she felt tears prick behind her eyes. This was another side to the man, one he kept under lock and key.

"Nicola?"

"Yes, Connor?"

"The car I was after for you—are you free tomorrow evening to have a look at it?" She said she was. "Good. I'll pick you up and take you there. Shall we say eight o'clock?"

She said thank-you, that would be fine. He was silent after that. Other people came to the summit, some walking their dogs; young couples, hand in hand; one or two children. *People must think we're lovers.* The thought buzzed into her head like a bee into the center of a flower. She shook her head to make it go away.

His breathing became regular and rhythmic. He was deeply asleep. The long, weary night had caught up with him. She studied his face and her heart, her mind, her desire reached out to him. His mouth held a sensitivity she had not noticed before and she wanted to rest her lips against it. She wanted to trail her fingers over his cheekbones, press away the hardness of his chin and push his straying hair from his forehead. Her desire grew so strong it became a pain.

She sat beside him until the clouds had gathered into a continuous black blanket, cutting off the sun and bringing premature twilight. She grew chilled, but nothing would induce her to leave him. She put away her materials and sat, knees drawn up, watching the view slip behind a veil of mist.

It began to rain. She grew alarmed. He was uncovered and unprotected. She had to wake him, she couldn't let him lie there getting soaked. Her hand rested on his shoulder. "Connor." He did not move. She called him again. He stirred faintly but settled down again. "Connor!" Her fingers pressed against his cheek.

His hand came up and covered hers, holding her palm

against his face. She pulled her hand free and moved away, but he said softly, "No, no, don't go. Come here." He reached out and caught her face between his hands, pulling her down until her lips covered his. She tried to break free. His eyes were closed and he didn't know what he was doing. He was still dreaming, he thought she was his girl friend. . . .

It was useless to resist because his arms held her prisoner now, pressing her against him. For a few moments she submitted, then wrenched herself away, breaking off the kiss. In the semidarkness she could see his eyes were still closed.

"I'm not Velma," she choked.

His eyes came open. "No, you're not Velma."

"Then why did you do it?"

He rolled on to his side and he was smiling. "One day I might tell you—if the opportunity ever occurs."

Her body was throbbing with excitement and anger. She began to gather up her belongings.

"Thanks for staying with me."

"Like a faithful hound, I suppose you're thinking, who wouldn't desert her master."

He grinned. "You said it. 'Faithful'," he said lazily, mockingly. "That's a word I like."

She did leave him then, running down the hill in the rain and the darkness, but she took with her the feel of his mouth against hers.

MRS. HENDERTON was hovering around the entrance to the house when Nicola got home. The inevitable cigarette was between her fingers.

"Just a package of tea, dear." She held out the money.

Nicola shook her head helplessly. "It's against the law, Mrs. Henderton."

"I'm a good customer, dear, aren't I?" she pleaded. "It's just that I've got a bad memory."

Nicola sighed. "Well, this once, but no more. Pay me in the morning."

The woman smiled the smile of the victor, followed

Nicola into the hall and put away the money. She took
the tea after dropping her cigarette and, to Nicola's fury,
grinding it with her heel into the doormat. Her humpty-
dumpty shape rolled away into the darkness.

One day, Nicola thought apprehensively, *someone
will get into trouble because of that woman, and whoever
or whatever it is, all the king's men will not be able to put
it together again.*

She was too restless to think about bed, so she decided
to cut out Mrs. Mitchell's two-piece suit. Midnight
brought her to the point of exhaustion, but was she tired
enough to forget those moments on the hill in Connor's
arms?

When she did sleep, in the early hours, she dreamed of
Connor. He was in her mind all day and when he called
for her in the evening, it was as though she had never left
him.

"Hallo," he said, smiling, "recovered yet?"

"No," she answered flatly, and he laughed. "I've decided you didn't know what you were doing. You were
half asleep and I'm convinced now you thought I was
Velma."

"Think away," he commented, seeing her into the car.
He treated the matter so lightly it was plainly of no importance to him.

As he drove he told her the name of his friends and she
asked, half afraid of the answer, "How much are they
wanting? If it's too much . . . ."

"We'll discuss terms when the time comes. We've got
to discover first whether the car suits you."

The front door of a house with a doctor's office built
onto the side was opened by a cheerful young woman,
fair haired, round faced, casually dressed. She greeted
Connor warmly. Behind her a man hovered, and Nicola
assumed he was her husband. A small child in a crib
banged on an upstairs window, and when his father
called up to him to stop, he went on banging.

Connor said, "Dulcie, Mick, Nicola Dean, a friend of

mine.'' She noticed with a flick of pleasure his description of her. ''Nicola, Dulcie and Mick Styles.'' They shook hands.

''The car's in the carport,'' Dulcie said, leading the way.

It was small and white and seemed in good condition. ''We've looked after it,'' said Mick, patting its roof. ''Had it serviced regularly. We're only selling it because it's getting too small for our needs.''

Nicola said it looked just what she wanted, but—

''Sh-sh,'' Connor's arm went around her waist, ''don't sound too enthusiastic, otherwise they'll want twice the price they're already asking.'' He bent down and whispered loudly in her ear, ''Find something to criticize, quick!''

They all laughed and the Styles' watching and wondering eyes betrayed their line of thought. Connor, Nicola decided, was proving an excellent actor after all. This evening he was putting on a commendable performance.

''Try it out,'' Dulcie suggested. ''Why not go for a test run, the two of you?''

''Nicola,'' Connor ordered briskly, ''get behind that wheel.'' He bundled her in, fixed the seat belt across her body and got in beside her. Dulcie thrust her head through the window and explained the controls. Then she withdrew and they both waved as Nicola backed out of the driveway.

''Into the country,'' Connor directed, and soon they were driving between hedgerows and making for the hills.

''It's fabulous,'' Nicola cried. ''I've never driven such a—well, such a willing car!''

''And the woman who's driving it,'' came mockingly from the man at her side, ''is she 'willing,' too?''

''Don't distract me,'' she muttered, ''with such a leading question.''

''Meaning,'' Connor laughed, ''the time is not yet ripe. I'll postpone it till later.''

"Then the answer will be no," Nicola said sharply.

"Will it?" he murmured.

At his suggestion, she turned into a quiet side road and pulled onto the shoulder. As she switched off the ignition, the country silence descended. Connor turned his head and she knew he was watching her. With the fresh unpolluted air breezing in through the open windows, untidying her curls and lifting his tie, a tension had stolen in, too, hand in hand with an undercurrent of mutual and disturbing awareness.

His "Well?" broke the tight silence and slackened the tenuous thread, delicate as a silkworm's, that had formed between them. Her eyes, she knew, still held the brightness of exhilaration as she turned to him. "I'd love to buy it, Connor, but—how much do they want?"

He told her and she went slack. "Out of the question, even if I used all my savings." She sighed. "So that's that. I'll have to look for a cheaper one. Thanks, all the same, for thinking of me." She reached for the ignition key, but his hand came out and stopped her.

"I have a proposition to make." Her head jerked around and he laughed. "Not that sort!" Then his expression altered and he looked at her estimatingly. "Suppose I did propose that, what, I wonder, would your answer be? After all, you owe me something. I saved your life."

Indignation made her burn. "What are you doing, placing me under an obligation, then testing the extent of my permissiveness?"

"Maybe I am. For one of your generation, your character has so far proved remarkably free of flaws. You're almost too good to be true. There must be some blemish, some vice I haven't unearthed."

Absently she pulled at the seat belt, testing its efficiency. "You sound disappointed."

"Not disappointed, perhaps, so much as challenged." There was a disturbing expectancy in his voice.

Nicola smiled down at the buckle that controlled the

tautness of the bands protecting her body. "Are you trying to corrupt me?"

"Corrupt the pure Miss Nicola Dean?" he grinned "Perish the thought!" He shifted sideways, putting a greater distance between them. "Now, Miss Dean, to business. The proposition I wish to make regarding the purchase of this car—"

She sat, her hands resting moistly against the lower part of the steering wheel, staring through the windshield, watching the birds circling in the evening stillness, the insects crawling over the glass in a futile search for a place to enter.

"I suggest," he was saying, "and hear me out before you move in to the attack—that I lend you the money to pay for this car." Nicola took a breath, started to protest, but his fingers reached out and closed her lips. "Lend, I said, not give, you understand?" She nodded, tasting her lips where he had touched them. "Then, in regular instalments, you can pay me back. You could make out a bank order if you wish, so that the monthly amount is paid automatically into my bank account. How does that idea strike you? It would be a straightforward loan."

She was overwhelmed by his generosity and told him so. "But it would have to be with interest. I'd insist."

"If you added interest, I should let it accumulate and return it at the end. So, no interest."

She looked at him. "But why?"

"Why? Because I don't want to have to repeat my rescue act, that's why. If you bought the sort of car you could afford, it would let you down again as the van did, and next time the consequences might be even more disastrous."

"But what will you tell your friends?"

"Dulcie and Mick? Simple. When we get back, you write the Styles a check. Later, when we return home, I shall write you out a check. Tomorrow you deposit my check into your account. They won't deposit yours at once. I know their ways and they're dilatory about money matters. By the time they get around to it, my check to you will have cleared.''

''It's very—''

''—kind of me. I know. Amazing what a pair of gentle blue eyes and a mass of auburn hair does to a man. Drive on, Miss Dean.''

When they pulled up outside the Styles' house, Dulcie and Mick were watching for them. When they heard Nicola had decided to buy the car, they invited her and Connor for a drink.

The house was almost an extension of their personalities. There was an impression of cheerful disorganization. Toys littered the floor where their small son had dropped them. Magazines were strewn over armchairs and couch and every flat surface was covered with papers, magazines and even baby clothes.

They spent the evening talking and laughing. Connor was animated, almost exuberant. He abandoned his usual reserve and Nicola saw, with astonishment, that she must fit yet another piece into the mosaic of his character.

When eventually the Styles let them go, Nicola opened the door of her new car with a swaggering pride. She glanced into the rearview mirror and saw Connor get into his car, which was parked behind hers. Mick jerked his thumb in her direction and called out jokingly, ''When are the wedding bells going to ring, Connor?''

In the mirror, Nicola saw Connor move his hand negatively from side to side. There was no mistaking the haste with which he was dismissing the whole idea.

He followed her all the way back and parked outside the store. In the living room his eye was caught by the framed pictures on the walls and Nicola watched him inspecting each one.

''What are these beautiful creations?''

''All my own work.''

He stared. ''*You* did them? Explain yourself.''

''That—'' she pointed to a picture of ballet dancer ''—is machine embroidery.'' There were three figure depicted in the work, a male and two female dancers, the women wearing elaborate net appliquéd dresses with full-length skirts scattered with sequins. "Those—" indicating two others "—are hand-embroidered." One, her favorite, she explained, showed a young girl in a long sequined dress surrounded by softly colored flowers; the other portrayed sprays of flowers and grasses in an appliquéd, elaborately decorated vase. "I'm proud of those. They were all shown in an exhibition. They were part of the work I had to do to obtain my qualification."

He turned from studying them. "What qualification?"

She tidied the sideboard, which was already tidy. "I'm a graduate of the Royal College of Art."

"You're what? But that's equivalent to a degree!" He came to stand beside her. "My dear girl, why didn't you tell me?"

"You never asked. I've also got a Dip.Ed—a diploma in Education."

He stared. "You have? After all the things I said about you to my mother, about your amateurism, your lack of experience . . . . And you let me!" There was a short, tense silence in which Nicola refused to meet his eyes. "Will you accept my profound apologies for what was spoken in complete ignorance of the facts?"

"Of course. How were you to know?"

"And you gave it all up, to serve in a store?"

"What about you," she challenged, looking at him now, "haven't you got excellent qualifications and didn't you give up a good position at the hospital to take on your father's practice?"

"Yes, because my mother asked me to."

She smiled at him. "So did mine."

"Snap!" They laughed and Connor asked, "Are those pictures for sale?"

"Sorry, no."

"Not even to me?" Nicola shook her head. "Oh." There was no mistaking his disappointment. He took out his checkbook.

"You're not surely offering me money for one. . . ?"

"My sweet girl, I wouldn't insult you. The check for the car, remember?" He wrote it out and gave it to her.

She smiled at him again. "I don't know how to thank you."

"You don't?" he asked softly, putting away his pen in the manner of one clearing the decks for action. His hand came out and as she unsuspectingly put hers into it, it occurred to her just too late that his action might not have been entirely motivated by the completion of a business transaction. He said, proving her right, "We must seal the bargain, Miss Dean." There was a glint in his eyes. "I always was a believer in mixing business with pleasure."

He pulled her toward him and she made a futile bid for freedom, trying to keep him at bay by firing at him a barrage of accusations. Indignantly, she said, "So you want a reward for your beneficence? I suppose, because you've now done me two good turns, mere verbal thanks are not enough." She added, panicking because he showed no sign of being deflected from his purpose, "I thought doctors were above this sort of thing."

"You did?" He was really amused. "At this moment, my sweet innocent, I'm not a doctor. I'm a man." He eyed her mouth with the anticipation of a dog licking its lips prior to getting its teeth into a long-awaited meal. "I want a reward, partly because I honestly think I deserve one, and," his finger traced the curve of her lips, "partly because what you gave me yesterday evening on the hill was so enjoyable. Also," his tone altered subtly, "so full of promise. I therefore insist on an encore."

His arms tightened and his mouth approached and hovered. "Let's get this clear. I state categorically that I am wholly aware that you are not Velma Westlake. You neither feel like her," his hands wandered momentarily, "nor do you kiss like her. I'm of sound mind, the balance of it is not disturbed and the girl in my arms is Nicola Dean, accomplished, sweet—and unbelievably virtuous. I also declare that it is not my intention—at this particular moment—to violate that virtue." For a few seconds his eyes mocked her, then his lips found hers.

He took his kiss and then another. One for each of his "good deeds." She did not fool herself that they held for him any significance. She remembered—she had never forgotten—what he had said to his mother on the evening of the accident. "Kisses are cheap. They're so easy to give and they cost nothing."

When he let her go, she felt with her hands for the nearest chair.

"Good night, Nicola," he whispered, but she did not reply.

CHAPTER SIX

NICOLA tacked the jacket and skirt she was making for Barbara Mitchell, then phoned her to ask if she might bring it over to her house for a fitting.

"Do come now," she urged. "Connor's out and I'm feeling neglected." Nicola said she would be on the doorstep in ten minutes.

Before she left, she removed one of her pictures from its place on the wall. She had decided a few days before to make the supreme sacrifice—to give Connor one of her embroidered pictures, her favorite, the one he had liked so much. As she wrapped it with loving care, she told herself it was the least she could do in response to his kindness, the friend-in-need act he so often put on for her benefit. If there was another reason why she was giving him the one she liked best, she would not admit it even to herself.

When Mrs. Mitchell threw the front door wide, Nicola handed her the parcel. "For Connor. Would you give it to him, Mrs. Mitchell? He admired it the other day."

"Not—" her eyes shone, guessing in advance, "—one of your beautiful pictures? My dear, how very kind!"

Nicola said shyly, "Connor's been so good to me, this is the only means I have of repaying him." They moved into the living room. "He saved my life, not that one can repay anybody for doing that. Now he's helping me to buy the car—he told you?"

"He did. But when he rescued you, he only did what anyone else would have done. And the car—well, he has the money, so why shouldn't he help someone in need—and a friend of the family, at that?''

There it was again, "friend of the family.'' The matter-of-fact way in which Mrs. Mitchell explained away her son's actions put everything into perspective, destroying at one blow any hopes Nicola might secretly have cherished that he might have had another motive behind all he had done for her. But, she thought, for heaven's sake, what motive? A helping hand, a kiss or two prompted entirely by a perfectly natural uprush of physical desire. . . .

"Connor's on call this evening and the patients are keeping him busy, but as soon as he comes in I'll give it to him. I'm sure he'll be delighted.'' Mrs. Mitchell seemed loath to let her go, so after the fitting, Nicola stayed for a while. "I've had a letter from your mother,'' Barbara said. "Do try to persuade her not to come home yet. I've written to her saying how well you're coping.''

Nicola caught herself watching the door so often she felt sure Mrs. Mitchell must have noticed. But the son of the house did not put in an appearance.

She was nearly ready for bed when the phone rang. She raced down the stairs. "Nicola? My mother's just given me your picture. My dear, how can I thank you? What a wonderful gesture! I know how much you value that particular one, and to give it to me . . . .''

"It's true it was my favorite, but—anyway, I hope you like it.''

"Like it?'' There was a brief silence, then, "I shall cherish it more than I can say.'' He seemed to need to take a breath. "I must apologize for phoning so late, but I got involved in an emergency dash to hospital. Heart case. And to set your mind at rest, the man survived. I'm glad I caught you before you went to bed. Tomorrow evening there's a small, rather select party at the hospital. One of the doctors has acquired a higher qualification and is celebrating. Are you free, because I should like to take you?''

"Take me, Connor? But are you sure?"

"Sure? Of course I'm sure." He seemed a little on edge and Nicola supposed he was tired. "Can you come?"

"Yes, I can. It's very kind of you."

"It is, isn't it?" he joked. "My 'kindness' knows no bounds, especially when there's an attractive, winsome, charming young woman within arms' reach to lavish it on!"

Nicola could not tell him how enticing his arms were. Nor could she say to him, "I wish you would keep your arms to yourself."

THE DRESS SHE WORE for the party was blue, low-necked and classically cut. Here and there she had embroidered miniature flower motifs, giving the impression that they had been scattered at random. When she opened the door to Connor, his eyes made eloquent comment, but all he said was, "You look good."

On the way he explained that most of the senior doctors on the hospital staff would be at the party, together with their partners.

"Your mother told me you held a senior post when you worked there," said Nicola.

"I did. I still act in a consultant capacity."

"Would you like to return to hospital work one day?"

He answered carefully. "I should like to go back to it as much as you would like to return to your teaching."

She gazed out of the window, watching the countryside give way to the town scene. She said, on a sigh, "Which is—very much."

Connor parked in the grounds of the hospital in an area reserved for medical staff. They entered the building by a private door, but even so he was recognized with apparent pleasure by staff of varying grades who passed them in the corridor.

"Here we are," he said, indicating a door through which the party spirit was already penetrating. But Nicola was paralyzed with fright. Connor saw it and put his arm around her. "They're not carnivores," he whispered, "they're just medicos. And underneath all that, they're men, some of them with unmistakably lecherous leanings, despite your determination to deify them. So be on your guard!"

She smiled up at him, although her nervousness had by no means been dispelled by his words. He opened the door. The silence that greeted their appearance was sudden and profound. All noise, all action, ceased. There seemed to be eyes, nothing but eyes, all converging on them.

"Connor!" someone said, and the spell was broken. "Come in, man. Good to see you again."

"Darling!" Velma came forward, hands outstretched, her body swathed from décolleté neckline to sandaled feet in emerald green velvet. A chunky silver necklace and matching pendant earrings provided their own touch of drama. The red hair was upswept and kept in place by a green velvet band. She had outdressed every other woman in the room.

Each studied movement of her swaying body had a special meaning, the outstretched hands themselves spoke a language which even Nicola could understand. "This man you're with," they said, "is mine. He bears a notice around his neck, which says strictly private, keep out."

Connor ignored the outspread, scarlet-tipped fingers. They fell, slowly curling, to her sides. She swung around to face her audience. "Everyone," she declaimed, "meet Miss Dean, the girl from the village store. She serves behind the counter. Don't you, Miss Dean?"

The color rose through Nicola's body like alcohol in a thermometer, reaching its limits as it met her hairline. Connor's grip around her bare arm savaged her flesh, and she winced, but his hand remained where it was. The smiles of welcome, which had sprung so spontaneously to the watching faces, became painted and artificial. Velma's poison had taken effect.

"Shall we begin again?" said Connor, applying with

speed—doctor that he was—an antidote to the venom. "This is a friend of mine, Nicola Dean, ex-schoolteacher, accomplished needlewoman, so accomplished she publicly exhibited hand-embroidered pictures of her own design and making."

"They were framed, Miss Dean," Velma asked ingenuously, "the sort you hang on the wall for family and friends to admire? Samplers, weren't they called in olden times, things sweet young ladies used to sit and sew because they had nothing better to do with their time?"

There was a ripple of laughter and Velma went on, "But then you're a sweet young girl yourself, aren't you, Miss Dean? You look far too good for this decadent century. You like old-fashioned things, perhaps?"

Every eye shifted from Velma to Nicola, every ear seemed to be listening for her reply. "I'm not exactly enamoured of the present day, Miss Westlake," she said. "How clever of you to guess. And you're so right, I do like old-fashioned things, especially old-fashioned good manners!"

The watching eyes brightened with admiration, the polite smiles broadened into hearty laughter. "That," said one of the men, "has put you in your place, Velma. Connor, we admire your taste—in handmade women as well as handmade pictures."

Connor responded with a deep bow and straightened, closing the gap, small though it already was, between Nicola and himself. Velma watched the action like a driver about to be beaten to the last remaining parking place. She moved swiftly, parting them forcibly and taking her place beside Connor.

"Darling," she said, "how nice of you to keep your promise. You've brought a partner for Grenville. Grenville," she stretched out a hand, which, this time, was not ignored, "come and meet your girl friend for the evening, provided without charge by the man in my life."

A pale young man detached himself from the decor and attached himself to the outstretched hand. Nicola stood alone. She felt like a space walker whose lifeline had snapped and was now spinning, beyond human help, in outer space. Now she knew why Connor had brought her. She was there to make up the numbers.

The pale young man, however, looked delighted with the surprise package that had been wrapped, sealed and delivered on his doorstep for the evening. He extended his hand towards Nicola. "Grenville Lennon. Are there any more at home in your village like you?" The others laughed. "I hope," he went on, "you don't object to a man who looks disgustingly anemic but isn't, and who smokes like a flaming chimney but shouldn't. Ask friend Connor there what he thinks of cigarette smokers—him and his damnable chest diseases!" He put his arm around her. "All the same, you're landed with me now. Come and be introduced."

Since Connor made no move to keep her with him— Nicola supposed he was either immobilized by Velma's grip or, more likely, delighted to get the girl he had brought to the party off his back—she let herself be taken around the room by her newly-acquired, but strictly temporary, boyfriend.

One by one the men, of varying ages, girth and stages of hair loss, rose, nodded, smiled and shook hands, doctors every one. Their partners, wives, fiancées or women friends were included in the introductions. Room was made for Nicola and Grenville on one of the long couches and Grenville wedged himself in beside Nicola like a book being forced onto a shelf on which there was manifestly no room for it.

It was some time before Nicola could overcome her chagrin and bring herself to look for Connor. He had brought her on false pretences and it would take her a long time to forgive him for that. Yet she had to admit that she had no real grounds for resentment. When he had invited her he hadn't said, "I'm taking you as my girl friend." Obviously he had taken her as a "friend of the family," or even to repay her for the picture she had given him.

When eventually she managed to pick him out from the

other guests, she found him lounging in a deep armchair with Velma on his knee. She was straightening his tie and gazing into his eyes and displaying to whoever might be interested and "Miss Dean from the village store" in particular, that Connor Mitchell was her property and was not on the market for sale, rent or auction.

Drinks came past on trays, nuts and potato chips stimulated a thirst that had not existed until they appeared.

Grenville chain-smoked, still squashed beside Nicola. He wouldn't move for the world, he said, life could offer him no greater pleasure than to be stuck with invisible adhesive to the side of Miss Nicola Dean. He joked with the others about the good company he was keeping, and how bighearted it was of Connor to have made him a present of the angel on the Christmas tree.

He was in high spirits, so Nicola turned her face firmly away from the bestower of the "gift"—who anyway seemed to be basking in the sunshine of his girl friend's smile—and did her best to catch Grenville's mood.

"You're in excellent form tonight, Grenville," one of the wives commented.

"Who wouldn't be," he answered, "with a sweet little village maiden sitting so close to me you couldn't even get a medical report between us?" His arm went around Nicola's waist. "Come closer, beautiful," he whispered, "come closer to Uncle Grenville."

Nicola laughed with the others. "I couldn't even if I wanted to," she said. There was more laughter.

"Don't underestimate the girl," said a doctor the others called Johnny. "There's more in that statement than meets the eye. You haven't got her helpless in your clutches yet. You'll have to work a bit harder."

"Which I intend to do before the evening's out," said Grenville, pressing his cheek against her hair.

Nicola tolerated his advances—she had her reasons. Not only was he such a pleasant man, despite his utterances of lustful intentions when the party was over that she didn't believe anyway, but it seemed from Connor's expression that her unprotesting acceptance of her companion's ardor was annoying him beyond words. Let him be annoyed, she thought furiously. He didn't want her company, he had only taken her with him so that Grenville would not be the odd man out.

The music on the stereo changed from sentimental sweetness to an irresistible beat. One of the men persuaded his wife to dance and others followed.

"Do you dance, beautiful?" Grenville murmured.

"I can," Nicola answered primly, "but I don't often indulge."

"Indulge now." Grenville eased himself into a standing position, caught her hand and pulled her up to mingle with the others.

As they swung and swayed to the music, Nicola made an effort to put aside her reserve and matched her movements to Grenville's and, as his were uninhibited in the extreme, she had to push her reserve quite out of reach.

With a quick flash of triumph she met Connor's eyes. His devotee seemed to have deserted him. He was alone and was sprawled in the chair, as he often was at home, head lolling on the upholstery, watching her with an estimating, sarcastic expression that narrowed his eyes and turned his lips into a tight, cynical smile.

It was plain to Nicola just what he was thinking of her, as plain as if his thoughts were scrawled on a banner held up by a demonstrator at a rally. *Well*, she thought, *I'll show him another side of me tonight, one he doesn't know exists. At least it will surprise him, even if it displeases him.* And it looked as if he was very displeased with her at that moment.

Whether it was the effect of the wine she had had, or the irresistible throb of the music, or merely the desire to provoke the man whose eyes clung to her like barnacles to a ship, she deliberately exaggerated the swaying, twisting, seductive movements of her body.

Flushed, panting a little from her exertions, she waited with Grenville for the music to start again. It became romantic and Grenville held her close, resting his cheek against hers. She knew she had asked for it, so she did not hold him off. *Why should I?* she asked herself. *Why shouldn't I exploit my femininity to its limits like Velma?*

Her life, she told herself in an effort to justify her behavior, was unexciting and uneventful. Usually she liked it that way, but tonight was different. She would enjoy the party to the fullest, whatever the consequences. Connor didn't want her, Grenville did, so Grenville would have his fun.

A finger tapped on Grenville's shoulder. "Excuse me," the intruder said. "My turn, I think?"

"Now look, Connor," said Grenville, irritated like someone disturbed from an absorbing book, "she's my partner. You've got Velma, have your fun with her, pal. . . ."

Connor ignored him, turned Nicola by the shoulders and pulled her none too gently into his arms.

"You might," she said, watching Grenville slouch away, "have *asked*." Her partner had nothing to say, so she went on prodding his conscience. "Grenville's such a nice person, it was hardly fair. . . ." Connor stayed silent, but she refused to be put in the corner like an ill-behaved schoolchild. She was determined to make him talk, so she looked up at him brightly and said, "It's a nice party, isn't it?" The question, she knew, was a stupid one, worthy of the infant he was trying to turn her into.

"Is it?" The words carried over her head which was where his indifferent eyes were staring.

"I never thought," she persisted gaily, looking around at the assembled company, "that doctors could behave so uninhibitedly."

At last she had caught his attention. "No?" he drawled, looking down at her with lazy eyes. "You'd be surprised just how uninhibited doctors can get, given the opportunity. Try it. Try me some time. I'd be only too willing to give you a practical demonstration. Come to the top of the hill one night when everyone else is in bed. Then we wouldn't be interrupted.''

She had got the answer she had asked for, nevertheless she held herself away, but he laughed softly and tightened his grip. When the music stopped Nicola left him standing alone. Grenville was waiting for her his arms literally outstretched. Defiantly, she walked into them.

He joked, "I feel as though you've been away for a week." He pulled her down beside him and put his lips to her cheek. Her instinct was to turn away, but she saw the derision pulling at Connor's mouth, so she allowed Grenville's lips to linger.

Velma returned from wherever she had been and swooped on Connor, saying, "Why so pensive, darling? Are you angry with me because I've been so long?"

He detached himself from her clinging fingers and walked out of the room. Velma frowned. After a moment's thought, she followed him. The party closed ranks and went on without them, the music became dulcet and less demanding. Food was wheeled in, drinks flowed freely.

For the rest of the evening Grenville either danced with Nicola or sat beside her, holding her hand. She had not drawn it away when he had tentatively taken it. He told her about his job, and said he was specializing in ophthalmic surgery.

He had a fiancée, he confessed. She had gone abroad for a year. It was too long, he moaned. He shifted along the couch toward her. A man naturally got lonely, didn't he? He'd been faithful—up to now. He put his arm around her neck. A man couldn't stay faithful forever, could he?

Only half listening to Grenville's mutterings, Nicola began to fret about Connor's absence. Had he abandoned her to Grenville? Velma came back and Nicola revived, looking for Connor. When he did appear, Velma did not join him. They seemed to have quarreled.

Connor stood in a corner, hunching his shoulder

against the wall, glass in hand, detached, remote, looking on with cynical amusement. He seemed to derive the greatest entertainment from watching Nicola and Grenville.

Nicola tried to build around her a wall of unconcern, a barrier so high Connor's frank disapproval could not scale it. But the scorn in his eyes deepened in proportion to the increase in Grenville's ardor to such an extent that the barrier collapsed as if it were constructed of toy bricks.

It was useless now to pretend that she was unaffected by Connor's mounting criticism of her behavior. Her mind jumped into the immediate future, the drive home and the reckoning. She doubted if Connor would spare her. She had already sensed the streak of ruthlessness only just below the surface of his personality. She remembered how he had cut her down to size the day she had slammed the door in his face, yet he had told her that "had been nothing" compared with the anger that he was capable of if sufficiently aroused.

Grenville lifted her hand to his lips. "We mustn't lose contact, beautiful," he murmured. "Give me your phone number."

"Nicola." The word was spoken like the smash of a wineglass on a stone floor. "The party's over. We're going home."

"But, Connor—" He was standing over her, implacable, stubborn, angry.

Grenville struggled to his feet, pulling Nicola with him. "Now, look here, Connor, you can't do this to me. You presented me with this delectable dish on a plate and now you want to snatch it away before I've even begun the meal! I'll take her home—"

"That's life," Connor answered curtly. "Nicola," he looked at his watch, "you have three minutes to say your goodbyes." He went to the door and slammed it behind him.

She looked helplessly at Grenville. "I'm so sorry. It's

been such fun. I have enjoyed meeting you."

"You can say that again, sweetie." He took out his diary. "At least give me your phone number."

"Sorry," Nicola said, but he persisted. How could she shake him off? "I've—I've got a boyfriend already, you know."

"So what? You can run to two, can't you?"

She laughed. "Too busy." She looked around apprehensively at the assembled, illustrious company, at the consultants and specialists, all top men in their own spheres. They still intimidated her, despite the "human weaknesses" so many of them had displayed that evening. "Grenville, will you help me say goodbye? I can't just slip out without a word."

He put away his diary. "That's simple." He took her hand and led her to the door. He turned and shouted, "Nicola's going, everyone. She says good-night and thanks."

There were shouts in reply, a few hands waved, someone said, "Come again," and the party turned in on itself, forgetting them.

"Don't bother to see me out, Grenville," Nicola said, but he continued to walk with her to the exit.

They found Connor leaning on his elbow against his car, staring into the distance. Grenville said urgently, "At least tell me your surname, Nicola."

"Dean," said Connor, without turning, "address, Dean's the grocers', High Street, Roydon Kingsley." In the same indifferent tone, he went on, "Serves behind the counter by day. Available every evening."

Grenville turned to Nicola, his eyes like car headlights. "Available for what, beautiful?"

"Use your imagination, man," Connor drawled, still lounging against his car. "What do you think? Hasn't she been giving you the big green light the whole evening?"

Nicola said desperately, "Connor, will you *shut up*?" To Grenville, "I—I told you, I've got a boyfriend."

"Think nothing of it, Grenville," Connor interrupted,

"he's so far away, somewhere in the northeast of England, he won't trouble you."

"And that's where you're wrong," Nicola shouted, in her anger committing herself to far more in her friendship with Terence than she intended. "I happen to be in love with him."

Connor turned at last, slowly, eyebrows high. "You are? That's news to me."

"I don't tell you all my business." She was frightened by the way the situation was growing out of control. "Now will you take me home?" She turned to Grenville, saying with defiance, "Good night, Grenville. Thanks for being so nice to me this evening."

He caught her by the shoulders and kissed her firmly on the mouth. "It wasn't difficult to be 'nice' to you, beautiful. I'd like to have been a lot—er—nicer, but with Connor here acting as a self-appointed watchdog, I didn't stand a chance."

Connor maintained an unbending silence as they drove through the darkness. Nicola was reminded of their first journey together in the taxi, when he had barely addressed a word to her. His profile now was as uncompromising as it had been then, his mouth set in the same unforgiving line, his chin as firm and mulish.

When at last he did shatter the silence, the glance he flicked at her was as icy as it had been at the first accidental meeting. "For a woman in love," he jeered, "you're surprisingly willing to kiss another man. And I don't only mean Grenville Lennon."

"If it's you you're talking about, then I didn't have any alternative, did I? You practically forced me to kiss you. Anyway, I owed my life to you, so—"

"So you kissed me out of a sense of duty?"

She rounded on him, almost in tears. The evening she had looked forward to with so much pleasure had been a fiasco. "What if I did? You called it your 'reward.'"

"Well," he said grimly, "I've seen you in action tonight, and my word, it was an eye-opener!"

"I don't know what you're talking about."

"Don't you? I never knew you were such an expert at leading a man on. And it was all for nothing, wasn't it? I suppose you can't forgive me for depriving you of your night of debauchery. I called you 'unbelievably virtuous.' 'Unbelievably' was right." He was silent a moment, then, "Just out of interest, did Grenville tell you he's engaged?"

"Yes," she answered sullenly.

"Which makes your behavior all the worse."

"But what did I do?"

"You can't see that you spent the entire evening raising his hopes? Then it must be so much a part of your normal behavior pattern that your provocative response to his advances must have been automatic."

"I was *not* provocative! You're reading far too much into it."

This time the silence remained unbroken for the rest of the journey. He pulled up outside the store and as Nicola prepared to get out of the car, she made a final attempt at reconciliation. "Thank you for taking me to the party, Connor. I did enjoy it, in spite of your—your quite unjustified accusation."

In the light of the street lamp, he could not have failed to see her tears. His only response was to turn away. He said, each word coated with a layer of frost, "I wish I'd never taken you."

CHAPTER SEVEN

THE VILLAGE was alive with rumors. Someone, the story went, had bought the store next door to Dean's. The name of the buyer was a closely-guarded secret, but everyone guessed it was the supermarket chain.

As Nicola served behind the counter the day after the party, she listened with alarm to the customers' gossip. If it was true, she knew that any time now she would have a phone call or visit from the firm's representative. And this time, there was no doubt about it, he would put on the pressure.

She wished she had someone to advise her. If last night's party and its disastrous consequences had never happened, she would have gone to Connor, but when she remembered their quarrel on the way home, her pride said an unequivocal *no*.

It was Joy who phoned that evening with the news that turned Nicola's world inside out. "Know who's bought the empty store, Miss Dean?" she asked. "It's Dr. Mitchell, that's who bought it."

"Dr. Mitchell, Joy, Dr. *Connor* Mitchell? You must have gotten it wrong. Why could he possibly want to buy the shop next door?"

"I haven't got it wrong, Miss Dean. Mrs. Henderton heard it from Mrs. Rowley and Mrs. Rowley heard it from Mrs. Dover, the wife of the real estate agent in the town who's handling the sale. It's definite. Contract's signed and everything's tied up."

Nicola sat on the stairs, trying to take it in.

"Did you know, Miss Dean," Joy went on, "that the

doctor owns quite a bit of property in the town? It was left to him by his father. Dr. Henry Mitchell was quite rich, you know.''

"No," Nicola said weakly, "I didn't know."

Joy said, "If Dr. Mitchell sells the shop to that chain—and I can't think of any other reason why he should buy it—it won't be good for our business, will it, Miss Dean? Just think of Dr. Mitchell doing such a thing! He seemed far too nice."

"Did he?" Nicola asked vaguely. "I mean, yes, he did. But he isn't nice, is he, Joy, if that's what he's going to do? If it's true, we might as well close the store right away."

"Sorry to upset you, Miss Dean, but I thought you ought to know."

"Thanks, Joy, for telling me. . . ." Nicola sat for a long time staring into space.

Could Connor really have done such a thing to her, not to mention her mother? Yes, he could. He had his theories about the future of the village stores and how they should be done away with.

This was an ideal chance, wasn't it, for him to put his ideas into practice? Out with the unhygienic family grocer and his over-the-counter sales. In with the pre-packed, clinical cleanliness of the faceless, impersonal choose-it-yourself shelf display. Connor was ruthless when he chose to be. Doctors are human, he'd told her. So much for Dr. Connor Mitchell's humanity!

There was no doubt about it, tomorrow she would have to sink her pride and phone him and make him tell her the truth. She couldn't let the threat of a takeover bid hang over her, tormenting her every waking moment. If the worst were to happen, her mother would have no alternative but to sell out to the chain, thus leaving the whole site free for development.

How could they carry on their small, insignificant business next door to the offspring of a giant company? She wondered if she should telephone her mother and ask her advice, but decided it would be premature. First she would talk to Connor and try to discover his intentions.

She went to bed feeling uneasy and disturbed and was drifting into a shallow doze when the door bell rang, amplified into a soul-shattering clangor by the sensitivity the mind acquires in the limbo between wakefulness and sleep.

In a moment of terror, she fought off the covers, swung her legs to the floor and waited. Had it been part of her dream? The bell rang again. A caller, at this time of night? Was it Mrs. Henderton with one of her maddening requests? But surely even she wouldn't call at such a late hour?

The bell rang again, this time insistent and repetitive, in the nature of an SOS. She tiptoed across to the window, but there was nothing to see. The caller, whoever it was, was hidden by the small roof over the porch. She had felt no anxiety, until that moment, of being alone at night, but now, shaking with an irrational fear, she prodded her feet into furry mules and cocooned herself in her short wraparound dressing gown.

The bell was ringing continuously. Whoever it was was determined to gain entry, even if he woke the entire village in the process. As she went downstairs, she took a last desperate gulp of courage and opened the door.

It was Terence, suitcase in hand and a pathetic smile on his face. Weariness blanketed him and he was trying hard but unsuccessfully not to look sorry for himself. "Hallo," he said, "I've just arrived."

There was, Nicola decided, absolutely no answer to that. Her stare was wide and fixed, like a doll's whose eyelids had stuck in the open position. What on earth was she going to do with him? A car came to rest at the curb. It was familiar and it was yellow. At that moment in time she would have given anything in the world for it to have been any other color. The driver wound down the window. Her heart gave a drunken lurch, clawing at her ribs in an effort to right itself.

Terence was sublimely unaware of the emotional maelstrom his midnight appearance was causing to the girl on whose doorstep he was standing. He was also supremely ignorant of the man glowering, like a massive rain cloud, in the background.

He said, his voice booming to and fro across the black silence of the village night, "Sorry to disturb you so late, Nicola, but—well, I was wondering—could I stay the night with you?"

What a question, and what a time to be asking it! A yellow door opened and slammed. Footsteps drummed across the pavement. A voice six feet or so above them growled, "I'm on my way home from a late call. Anything wrong, Nicola?" He gave a hostile, I'll-soon-deal-with-him look at the newcomer and said, "Having trouble?"

"N-no, it's all right, Connor, everything's under c-control." The words fell over each other, her tongue being in the same drunken state as her heart. "It's—it's Terence, Terence Stevens, my—my boyfriend." She cursed her own hesitancy and the guilty flush that made her cheeks shine out like burning beacons even in the dimness of the hall light.

There was, in Connor's narrowed, assessing eyes, the look of someone making a diagnosis. He was collating the evidence: the suitcase, the expectation of welcome in the young man's eyes; the weariness in every line of his body which indicated a long journey ended and an arrival greatly anticipated by both parties; the expectation evident in the traveler's smile of the comfort and loving attention that would be meted out to him as soon as the door was closed by the girl he had come so far and so late to see.

The analytical gaze was turned onto Nicola and now he sought for her symptoms, looking her over from disheveled hair where the pillow had already ruffled it, to cosily slippered feet. His glance dwelled long and appraisingly on the short, filmy nightdress under the dressing gown, which, in her agitation, she had allowed to fall apart, like curtains across a stage opening to reveal the scenery behind it.

Her guilty flush deepened as she saw where his thoughts were leading, and she gathered her dressing gown around her tightly. Because he had made his assessment as a man and not as a physician, his diagnostic powers had led him in the wrong direction and therefore to an incorrect conclusion. But, Nicola asked herself, could she really blame him? The situation was fraught with compromise and suggestion. She knew that every hasty action she made to demonstrate her innocence only served to underline in his eyes how deeply implicated she was in what he had obviously interpreted as intrigue and brazen immorality.

"Go in, Terence," she urged, moving aside to let him pass. Connor stayed where he was, one foot planted firmly on the pavement, the other resting in an intimidating, browbeating kind of way on the doorstep. "He's—he's just arrived, Connor," she volunteered weakly.

"And you're providing him with a bed for the night?" The question was an innocent one, but the way Connor said it turned it into an insinuation of wanton behavior beyond all belief.

"He's asked me to, so of course I will." Now she sounded belligerent, which was not what she wanted at all, but she was so nervous she had no control over how her words came out. "He is, after all, my boyfriend. I—I happen to be fond of him." *Which is true*, she thought, leaving aside *the fact that I don't love him*.

"Fond of him enough to offer him all the womanly comforts, of course?"

"I don't see what the hell it's got to do with you!" she cried, provoked by his insinuations into a turn of phrase completely out of character. "This is *my* home, he's *my* boyfriend, so I can offer him whatever 'comforts' I like—and he wants."

Connor's lip curled and the derisive look he gave her seared her like a naked flame. "Nicola Dean, the chaste, the pure, the undefiled!" He swung away and drove into the night.

TERENCE TOOK NICOLA into his arms. She remained acquiescent and passive because she had nothing to give him. Her body felt as empty as a ransacked house. Connor had acted the ruthless bailiff and had evicted all feeling. Her skin felt blistered and scorched by the contempt his eyes had held.

The arms she wanted around her were not these arms, the kiss she let Terence give her was not the kiss she longed for. But Terence was tired, he had had a long journey and it was late. Now it was tomorrow morning and he had made his way to her like a lone voyager making for the coastline of his homeland. She had to welcome him, if not with open arms, then with a smile full of simulated happiness and love.

He was hungry, so she cooked him some food. Then she made up the spare bed and unpacked his suitcases. She was dropping with fatigue, but she had to hide it and show an interest in all his news. He had been sent on a course, he told her, on the new approach to the teaching of history. The conference hall was in Shrewsbury.

"I was going to write and tell you, but somehow I didn't get around to it. I intended to come in a couple of days' time, but the car started giving trouble. Then, without warning, I was offered a lift for this afternoon. I didn't have time to let you know. I just said 'yes, please' and—well, here I am. Pleased to see me?" She nodded and returned his look of affection. "It's good to see you, love," he said. "It's been a long time."

He kissed her again. She saw with compassion that his face, normally alert and cheerful, was lined with weariness. He was tall and thin, painfully thin for such a healthy young man. His light brown hair was wavy and looked permanently untidy. His clothes barely veered from the conventional, except for an occasional dazzling tie when he felt in the mood. He was good-natured and easy going and Nicola wished she felt deeply enough about him to love him. But it just wasn't there; never had been, she knew now. The appearance of Connor Mitchell in her life had proved that.

"Tomorrow," said Terence, "I'll get myself a room in a guest house in the town."

What could she say to that except to dissuade him? "You can stay here. You could take the morning bus to town and come back here every evening. How long does the course last?"

"A week." His eyes brightened. "Could I stay with you? Would you like me to?"

What could she answer? "Of course I would."

Later, when she rolled into bed, she could not settle down. Her fatigue-wide eyes stared into the darkness, but all she could see was the reenactment of the doorstep scene, the scathing, disgusted glare Connor had hurled at her as he had gone away. He had been contemptuous enough after the doctors' party about her behavior. What he would think of her now, unjustified though his censure was, she didn't dare to think.

Her mind, in its blind groping for the rest, turned to the matter of the store next door. She twisted uneasily to her side and told herself she would have to discuss the matter with Connor. No good listening to her pride, no use trying to think of answers to the accusations she knew he would make. She would need all the courage she possessed to face him, but face him she would.

Daylight was coloring the walls of the room. It was heralded with dismay by Nicola, and joy by the birds in the trees, before sleep finally conquered. The alarm woke her cruelly early, and when she looked at herself in the mirror, she turned away in distaste. It would take a lot of makeup to disguise those shadows under her eyes, and that pinched, dull look in her cheeks.

IT WAS SATURDAY, so Connor would only have morning office hours. Since she did not think it right to take advantage of her friendship with his mother and ask to see him at home, Nicola phoned the office.

"It's not about my health I want to see Dr. Mitchell," she explained to the receptionist. "It's business."

The receptionist was doubtful. "He's very busy on Saturday mornings, Miss Dean. Hang on a minute and I'll ask him." She soon returned. "He says come at the end of his office hours. Ten o'clock prompt."

Nicola gave Terence some breakfast and left him working at the dining-room table, his papers spread all over it.

She drove into town and when she arrived the waiting room was still half-full. There were magazines on the table and she chose one, flicking through it without seeing a word. There were two doctors on duty that morning, Connor and her own doctor, Dr. Muirson.

As each of his patients left, Connor came to the door calling for the next one, but not once did he acknowledge by a smile or even a look that Nicola was there.

Dr. Muirson's office hours ended just before Connor's and at last Nicola found herself alone. The strain was becoming unbearable. Her heart was pounding, her cheeks were flushed, her throat parched, and she knew she was in a state of near-hysteria. With an odd twist of her mind, it reminded her vividly of the day she had sat petrified in the van watching the train hurtling toward her. Now, ironically, Connor himself was the "train" and there wasn't a rescuer in sight.

"Miss Dean?" the receptionist recalled Nicola from her reverie. "The doctor will see you now."

When she stood to go into the office, she would have been glad of a wheelchair. He was writing and did not look up. She hovered, gripping her handbag, awaiting his attention and gazing at the chair opposite him with longing. As if sensing her need he raised his hand, not his eyes, and motioned her toward it, then he continued with his writing. If the strain in the waiting room had been bad, this, Nicola reflected, was a thousand times worse.

But at last he threw down his pen and leaned back in his swivel chair, looking her over with a very masculine eye—it was, after all, outside office hours. He said, "You have ten minutes." Each one of his actions seemed calculated to emphasize her inferiority. When she brought herself to meet his eyes, he said, "You look tired."

"I am. I was up late."

"I'll bet you were. Active into the small hours, no doubt, after such a long absence from your loved one."

"I know what you're thinking, but you're wrong."

"Am I?" Two words, but with a wealth of insinuation behind them.

"Anyway, what I do and don't do with my boyfriend is my own private affair." No, no, that was the wrong word. He smiled cynically. She tried again. "What happened between us is none of your business." That was wrong, too, she could tell by the mockery in his face. All her words, all her remonstrations so far, even to her own ears had seemed to confirm her "guilt." It was clear that to him they undoubtedly had.

He inclined his head. "Agreed. Your own *affair* entirely." He swiveled slowly from side to side and said softly, as if to himself, "So the sweet pure Nicola Dean isn't so pure after all."

Words gathered, words with which to defend herself, but the situation was so hopeless—hadn't she by her thoughtlessness, as good as condemned herself?—that she let the words remain unspoken. He waited, playing idly with the rubber tubing of his stethoscope.

"I've come to see you," she faltered, "because of a rumor going around the village about the empty store adjoining ours."

There was an infinitesimal pause, then, "Well? And how does that concern me?"

"You know damned well how it concerns you," she blurted out, maddened by his indifference. "People are

saying that you've bought the store and," she rushed on
in spite of the raised eyebrows, "that you're going to sell
or lease it to the supermarket chain."

"Now tell me—" he leaned forward "—since you
seem to know so much, which is it to be—that I lease the
store to the chain, or that I sell it? It can't be both."

"So you admit you're the owner?"

"I do."

"Then it's true." Her muscles contracted at his
treachery. "And it's probably also true what they're saying about your conniving to bring the supermarket into
the village." She waited eagerly for his denial, but to her
dismay it did not come. "How could you?" she cried.
"You know the store is our livelihood—at least, it's my
mother's. How could you be so callous and self-
seeking?"

"You're making strong, and if I may say so, rather
abusive accusations. I take exception to them." He
picked up his ballpoint pen, idly clicking it. "One thing
you and your mother will have to face up to sooner or
later is the inevitable. Whether you like it or not, people
want new ways, new methods. Women want pre-
packaged goods these days. And, in my opinion as a
physician, it's a damned sight healthier than food displayed as you do it, uncovered on the counter. That store
of yours has never, to my knowledge, been modernized,
except to have a refrigerator and display deep-freeze in-
stalled."

"We haven't the capital to modernize. Anyway, we
keep it clean. We're particular about it."

"*You* may think it's clean, but hardly what I would call
clinically clean as a food store should be. Its age alone
precludes that."

"So," with an effort she kept her voice steady,
"you're going to let this company get a foothold in the
village. You're going to make my mother suffer so that
you can put your grand theories and beliefs into practice."

"You know—" he threw down the pen and clasped his

hands on the desk "—you're assuming an awful lot. Just like a woman, you've jumped from one conclusion to another, without pausing at any stage to discover whether your assumptions are correct. "Now—" he looked her in the eye "—let's get this clear. One, I am now the legal owner of the empty shop adjoining yours. Two, I have plans for that shop, but what they are is no one's business but mine. Beyond that, as circumstances are at present, I am not prepared to go."

Now she knew the truth and it hurt. Her lip quivered. "You know how much I wanted that store. You knew I was longing to be able to buy it one day and use it for my own purposes. And yet you disregarded all my hopes and wishes and bought it yourself."

He leaned back and moved his chair slowly, infuriatingly, from side to side. "My dear girl, did you really expect me to hold back on the purchase of the store because of some vague sentimental longings you might entertain of buying the place for yourself one day in the very distant future? In the hardheaded, hardhearted world of business, such consideration would be laughed at."

She answered, her voice low and intense, "I never realized until now just how hard and unscrupulous you are."

Anger leaped into his eyes like a tiger onto a victim. "You," he said, between his teeth, "are in no position to pass judgment on my character. If I were to tell you just what I thought of you, by the time I'd finished with you, you would barely have the strength to stagger out of this room."

"You're wrong," she cried, "you don't know what you're saying."

The phone rang. He listened, asked the receptionist, "What are the symptoms?" and listened again. "Put her through to me, will you?"

He closed his hand over the mouthpiece and said, icily, "If you'll excuse me now? I have a number of calls to make before lunch. . . ."

Nicola left him with a brief, "Thank you for seeing me," and went out into the cool morning air.

TERENCE HELPED behind the counter that afternoon. Nicola introduced him to Joy, who took him around the shop showing him where the things were stored and how to use the cash register.

Customers asked, "Got a new assistant, dear?"

"He's a friend of mine," Nicola explained. "He's staying with me for a few days." Eyebrows rose, but the smiles and nods were friendly enough.

That evening she told Terence her problems about the store next door. They talked the matter over, then Terence suggested that Nicola should phone her mother. "After all, the business is hers, so she really should be consulted."

Nicola was glad to hear her mother's voice again. "I'm feeling fine, love," Enid told her. "I'm thinking of coming home soon. How are things with you?"

When she heard about Terence, she said she was delighted to hear Nicola had company. Nicola felt a rush of gratitude for her mother's implicit trust in her—and in Terence. Then she told her mother about Connor Mitchell's surprise purchase of the shop next door and the plans he was rumored to have for selling it again.

"Does he know you wanted it for yourself, Nicola? He does? Well, this is my suggestion. He's a reasonable man—"

"No, he's not!"

"Oh, I think he is, dear, deep down. On the surface he's a bit brusque at times, even his mother admits that, but he's quite a nice young man, really." Nicola laughed ironically. "I suggest you go and see him again and ask if he'd be willing to lease the store to you."

"You mean ask if I could become his tenant? But I couldn't do that! After the things he said to me, it would be too humiliating."

"What sort of things, dear?"

"Well, er . . . ." What could she say? "About people in the village wanting new ways, and so on."

Enid sighed resignedly. "He could be right, but that doesn't stop you going to see him, does it? I'm sure he'd consider the suggestion seriously before he took such a drastic step as selling to someone who would virtually put us out of business."

It was a suggestion Nicola had been half expecting—and dreading. She supposed there was really no alternative. She would have to lower her pride, seek a second appointment and ask another favor of Connor Mitchell.

It took her two days to find the courage. She told the receptionist she was sorry to trouble Dr. Mitchell when he was busy, but please could she see him again? There seemed to be someone with the receptionist to whom she addressed the question.

A violent expletive, spoken by a familiar male voice, exploded in the background. The words, "What the blazes do you want now?" erupted out of the receiver.

"I'm—I'm sorry to be such a nuisance, Dr. Mitchell, but I've had a word with my mother and—"

"Don't come here again. The last visitation you made put me behind for the rest of the day." Nicola bit her lip. If she had not been acting on her mother's instructions, she told herself mutinously, she would have slammed the phone down.

"I shall be at home this evening," he said. "Come at eight o'clock." He rang off, ignoring her words of thanks.

When Terence returned from town that afternoon, he served in the shop again. He enjoyed doing it, he said. It was a realxation after the mental effort of working on the course. He and Joy had taken to each other. He seemed to like her cheerful matter-of-fact manner and she in return liked his serious, almost dedicated approach to everything he tackled. She would laugh at his mistakes—he took her amusement in good grace—then she would set him straight.

After the evening meal Nicola left Terence working on his notes and drove slowly along the village street. She passed young men straddling bicycles and joking with girls under the ancient oak tree that dominated the path of grass outside the church. She bumped over the hump-backed bridge that spanned a tributary—here little more than a stream—of the River Severn. She was on her way to keep her appointment with the man who, unaccountably, had become her enemy. She had brought with her the finished outfit she had made for his mother. She at least, if not her son, would give her a warm welcome.

But it was Connor who opened the door, unsmiling and cool. To Nicola's dismay it seemed he was alone. She said, stepping inside, "I've brought the two-piece suit I've made for your mother."

He took it and put it on the hall table.

"How much does she owe you?"

His peremptory question startled her and in her nervousness she shook her head vigorously. "It doesn't matter. She can give it to me when I see her."

"Come into the living room," he said.

She took the armchair he offered and he sat opposite her. "Is your boyfriend still living with you?"

Nicola noted the malicious subtlety of his phrasing, but forced herself to remain calm. "Yes. He's here on a course. He returns every evening. I told him it was silly to take a room in the town when I lived so near—"

"You don't have to explain to me," he said curtly. "It's your life you're living, it's your business entirely what you do with it."

He hauled himself out of the chair and paced the room. He said bitterly, as if he had with difficulty been reining in his thoughts, but had at last been forced to give them their head, "My word, if ever I was mistaken in my assessment of someone, it was you. My belief in my own judgment has suffered a severe jolt." Having started on her, it seemed he was not going to stop.

"Miss Nicola Dean," he intoned, "pure and unsullied, just a sweet old-fashioned girl with sweet old-fashioned

morals. The girl who hates the twentieth century because
of its poor standards, yet here she is behaving as amor-
ally as all the rest. The irony of it! I might have forgiven
you a little more readily if you hadn't been so damned
hypocritical about it.''

Nicola shook her head miserably. "Circumstantial
evidence. You're being very unjust. What you're implying simply isn't true.''

He moved his hand in an abrupt dismissal. "Don't give
me that. You and your boyfriend, with whom you admit
to being in love—'' how she regretted that statement now
''—sleeping in the same house alone for how long . . . a
week, ten days? And you expect me to believe you've
spent every night in separate rooms, sleeping in separate
beds, and that you've successfully kept him at bay, on
the other side of your bedroom door?''

"Two and two,'' Nicola told the carpet, "don't always
make four.''

He gave a short, derisive laugh. "Go back to school.
Your arithmetic's slipping.'' He stood up, pushing his
hands into his pockets. "What did you want to see me
about?''

Nicola felt she had made a bad start, and fought to find
the right words with which to introduce the subject. With
his cold stare on her, how could she even begin to ask a
favor of him?

"A few days ago,'' she said, "I telephoned my
mother.'' She paused, seeking inspiration, but none
came. He maintained his frozen silence.

"She—she made a suggestion.'' Another agonizing
pause. "She suggested that if I came to see you and
asked you to reconsider your decision to sell the store to
that supermarket chain—'' there was a sharp, inexplicable movement from him, but she plunged on ''—you
might . . . change your mind.''

She darted a look at his face, but it told her nothing.

"She also suggested—'' she realized she was twisting
her hands in extremely painful positions and im-

mediately untwisted them "—that I might ask you if you would consider something else." She stopped again, needing encouragement. He took pity on her and provided it.

"And that is?"

"That you . . . might . . . possibly . . . consider . . . leasing the store . . . to me, at a rent to be decided on by you."

Now it was out, but for a long time there was no response. Then he moved and she looked up to find a drink being thrust into her hand.

"It's obvious you need reviving."

She murmured her thanks and took a few sips. He drank and asked, "And did the idea appeal?"

Now she looked up, eyes wide, lips parted in anticipation. "Yes, of course it did. It would be a dream come true."

He leaned against the mantelpiece. "Tell me, if I agreed to do this, what would happen to the store when you marry?"

"When I *marry?*"

"Sorry, silly of me. In your relationship with your boyfriend, marriage is expendable, doesn't enter your thoughts. Doesn't need to, does it?"

She let his comments pass. There was really no answer to them, and anyway, what was the use of telling him yet again that she hadn't allowed Terence inside her bedroom, let alone her bed?

"Now," his fingers drummed on the mantelpiece, "rentwise I should want the market price." He named a figure and she winced. "Would you be prepared to pay that?"

"It's a . . . a little more than I expected. It's rather high."

He planted himself in front of her, legs apart, elbows cupped in his hands, and there was an odd smile on his face which worried her. "For certain, er, considerations I might be prepared to reduce it."

She answered indignantly, "What do you mean?"

"My dear Nicola, you surely aren't *still* pretending to be the personification of maidenly virtue? You may have fooled me in the past, but not anymore."

This she would not take. "So you're testing me, are you, no doubt basing your 'experiment' on my alleged intimacy with my boyfriend?" She stood up, her face flaming. "You can keep your shop! Where business is concerned you and I obviously don't speak the same language." She went to the door and wrenched it open.

"*Come back here, woman!*" She stopped in her tracks and turned. "Precipitate and unthinking as ever, aren't you? In that at least I was right. Sit down." She complied, but he remained standing. "You can rent the store. I'll agree to that."

She was studiedly cool. "Thank you, but it's no good. I couldn't afford the rent."

"I'll halve it."

She stared up at him, unable to believe his change of heart. "Are you sure?"

"I'll get my lawyer to draw up a contract that will be signed by both of us, I as the landlord, you as the tenant. Does that satisfy you?"

She stood unsteadily. "That's wonderful!" His generosity and the near achievement of a long-cherished dream brought the moisture to her eyes. "It's very kind of you."

"Let me contradict you," he answered stiffly. "This is not 'kindness.' It's business." His tone was brusque and unsentimental. It dried her eyes as effectively as a parching wind blowing across a desert. It also brought her racing heart to a crash stop against the cold-blooded, impossibly tough side of his nature.

They moved into the hall. "You'll hear from my lawyer in due course."

They looked at each other. She sought compassion, if only the compassion of his calling, but his eyes were the steely gray of a rolling winter sea. They tossed her about like so much driftwood.

Nicola could neither understand nor bear his unforgiving attitude. She remembered with intolerable longing his past kindnesses, his sympathy, the delight of his kisses, all now so much part of the past they might have happened between two different people.

She told herself, whipping herself to anger like a child spinning a top, he was condemning her without trial or jury, punishing her without a shred of justification, and all because of a grossly false assumption on his part that she and Terence had become lovers. Bitterness at his mistaken indictment of her morals, coupled with the knowledge of her own innocence, made her imprudent, reckless and abusive.

"I suppose," she burst out, "any time now you'll be demanding your 'reward' as you did once before. After all, you've already tried to buy me off with improper suggestions. Just think of the bighearted concessions you've already made to me, your charity towards a poverty-stricken friend of the family; your benevolence in slashing by half the rent of the store you're so graciously allowing me to occupy; your role as benign moneylender—my car, remember? Any time now there'll be a demand for 'payment' for all those incredible acts of self-sacrifice!"

She could see she had gone too far. Too late now to conciliate, to apologize. His lips almost disappeared. He took a breath and snarled, "If that's not as blatant an example of ingratitude as I've ever come across, if that's not brazen provocation, if that's not literally asking—no, *begging* for it, then I don't know what is! To hell with your precious boyfriend, you're going to get it!"

With his foot he slammed shut the half-open door and gripped her around the body. There was no mistaking his intention—of taking his revenge, not only for her remarks but for something else, she was sure. There must have been some other explanation for the viciousness with which he grappled with her.

She struggled, made a last-minute attempt to placate, throwing her head from side to side in denial. "I didn't

mean it, Connor, please believe I didn't mean it. . . ."
But she might have been talking to herself.

His mouth bore down upon hers in a merciless kiss that
reduced her struggles of a moment ago to a state of utter
submission. Then he let her go with a suddenness that
startled her. She leaned sideways against the door and
hid her face.

He was silent for a few moments, giving her time to recover. The he pulled her away from the door and opened
it wide. She walked unsteadily, blinded by tears, along
the crazy-paved path and before she reached the gate,
the door had been slammed behind her.

CHAPTER EIGHT

TWO DAYS LATER Nicola received a letter from her mother, "I'm coming home," she had written, "but only for a few days, to collect some more clothes. Your Uncle Will is being sent to Switzerland for a couple of months on business and Aunt Sheila's going with him. They've invited me to go along, too, at their expense, and I'd love to, because it would be a wonderful chance to stay with Lucille and family. But I thought it advisable first to get the doctor's approval. Would you be a dear and phone him? Tell him my chest is a lot better and I'm feeling fitter now than for a long time."

Nicola's first thought was, *I can't do it.* But she knew she would have to sink her pride, the pride he had pulverized to powder the other evening, and speak to Connor Mitchell.

The receptionist, after a brief absence said, "I'm putting you through, Miss Dean."

"Yes?" came the hard, impatient voice.

"Once again I'm sorry to trouble you, Dr. Mitchell." Did she have to sound so differential, did her heart have to throb like a ship's engine, she wondered. "I have a question to ask on my mother's behalf." She explained the position.

"Tell her yes. It would do her the world of good." A brittle silence followed and she filled it by asking with ridiculous timidity, "Is there any news of the store, Dr. Mitchell? Will I be able to move my things in soon?"

"All in good time," was the stringent reply. "These legal matters progress slowly but surely. A little patience on your part wouldn't come amiss."

Nicola choked, "You never let an opportunity pass of putting me in my place, do you? I asked a civil, reasonable question. I must have been off my head to expect a civil, reasonable answer from you in return!"

All she got for her pains was the deafening clatter of his receiver in her ear.

After tea, she phoned her mother and passed on the doctor's message. "Thanks, dear. I'll be home on Monday. Will I see Terence?"

"No, he goes back on Sunday, the day before you arrive. I'll meet you at the station. It'll be good to see you again, mom." She couldn't hide the catch in her voice.

Later, as the evening was fine, Nicola and Terence went for a walk to the top of the hill. She took a chance on seeing Connor. What did she care, she asked herself, if they found him up there? But they had the hill to themselves.

Terence talked about his course, which was over now. He said how much he had enjoyed seeing her again. He had liked serving in the store, too. "Joy's a nice girl, isn't she? I suppose she has a line of boyfriends?"

"No, only one, I think, and I doubt if it's serious. Just a boy-and-girl affair. She's only seventeen."

"Is that all? She looks older."

On the way down, Terence took Nicola's hand. It was for him an unusual display of affection, and it surprised her because he had kept his distance for most of his visit. Apart from a chaste, ritual good-night kiss, he had shown no particular desire to touch her or make even mild love to her as he had done in the past. He had acted the friend, almost the brother, but certainly nothing more, which made Connor's assumption that they were lovers all the more ironic and hurtful.

It was, Nicola supposed, inevitable that they should meet him. He was climbing the hill with energetic strides as they went down, fingers entwined. He merely nodded and passed by, stony faced.

On the last evening, Terence asked Nicola if she would

object if he went for a walk. "Of course not," she told him, surprised and a little puzzled. "Want to say good-bye to the village?"

"Yes," he laughed—was there a hint of embarrass-ment in the sound? "I've enjoyed my visit tremendously. It's been so good of you to look after me." She thought, with wry amusement, he sounded like a lodger thanking an attentive landlady.

Next day was Sunday and she drove Terence to the station. Having no reason for rushing back, Nicola took the return journey slowly. As she went along, she ex-amined her feelings. There was no sense of loss at Terence's going; if anything, rather a sense of relief, even release. He was a nice young man, gentle, harm-less, uninspiring and unexciting. But there was no doubt about it—he was not for her. And she was sure that by the end of their week together, he had known it, too.

ENID WAS HOME for a few days collecting suitable clothes to take away with her. One evening Barbara Mitchell called. Connor brought her and Nicola took it for granted that, having deposited his mother on the doorstep, he would drive away. But he followed her in.

He greeted Nicola with a lingering, sarcastic look that made her blush, then spoke to her mother. "Just thought I'd take a look at the patient before she goes off on her long journey."

"That's very good of you," Enid said. "Do I pass the test?"

"Er—" He looked at her keenly. "Yes. The break you've had already seems to have done you a power of good."

"You're a bit pale, Nicola," Mrs. Mitchell com-mented. "There's a lot of illness about, isn't there, Con-nor? Some mystery bug. Tummy trouble. Hope you're not catching it, dear."

Connor transferred his gaze to Nicola and looked her over with a dauntingly professional eye. "Very doubtful.

Missing her boyfriend, more likely. Extraordinary what frustration can do to a woman!"

Only Nicola knew what he meant, and only he knew why she gave him such a crushing look, which he deflected with a smile.

"You're feeling all right, aren't you, Nicola?" her mother asked, worried now. "You'll be able to cope if I go away again?"

"Of course I will! I'm perfectly well."

"You go off on your jaunt with a clear conscience, Mrs. Dean," said Connor. "I can keep an eye on your daughter." He turned to the daughter in question, eyebrows raised provocatively. "Can't I, Nicola? Healthwise, of course." His grin was wicked, and Nicola was sure he was reminiscing.

Her mother, unable to see his face, took his statement at its face value. "You're conscientious, Connor. I sang your praises to my daughter as soon as she came home. I told her she couldn't do better than to have you as her doctor, too, but—"

"But one glance at me—" he took her up "—and she made a beeline for the list of one of my colleagues!" He shot Nicola a sly glance. "Know what she said when she thought I couldn't hear? That she wouldn't have me as her doctor for the whole world!"

"Nicola! You didn't!" Embarrassed, Nicola gave Connor another scathing look and said it was true. "But why, dear? The people of this village don't know how lucky they are to have a doctor of Connor's caliber to treat them."

"Don't try to talk her into coming on my list, Mrs. Dean. I have the right to refuse any patient I take a dislike to, you know, and I might turn down her application."

"Connor!" Now it was his mother's turn to be shocked. "How can you say such a thing? Nicola's a sweet girl. . . ."

"Is she?" Connor pretended to joke. But he turned unconvinced, narrowed eyes toward the girl of whom they were talking. "You could have fooled me."

His mother said soothingly, "You know very well you like her, dear. . . . Now, Enid—" they drifted into the living room, leaving their respective son and daughter alone "—tell me all about this wonderful holiday you're going to have. . . ."

Connor folded his arms and contemplated the pain and indignation Nicola could not hide. "Yes," he murmured, " 'like'—such a convenient, nebulous word. I like dogs, for instance, but it doesn't mean I want to own one. I like flowers, but I don't want them around me all the time. I even like women—in their proper place." His mocking smile grated and she fell into his trap.

"Which is?"

"Where all men—real men—like them. My dear girl, you surely know where that is by now?"

She swung away. "Excuse me. I have work to do."

She went into the dining room, longing to close the door on him, but politeness prevented her from doing so. She hoped her words and her decisive action would tell him clearly that she did not want his company.

But he followed her, sat on a corner of the table and watched her embroidering a baby's dress. "Still taking orders for customers?"

"What does it look like?" she snapped.

"Well," he taunted, "Terence has been staying here, hasn't he? I just wondered if—"

"Go on wondering." She glowered at him. "I don't care what you think! I—oh, damn!" She thrust her finger into her mouth and with her other hand, pushed the sewing aside.

He pulled the finger from her lips and inspected it. The needle must have penetrated deeply because the blood spurted out. "Major surgery required," he said, grinning. "Get an ambulance!"

She snatched her finger back and wound her handkerchief around it.

"You *would* make a good nurse," he jeered. "That's hardly a sterile dressing. Have you a box of adhesive strips? Where do you keep them?" She told him. He selected one of a suitable size and pressed it around her finger. "Private medicine. I'll send you my bill."

She thanked him, blunting her gratitude by saying she could easily have done it herself, and resumed her sewing.

"Remember Grenville?" he asked, idly rolling a reel of cotton to and fro across the table.

"Clearly. He was such a nice man."

"He asked about you the other day. He thought you were a 'nice' girl, until I told him you had your boyfriend living with you for a week. You won't be hearing from Grenville again. I left him shaken to the roots."

"Then—" she glared "—you obviously gave him a totally wrong impression."

"Did I?" he murmured skeptically, unwinding a few feet of cotton from the reel and solemnly winding it back again. "I don't think so. Mick and Dulcie have been asking about you, too."

She looked up, anxiously. "You didn't give them the wrong impression, surely?"

"They merely asked how your car was going. I told them very well." He picked up some strands of embroidery silks, but she removed them from his hands and put them out of his reach as if he were an interfering child. He grinned. "Still got the remnants of the schoolmarm in you, haven't you, despite Terence's liberating activities." He looked for something else to fiddle with and picked up a pair of scissors, but she whisked these away from him, too. He laughed out loud.

When she handed him a tape measure to take their place, he unwound it, then rewound it, settling himself more comfortably on the table. "I suppose you've heard the rumors circulating around the village about you and your boyfriend?"

She asked edgily, "What about us?"

"He lived here with you for nine whole days, didn't he? Well, they put two and two together, as I did."

Nicola flushed angrily. "And like you, they didn't get their addition right." He gave a short cynical laugh.

After a thoughtful silence she smiled and said with rebuke in her voice, "Even if I had committed the—to you—unpardonable sin of sleeping with my boyfriend, why are you so narrow-minded about it? Who's being old-fashioned now?"

He stood as if the table had been jerked from under him. "So you admit it's true? It did happen?"

She held her breath at the blunder she had committed, answering in a strained, high voice, "I'm admitting nothing."

"Whether you intended to or not, you've as good as admitted it."

How could she clear herself now? "I tell you, I *haven't* admitted it!"

Her mother called, "Nicola, be a dear and make us a cup of tea."

Nicola thrust aside her sewing and went into the kitchen, still angry at her own unthinking stupidity as much as with him for misinterpreting her words. "The others are in the living room," she said pointedly, but Connor followed her again, taking up a corner position on the kitchen table. He watched her for a while in a preoccupied way.

"How's Velma?" she asked, busy with the kettle and cups.

"Couldn't tell you. I'm making myself, shall we say, inaccessible to her for the moment."

"Playing the elusive male?"

"Exactly. She's been taking too much for granted. I'm trying to get her to ease off."

"By running away? That's hardly advisable, surely? It might well have the opposite effect."

"So speaks the voice of experience! You think if I were to chase her, it would make *her* run away? Very doubtful psychology. Too risky, anyway. I'm selective. I only chase the ones I really want."

She looked up and caught his provocative smile. "And you always get what you want, of course?"

"Invariably," he replied, still smiling. He stood up.

"But I've grown a little tired of the female species. I'm proving—to them and to myself—that I can live without them." He counted the cups on the tray. "Leave me out. I'm off."

He went into the hall, called good-night to the two mothers and left the house. Then Enid and Barbara laughed at some shared joke and their laughter seemed to mock the emptiness that Connor had left behind.

ON THE DAY her mother left for her holiday in Switzerland, Nicola took her to the station. Enid was to meet her sister and brother-in-law in Birmingham and they were continuing their journey together from there.

It was June and the weather was beginning to behave as if it were summer at last. The unseasonal chill had given way to a soft, pleasing warmth.

Customers were coming into the shop with worrying accounts of the illness that was sweeping the village. One by one, they said, relatives and friends were going down with it. The doctor was puzzled as to the cause of the outbreak. He called it a form of food poisoning, and had said he would go to any lengths to discover the source of the trouble.

One morning Joy did not arrive for work. Mrs. Atkins phoned. Joy had been taken ill in the night, she said. "Dr. Mitchell's been. He says there's something going around. Take care you don't get it, dear," she told Nicola, "or you'll have to close the store."

So Nicola was faced with the daunting prospect of running the business alone. By the end of the first day, she wondered how she was going to find the strength to carry on next morning. But she did find it, although by closing time she felt too tired to eat or even to read. When the phone rang, it took all her willpower to stir herself to answer it.

It was Connor, and despite her exhaustion, her pulse leaped at the sound of his voice. Was he checking up on how she was managing as he had promised her mother, especially now Joy was away? She would tell him how tired she felt. He would encourage her, she was sure, and give her advice on how to ease away her fatigue. Whatever he thought of her, he wouldn't refuse to be a friend in need. . . .

"I expect you're busy with your sewing."

"Well, actually, Connor, I'm feeling too—"

"If so, I'm sorry to disturb you, but the matter I want to raise is of vital importance." Nicola tried to gather her scattered wits together because he sounded so serious she knew she must try to listen intelligently.

"You're aware, I believe," he went on, "that there's an illness going around the village. It's not a virus as I first thought. It seems to be some kind of food poisoning. I'm sorry to have to say it, but it's my belief that it's your store that is the source of the outbreak."

Her sagging limbs stiffened at his terseness, and his outrageous accusation. "How could it be?" she snapped. "I told you, we're most careful to keep the premises clean."

"You may think the place is clean, but you can't deny the building's old, your method of display dates back some decades, your way of shielding the food from flies and dust is little short of primitive—"

"You're wrong," she cried, "you're prejudiced. You don't like me, so you're only saying all this because you want to make this store—make *me* a scapegoat. . . ."

"If you'll stop talking in personal terms and become more objective, if you'll drop your emotionalism and look at the problem rationally. . . ." His voice, patient, but holding a warning, quietened her. "I've thought about it exhaustively and I've come to the only possible conclusion—that the source is your store. I've therefore contacted the public health authorities and in the morning a couple of men will be calling on you to collect samples of your goods—especially the food that you display inadequately covered—and take them away for analysis."

"And," she whispered, "if they discover we're the cause, what then?"

"There are two or three things they can do. They can demand a complete inspection of the premises and if they find them below standard, they can insist that the place is cleaned up so that it reaches the required standard. They could insist that the place is modernized, or if the circumstances are bad enough, they could close you down."

"I see." She put a hand to her head. "Then there's nothing I can do except wait, is there? Nothing at all. . . ." Her voice wavered. That this should happen now. She tried to speak to fill the silence, but could find nothing to say.

"Nicola, are you there?" She made a sound to reassure him. "Are you all right?"

No, she wanted to tell him, *I feel terrible. I'm tired to the center of my being, so tired I can hardly hold this phone.* She replaced the receiver, hid her face in her hands and cried until there were no more tears to come.

IN THE NIGHT she was ill, so ill she could hardly crawl back into bed. But then the daylight crept into the room, and daylight came impossibly early, she couldn't sleep any more, nor could she even doze as she had been doing since the early hours. The pain had not left her and she lay exhausted, curled up under the covers, telling herself that somehow she must find the strength to open the store and get behind the counter.

When the men came from the public health department, she was sitting on a high stool, dreading the arrival of the next customer. The men apologized for having to trouble her, told her to stay where she was and they would help themselves. They took samples of all exposed food: cakes, bread, sliced meat. They selected various tins, especially of meat, apologized again for having disturbed her and staggered out under the weight of their booty.

When some time elapsed before another customer came in, she decided to take advantage of the lull and rest in the house.

Five minutes later the store door opened. Nicola pulled herself out of the chair and walked unsteadily through the doorway from the house and found the customer was Connor. He was walking restlessly up and down, as if impatient at the delay. He stared, then walked toward her until only the counter separated them.

"You're ill!"

She clung to the counter for support and said tonelessly, "Can I help you?"

"I had my suspicions last night when I phoned you. Why didn't you tell me?"

"You didn't give me a chance. You'll be glad to know that the public health men have called and they've taken a large selection of goods."

"At this moment, I'm not interested in public health, I'm interested in Nicola Dean's health, which seems to be in a bad way."

"Why should you worry? You're not my doctor."

He ignored the rudeness. "Have you caught this illness that's going around?"

She ran a thumb nail along the scratch marks in the plastic-topped counter. "I think so." Then defiantly, "But I'm carrying on. I've *got* to carry on. And you can't stop me."

"No? I'm going to have a dammed good try. Go into the house at once and sit down." She did not make any attempt to do as he told her, but remained silently opposite him, wishing that he would go away and leave her alone to have a little peace and quiet to recover her strength. He sighed with exasperation and came round the other side of the counter. "Did you hear what I said to you? If you don't go into the house immediately, Nicola, I'll carry you there."

She heard the authority in his voice and, as there were

still no customers, she decided to obey him. In the hall, at the foot of the stairs, Connor said, "On second thoughts, you'd better go to bed and get some sleep."

Although she felt so weak that she could hardly stand, Nicola was still unwilling to tamely accept his advice. How dared Connor presume to order her about as if she was no more than five years old? "I'm *not* going to bed," she told him as firmly as she could in her debilitated state. But he would not let her go past the staircase.

He treated her like a willful infant. "Up you go, Nicola." His voice was patient.

She shook her head, clinging to the bannister post. Then, because she had used up so much energy in arguing with him, her strength gave out and she sank onto the bottom stair. She covered her face with outspread fingers and started to cry. "I'm sorry," she sobbed, "I can't help it. It's the weakness."

A sound of extreme irritation came from him and he lifted her into his arms. As he climbed the stairs her cheek rested against his shoulder and her eyes were closed. With the utmost gentleness he lowered her carefully on to the bed.

She struggled to sit up, determined to defy him to the last, but realizing that she hadn't the strength to make the trip downstairs, she sank back exhausted. Perhaps she would feel better after a little rest.

"Get undressed," he ordered. "You're ill, Nicola, and it's no use trying to deny the fact."

"No, no," she protested, "I'm sure I'll feel better in a few minutes. I just felt rather dizzy. I'll be all right soon. There's absolutely no need for me to go to bed."

"I suppose you think that you know better than a qualified doctor?" he asked her with dangerous calmness. Nicola knew when she was beaten and gave up the struggle to defy Connor. She had no chance of scoring over him, feeling as she did at the moment. She closed her eyes and let her head sink back on the pillow, hoping that he would take the hint and leave her alone.

But Connor did not seem ready to leave and she

opened her eyes again to find him looking down at her with something strangely like anxiety in his expression. He reached for her pulse and Nicola closed her eyes again at the touch of his hand. She wanted to be gathered into his arms and comforted, she wanted the feel of his lips on hers easing away the pain. She wanted his hands to touch hers with the tenderness he had shown when he was helping her just now.

He removed his hand from her pulse and was once more the briskly professional medical man, whose manner she hated so much. "Until you can get help the store will have to be closed." It was impossible to argue on that point and Nicola made no attempt to do so. "I'll ask my mother to come in and look after you until you're on your feet again."

"Oh, but," her eyes sought his, "I couldn't possibly let your mother put herself to so much trouble for me, Connor. I'm sure she's far too busy to be bothered with an invalid on her hands."

"With your mother away, do you think we could let you lie here alone without any help or attention? Of course my mother will come and look after you. She wouldn't dream of leaving you to fend for yourself."

"It's very kind of you," she said weakly. She was feeling much too ill to argue any further with him and was forced to admit that she wasn't likely to be able to look after herself until she could stand unaided without that terrible feeling of weakness attacking her limbs.

"You're a friend of the family. I can hardly do otherwise."

Her heart lurched at the familiar phrase. "Thank you for helping me."

"It's my job," he said tersely. "Will you be all right if I leave you for a while? I must make the necessary arrangements with my mother."

"Don't worry about me," she answered wearily.

He went to the door. "I'll tell Muirson about you. He'll probably call later."

"Dr. Muirson?" She tried to keep the desolation from

her voice. Did he dislike her so much he couldn't bear to have her as his patient even temporarily?

"Yes, Muirson," he sounded surprisingly abrupt, "since you so object to me in the role of your medical advisor."

"But—" she began, but what was the use? "Thanks," she finished. He nodded and left her.

FOR THE NEXT three days, Barbara Mitchell took over the running of the house, sleeping in Nicola's mother's bed and looking after her as if she were her own daughter. She even managed to find two women in the village to take over the shop.

"How has Connor been managing?" Nicola asked on the second day. She was feeling better and had taken a little food.

"Coping well, dear. He's a very self-sufficient man. I didn't consciously bring him up like that, it just happened. He doesn't seem to need people around him as others do. He's a little like his father was in that respect."

"Has he—has he been busy?" Perhaps, Nicola thought, willing her to say yes, that was the reason for his absence.

"This illness in the village has had him out quite a lot, but it's easing off now, and he's had a little more time to himself."

So, Nicola thought miserably, *his work has not been the reason.* Dr. Muirson had called, prescribed some medicine, and had said the illness should clear in a day or two.

Joy came back to work and, with her mother's help, ran the shop. Slowly things returned to normal. Nicola regained her strength and eventually joined Joy behind the counter. Mrs. Mitchell went home to her self-sufficient son, with strict instructions that if Nicola ever needed help again, she mustn't hesitate to ask.

A few days later a letter came from Connor's lawyer

asking Nicola to sign the contract that would make her the tenant of the premises next door. The contract would be renewable yearly, and would be leased at the mutually agreed rental. Overjoyed, she signed the document and sent it back by return. Connor called during the afternoon. Joy served him, then he waited until Nicola was free.

"You received the contract this morning?" he asked, as she took him through to the house.

She glowed with pleasure and told him, "Yes. I can't thank you enough."

He smiled at her enthusiasm, raised a hand and lifted aside a stray curl that had fallen too near her eye. Then he moved away. "I wish you luck with your new venture. Remember, whether it succeeds or not, whether you marry your boyfriend or not, the store is yours for a year. You keep paying the rent until the contract ends. Understand?"

"Oh, dear—" she pretended to be worried "—are you going to be a hardhearted landlord?"

"Absolutely wicked, Miss Dean." He twirled an imaginary moustache. "If you default on the rent, I shall demand reparation in the traditional way. I shall have no mercy on you."

"Knowing you," she said, smiling, "and judging by past experience, I shall expect none."

"Good. At least we know where we stand. When are you taking possession?"

"I'll have to order fittings, shelves, display cases and so on."

"So you're doing the thing properly? What, may I ask, are you using for money? Boyfriend subsidizing you?"

"*No!* My savings."

"So you're sinking everything you've got into it? Is that wise?" Nicola frowned, uncomprehending. "Shouldn't you be consulting the man in your life? One day, presumably, you intend to legalize your relationship with him?"

She answered frigidly, "That, surely, is my concern."

"Not entirely." His voice was as cold as hers. "It's my property you're renting. When you marry, what will happen to the business you'll have so painstakingly built up?"

Her lips tightened. It was a reflex action to stop them from trembling. "I shall meet that problem when, and if, it arises."

"I see." His eyes reflected the ice in his voice. "As I said once before, it's your life, so you can live it—and mess it up—as you please." He went out, slamming the door.

CHAPTER NINE

WHEN the clearance came from the public health authorities, it virtually exonerated the store from blame for the food poisoning outbreak. Nicola felt she had to tell Connor how delighted she was. But when she phoned him, catching him at the end of his morning surgery, his terseness cut off her pleasure.

"The blame," he cautioned, "hasn't been entirely removed from your shop. You've been selling the cold meat that contained the bacteria that caused all the trouble."

"I know, but it was tinned meat. All we did was open the tins and slice the meat. It wasn't our fault—"

"All right," he sighed, "I'm not blaming you, so you can calm down. But I hope you understand that all of that particular brand of meat must now be cleared from the shop and that no more of it must be sold to the public."

"I understand," she answered testily. "Give me credit for some intelligence!" The delight she had felt at having been vindicated from blame had gone still, like ginger ale exposed too long to the air. The bubbles had vanished, the liquid was dead. "I was so pleased when I heard we were cleared." She added, in a pathetic voice, "I thought you would be, too. I should have known better."

He made a noise of exasperation. "Women!" he breathed. "To me, it's all in a day's work. But if it pleases you, I'll have a medal cast and present it to you with due ceremony."

She sighed. Did the two words "Nicola Dean" invariably have to bring out the cynicism in the man? With a slow, heavy movement she replaced the receiver.

A fixture firm came from the town and said they could start on the work in a few days. Nicola spent the intervening time scrubbing the floors of the empty store and washing down the paintwork. Joy offered to help, but Nicola refused, saying she wanted it to be "all her own work." She had noticed how much happier Joy had been looking lately and decided she must at last be getting serious with her boyfriend.

When the fixture fitters moved in, there was nothing for Nicola to do but wait impatiently for the work to be completed. In the evenings she often went to the top of the hill, hoping to see Connor there, but he never came. She remembered the day they had agreed to "share" it, as if it had been theirs to divide and allocate. He had obviously lost interest in the place, otherwise why had he neglected it?

One evening she saw him driving through the village with Velma beside him. The girl friend, it seemed, had been reinstated. He must have recovered from his aversion to women and discovered, probably to his chagrin, that he could not live without them after all.

When the workmen had gone, Nicola stood in the middle of the emptiness and gazed around. It was a dream fulfilled, a place of her own to fill to overflowing with the products of her own two hands.

One Saturday, after tea, Nicola was working on a baby's dress that a devoted grandmother had ordered for a newly-arrived granddaughter, when the doorbell rang.

Mrs. Henderton stood on the step, a cigarette as usual between her lips. She removed it. "So glad you're in, dear. Just a bag of sugar, that's all."

This time, Nicola told herself, I'm standing firm. She smiled and said, "Sorry, Mrs. Henderton, the shop's closed."

"But, dearie, it's Sunday tomorrow and I can't go all Sunday without sugar, can I?" Nicola hardened herself to the woman's wails and shook her head. "If your mother was home," Mrs. Henderton persisted, "she'd give it me, you know she would."

Nicola sighed and let her in, reproaching herself as she did so for giving in so easily. She told the woman to wait in the kitchen and made her way to the shop. She lifted down a box of sugar and returned to the kitchen, thrusting it into Mrs. Henderton's eager hands.

"Pay me on Monday, Mrs. Henderton," Nicola said wearily, "and honestly, I do wish you wouldn't do this. You'll get me into terrible trouble one day."

"Of *course* I won't dear." Mrs. Henderton was purring now she had got her own way. She threw her cigarette aside, regardless of where it would land. It fell, still alight, inside the sink where it sizzled and spluttered and destroyed itself in the drops of water left behind in the dish basin.

Horrified, Nicola watched the careless action, wishing the woman would confine her slovenly, dangerous habits to her own home. Mrs. Henderton bore the sugar away in triumph. Nicola showed her out, wondering whether she really had been short of sugar or any of the other things she had asked for after hours, or whether she made the demands merely to test her strength of will against that of the owner's daughter. So far she, the customer, was winning hands down.

As Nicola picked up her sewing the doorbell rang again. Surely, she thought, it's not another illegal customer? It was Connor, and the sight of him had her heart pounding. He came in.

"You look tired. You're working yourself to the point of exhaustion even before the store opens. I must have been mad to sponsor you in such an idiotic venture."

"There's no need for you to worry about my health. I can look after it myself."

"Unfortunately, it seems you can't. Do you never let up? Come on, you're coming with me to our hill. You need fresh air in your lungs. The shadows around your eyes grow darker each time I see you."

She should have known, Nicola told herself, that he would look at her with the eyes of a doctor. What else had she expected?

They walked through the tranquil village, acknowledging the smiles of passersby. Connor raised his hand in answer to the numerous, "Hello, doctors" while Nicola responded to the "Evening, Miss Deans." The speculative glances they received made her wonder how Connor was taking them, but he did not appear to be in the least affected.

They turned along a narrow lane leading up and away from the main street, and began to climb. The trees cast shadows over the sun-yellowed path and the evening warmth caressed Nicola's bare arms. The slope became steeper and her pounding heart—racing because for the first time ever she was climbing the hill with the man she loved—labored disturbingly, making her fight for breath.

Connor, concerned, looked at her. "What's the matter? Finding it hard going? At your age? You must be out of condition. You haven't any record of heart trouble, surely? I must look up your medical notes. Here, give me your hand." He took it, entwining his fingers with hers.

"It's a pity," she gasped, "you haven't got your stethoscope with you, isn't it? You could examine me here and now, make an instant diagnosis, whisk me off to the hospital and put me in an oxygen tent, or wherever it is you put chronic heart patients."

His grip on her hand increased. "Any more sarcasm from you, young woman, and—" he paused "—you know that fallen tree you're so fond of? I'll put you across it face down and give you the spanking of your life. A heart condition is no laughing matter."

"Connor," she looked up at him earnestly, "I'm really perfectly healthy. I haven't got a heart condition. Except—I mean, unless you . . . ." She had got herself hopelessly involved. How was she going to talk herself out of this one?

"Go on," he said, letting her out more easily than he knew, "unless you regard being in love as a heart condition. All right, so we're back to Terence. You're pining for him, which has a psychological effect on your physical health, and all that rubbish!'' He uttered the last four words with surprising ferocity. "Is he returning the compliment and pining for you?''

In answering such a question she could only prevaricate. "I don't know. I haven't heard from him lately.''

She hoped that would satisfy him, but he said, with cynicism, "That's the trouble with giving a man too much too soon. They lose interest if they get what they want too easily. Will women never learn?''

"Thanks for the lecture on male psychology, but it was misdirected.''

"Just how long are you going to keep up this pretense of unsullied virtue? As a pose, it's wearing a bit thin.''

"There are times,'' she said, trying to free her hand, "when I hate you.''

He stood stock still and pulled her around to face him. "You want me to go?''

"Go?'' she repeated, horrified. "Of course I don't want you to go.''

They walked on. His smile was a cocktail of triumph, malice and mockery. And of satiated male pride. Nicola thought it was time to change the subject. "I'm looking forward to the grand opening of my store.''

"How are you going to manage, staffwise?'' She shrugged. "Haven't you given it a thought?''

"Yes and no. I'm hoping to be able to divide my time between the two.''

"That's crazy. You'll have to employ an assistant.''

"But that would put up the running costs. Anyway, I'm not sharing my store with anyone.''

He said with a touch of indulgence, "You sound like a little girl who's been given a dollhouse for Christmas.'' Then, more sharply, "If you want to monopolize your own business, you will have to employ someone else to help Joy with your mother's.'' She began to shake her head, but he insisted, "There can't be any argument, Nicola. Otherwise, you'll crack under the strain. Ask Mrs. Atkins, Joy's mother. Even if she only worked part-time, it would take a load off your shoulders." He put his arm around her waist as if he thought it would add strength to his argument. "Will you do that?"

She looked up at him. He seemed really concerned—for her health as a patient, of course, nothing else. "I . . . might," she temporized, "I'll think about it."

With that, he said he supposed he would have to be satisfied.

They had reached the summit, and as she breathed, and gazed, and turned her head, Nicola felt herself opening out like petals under the influence of the sun. The view, with this man beside her, was heady stuff and she felt free, elated and liberated from her cares. The scene, as always, drew her eyes by its sheer beauty, her ears by the country sounds that abounded and carried high into the still air. It appealed to her sense of smell, which was assailed by the multitude of summer scents arising from the foliage, the elusive fragrance drifting from the trees, the merest hint of evening mist. The essence of her expanded of its own accord to encompass the width and breadth of the landscape below.

She let her eyes slide sideways to Connor, wondering if he shared her delight. His profile looked composed and at peace. "Medicine, indeed," he murmured. "Therapy in itself. Yet if I wrote this as a prescription, the dispenser would think I'd taken leave of my senses."

He pulled her across the fallen tree and lowered himself to sit with his back against it. He tugged her down beside him, then folded his arms and closed his eyes.

"This," she said playfully, a little upset at being cut off from him like someone pulling the curtains to keep out prying eyes, "is really my territory. Shouldn't you go over there to yours? Don't you remember the pact we made when we first knew each other?"

He paused before answering and a hint of a smile preceded his question, which he asked without opening his eyes, "Do you want me to?"

"No." The answer was spontaneous and unpremeditated and she realized she had given herself away. Why hadn't she paused as he had done?

But he was still. He had about him that profound stillness he could achieve so easily and that Nicola had found herself envying in the past. She looked at him—she could look her fill because his eyes were still closed—and he showed no sign of emotional disturbance. But why should he, even if he had guessed her feelings for him? He was no innocent, of that she was convinced. So many women must have been attracted to him in the past—he was, after all, in his mid-thirties—that yet another would be of no consequence.

She leaned back against the tree and shaded her eyes, looking at the Welsh mountains rising majestically in the far distance. Then her eyes shifted to contemplate the hills nearer home. They wandered over the fields flourishing with the ripe corn and barley that would be ready for harvesting in a few weeks' time. From the hamlets and villages that were splashed at intervals over the landscape there arose, now and then, a thin wisp of smoke, telling of the chill in the air that the elderly felt even at this time of the year. Hillocks, smooth and green, tolerated long-sufferingly their own patches of woods, swarming and straggling in disorder, like a tired army trying in vain to conquer a summit.

More distant and more forbidding were the barren moors, stretching, regardless of borders and the political barriers erected by the minds of men, across into Wales. For a long time she gazed, drinking in the beauty as if she were dying of thirst. The incredible serenity of the man beside her lulled her into a waking dream. They were there, they were together, alone, indivisible by time, people or the events of the rest of the world.

Their personalities, usually so different, seemed on this hill to fit together as perfectly and as satisfactorily as interlocking pieces in a complicated jigsaw. Was it an illusion, brought about by the charm of the surroundings, was it a dream from which any time now there would come a rude awakening? Why couldn't this moment go on forever, stretching into infinity, like space, like time?

Connor stirred and by pure reflex her pulses sprang to life. She whispered, "Have you been asleep?"

He smiled, felt for her hand and held it. "No. I haven't once lost consciousness. I've been basking in the aura of a quiet woman. I sought refreshment in her peacefulness and found it." He turned his head, still smiling. "I've been drinking at the fountain of your silence."

His fingers entwined with hers and her body leaped instantly from its state of calm to a clamoring agitation. A longing to be held in his arms, to hear him say the words of love that she wanted so desperately to hear, to be loved by him, erupted in her brain and—because it was beyond her power to stop it—spilled out of the look she gave him. Nicola had her pride and at one time she would have given anything to prevent Connor from knowing how she felt about him. But suddenly it didn't matter anymore. She was past caring whether he despised her for loving him. It was no use for her to try to hide her state of mind. She didn't even want to.

Their eyes met and now there were no barriers between them. He had only to look at her to realize that. Dusk was falling and around them the night insects were beginning their humming and buzzing, accompanying the birds in an orchestra of sound. Nicola was barely conscious of the noise that they made. Connor was all that mattered to her.

He reached out for her and in his arms was heaven. Her dream had materialized, they were together as only a few minutes ago she had imagined them to be. Gently he caressed her cheek with his lips, then his mouth met hers and his arms tightened around her, drawing her more closely to him. The kiss he was giving her was received and returned, growing and changing into an insistent demand to which she responded warmly.

Then, suddenly, he released her and she felt weak, inert, and flopping like a discarded rag doll. It was self-discipline—or perhaps it was indifference or boredom on his part—that had called the halt. Nicola wondered what she had done to make him release her so abruptly. She thought that she could have done nothing to stop him, because it had simply not been within her power to do so.

He turned away from her. The action—was it rejection—brought her to her senses. What exactly had he been trying to discover when he kissed her? Had he been testing her again—after all, in his opinion, wasn't she deeply involved with Terence—and putting theory to the test? What would he think of her for responding to his advances when she was supposed to be commited to another man? He would despise her as always, she supposed. "I suppose," she said, sitting up and clenching her fists around her knees, "that because I've allegedly been involved with Terence, you thought I'd be easy game for you?"

"You were not exactly unwilling to fall into my arms, were you?" he answered languidly. "I suppose from that angle you could be considered easy game for me."

"And of course my opinion doesn't really matter," she said with fury.

"Of course not." He rolled over on his side and smiled at her in a tantalizing way.

"Go on," she said bitterly, regretting the whole episode now that he was treating her in this fashion, "tell me I made a fool of myself."

"You said it, my dear." He leaned on his elbow and plucked two or three pieces of grass, which he proceeded slowly and deliberately to tear to pieces. Then his eyes flicked up to hers. In the semidarkness it looked as though he was enjoying the conversation. "What are you trying to do, pick a quarrel with me? Pity to spoil the accord between us." His tone was lethargic, like his manner. Had the kiss, the lovemaking, meant nothing to him at all? At the time, Nicola thought, he had seemed as moved as she was, but it was obvious that she had imagined it. She had imagined so much that evening. Her imagination had taken her for a ride, deep into unknown country.

His hand reached up for hers. "Come and sit nearer to me."

Was he about to "test" her again? It was almost dark now and she was beginning to think that it was time she returned home. It was chilly out on the hill at night. She was suddenly afraid of what he was going to say to her.

She shook off his hand and stood up. He got up, too, brushing off the clinging leaves. He sighed. "Ah, well, it was fun while it lasted."

"Fun?" She turned on him. "*Fun?* Is that all it meant to you?"

"Why," he murmured, putting his arm around her waist and pulling her toward him, making it virtually impossible for her to get away, "did it mean more to you than that? With Terence's ring virtually on your finger? You surprise me."

She had no adequate answer. They walked down the hill in silence, the darkness slowing their descent a little.

Connor said, as if he had been turning the subject over in his mind. "I suppose I was a replacement for Terence. That must have been why you kissed me back so passionately. You're missing Terence so much you imagined you were kissing him."

Nicola remembered with a shock how, that evening on the hill when he had woken from his sleep and kissed her, she had accused him of imagining she was Velma. So the wheel had turned full circle. The misunderstanding was complete.

As they reached the main street of the village, Connor broke away, probably, Nicola decided, because he did not want to mislead the villagers as to their relationship.

He stood on the pavement outside the door and looked down at her in the dusk. "Next weekend," he said, "there's a dance at the hospital. Would you like to come with me?"

Her heart bumped. "You're asking *me* to go with you?"

He frowned. "Yes. Why not?"

"It's just . . . ." Was it dark enough to hide her excitement? "Yes, please, Connor, I'd love to. Is—is Velma going to be there?"

"No. She couldn't get away. She's on duty."

"Oh." Nicola thought, *now I know why you've invited me—as a substitute for Velma.* But she said levelly, "I'll look forward to it."

"Good. So shall I." He walked off with a brief wave.

Nicola let herself into the house. He would look forward to it, he'd said. He hadn't meant it, of course, but it was such a pleasant thought she fooled herself that he had.

NICOLA was so excited at the prospect of going to the dance with Connor, the knowledge that she was second-best in his choice of partner made little difference to her happiness on the day of the dance.

The hours had dragged and she thought the evening would never come. But come it did, and after a bath and a light meal—as her excitement had grown, so in proportion had her appetite lessened—she took her dress from the wardrobe and spread it out across the bed.

It was a glittering silver blue, simple in design but cut to enchance the wearer's shapeliness. She had bought shoes and a handbag to match. She looked at herself and knew with a spurt of pleasure that, second choice though she might be, in that dress she would not let Connor down in front of his friends and colleagues.

It was too early to put on her makeup, but she did so, nevertheless. She combed her hair so that the curls, those curls she despaired of and that escaped so often from control, framed her face.

The doorbell rang. Nicola was puzzled. It was much too soon for Connor to be calling for her. Mrs. Henderton, she thought, that's who it is, asking another of her maddening favors. Now of all times, for her to come! She shifted the long skirt so that she would not trip over it and ran down the stairs.

She pulled the door open angrily and said, "I'm sorry, Mrs. Henderton, but the answer's no, absolutely n—" She gasped *"Terence!"*

He was standing on the doorstep, suitcase in hand, an uncertain, questioning smile on his face. Terence, to arrive now, when in half an hour's time Connor would be calling! He hadn't, surely, come to stay? But of course he had. There was his suitcase, there was the expectation of welcome in his eyes.

"Come in, Terence," Nicola said, her smile as feeble as her tone. He stepped into the hall and she closed the door. He gazed at her, opening his mouth to speak, but nothing came out. Nicola supposed that to him, who had never seen her in anything but everyday clothes, she looked as though she was dressed for a part, and in a way she was—the part of Connor's second-best girl friend.

But how, she asked herself distractedly, could she go to the dance now? The excitement had been roaring in her ears all day like a fire out of control, but Terence, standing there travel-weary, waiting for her to make a speech of welcome, acted on the excitement like a fireman's hose, deadening the flames until at last they were out, right out.

In the end it was Terence who broke the silence. "Sorry to turn up unannounced, Nicola, but I was offered a lift again, so I had no time to warn you. I— wanted to see you again." He looked at her from top to toe. *Well, he's seeing me again,* her mind shrieked hysterically. *Can't he go back now?* "It didn't occur to me you might be going out."

"Going out?" She knew she sounded dazed, but there had to be an answer somewhere. What should she do with Terence? It was unthinkable to leave him alone all the evening when he had come so far for her sake. She could not understand why, after their rather cool parting last time, he had decided to resume the friendship. He had an odd way of showing his affection, she reflected distractedly. She had not heard a word from him since their last meeting.

"Going out?" she repeated. "Well, I was. I was going to a dance, but it doesn't matter. I'll tell Connor I can't come—"

Terence broke in. "Good heavens, you mustn't let the man down at such short notice. Isn't Connor, er, Dr. Mitchell?"

She nodded. "He was hard up for a partner, so he invited me to the hospital dance."

"Then go, Nicola. Don't worry about me." He seemed oddly eager to be left alone, she thought. For a man who had come such a long way only to find the girl he had traveled across England to see was going out with another man, he was being surprisingly accommodating. But, she told herself, knowing Terence as she did, she shouldn't have been surprised. He was not easily thrown off balance. He would, she knew, be perfectly happy watching television or reading until she returned.

She looked at her watch and, panicking, saw that in only twenty minutes Connor would be calling for her. And if he arrived early. . . . Come what may, she had to be ready, ready to run out to the car. And come what may, he must not come into the house and find Terence there again. She had to keep that particular person's presence a secret as long as possible. She could not stand Connor's scorn and contempt for the second time around.

A bed, she thought, she must make up a bed. "That is, if you're going to stay here?"

There was an odd pleading in his eyes. "Well, if you wouldn't mind. . . ."

Of *course* she didn't mind, she told him, forcing a smile. He looked so pathetically pleased, her annoyance at his bland assumption that he would be welcome at no matter what time he put himself on the doorstep receded, and she began to feel just a little sorry for him.

"If you'll excuse me?" she asked, one foot on the stairs. "You can have the spare room again."

"Don't worry about a meal," he called. "I had a bite on the way."

Thank goodness for that, she thought, as she whisked sheets from a drawer, unfolded blankets and found pillows. The bed was made in record time. Two minutes to run the comb through her hair again, another to put on her coat and as soon as Connor's horn sounded outside, she would be ready.

Downstairs, she asked Terence, "What will you do all the evening? I might be back late."

"Oh," he looked vague, "I might go for a walk." Another of his walks? She remembered his last evening there. He had gone for a walk then. Perhaps he was becoming attached to the place, if not to her!

"If you do," she said, "you'll find my mother's front door key in the kitchen drawer. Take it with you so that you can let yourself in again."

"Thanks," he answered, as though he meant it.

Connor's horn sounded, and her heart started up like a racing car revving before the getaway. She called, "Sorry, Terence, to have to leave you," lifted her skirt clear of the ground and, feeling like Cinderella as the clock struck midnight, ran out to the waiting car. She threw herself into the passenger seat and, gasping for breath, turned wide-open anxious eyes to Connor's.

He laughed. "Why so worried? It is a collection of medical men you're going to socialize with, not a gang of criminals."

She forced a smile and to her infinite relief, he drove on. Her secret was safe—for the moment. When they returned, it would be dark and with luck, it would be so late Terence would have gone to bed.

It was an evening to remember. Dulcie and Mick Styles were there and Grenville and his fiancée. Soon after Nicola and Connor arrived, Grenville came toward them. He introduced his partner as Moira and held her hand out to Connor as though he were presenting him with a trophy. "One dance, Connor? A fair swap?"

Connor took Moira's hand—she was a pretty blonde—but he made a great pretense of unwillingness at being parted from Nicola.

"Anyone would think," she said to Grenville as he led her to the floor, "that Connor meant it. But I'm only here because Velma's on duty."

"You are?" said Grenville close to her ear. "You could have fooled me!" She did not ask him to explain that cryptic statement. "You know," he murmured, "I don't believe a word Connor told me about you."

Her heart sank. "He's said some bad things?"

"They weren't very complimentary. I said you were a nice girl. He said you weren't. And told me why."

Connor passed them with Moira. Instead of smiling at him, Nicola turned her head away. As she did so, she caught the beginnings of a frown on his face.

"I can guess what he told you," she said. "He was wrong."

"I knew it!" said Grenville.

"Thank you for believing me," said Nicola. In response he held her closer.

Grenville reclaimed his fiancée and left Nicola beside Connor, who put a drink into her hand. "What's gotten into you?"

She did not answer; instead she stared into her glass.

"It must be pretty bad if it's deprived you of the powers of speech." She looked at him and he commented, "You're upset. Why?"

She told him and added, "How could you?"

Now Connor studied his drink. "Pity he had to bring up the past. For myself, I've forgiven and forgotten long ago."

She blazed, "*Forgiven?* For what? For something that only happened in your own rancid imagination?"

"Nicola!" Dulcie came across the room and Mick was close behind. "Lovely to see you."

"So you got the girl of your choice?" Mick said cheerfully to Connor. To Nicola, "He told me he was inviting you."

"Second choice," she answered, flashing a misleadingly sweet smile at Connor, "not first. His girl friend is on duty."

"When I want you to answer for me," Connor said crushingly, "I shall give you due notice. Until then, I'm perfectly capable of speaking for myself."

"They're quarreling," Dulcie said delightedly, "like an old married couple." Then, seeing Connor's venomous expression, she hastily changed the subject. "How's the store going, Nicola? Connor told us about it. Is it open to the public yet?"

"I throw the doors wide on Monday and hope the hordes will come trooping in!"

"They will," Dulcie assured her. "Anything hand-made or homemade draws the multitude like gold dust these days."

"What I should like to know," said Connor, the coolness of his tone showing that he was still annoyed, "is once the demand begins, how she's going to keep up with the supply. I assume," he turned to her, "you won't be stupid enough to think you can cope single-handed."

"You mean employ someone to *make* the things for me?" she asked, aghast. "But of course not. That would defeat the whole object. It wouldn't be my own work, would it?"

"So you're going to set up a kind of one-woman factory?" Mick asked. "That's all very well, but what happens if you get swamped with orders?"

Nicola shrugged. "I'll just have to cope, won't I?"

"You've got it coming," Mick remarked.

"She's got a lot coming to her," Conor said with asperity, "if she's fool enough to think she can manage alone—a breakdown in health, for one thing."

"You're too pessimistic for words," she answered. "My health is excellent, thank you."

The music began again and Connor said, taking her glass and putting it aside, "For heaven's sake stop talking and let's dance."

Mick laughed and called after them, "You're on the right lines, Connor. Take a tip from a married man. Caveman tactics win every time!"

The music was romantic, the lights were turned low, colored beams played over the dancers. One or two couples in the shadows were kissing.

"Nicola?" She looked up at Connor, seeing his features glow in the multicolored semidarkness. It was primitive and it was exciting. She felt the hardness of his body pressed to her own, felt the pressure of his arms increase, and the magic came back to the evening. With it came the longing she had felt when they had kissed so passionately on the hill.

That evening it was the longing that had betrayed her, this time she had to hide it at all costs. She pried her eyes from his, but she had left it just too late. He must have read the message there. He whispered her name again and as her head came up, his lips came down. The kiss was short, intense and curiously possessive. Her heart thundered, creating waves of sound in her ears that blotted out the music.

In the moment in which their lips had met, the colored lights had played on them. Now the other dancers were looking at them with a deeper interest. But, oddly, Connor did not seem to mind. Why should he, she thought miserably, when to him, a kiss meant nothing, cost nothing? His words.

There was a buffet supper. Nicola was introduced to so many people she scarcely took in their faces, let alone their names. There were consultants and their wives, young doctors and their girl friends, general practitioners who, like Connor, had some association with the hospital, either in the past or the present, nurses and yet more nurses.

Connor seemed to be known to them all, and it was clear he was popular. Now and then someone drew him aside briefly to talk shop, but even so he kept hold of Nicola's hand. The sense that she was existing in some no-man's-land, in a kind of prolonged and unbelievable dream, persisted the whole evening. Even when the dance was over at well beyond midnight—if she really had been Cinderella, she thought, she would have been in trouble—the feeling of unreality persisted.

Connor pulled her behind him and into the car.

The dance was over. In the darkness of the early hours, the dream began to fade. Tomorrow—no, today—Connor would go back to Velma, just as, at that moment, she, Nicola, was going back to Terence. Terence, the submarine lurking under her calm sea, unseen, unheard, but liable at any moment to torpedo her happiness and blow it sky-high.

What was she going to do about Terence? All the evening she had thrust the thought of him to the back of her mind. He was something unpleasant to be dealt with in the unrelenting light of day. There was so little time left with Connor. He would not hear of Terence's presence until the village grapevine started functioning, but when it did, the news would make the local gossips' headlines.

She rested her head against the seat and closed her eyes. Connor's hand covered hers. "Tired?" His tone could have been interpreted as any one of three things—paternal, medical or intimate. She knew which of the three interpretations she preferred.

But she had to tell him the truth. She couldn't say, "I'm worried to death about what you'll think of me when you know Terence has come back to stay with me."

"Yes," she agreed, "very tired. But," she had to add the words, because she knew it might well be the last time she could convey to him how she felt, with any hope of his believing her, "very happy."

As they turned the corner into the village street, Nicola put a hand to her mouth. It couldn't be true! There were lights on all over the house. Terence was not only still up, he was telling the whole world of his wakefulness.

"Why," came Connor's deep-frozen voice, "the lights of welcome? Is your mother home?" He knew very well that Enid Dean was enjoying life to the full in

her daughter's house in Geneva, so the question was re-
dundant. There was no need to tell him—he knew the
answer already.

Oh, Terence, Nicola thought, near to tears, *you might
have left me my dreams just for tonight. Did you have to
destroy my happiness so quickly, so cruelly, before I had
had time to hide my memories deep in the ground, like a
squirrel storing nuts—memories to take out and feed on
in the coldness of the winter to come?*

CHAPTER TEN

"Is your mother home?" The question, repeated in a hard biting tone, had to be answered.

"No," she answered, so quietly the word was barely audible. "This evening Terence came to stay."

It took a long time for Connor to respond. He sat as still as if his whole body had suddenly been affected by frostbite. The words, when he spoke, turned into icicles as they came from his lips. "And you didn't tell me?"

"No, I didn't tell you." She could not bring herself to look at him. Instead, she gazed at the house as ablaze with lights as if each room were on fire. "I didn't want you to know. I knew you'd think, as you thought before, that I was indulging in a clandestine affair."

"*Clandestine?*" My God, what's clandestine about it? You might as well go around with a loudspeaker announcing it to the whole damned village!"

"I know you won't believe me," she said dully, "but there's nothing to announce."

He made a violent movement with his hand. "Don't go on playing the hypocrite with me. I'm sick to death of your deceit, your sanctimonious pretense. If you were to admit honestly that he was your lover, I might have a little more respect for you." He stared at her in the darkness as if he were remembering something. "No wonder you were so agitated when you ran out to join me! And I, fool that I was, thought I might have been the attraction!" He paused and asked, icily, "Why did you bother to come? You didn't have to leave the man. I could have found another partner. To me one woman is much the same as any other. They all serve the same purpose." If he had knocked her to the ground he could not have hurt her more.

He raised his eyes and said cuttingly, "He's in the right place, awaiting your return."

With immense weariness she followed his eyes. Terence was at an upstairs window, gazing out, looking for the car that he must have heard coming along the main street. He saw them and drew the curtains across. Nicola knew, and Connor knew, that Terence was in her bedroom.

He turned on her. "And you had the audacity this evening to accuse me of having a 'rancid' imagination! I began to think that maybe I'd been wrong about you, that I'd grossly misjudged you. I had even started to like you." She winced at the lukewarm word. "I must have been mad!"

She said bitterly, "I suppose you're regretting now that you saved me that day on the level crossing, only to watch me degenerate into living a life of unbounded iniquity and sin."

He leaned across and opened the door. It was an act of dismissal. He sat, looking straight ahead into the darkness beyond the windshield, waiting for her to go.

"Good night, Connor," she whispered, "thank you for this evening."

He made no response. It seemed he had nothing to say to her anymore.

THE SUPERMARKET representative telephoned next morning. "Just checking," Mr. Goodman said, "to find out if the position is the same. Or have you changed your mind?"

"Sorry," said Nicola, "no change. My mother and I are more determined than ever to stay on now. You see—" it slipped out, her pride was to blame "—I'm renting the store adjoining the grocery store now, for my own purposes, handmade goods, drapery. . . ."

He was on to the information she had given him free

before she could tell herself what a fool she had been. "You're *renting* it, did you say? Presumably—" half to himself "—on a contract that will at some time expire. May I inquire who the owner is?"

If she didn't tell him, she thought, someone else would. "It's Dr. Mitchell, the local GP."

"Ah, yes, I've heard of him. Thanks for telling me, Miss Dean." He hung up.

What was the man up to, she wondered. Now she was afraid. Would he try to talk Connor around to canceling her tenancy? It wouldn't be difficult, she thought pessimistically, considering the state of siege that existed between them again. Wouldn't Connor do anything to get even with her, to show his contempt for her in material terms? He might even insult her by offering money to buy her out and end the contract prematurely. The thought depressed her beyond words.

Terence helped in the shop all day. He seemed to get on well with Joy and Nicola left them to it while she put the finishing touches to her own shop. Come what may, she was determined that Nicola's would open on Monday. It occurred to her that Terence's week's holiday would prove useful. His help in the grocery section would tide her over the first few days of Nicola's existence. She would be able to spend all her time there, instead of having to divide it between the two shops.

Terence seemed touchingly eager to please, to tackle household jobs, to help in every way Nicola's preparations for the opening of the shop. On Sunday they took an hour off and, as Terence seemed to have taken to walking as a pastime, they went for a walk. Not to Nicola's hill— she avoided that as though it were as unsafe as disputed enemy territory. They wandered instead through the oldest part of the village.

But far from being satisfied, on their return Terence seemed more restless than ever. He kept wandering to the window and staring out of it, like a prisoner committed to spending the rest of his life in solitary confinement.

That night Nicola slept badly, but since the dance that was nothing new. In the stillness of the small hours, the extra responsibilities she was taking on seemed formidable. The seeds of doubt Connor had sown about her ability to cope without employing an assistant had not only taken root, they were threatening to overgrow the garden. He was right, of course, she would have to ask Mrs. Atkins to work part-time, at least until she had things sorted out.

Terence insisted on helping in the shop again on Monday morning, and, he announced, would continue to do so for the rest of his stay. Somehow, he said, he would have to repay her for her kindness in having him. *Kindness?* she thought. *If we're supposed to be in love, there should be no "kindness" about it.*" She was still puzzled as to why he had come.

Nicola asked Joy if she thought her mother would be willing to assist in the grocery shop for a month or two and Joy promised to ask her. Mrs. Atkins agreed and sent a message saying that "if Miss Dean would give her two or three days to get her domestic affairs in order, she would come to work for her with pleasure."

Business was slow at first and Nicola was able to spend more time than she had anticipated with Joy and Terence, but they worked together so efficiently, she felt unnecessary.

The doorbell of Nicola's sounded and Nicola ran into the shop to serve the customer. The woman was the first of many. The news seemed to be circulating fast that Nicola's was open at last. Favorite items proved to be the homemade cakes and biscuits, but jams and preserves were not far behind.

By the end of the day all the perishable goods had been sold, and Nicola realized that she would have to spend the evening making fresh supplies. The children's clothes had sold well—too well, she told herself ruefully, seeing evenings of work ahead trying to keep up with the demand.

That evening the house was filled with the smell of cooking. She told Terence firmly that there was nothing he could do to help, except perhaps later with the washing up.

"You could go for a walk," she suggested. "It's a fine evening."

He agreed eagerly and was out for some time. Nicola did not like to ask him where he had been, and he did not enlighten her.

Next day the number of customers patronizing Nicola's had doubled, and the cakes and biscuits were sold out by lunchtime. Nicola panicked. If this went on she would have to spend every evening from now until eternity cooking and making jam. The idea was frightening. She had started an avalanche and it was engulfing her. How Connor would have laughed if she had been able to tell him . . . not with humor but with an "I told you so" triumph.

The last customer of the day was a woman Nicola recognized as being Barbara Mitchell's daily help. Her name was Mrs. Wilkes. She was pleasant but a chatterbox, and she talked for some time after she had bought her cakes. Nicola drew a bolt across the shop door as she listened, and turned the Open notice to Closed.

"Heard the rumor, dear?" she was saying. Nicola shook her head. Another rumor? What now? It made her wonder what kind of rumors were circulating about Terence and herself.

"Well, you know the doctor owns some land in the village?"

Nicola swung around. "Dr. Mitchell? No, I didn't know."

"It's the bit next to Varley's farm. Largish piece. Well, a man called on him this morning after the doctor came back from his office in the town. I heard them talking. Keep it to yourself, dear, but the man was asking if the doctor would agree to sell that piece of land to his firm. Something about a—"

Nicola paled. "Not a *supermarket*?"

"That's it, dear." Mrs. Wilkes looked disappointed at having been deprived of imparting the news. "How did you know?"

Nicola told her, adding, "They must have done some research on the village and discovered that the man who owns this shop also owns some land."

"Well—" Mrs. Wilkes went to the door and waited for Nicola to let her out "—if the doctor does take it into his head to sell to them, it wouldn't do your business any good, would it, dear? What a problem for your poor mother, and her so far away and enjoying herself—isn't she—on holiday."

Mrs. Wilkes went out and Nicola bolted the door again, leaning against it and wondering what to do. Yet another worry to add to all the others! As she did the cash, weary and depressed, she supposed she would have to see Connor and plead with him once more, if only for her mother's sake, not to sell to the supermarket people. But she had to admit that there was nothing they could do about it if he had made up his mind.

He would have no compunction in depriving them of their livelihood now: now that he thought so badly of her, now that his belief in her "immoral and hypocritical" conduct had, in his eyes, been confirmed by Terence's reappearance.

Immediately after tea she began her nightly baking session. Terence went for his usual evening walk. The fact that it was drizzling with rain had not deterred him. On a sudden impulse, Nicola went into the hall and dialed the Mitchells' number. She knew that if she did not take the plunge and immerse herself all over at once in the cold, cold sea, she would lose her courage altogether.

As she stood waiting for the call to be answered she closed her eyes and concentrated her thoughts on the cakes she intended to make. Anything to keep her mind off the man she was trying to contact. To her relief, his mother answered. "Anything wrong, dear?"

"No, I'm quite all right. It's just that . . . I wondered if Connor could spare me a few minutes one evening."

"I'm sure he will, Nicola. I'll get him to come and speak to you." She must have held the receiver away from her, thinking that in doing so Nicola would not hear her speaking to her son. "It's Nicola, Connor. She wants a word with you." There was a pause, then, "But why won't you speak to her? Have you two quarreled or something? She wants to see you one evening."

An explosive string of words came from the distance, each one a rifle shot seeking to down a hapless bird. "For God's sake, *what does the blasted girl want now*?"

"*Son!*" Mrs. Mitchell's high-pitched miniscule voice crept out of the receiver. "Don't talk about Nicola like that. I won't have it!"

Nicola bit her lip.

Mrs. Mitchell said, "He's—he's busy, dear. Sorry he can't come to the phone. He says tomorrow at eight o'clock. Is that all right?"

Nicola said it was fine and thanked her for her trouble. She returned to her baking, working mechanically, putting no thought into the cakes and their decoration or fillings. Her hand felt as heavy as her heart and if the customers were not so well pleased with her products next day she would just have to apologize and explain that with handmade goods, you couldn't expect perfection every time.

Next day was early closing and before Joy went home she told Nicola that her mother would be starting work first thing next morning. Nicola sighed with relief at the thought of getting that extra help at last. She spent the afternoon baking again, and added jam making to her list. Afterward, she got down to some sewing, spending the waiting time between the evening meal and her visit to Connor cutting out a baby's dress for a customer.

Terence passed the time reading, drying dishes for Nicola and generally mooning around the house and gazing out of the window. She wondered what was wrong with him, if he were ill, perhaps.

When she left the house on her way to the Mitchells', Terence left with her.

"Off for my walk," he explained, his tone almost apologetic.

"That's all right," Nicola answered airily. "You've got mother's key in case you're back before I am?"

He nodded and went off whistling. She shook her head, completely mystified. As she approached the Mitchells' house, she wished she felt as jaunty as Terence obviously did. With a tremor she could hardly control, she lifted her hand to knock at the heavy wooden front door.

Barbara Mitchell opened it. "Why, Nicola," she said, "it seems so long since I've seen you!" They embraced and Barbara kissed Nicola's cheek. "How's your mother? Have you heard from her lately?"

"She writes every week," Nicola told her. "She said in her last letter that they would probably be home within the month."

"I expect you'll be so glad to see her again."

Connor hovered and his mother said, "She won't be very pleased with you. You look so pale, dear. In fact, you look quite ill. Are you sure you're all right?"

Nicola avoided Connor's eyes. "Yes, thanks. I'm busy with the two shops."

"Overdoing things, of course." The words came from the man of the house and there was not a grain of sympathy in them.

"*Are* you, Nicola?" His mother made up for his lack of feeling. "I wondered if you were taking on too much with the new store of yours."

Nicola sidestepped a little by saying, "People seem to like my produce. I sell out every day, so every evening I have to replenish my stocks. I make more cakes and biscuits—"

"Every evening, dear? Don't you ever relax?"

"I can't, Mrs. Mitchell. Customers would grumbl next day if they didn't get their supply of homemad cakes."

"No wonder you look like death," said Connor cal lously. "I warned you. But it's in character."

That was too much. Her temper, already frayed b worry and fatigue, became threadbare. She tore the re mains into shreds and threw them at him. "You know nothing about my character. You think you're so clever but you don't even know the first thing about me. If yo did, you'd have the sense not to think—to think . . . ."

His mother's presence placed an embargo on what sh had been about to say, but Connor narrowed his eyes an said nastily, "I beg your pardon?"

Whether it was a question, a request for elucidation, o a reprimand for her rudeness, Nicola could not decide But as a preliminary to the plea she was going to make the appeal to his better nature, it was clearly not a goo start.

"Connor, she's tired. You must make allowances. It' not like Nicola to get angry." Her son gave a short, sa castic laugh. "Take her into the living room, Connor—"

"I'll see her in my study, mother." His voice, quiet firm, made his mother look at him curiously. He said t Nicola, "Come this way, please." She might have been stranger making a business call. Well, this was a busines call, wasn't it? *But*, her heart cried out, *I'm not . stranger!*

He closed the door, slipped his hands into his jacke pockets and said, "Well?" He looked her over coldly and her gaze flickered away from his and roamed aroun the small, neat room he had referred to as his study There were laden bookshelves, a desk with a blotter an telephone, a medical bag lying open as if he had been ir specting it and perhaps replenishing its contents. Th carpet was deep, tufted and green; there was a sink an towel, scales, an examination couch partly hidden b curtains along one wall.

This was probably where he brought his private patients, if he had any private patients. Her eyes came up against his and she realized with a shock that despite the kindness he had shown her, his financial help and his generosity and in spite of the fact that she owed her life to him, there was so much about him she did not know.

Perhaps he saw her lost look, and in that respect only he took pity on her. "You'd better sit down. You seem fit to drop. You'd better see Muirson for a check up."

She shook her head resolutely but accepted his offer of a seat, taking what she assumed to be the patients' chair. He stood where he was, looking down on her, a position she guessed he would maintain because it would make her feel at a disadvantage.

"I'm sorry to break into your evening," she faltered, "but I—heard a rumor—"

He gave a sharp, cynical laugh and leaned back against the door, crossing one leg nonchalantly over the other. "It's getting monotonous."

"I'm sorry you're taking that attitude," she flared, "but although what I've heard may be amusing to you, to me—and to my mother—it's deadly serious."

"Oh? And what have you heard?"

"I was told that you own a piece of land next to Varley's farm."

"I do."

"I was told that you—that you've been approached by the supermarket representative and asked to sell that land to his firm."

"And who gave you that information?"

She looked down at her clasped hands. "I'm sorry, I can't tell you."

"Very loyal of you, but I can guess."

Her eyes sought his. "So it's true?"

"Yes—" he straightened himself lazily, but his hands did not leave his pockets "—it's true. I have been approached."

"Well?" she held her breath, waiting for him to continue, but had to watch him walk silently to the window and gaze out at the dull, fading July evening.

"And," she could hardly stand the suspense and spoke to his back, "what have you decided?"

"That is entirely my business," was his implacable reply. His cool, even tones put her in her place more effectively than if the words had been spoken in anger.

But her anger was aroused. "Excuse me, but it is *not* only your business."

He turned slowly and leaned back against the window-sill, regarding her with raised eyebrows. "Is it not?"

"No!" She did not care now if she was being rude. She was fighting for her—and her mother's—interests. "If you sell the land and it's developed as a supermarket, you know very well it would put my mother and me out of business. We couldn't possibly stand up to the severe competition of such an establishment with all the financial advantages they would have over us."

He stayed maddeningly silent.

"And if you were to sell the land to them," Nicola plowed on, "my mother and I would be far worse off than if we had sold our business to them. We wouldn't receive any recompense, any financial compensation at all."

"In other words, your mother would have nothing to retire on?"

"Nothing, absolutely nothing," she declared emphatically. Then she played back in her mind the question he had asked. It was a reasonable question. She sought his eyes. Was he at last seeing reason? She received her answer straight away, and it was plainly in the negative. It was also cynical and callous.

"That's too bad." He walked away from the window and settled himself on a corner of the desk. Nicola had the feeling that he was enjoying himself, taking pleasure in baiting her, in making her struggle and flounder like a fish on a line.

As if she actually had a fisherman's hook through her

body, she pressed her arms together across her middle. She had to do something to keep back the tears. "Have you lost *all* feeling, all compassion, even for my mother? Have I got to write and tell her, even while she's recuperating on holiday, that the business is doomed, that there's nothing for her to come home to but bankruptcy and ruin?"

He said softly, goadingly, "You're getting very melodramatic. Aren't you overdoing the pathos a little?"

She jumped from the chair. Now the tears broke through. "If you aren't the most unspeakable—"

He strolled across to her, put his hands on her shoulders and pushed her down again. "If you'll listen for a few moments, instead of filling the air with bloodcurdling, heartrending oratory . . . ."

Nicola subsided into the chair, but flung at him, "And I wish you'd stop being so damned cynical!"

It was greeted with raised eyebrows but no comment. At last he found his way to his seat behind the desk. "Now." He paused, frowned and picked up a pen that was lying beside the blotter, and started laboriously to fill in the outline of a doodle he had made at some other time. "For your mother's sake," he flicked his eyes up to hers and down again, "and only for her sake, I'll tell you the true position. I have been approached yet again by the firm in question, this time with a view to purchasing my land."

He paused, as if intent on tantalizing her. He started on another doodle. "I told them I was not interested in their offer—" he stopped again, presumably to give her time to relax, which she did, visibly, "—and I also told them that I had plans of my own for that piece of land. I did not divulge those plans to them." He looked at her fully. "I will to you. I intend having a house of my own built there in the not too distant future. My mother will, of course, continue to live here."

She had to ask, although she dreaded the answer, "You're—you're getting married?"

He did not reply to the question directly. "I certainly
don't intend to live there alone. The house will be built
with a wife and family in mind."

"Of course," she breathed, "Velma. . . ."

He did not deny the implication contained in the unfinished sentence.

Nicola stood up. She had got the assurance she had
been seeking, even if her heart was slowly eroding under
her ribs. He was getting married. . . .

But he had something more to say. "That picture you
gave me."

"My—my embroidery?"

"Yes. I saw no point in keeping it. I told my mother I
would be returning it to you. She said she wouldn't allow
me to insult you in such a way, so I gave it to her instead."

Nicola gripped the chair back as if without its support
she would fall to the ground. "Just how *brutal* can you
get?"

"I warned you once."

"Yes. And demonstrated. I had an example some time
back of your physical brutality—one I won't easily
forget. But this—this is, if anything, worse. It's *mental*
brutality. It's gross insult brought to a fine art. And all
because of a false supposition on your part."

"Prove my supposition is false."

"You know I can't."

"Which leaves you free, doesn't it, to protest as much
as you like. It doesn't follow that I'll believe you."

"Would you like me any better," she challenged, "if I
told you, 'Yes, I let my boyfriend sleep with me every
night'?"

His expression became savage. "Thanks for telling
me the truth. At last."

"The *truth*? It's not the truth!" But she could see she
had made no impression. "Once you didn't agree when I
said you were kind. How right you were." She ran to the

door. "You're cruel, you're hard, you're cold to the very core. You're not fit to be a doctor!"

His eyes gleamed and caught fire, but she was into the hall and out of the house before he could lay hands on her.

CHAPTER ELEVEN

FIRST THING next morning, Mrs. Atkins arrived. Joy was with her. They put on their overalls and tidied the shelves. Someone came into the shop from the house.

Nicola's back was turned and she heard Mrs. Atkins say, "Hello, Terence."

Nicola swung around and stared, first at Mrs. Atkins, then at Terence. He was blushing from top to toe. Joy exclaimed, aghast, "Mother!"

"I didn't know," said Nicola, feeling cold in the pit of her stomach, "that you two had met."

Mrs. Atkins stammered, "Oh, oh dear! I've gone and said it now. I've let it out." To Joy, "Sorry, dear." To Nicola, "Sorry, Miss Dean." Back to Joy, "Hadn't you better tell Miss Dean the truth? I said all along it wasn't fair the way you two have been going on under her very nose." To Terence, "And you living under her roof, Terence, and accepting her hospitality. Come on, one of you must tell her what's happened between you two."

NICOLA AND TERENCE were lingering over their coffee after the evening meal. Terence was saying, as if the mere action of talking about it gave him pleasure, "The first time I came to stay here, when I was attending that course, Joy and I fell in love."

Nicola nodded. She knew the story now, but she let him talk. It was better than sitting silent, while he occupied himself with thoughts of his loved one.

"I know I've said it before, but I'm really sorry, Nicola. I wouldn't have let it happen if there had been anything lasting between us two, but it was probably as obvious to you as it was to me that there was something missing.''

"Don't *worry* about it, Terence," she assured him for the twentieth time. I'm glad for both your sakes. I truly am.''

"We wrote to each other a lot," he went on, as if Nicola had not spoken. He was in no mood to listen to anything but his own voice talking about his beloved. "I should have been honest with you from the start, but I didn't see how I could stay under your roof and yet tell you all I wanted to do was make love to another girl!''

Nicola laughed, but was thinking, "There's a pub in the village where you could have stayed." She was silent, though, because she did not want him to think she was reprimanding him.

Neither could she tell him, "Your coming here for the second time has wrecked my future happiness. By acting so selfishly, you've driven the man I love away from me forever.''

"Is it all right," he asked, "if I stay till Sunday?''

"Perfectly," she told him yet again. She looked at her watch, asking with a smile, "Isn't it time you went for your 'evening walk'?''

He had the grace to blush and pushed back his chair as if he could hardly wait to get to his ladylove's side. Nicola spent a lonely, sad and work-filled evening, brooding rather pointlessly over what might have happened between Connor and herself if Terence had been honest from the start and had not tried to keep his love affair with Joy a secret.

On Sunday afternoon Nicola took Terence and Joy to the town. They planned to have a meal together before Terence caught the train. They had told her they were unofficially engaged and did not want to wait too long before getting married. They hated being so far apart.

She left them and drove home, feeling an unbounded envy for their happiness. She hoped it would all work out for them. Joy was young, but she was sensible and seemed mature enough to know what she was about. Already she had brought Terence out of his shell. He had changed radically from the diffident young man Nicola had known when she had worked with him in the old days.

In the week that followed, Nicola often saw Connor driving past, sometimes alone, sometimes with Velma. As far as he was concerned, neither Dean's nor Nicola's existed. Yet, she argued hopelessly, she was bound to him by so many things—by her mother's friendship with his, by the fact that he had once saved her life.

She told herself, trying frantically to rationalize, a doctor saved so many lives in the course of his work, what was just one more to him? But it was not possible to argue away the fact that without his help she would have had neither the car nor the store. And without him she would never have experienced the joy, the wonder and the pain of love.

Now and then their cars passed each other going in opposite directions. On one occasion he overtook her. He must have known it was her car by the registration number, out he gave no sign of recognition. It seemed that he had, without effort, without scruple, put Nicola Dean out of his life.

THE FOLLOWING SUNDAY, feeling too lazy, or too weary, to work, she gazed out of the window and wondered what to do about her restlessness. And her loneliness. In less than two weeks her mother would be home, but there were still eleven days or so in which to endure this misery and solitude.

Loneliness had never been a problem in the past, because she had always enjoyed her own company. But now part of her was missing—the part she had given to Connor, and which he had thrown away as unsentimentally as someone leaving a discarded car to rot by the roadside.

The evening sun brought to mind a vision of the hill. It

tugged like a magnet. She pulled on slacks, found a jacket and went out. She walked along the village street, with its desperately respectable cottages; desperate because they clung so valiantly to the respectability with which they had been endowed in centuries past; but which, with their need of repair—roofs, guttering, rusting window frames—would have left them long ago if it hadn't been for the pride of their owners. It was a pride that had the houses painted white or pink or delicate yellow, with trained plants and flowers to climb high over the bulging walls, hiding the ominous cracks and adding a gentle perfume to the air around.

Inside the front rooms, with their gilded picture frames, oak dressers and shabbily comfortable furniture, the inhabitants, many of whom Nicola knew, were sitting content, at peace, reading, sewing, or watching television.

A powerful longing for their unquestioning serenity, their contentment with their lot, made her clench her hands in her pockets, kick unoffending tufts of grass growing on the edge of the pavement and quicken her footsteps. Her envy was too powerful to let her linger, watching other people's happiness.

She found herself alone on the hill. Now and then an excited, panting dog heralded the coming of its owner, both passing on and pursuing their routine evening walk without a moment's pause to admire the view. Then even the dogs stopped coming. The view, which had once brought her repose and refreshment, seemed to have lost its power to soothe. Her eyes raked the landscape constantly, settling for long on nothing, seeking, seeking for—what? Lost hopes, lost love?

Someone was coming. Her eyes stopped their searching and fixed unseeingly on the distant Welsh hills. Her ears, alert and waiting, picked up the footsteps. Her brain told her whose they were, her common sense lost its battle with her emotions and her heartbeats responded frighteningly to the new presence.

Slowly she let her head swivel around, feigning disinterest. Nicola knew he had seen her because he was standing only a few yards away. His eyes were scanning the view, like a movie camera shooting a film, alighting on nothing for very long, eager to pass to the next item worthy of recording. His features were composed, his expression coldly serious.

He did not even glance at her. He moved a few yards away and sat down, pulling at the grasses beside him. He was respecting their arrangement. He was keeping to his territory, while she stayed in hers. There would be no trespassing, no illegal entry on his part, either by word or deed.

But words, she told herself, were the only thing she had left. Could she reach him with those? Dared she try to explain, if nothing else, to put herself in a better light in his eyes? She would gain no material benefit, apart from the knowledge that she had at least made an attempt to vindicate herself. If she could do that, she would live the rest of her life in reasonable contentment—lonely, sad, but absolved.

He lay back in his favorite position, one arm raised to support his head, the other stretched loosely beside him. Nicola was gripped by panic. If he went to sleep now, that would be the end of any chance of communicating with him. There might never be another. Soon he would be married and with Velma as his wife, Nicola Dean would become so unimportant to him he would not care about her anymore. Whether or not she had been guilty of breaking all the moral laws conceived by man, it would no longer worry him and she would remain, in his mind, guilty of everything that he had accused her of.

In the gathering dusk, she looked at him. His relaxation was so deep he was scarcely breathing. He was clearly free of the turmoil that had her in its grip. His heart was not racing, his cheeks were not flushed, his hands weren't moist and gripped together until it was possible to feel the bones beneath the skin.

Now she had to make up her mind. She spoke his name, but the word was whispered because her throat was sandpaper rough. Perhaps he hadn't heard.

"Connor?" This time a little louder, loud enough for him to hear if he had been listening. But it was plain that he was not. She tried again. "Connor, are you asleep?" No answer except for the faintest movement of the fingers, searching for more grass to pull at.

"Connor," she ventured again, shifting nearer, "will you listen to me? Will you give me a last chance to clear myself?" No response at all. He was all set to ignore her.

But ignored she would not be. "Connor—" her voice rose slightly and involuntarily she had allowed a note of appeal to creep in "—Terence has gone. I'm alone again."

"What do you want me to do," his voice rasped into the summer twilight, "take his place beside you in your bed?"

"Connor!" She could not allow herself to be put off by his deliberate misunderstanding. "Please believe me when I tell you that there's nothing between Terence and me, there never was, there never will be. He has never been my lover. I've never loved him and he has never loved me."

"My God," he said disgustedly, turning away onto his side, "what do you think I am, the editor of a problem page in some women's magazine? Go and find someone else to pour out your heart to."

"*Connor!*" she shouted, crying now as though he had hit her. "The only reason Terence came back was to see Joy. They love each other. They're going to be married."

His body stayed as it was, rigid, uncompromising and utterly unmoved. She hauled herself upright and stood over him. "Why don't you believe me?" she cried out, the hopeless words echoing and dissipating drunkenly over the countryside. "Why have you shut your ears to the truth? The truth, Connor, the *truth*!"

Crying so passionately she could hardly breathe, she

ran away from him, down the hill, through the trees and along the path until it met the main road. She was glad of the darkness because it hid her distress from passersby. She let herself into the house and threw herself, sobbing, onto the couch. She stayed there for a long time, until passion gave place to a hopeless exhaustion.

The doorbell rang. Nicola lifted her head. Hope, so intense, so painful she flinched from it as if it had been a knife thrust into her, had her rigid and waiting. The ring came again. Connor? *Was it Connor?* Had he believed her after all?

Mrs. Henderton stood on the doorstep, a smile on her face and a half-smoked cigarette between her fingers. Nicola was weak with disappointment.

"Yes?" she asked wearily. If, Nicola thought, she were to ask for the whole shop she'd give it to her. But all she wanted was a box of cornflakes.

"Got to have them for breakfast in the morning. You don't mind the favor, do you, love? Just this time," she wheedled. As usual she held out the money.

"Pay me in the morning, Mrs. Henderton," Nicola said automatically. "Wait in the living room, will you?"

Nicola left her to go through to the store, turning on the lights and taking the box from the shelves. The smoke from Mrs. Henderton's cigarette had followed her. It was probably filling the entire house. She wished the woman would keep her cigarettes to herself. Mrs. Henderton took the giant box of cereal eagerly, with both hands outstretched, like a successful student receiving an award for good work.

Nicola closed the door on the satisfied, if illegal, customer, wondering what the woman had done with her cigarette—eaten it, perhaps? The smell lingered even if the smoker had gone. She trod slowly up the stairs, finding it an effort to lift one foot above the other. Her bed was a comfort, a refuge, a safe harbor in a tumultuous storm. She lay facedown and drifted into a deep, hopeless, exhausted sleep.

CHAPTER TWELVE

SOMETHING WOKE HER, some sixth sense, perhaps, the instinct for self-preservation. In the darkness her eyes came open and she listened. Then her sense of smell started working, overriding all other senses, warning her, urging her to act.

Her eyes smarted, her ears told her of a frightening noise outside the door, a crackling, a roaring, the sound of timber burning, breaking away and collapsing. The smell was creeping in and it was overpowering. Smoke . . . . *Smoke! The place was on fire!* But how? Why? Since when? She groped about in her mind. Mrs. Henderton—her cigarette—when she had taken the cereal the cigarette had gone. Last time she had thrown it into the kitchen sink. Once before it had been the doormat. This time—where? The wastepaper basket? The carpet? Anywhere was good enough for Mrs. Henderton!

Nicola struggled to the door, opening it only to choke and cough with the smoke and fumes that hit her on the landing. She retreated, terrified, but there was no escape by going back. Somehow she would have to get through that terrible barrier and down the stairs.

On the landing she lurched about, trying to find the light switch. Someone must have moved it, it just wasn't there. She gasped for breath, but the air she took into her thirsty lungs was toxic, putrid. There were voices, she heard them dimly . . . voices outside, inside, in the street . . . in her head? She grew confused, petrified into a useless rigidity.

From the bottom of the stairs someone called her

name. "Nicola!" She couldn't see who was calling. The smoke was so dense, her stinging eyes too blinded, her throat too dry to reply.

"Nicola!" It was a man's voice, shouting, desperate, a familiar voice, but she couldn't place it. She was sure it was a man she longed to reach, but he was separated from her by an impenetrable fog. She strained to touch him, but he was too far away. She strained, but she hadn't really moved a muscle. Her mind was wandering, she thought she was moving. Up or down? She didn't know. She was floating, surely. . . .

"Nicola!" The cry echoed across a mountainside and died, reverberating. Why couldn't she answer? "Come down, girl!" the voice said. "Come down to me. If you don't come now, it might be too late!" But she couldn't obey, she couldn't lift a foot. Still clinging to the banister post, her legs began to give way and she slid to the floor.

"Doctor!" There were voices from outside. "Come back, doctor! You'll never get out of that alive!"

She began to sob. Life was ending, and it was such a pity because she had so much to do. . . .

"For God's sake, Nicola, do you want us both to die?" The man was coming, he was coming up the stairs, there was a handkerchief around his face like a surgeon's mask. He was coughing, he was choking. . . . "My beloved girl," a voice was gasping, "I want us both to live!"

Arms gathered her sagging body, strong arms that held her as though she was the most precious thing on earth. She was living that dream again, that dream she'd had on the hill. The man in her dream had a face now, a face she knew and loved—and would probably never see again.

They were going down, down, so far down she wondered if the descent would ever stop. . . .

THE GROUND beneath her was hard, a folded jacket was under her shoulders, a blanket over her legs. Her eyes came open and in the light of the street lamp, and another brighter, brasher light, she saw that she was surrounded

by people. They were silent, watching, waiting. Sirens
wailed, distant voices shouted orders. There was a sound
of equipment unwinding, engines revving.

A man leaned over her. On his face, which was very
near, there was reflected a restless, fluctuating red glow.
His hand pressed against her ribs, another held her wrist.
She tried to work out why he looked so worried, why his
jacket was off, his tie loosened, his hair awry.

"Nicola?" His voice was questioning, deeply anxious.

"Connor?" she whispered wonderingly.

His eyes closed, his head drooped, he seemed to sag.
"Thank God!" he muttered.

"You've managed it, doctor," someone said. "She's
conscious."

"Yes." His voice sounded deadly tired. "I've managed it."

"Hospital, doctor? Want an ambulance?"

"No, thanks. I think she's over the worst."

"Connor," asked a quiet feminine voice, "will she
do?"

"She'll do, mother," was the weary answer.

"Bring her home, son. She has no other, now."

What did they mean, Nicola wondered, *I've got no
home*. But she was too tired, her brain too lazy to solve
puzzles. Those strong arms lifted and carried her again.
Her head lolled against a solid masculine shoulder and
she clung to the man with all her strength. He was her
refuge now and when he lowered her into the backseat of
a car, she did not want to let him go. But with gentleness
he disentangled her clinging arms and she felt other arms
take over, soft motherly arms that offered protection and
kindliness.

"Nicola?" asked the woman, "You know me? I'm
Barbara, Barbara Mitchell."

Of course, that was who it was! "I'm sorry, Mrs.
Mitchell—" why did her voice sound so strange "—to be
like this."

"My dear, dear child, don't, *don't* apologize. . . ."

The wheels turned slowly over the surface of the roa
as if the driver were holding back the speed of the ca
Minutes later she was being carried again, up, up som
stairs this time, not down as they had gone before. Sh
was lowered onto a bed.

"A nightgown. I'll get one, son."

Someone was removing her clothes with deftness an
speed. Nicola opened her eyes and saw a man bendin
over her. "Connor," she whispered, trying to protes
but the words did not even make the journey to her lip:
The gentle reprimand in his dark eyes and the deep ser
ousness of his expression silenced her.

His mother joined him and with his help slipped th
nightgown over Nicola's head. The covers were pulle
up and the warmth they generated helped the life see
back to her exhausted body.

"I'll sit with her, Connor," said Barbara.

"Not on your life," was the son's reply. "You nee
your sleep. Besides, this is a job for an expert. I mu:
watch for shock symptoms. Bring the folding bed in her
I'll rest on that if I feel the need."

He spoke with authority and his mother did not argu
He left the room with her and Nicola felt that without hi
there was a terrible emptiness everywhere. When h
came back he rubbed her left arm and gave her an inje
tion. "It will help you sleep, my dear." He smiled, an
the smile was kindness itself. How, Nicola reproache
herself, could she have said all those terrible things in th
past about his brutality and cruelty? He was the kindes
most wonderful man she knew.

In the night she climbed back to the edge of consciou
ness and felt a hand on her wrist, another on he
forehead. She heard herself say, "I'm thirsty." Almo
at once those arms that she had come to rely on so muc
lifted her into a half-sitting position and a glass was put
her lips. She drank and lay back, drifting immediate
into a deep sleep.

WHEN SHE AWOKE in the morning, she was alone. The covers on the folding bed a foot or two away were creased as though someone had lain on them. Her eye wandered and she realized it must be Connor's bed she was occupying. As her brain threw off the drowsiness produced by the aftereffects of the injection Connor had given her, she groped for a reason for being there.

It did not take long for the truth to dawn. She heard again the burning and the roar, smelled the smoke, saw the hungry flames. Memories came stampeding in, trampling her tranquility underfoot and bursting through the barriers that her mind, in self-defense, had erected.

Barbara Mitchell came in and Nicola saw her own anguish reflected in her eyes.

"Don't worry, dear," Barbara soothed, sitting on the bed, now all doctor's widow and doctor's mother. "Connor will take charge of your affairs and your mother's, too, if she wishes. He's out all day, I'm afraid. You know that in addition to his work as a general practitioner he also acts as a part-time consultant at the hospital? Unfortunately, it's his day to attend there, but this evening when he comes home, you can talk to him. Tell him all your worries, he'll sort them out." She looked at the time. "He's at morning office hours now, but he told me to call as soon as you woke up. Do you mind if I leave you for a moment?"

She went out and Nicola heard her talking. "She's awake. A little dazed. I think it's all come back. Food? Of course, if she wants it. . . . Don't be late this evening, son." This last with a touch of pleading.

She returned, a little breathless from climbing the stairs. Nicola guessed that she thought it expedient not to use the telephone extension in Connor's bedroom while his patient was in there.

"Dr. Muirson will be dropping in to see you this morning. He's your own doctor, isn't he, dear?"

So once again Connor had passed her over, out of his care. Well, she acknowledged, she had only herself to blame. She knew now how wrong she had been in refusing to go on Connor's list of patients. She struggled to sit up and Barbara helped her.

"I have a bedjacket," said Barbara. "I'll find it." It was blue and soft and covered Nicola's bare shoulders. "Your hair, dear, you'd like me to tidy it?" She returned with a comb and used it gently. "What a beautiful auburn color," she murmured. "Pure gold, Connor calls it. There, you're beginning to look like your old self again, although you could do with a lot more color in those cheeks." She put the comb in her pocket. "Tonight I'll make up the spare bed. It's a more feminine room than this. Now I'll get you some breakfast."

"I'd rather talk than eat," said Nicola, smiling with difficulty.

"No, no, eat first, my dear, then you'll have the strength to talk!"

"You're so kind to me," Nicola whispered.

Barbara's eyes moistened. "Oh, my dear . . . kind?" She shook her head and left the room.

After breakfast the tray was removed, the blankets from the folding bed put away, the room tidied. Then Mrs. Mitchell pulled up a chair, clasped her hands and said, "You talk, I'll listen."

Her smiling expectancy made Nicola smile, too, but she could not keep up the cheerfulness for long. Despair was taking over. She steeled herself to ask, "Mrs. Mitchell, has everything gone?"

It was a question she seemed to have been expecting. She had a ready answer. "Not everything, dear. Your mother's shop was badly damaged, but not completely destroyed. But the house, I'm afraid—" she shook her head "—very little left."

Nicola's heart sank against the pillows. "My—Connor's—store?" She had to drag the words from her lips.

"That could have been worse. Most of the stock escaped serious damage." Her smile was reassuring. "So all your hard work was not entirely wasted."

Nicola said, her voice flat, "My mother will have to be told."

"Yes, in due course. Connor and I discussed it. He'll contact her. You know the phone number? Good. When she returns, she can come and live here with you for as long as she likes."

"We shall have to find somewhere soon. We mustn't take advantage of your generosity."

"Don't talk nonsense," said Mrs. Mitchell briskly.

Dr. Muirson called and examined Nicola for any ill effects. He told Mrs. Mitchell that "the patient should be kept quiet, but after a few days' rest, she should be fine again." He left with a cheery wave of the hand.

Nicola slept fitfully for the rest of the day. She tried not to dwell on her future, or her mother's. As evening approached, she became determined to stay awake, but even so she drifted off. The day had no end and Connor was so long in coming.

A sound disturbed her and her eyes came open to see him standing beside the bed. Her heart throbbed painfully, but she managed a smile, its main purpose being to bring one to his serious face. She succeeded and he responded with a faint one of his own. Then the two smiles, so small, so weak, struggled, gave in and collapsed, like newly born foals trying unsuccessfully to stand on own feet. They had both attempted so much more than they could manage.

Nicola looked up at him, seeing his broad shoulders, the tough masculinity of his body, sensing the power of his intellect and the strength of his will and she longed for him with every particle of her being. Her very weakness cried out to be infused with his energy, his vigor. She knew that he and only he could give meaning and direction to her life.

But the knowledge that he was not, could never be, for her—that their paths, however close they might be running at that moment, were destined never to merge and become one—brought despair to her heart and the beginnings of tears to her eyes.

"Nicola?" he whispered, and the concern in his voice and the kindliness of his manner was her undoing.

The tears began in earnest and she rolled onto her side to keep them to herself. But he stooped and turned her and sat on the bed and gathered her into his arms.

"C-Connor," she sobbed, "oh, Connor, everything's gone, there's nothing left. . . ."

He let her cry, stroked her hair and, when the storm had passed, put her back against the pillows. She dabbed at her eyes and said she was sorry.

He smiled. "I'm not. I've been waiting all day for that to happen. I hoped I'd be here when it did."

"You mean you *wanted* me to cry all over you?"

He answered indirectly. "I wanted the shock to come out. You were too passive for my peace of mind."

"Connor," she ventured, "what does it look like?"

"The shop? Like any building after a fire. Burned, ravaged, painful, like an open wound. How did it happen, Nicola?"

She told him how Mrs. Henderton had made one of her many illicit calls and that she was convinced the woman had thrown down her half-smoked cigarette, which she assumed had been the cause of the fire.

"I can't be sure, of course, but I can't see how else it started. When she'd gone, I went to sleep on my bed. I hadn't undressed." She avoided his eyes. "I—I was emotionally exhausted and I must have been sleeping deeply."

He frowned, and prowled about the room. "I had to give you the kiss of life. You'd lost consciousness. You were suffering from the effects of carbon monoxide poisoning, which is why you were so confused and couldn't move. If I hadn't got you into the open air at once, the damage would almost certainly have been incalculable—and irreversible. Not to mention the physical danger you were in." There was a long silence. "When I think," he said softly, "what might have happened if I hadn't been coming to see you—"

Nicola stared. "You were coming to see me? Why?"

"Because of what you told me on the hill, because I had to hear those words again and again so that I could be sure they were true."

"They were true."

He lifted her hands and played with her fingers. "I'm sorry for being so rough with you in the past, Nicola. At times I was motivated by a force so powerful it warped my outlook and defied my attempts to control it. I'm afraid I have two sides to my nature."

She smiled and shook her head. "Wrong. Many more than two."

"Oh?" He came to life and sat on the bed. "You've made a study of me, done a piece of psychological research?"

"Yes, I've analyzed your character, taken it apart—"

"And put it together again with something missing, like an amateur watch repairer?"

She laughed. "I must admit I found you so complex I didn't even begin to put you together again!" His hand still held hers. "Whereas you not only took my character to pieces, but quite without mercy, you lifted up each piece in turn for me to inspect, and every single part had some terrible defect."

He looked at her ingenuously. "I did? I gave you that impression?"

"You know very well you did. You wanted to annoy me."

"There were times, I honestly admit, when I desperately wanted to annoy you. To have my own back."

This puzzled her but she did not question him. He looked so tired; he had probably been up most of the night watching over her. Involuntarily she lifted her hand and smoothed his hair. Then she realized what an intimate gesture it was, and blushed, but he didn't seem to mind.

"I'm sorry," she said, "I shouldn't have done that." Then she added with apparent irrelevance, but trying to imply that she accepted without question that she would never be allowed to get close enough to him to have the right to touch any part of him, "I know what you think of me."

"You do? Tell me what I think of you."

"That I'm permissive, immoral, a hypocrite. . . ."

Connor threw back his head and laughed. "If that's what you think I think of you, then you're a very bad psychologist, Miss Dean!"

She became serious. "The future frightens me."

"Why should it? You and your mother will rise— literally—from the ashes. She will retire . . . it's better for her health that she does. And you . . . well, you'll find other things to do."

"Yes," Nicola sighed at the bleakness of the prospect, "I'll probably return to teaching." He was silent. "So," she said thoughtfully, "the supermarket has won, after all."

"It was inevitable, Nicola. They would have found their way into the village with or without your co-operation. I don't want to imply that your customers were disloyal, but I think they secretly hoped the change would come."

She saw the truth in his contention and sighed. "Connor." He looked up. "You saved my life again. I don't know how I'll ever be able to repay you for all you've done for me."

"So we're back to rewards again, are we?" She went pink at the memories his words brought back. He put her hand from him and stood up. "I'll tell you how you can repay me." He looked into her puzzled eyes. "Marry me."

Her heart shot across her body like a comet with a dazzling tail. "*Marry* you?"

He looked hurt. "Don't say it as though it's the last thing on earth you'd contemplate."

"But surely, Connor . . .? You've helped me so much since we met, there's no need for you to take pity on me again and sacrifice yourself, your freedom, your—your girl friend for my sake.''

There seemed to be a minor eruption taking place inside him. Her body acted as a human seismograph, recording the tremors he set up. The shock waves were so violent they sent her back against the pillows.

"Take *pity* on you?" he shouted. "*Sacrifice* myself? What in God's name, woman, are you talking about?"

If she had been a rabbit, she would have considered it expedient to burrow into her hole. "What I—what I mean, Connor, is . . . well, no man should marry a woman he doesn't love to help her out of a difficult situation. I know you don't love me. . . ."

"Don't *love* you? Didn't I as good as tell you last night just what you mean to me?" She frowned, trying to remember. "When you didn't come down from the landing? When I had to hurl myself up the stairs to get you?"

She closed her eyes, hearing his voice, his anguished words, "Do you want us both to die? My beloved girl, I want us both to live!"

Was she his "beloved girl?" "Connor?" Her voice shook. "You love me?"

He strode around the room like a caged lion. Nicola thought, inconsequentially, if he'd had a tail, it would have lashed.

"My darling idiot," he growled, "what else do you think I've been doing all these weeks but love you? Why else was I consumed with jealousy when Grenville Lennon showed such interest in you? Why else could I cheerfully have throttled your late lamented boyfriend? Why else did I treat you so abominably when I thought you were having an affair with him? Why else have I alternately ranted and raged at you, and then behaved like a lover to you, taking every possible opportunity, no matter what shape or form, of kissing you? Why else have I helped you financially at every twist and turn, giving you what you longed for—a new car, a store of your own, which is why I bought the damned premises in the first place? Why else did I introduce you to my friends and colleagues at the hospital? Why else did I get so worried by what you were doing to your health by constant over-work, if not for love of you?''

"But—but, Connor . . . ." Was she really as stupid as she sounded? "I thought it was your kind nature.''

He shouted with laughter. "My kind nature? You re-garded it as *kindness*? My darling, how naive can you get? No man shows that sort of interest in a woman un-less he has very definite—not to say lustful—motives. What do you think a man's made of—stone? Every time you came near me, I wanted to touch you, to make love to you, to seduce you. Like this.'' He pulled back the bedclothes, scooped her up and swung her around to sit on his knee.

Then he wrapped her in his arms and she knew what it felt like to be a child's beloved teddy bear, crushed and loved until breathing became almost impossible.

But unlike a teddy bear, she could respond, and re-spond she did in good measure, answering his passion with hers and clinging to him with the last remaining fragments of energy he allowed her to keep.

When his mouth allowed her lungs to imbibe air again she gasped, "But, Connor—"

"There'll be no stopping me now, my darling. I've waited too long—"

"But, Connor—" she put her fingers over his lips to make him listen "—I haven't told you yet that I love you.''

"You haven't?" He laughed. "You're so wrong, sweetheart. If this isn't loving me . . . ." Then, as if he could not wait another minute, his head came down again and she discovered that submission to his kind of loving was paradise and the promised land rolled into one.

After a while he put her beside him, but kept his arm around her. "This is torment. We love each other, here you are in my bed. Here am I, desiring you as I've de-sired no other woman—" he took her left hand "—when will you marry me?''

"As soon as my mother comes home," she answered shyly.

"Then for God's sake, my sweet, get her back quickly."

She nodded. "Connor, every time I needed a doctor, why did you keep sending someone else? Why didn't you treat me yourself? I thought it was because you disliked me."

"Of course I sent someone else. Don't you know it's completely unethical for a doctor to make love to his patient? And my word, I certainly wanted to make love to you! No, my darling, it wouldn't have done at all. Whenever I did treat you, it was in an emergency. Then I passed you over. And you thought I disliked you? Come here, and I'll show you how much I dislike you." And she was back in his arms.

When she could speak she said, "Do you remember that evening I went to sleep on the hill?"

"Yes. I stood and watched you for a long time. And I remember my reactions, too." He whispered in her ear, "I desired you even then."

"That evening," she went on, "I dreamed of a man. I couldn't see his face, but whoever it was was holding me and trying to calm me. . . . It was you, of course. It was prophetic."

"Of course it was me. And it wasn't prophetic. It was wish-fulfillment on your part. I attracted you—be honest. Now," he settled her into a more comfortable position, "I think it's time I let *you* into a secret. Remember when *I* went to sleep on the hill and you stayed beside me and woke me when it rained?"

"And you kissed me?"

"Yes. You see, I'd had a dream, too. I dreamed you were my wife and I'd come home to you, tired out, troubled and depressed, and I had unburdened myself to you. You were beside me, in my bed, and I had reached out and pulled you to me. Like this." His arms went around her again, but even more possessively. "And there you were, in reality, next to me. You were touching me, calling my name. So I made my dream come true. I kissed you.''

"Which means," she whispered, "that we both had our dream on the hill—about each other."

They sat, arms entwined, quietly reminiscent, then Connor spoke again. "We'll have our house built on the land I own and we shall live there. My mother and, if she's willing, your mother, will live here."

"Darling," she breathed, "what a wonderful arrangement!"

"It is, isn't it? And you shall continue making your baby clothes . . . for our children. You'll continue making your cakes . . . for our family. And when the kids are old enough to go to nursery school, you can return to your precious teaching, if you still want to. Does that suit you, Mrs. Mitchell-to-be?"

She didn't answer him with words, only deeds.

The door handle rattled and Mrs. Mitchell came in. She took a breath and exclaimed, "*Connor!* My dear son, what are you *doing*?"

"Making passionate love to our guest, mother," he answered blandly. "What does it look like?"

Her eyes shone. "You don't mean . . . ."

"I do mean. I mean we're in love and as soon as Nicola's mother reappears on the scene—as you can see, the sooner the better—you will acquire a daughter-in-law. In other words, with all reasonable speed, Nicola and I are going to be married."

"Oh, my dears—" she kissed them each in turn "—I'm utterly delighted. Enid and I had hoped, you know, but we'd almost given up. Your relationship seemed to blow so hot and cold we thought nothing would come of it."

Nicola and Connor exchanged smiles. "You know what they say," Connor murmured, contemplating Nicola's lips like someone being offered a box of chocolates and wondering which to choose, "about the course of true love."

Mrs. Mitchell smiled. "*I* know when I'm superfluous! I'll go and get some tea. By the way, son—" she paused at the door, and her eyes twinkled "—Nicola's doctor said we must keep the patient quiet."

"Well," said her son with a wicked, anticipatory grin, "we must always do what the doctor orders, mustn't we?"

And as his mother went away, he proceeded to "keep the patient quiet," with her willing cooperation, for a very long time.